To Try Men's Souls

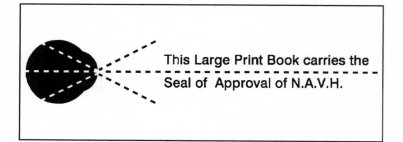

This Large Print Book carries the
Seal of Approval of N.A.V.H.

TO TRY MEN'S SOULS

A NOVEL OF GEORGE WASHINGTON AND THE FIGHT FOR AMERICAN FREEDOM

NEWT GINGRICH
WILLIAM R. FORSTCHEN

Albert S. Hanser, contributing editor

THORNDIKE PRESS
A part of Gale, Cengage Learning

GALE
CENGAGE Learning

Detroit • New York • San Francisco • New Haven, Conn • Waterville, Maine • London

GALE
CENGAGE Learning™

LIBRARY OF CONGRESS CATALOGING-IN-PUBLICATION DATA

Gingrich, Newt.
 To try men's souls : a novel of George Washington and the fight for American freedom / by Newt Gingrich, William R. Forstchen and Albert S. Hanser, contributing editor.
  p. cm. — (Thorndike Press large print core)
 ISBN-13: 978-1-4104-2397-9 (alk. paper)
 ISBN-10: 1-4104-2397-2 (alk. paper)
 1. Washington, George, 1732–1799—Fiction. 2. Paine, Thomas, 1737–1809—Fiction. 3. United States—History—Revolution, 1775–1783—Fiction. 4. Large type books. I. Forstchen, William R. II. Hanser, Albert S. III. Title.
PS3557.I4945T6 2010
813'.54—dc22   2009046329

Published in 2010 by arrangement with St. Martin's Press, LLC.

Printed in the United States of America
1 2 3 4 5 6 7 14 13 12 11 10

DEDICATION

It is humbling to write this dedication. For General George Washington and the "gallant few" — the 2,500 men — who crossed the Delaware River with him on the night of December 25–26, 1776, facing impossible odds, and by so doing, saved a nation.

ACKNOWLEDGMENTS

The genesis of this book is a curious one and might be of interest to some of our readers. More than a decade ago, our team (Gingrich, Forstchen, and Hanser) got together to talk about writing historical fiction, and the very first topic on the table, in fact one that we worked on for months, was the American Revolution. For a variety of reasons, our attention finally shifted to the American Civil War, and then the Second World War in the Pacific.

For our fans of the "Pacific War" series, please excuse this change of topics. We have not let that storyline drop and will indeed pick it up again in the near future; it is just that a unique moment occurred that we had to follow through on.

Shortly after the 2008 election, in a conference call with our remarkable editor, Pete Wolverton, it was Pete who asked us if we might be interested in a brief hiatus from our story focusing on Pearl Harbor and consider a topic related to the American Revolution. There seemed to be a certain resonance at that moment. Pete felt that a novel that looked back to the origin of our country and its struggle for freedom would be a timely subject that we should consider. Little did Pete know what he was unleashing; for in fact we already had a working outline and even some sample chapters filed away from more than a decade ago.

We therefore had an editor urging us to consider this topic along with research and writing that was gathering "dust" in the cyberworld of our computers, and thus the work started.

For Bill Forstchen there was a particular personal connection. After graduating from college early in the 1970s he had worked as a "reenactor" at Valley Forge and at Washington Crossing as a private in the Continental Army of General Washington. Some of the incidents that occur in the novel are real personal experiences that he observed, and even after thirty years, left him awed with the endurance of those who experienced it "for real," and most definitely left him "chilled" as well.

It is hard for any of us to grasp today the suffering experienced by Washington and his troops during that bitter autumn and winter of 1776. We who are so pampered with luxuries can barely comprehend the experience of marching all night — barefoot — in a freezing December storm, with little hope other than "victory or death" at the end of that road. We were a nation so reduced in poverty that men literally marched with the hopeful prayer that if they survived, their reward would be a pair of shoes, a warm meal snatched from an enemy's larder, and a few hours' rest under a dry roof. This they endured across all the bitter winters from 1775–1783. It is to this gallant few that we owe all that we have today.

It is why we felt compelled to write this book; to remember them — the barefoot privates with frostbitten and bleeding feet, and the general who never surrendered his hope for a free and independent nation.

We were also intrigued by the power of the pen during those dark days of 1776, and thus did the story of Tom Paine become part of this tale as well. There have been unique moments in history where the written and spoken word has indeed proven to be mightier than the sword: Lincoln at Gettysburg redefined the Civil War as a conflict about the meaning of the word "equality"; Churchill in the summer of 1940 roused a nation to fight what many thought would be a hopeless last stand against totalitarianism, but for which at least he and his stout English comrades would have died standing on their feet rather than submit on their knees; and Thomas Paine, who with but one short essay starting, "These are the times that try men's souls . . . ," fanned back to life the dying embers of a revolution. They show us that no matter how dark the hour, then or now, all that is required is a few gallant men and women who refuse to surrender.

As we wrote this book, there were many who were eager to help, and some who might not realize they were helping but nevertheless deserve our humble thanks. First and foremost our compliments to David Hackett Fischer. Our work is fiction. Fischer's remarkable book *Washington's Crossing* is the real history, and we urge you, if you have not already read it, to put it first on your reading list. Another work we highly recommend is Joseph Ellis's *His Excellency: George Washington.* Both Ellis and Fischer are recipients of well-deserved Pulitzers. We also must compliment David McCullough with his monumental study of John Adams. To list all of our references for this book would be near to impossible, but the three mentioned above are good starters.

As to the actual team that has worked directly with us, there are so many we wish to mention. First off, the team with St. Martin's who has published our previous novels on the Civil War and Pearl Harbor: our editor Pete Wolverton, his assistant Elizabeth Byrne and publisher Thomas Dunne. We are blessed to be working with you.

To our agent Kathy Lubbers who handles all the business aspects of a project like this, thus freeing us up to write, our sincere thanks. Also with the Gingrich team: Randy Evans, Stefan Passantino, Joe DeSantis, Vince Haley, Liz Wood, Chris Paul, Rick Tyler, and the remarkable Michelle Selesky were always on top of all the administrative details. And, the more than capable Sonya Harrison and her team: Lindsey Harvey, Bess Kelly, and Heather Favors.

Throughout the years Sean Hannity and Oliver North have helped in so many ways, and our gratitude must go out to them as well. A very special team is our close friends "WEB Griffin Sr. & Jr." Long before we started writing they were already an inspiration and through an interesting coincidence, "WEB Jr." Bill Butterworth IV, long ago, was Bill Forstchen's first editor and mentor when Bill started writing for *Boys' Life* magazine.

Lt. Commander Chris McConnaughay and Captain Bill Sanders USN, were always ready with a critical eye in reviewing our work, especially if any nautical details needed attention.

An extraordinary group that must be cited here are the staff and volunteers at the Mount Vernon historical center. General Washington's home is not a federally owned national park. It is owned and maintained by a private foundation. It is an endeavor worthy of the support of every citizen who wishes to honor the memory of the man who is "first in the hearts of his country-men" and his beloved wife Martha. Resting there as well, Washington's "servant" Billy Lee, who remained by his side throughout the war, a hero worthy of far more recognition. We especially want to thank James Rees, the director; Mary Thompson, the historian-librarian; and Sue Keeler, the extraordinary guide. We also want to ac-knowledge the amazing work of Gay Gaines who led the effort to raise over $100 million to build the extraordinary new educational center which every American should see to better understand their country's origins. The Mount Vernon Ladies' Association does a remarkable job of preserving the home and educating the nation about George and Martha Washington.

Our families, of course, had to "endure" this book as well. From Newt, as always, a heartfelt and loving thanks to his wife, Callista, and his daughters, Kathy and Jackie, and for Steve his beloved wife, Krys. For Bill, his ever-patient daughter Meghan, who learned long ago that "I'll be with you in fifteen minutes" usually meant several more hours of waiting, and Dianne St. Clair, who as an English teacher reviewed our writings with a critical eye.

The problem with an acknowledgments page such as this is all the names not mentioned. To list all would result in a manuscript at least a chapter in length, so please do know that our thanks are with you.

We hope that this book will serve in some small way as an inspiration. Thomas Paine so correctly named his pamphlet, *The American Crisis.* It was indeed a time of crisis. America, however, rose to the occasion at a time when so many naysayers claimed that it was lost. There is a fascinating point about the study of history, and that is to understand the context of the moment in which an event transpires. Long after the crisis is past, a multitude will step forward to claim they had a part in it. Or that all along they believed "things would work out." Or most telling of all, the doubters would exclaim that maybe their ancestors had "the right stuff," but the current generation no longer has the guts to see it through.

Thus it was said in 1776, in 1863, in 1944, and thus we hear it said today.

We can glorify a past and, rightly so, call those of that time the "greatest generation," but read carefully what contemporaries were writing and you will see how few truly did believe, at that moment, that we as Americans would see it through to victory. On that grim and terrible night of December 25, 1776, General Washington had but 2,500 men by his side out of a nation of more than three million. Those chosen few saved the Revolution and gave us a legacy of freedom. That spirit is still with us today, and we believe that even now we have a "greatest generation" who can and will face the same hardships if need be to insure freedom for the "greatest generations" yet to be born as Americans. That is the legacy we have written about. This is the legacy we must pass on to the America that we believe still can stand as the "shining city on the hill," and that is indeed the best hope for all mankind.

INTRODUCTION

THE MIRACLE THAT MADE AMERICA POSSIBLE:
WHY WE THINK THIS BOOK MATTERS FOR ALL AMERICANS

We first began discussing a Revolutionary War book about George Washington and the miracle of the American success about fifteen years ago.

Steve Hanser, Bill Forstchen, and I were all fascinated by the extraordinary leadership of Washington and the equally extraordinary success of his generation in creating the United States of America.

After years of reflection (and writing six history-based novels) we decided the Christmas Day campaign of 1776 would be the best place to introduce General George Washington to a modern audience. This was a campaign of extraordinary heroism, improbable good fortune, and involving a

17

series of events that led Washington and others to conclude that the outcome was a miracle indicating Divine Providence was on their side.

The events that transpired on the Christmas Day campaign — crossing the Delaware at night, marching miles through snow and ice in a severe storm with an army (one third of whom had no boots and had wrapped their feet in burlap bags) leaving a trail of blood as they marched, and then surprising a professional Hessian unit that should have been ready and waiting for them — came together to suggest a miracle in Washington's mind and in the minds of many contemporary supporters of the American Revolution.

We decided this time not to write our normal active history in which we change one critical decision in order to show how other things might have been changed because history is not automatic or inevitable or predetermined.

After studying and thinking through the Christmas Day Trenton campaign, we concluded that it was so improbable and indeed so miraculous that any change would only diminish it. We decided that given the current threats to American civilization from both without and within, the time was ripe for a novel that told the story of that miracle to help bring Americans back into contact with their Founding Fathers and with the faith and courage that made that founding possible.

Indeed, the real events of those twenty-four hours were so difficult — and the successful outcome so improbable — that it is almost impossible to improve on a simple retelling of that great courage in the face of overwhelming adversity.

There is much to learn from great historic nonfiction works, and as professional historians all three of us deeply enjoy reading well-researched and well-written history. However there are also human moments, personal encounters, insights, and relationships, which can best be conveyed in a fictional setting. We felt that a fictional account would help Americans today get some sense of the exhaustion, the desperation, and the determination of their ancestors.

America is a country of miraculous opportunity for all.

America is a country where for four hundred years events occurred which can only still be termed miraculous.

The poorest American has an opportunity to rise. The newest immigrant has an opportunity to rise. The son of a first-generation immigrant can and has become president.

One of the greatest weaknesses of modern America has been the collapse of the teaching of American history in our schools, and the loss of this sense of what a miraculous country America is and how fortunate we are to be Americans. The modern education establishment has deliberately ignored American-history and minimized the importance of learning about America. Yet America is essentially a cultural concept. Americans can come from anywhere but they learn to be American. A key part of being American is the memories we have of Thanksgiving, of Washington crossing the Delaware, of Lincoln at Gettysburg, and of the millions of Americans who have risked their lives for this country to be free and safe. We believe that this kind of accurate history about who we are and how we got here should be reinstated in our schools and taught to every student and to every first-generation immigrant.

We have to begin by acknowledging the extraordinary work of David Hackett Fischer. His *Paul Revere's Ride* and *Washington's Crossing* are two of the great modern studies of the American Revolution. No student of this period can read these two books without a sense of awe at his research, his understanding, and his writing ability. We write in his shadow.

The shock of American political and military effectiveness in *Paul Revere's Ride* explains much of the British failure to understand their opponents. It also explains a lot of the reasoning behind the Second Amendment's commitment to the right to bear arms. The Founding Fathers knew full well that without local militia they would have been subjected to British tyranny and would have been powerless to oppose it.

The meticulous intelligence, planning, and execution of the Christmas Day campaign is captured flawlessly in *Washington's Crossing.* As a work of nonfiction, it is without peer for those who would understand this great achievement.

We have been informed by Fischer's great works, but we were inspired by an entirely different source.

We were inspired to write *To Try Men's Souls* by a wonderful film we saw at the Mount Vernon education center. This magnificent new museum uses film in very pioneering ways to reintroduce George and Martha Washington to modern audiences.

It is a sad commentary on the anti-American-history bias of our modern school systems that students today have far less knowledge of Washington than their parents and grandparents. The Mount Vernon education center is beginning to fill that void.

The film about the decision to cross the Delaware makes clear what was at stake, how deep the odds were against American success, and how desperate Washington's decision to gamble was.

He commanded an army that had been defeated steadily from September 1776 on. It had been driven from Brooklyn across Manhattan to White Plains and then south past the Palisades and across New Jersey. It had shrunk from 30,000 to fewer than 2,500 effectives. There were another 2,500 in camp, but they were so sick they could not fight.

Morale was collapsing, and as enlistments expired, virtually everyone was choosing to go home. Without victory the army would disintegrate. As Washington warned his officers: "If we do not win soon there will be no army left. When there is no army left the rebellion will be over. When the rebellion ends we will all be hung. Therefore we have little to lose."

Crossing the ice-choked Delaware at night in three different places, and then marching in the dark to Trenton to surprise a professional Hessian military unit (among the finest in Europe) was an act of absolute desperation.

Some of the desperation was captured in the password for that night: "Victory or death." Washington understood this was potentially the last gamble of the Revolution.

Washington also understood the importance of morale and the power of a small number of determined people. Therefore he had Thomas Paine's new pamphlet, *The American Crisis,* read to his men as they boarded the boats that night.

One of the most interesting characteristics of the American Revolution is the wide range of personalities engaged. From the permanently optimistic Ben Franklin, to the disciplined John Adams, to his fiery cousin Sam Adams, to the intellectual Virginia planter Thomas Jefferson, there was an extraordinary diversity of personalities and backgrounds brought together in response to the perceived threat of British tyranny.

There may have been no greater contrast than that between General George Washington and the gifted propagandist Thomas Paine. Paine was from the poor neighborhoods of London. He was a natural revolutionary, deeply resentful of the wealthy and secure. Washington was probably the largest landowner in the colonies; a man of impeccable rectitude, considerable formality, and an intense, disciplined work ethic.

The two could hardly have been more different in their background and temperament, and yet they came together in a moment of need to inspire a movement of determined men with the energy, the conviction, and the courage needed to win despite all the odds.

No one should underestimate how great the odds were against Washington, the Founding Fathers, and the American Revolution succeeding.

There was no reason to believe the American Revolution would survive.

There was no reason to believe it would find a leader so patient, so determined, so disciplined, and so noble that his men would stick with him through defeat after defeat and that a Republic could be built on the shoulders of his moral force.

George Washington faced an almost impossible task, and the odds were overwhelming that he would lose. The British had grown used to winning. They had crushed the last Irish rebellion in 1693. They had crushed the last Scots rebellion in 1745. They were used to peasant uprisings in rural

England and routinely used the army to suppress the rabbles who dared break the law.

British arrogance and self-confidence had been vastly strengthened by the triple realities of commercial mercantile wealth, the even greater wealth of the early industrial revolution, and by having the most powerful navy in history.

The commercial mercantile revolution itself was a byproduct of the dominance of the Royal Navy. From sugar plantations in the West Indies, to the African slave trade, to the spices of Asia, the British merchant fleet was the largest and most profitable in the world. It existed in the protective shadow of the Royal Navy's dominance over all other navies combined.

The wealth, which had been coming from trade, was in the eighteenth century rapidly being augmented (and then overshadowed) by the enormous opportunities of the industrial revolution. From the early eighteenth-century invention of the steam engine (applied initially to pump water out of coal mines) to the rise of railroads, which were initially horse drawn, as efficient methods of moving coal, to a huge canal system (which still exists and on which Steve Hanser has navigated on vacation with great enjoyment) there was an explosion of practical invention and production, which was rapidly making Great Britain the wealthiest and most productive country in the world.

Finally there was military power.

The British Empire was at its peak. Just a decade earlier (in 1763) its French rival had conceded defeat in a seven-year world war. From North America (where Washington had played a role) to India to Europe and across the world's oceans the British and French Empires had collided in an all-out struggle for supremacy.

After a period of defeat the British switched leaders and elevated William Pitt, the Great Commoner, to be wartime prime minister. In a brief intense period of extraordinary leadership and decisive risk-taking (comparable to Churchill in World War II, but stunningly more successful), Pitt gambled again and again on brave leaders who forged victory. In 1759 Britain won a series of miraculous victories in India, Canada, and in the West Indies; terming it the *Annus Mirabilus.*

After the extraordinary worldwide exertion of the Seven Years' War, the British Parliament and taxpayers felt entitled to have a little help from the Americans. The London elites reasoned that they had spent all that money building an army and navy to protect North America. Now that the French had been defeated and had surrendered Canada to Great Britain, the Americans were safe.

It was now time for the American colonists to pay for their own safety.

There have been few moments of misunderstanding more decisive and more radical than that between the British elites and their American colonists in 1770.

The elites in London felt they were, well, "elite."

The colonists in America felt they were "free and equal Englishmen under the law."

The British elites sought to impose their will on the colonists in what they thought was a reasonable action by a naturally governing empire.

The American colonists resisted what they saw as a mortal threat to their very freedom and identity.

Modern cynics find it hard to understand the moral power of the American Revolution.

This was not just a fight over economics.

This was a fight over fundamental rights.

This was a battle of life and death over the nature and meaning of the American personality.

"Live free or die" was not just the slogan of New Hampshire. It was the way many — not all, probably only a third, but a deeply committed one third — Americans felt about what was happening.

It was this sense of fighting for their lives and their very freedom that impelled the colonists to more and more extreme measures.

The British elites believed this was a conflict about money and about minor irritations. They simply could not believe the colonists were serious about their rights as free men and women.

Thus when they sought to impose a tax on tea the British elites thought they could cleverly reduce the burden by granting the East India Company a monopoly so the price of tea would actually drop.

It was an enormous shock in London when Samuel Adams and his friends launched the original Tea Party in December 1773 and threw the tea into Boston Harbor.

Principle, not price, was the American objection to the tea tax.

No taxation without representation was a serious, life or death belief of those colonists who were finding themselves increasingly at odds with London.

The second great threat to American liberty was the power of the British judges and the dictatorial way in which they wielded that power.

Anger over the judges and a demand for trial by jury (so local citizens as jurors could set aside the judge's power) was the second greatest demand of the colonists.

This objection to the arbitrary power of the British elites grew gradually.

It was said that Benjamin Franklin went to London as an Englishman and after years of living there came back to Pennsylvania as an American. He had concluded that the British aristocracy would never admit him to their ranks and never treat him as an equal. He would spend the rest of his life teaching them how wrong they had been and how expensive arrogance and haughtiness could be.

The colonists initially had no thought of independence. They saw themselves as Englishmen defending their historic rights against a dictatorial government. Had the British elites listened to the complaints and analyzed the logic behind them they might have found a constitutional compromise in 1774. However when they decided to disarm the Americans by marching to Lexington and Concord to seize the militia's arms, they began a process of alienation, which seemed to inexorably lead to a crisis of identity.

In 1775 the Americans were frightened and threatened by the British military response, but they still responded as loyal subjects petitioning the king to intervene and create a new framework for peacefully living together.

However at each stage, as the British increased their military presence, the Americans increased their preparations for resistance.

The British occupation of Boston led to an outcry in all thirteen colonies. If the British could militarily occupy Boston and suspend the rights of Englishmen they could occupy any part of the Americas.

The threat to one had become a threat to all.

In response to the British challenge in New England, the Continental Congress in Philadelphia sought a unifying symbol. They found that symbol, and the instrument that would lead to victory, in the only man in the Congress who was wearing a military uniform.

Colonel Washington of the Virginia militia was one of the tallest men in the Continental Congress. He did not offer to be the military leader, but he did wear his uniform every day. He exuded calm and confidence. He had quite a remarkable number of experiences in the West (meaning western Virginia and western Pennsylvania) during the French and Indian Wars (as the Seven Years' War was known in America).

Colonel Washington had read quite a number of books on military matters. A leader as a young man he was now at the peak of his physical strength. Widely known as the best horse man in the colonies, Washington was so strong he could break a walnut between his thumb and first finger.

Washington represented stability, discipline, calm, determination, and martial knowledge. He also represented Virginia, which was the most important colony. If he went to New England he would single-handedly symbolize the resolve of all the colonies to come to the aid of New England.

In the months after the British occupation of Boston, the patriots went from exhilarating victory as the British sailed away, to exhausting administrative detail, to a brilliant forced march to Long Island (where he had correctly deduced the British would come next).

And then defeat after defeat and calamity after calamity.

It is at the nadir of the Revolution, the depth of defeat and despair, on a cold winter night during a bleak Christmas that we join General Washington and his diminished and demoralized but determined army on the banks of the Delaware.

CHAPTER ONE

Christmas Night
McConkey's Ferry, Pennsylvania
Nine Miles North of Trenton, New Jersey
December 25, 1776
4:30 P.M.

Cold.

It is so cold, so damnably cold, he thought, pulling his hat lower in an attempt to shield his face from the wind and the driving rain.

His woolen cape was soaked through, water coursing down his neck, his uniform already clammy. Though his knee-high boots were of the finest calfskin, they were soaked as well and his pants sopping wet halfway up the thigh as a result of his having slipped several times walking along the banks of the flood-swollen Delaware River.

Another gust of wind out of the east kicked up spray that stung his face, and he turned his back as it swept by, roaring through the treetops and up the ridge on the Pennsylvania side of the river.

"This damn storm will play hell with moving the artillery across."

General George Washington, commander of what had once been so valiantly called the Continental Army of the United States of America, turned toward the speaker, his artillery chief, Colonel Henry Knox. Rotund at what had to be three hundred pounds and powerful looking, towering several inches over Washington's six foot, two inches, the artilleryman was shivering, his spectacles misted by the rain. Knox looked pathetic, this bookseller turned warrior who should have been in his store in Boston, resting by a crackling fire rather than out on an evening such as this.

"They'll cross. They have to cross," Washington replied calmly. "This wind is just as cold for the Hessians as it is for us. They may not be very good at picketing in this kind of storm."

He wondered if Knox and the others gathered nearby, Generals Stirling and Greene, their orderlies and staff, were waiting for the most obvious of orders on a night like this, just waiting for him to sigh and say, "Return the men to their encampments."

He shook his head, shoulders hunched

against the spates of rain, which were turning to sleet.

He looked across the river, to the east, to
the Jersey shore.

In his haunted memories, memories that
did indeed haunt, he could see that other
river bordering New Jersey sixty miles to
the east . . . the Hudson, and just beyond
the Hudson . . . the East River.

Merciful God, was it but five months ago
we were arrayed there in our proud defiance?

Another gust swept across the Delaware,
but this time he did not turn away from it.

How hot it had been during those days of
August. How proud we were. How proud
and confident I was, he thought. He shook
his head at the memory of it. Our victory at
Boston and the British withdrawal from that
port had misled all of us into an absurd
overconfidence. We had marched to New
York in anticipation of the next British move
with the satisfaction of having driven off the
army of the most powerful country in the
world and were expecting to do so again
with ease.

On the very day that the Declaration was
read publicly for the first time, the vanguard
of King George's reply was coasting Long

Island, bearing toward New York's outer harbor.

He had second-guessed the move months before, and so had moved his army, fresh from their triumph at Boston, on the long march south to defend New York.

Filled with confidence, so many had boasted that if the British and their hireling Germans, commonly called Hessians, did attempt to return there, this new army of America would make short work of them.

Arriving in New York the Continentals had set to work with vigor, building bastions, fortifications, and strongpoints, ringing the harbor with hundreds of guns and near to thirty thousand troops.

Most of the troops he had commanded during the long siege of Boston had been New Englanders. It had been a difficult command and one, at first, not easily accepted. The men of Massachusetts felt one of their own should be in command, for, after all, was it not their state that had stood up first, and was it not their state where the battle was being fought?

It had taken the utmost of tact to manage them in a situation that would have caused any regular officer of the British army to howl with rage or derision or both. Yet manage them he did, slowly earning their begrudging respect.

As they set to work building their fortifications around New York Harbor, reinforcements flooded in from the other states, transforming the army. There were tough backwoodsmen from the frontiers of Pennsylvania, western New York, Virginia, and the Carolinas joining spit-and-polish regiments from the tidewater of Chesapeake Bay and unruly militia by the thousands from Jersey, lower New York, and Connecticut.

His army swelled until there were more men than the entire population of Philadelphia, America's most populous city. The worry then, added to when the invasion would strike, was simply keeping so many men fed, housed, and healthy and not at each other's throats. As to the feeding and housing, the need had been met, for the countryside was rich; supplies could be floated down the Hudson Valley and drawn in from the fertile Jersey countryside. As to health, that soon broke down as it would in almost any army that stayed in camp. Smallpox struck thousands, and hundreds perished, but such was to be expected even in the best tended of armies. As to stopping the men from going at each other's throats, that had proven near impossible at times.

Though he would never admit it within the hearing of a single living soul, the New Englanders struck him as a haughty and ill-bred lot, lacking in the refinements a gentleman planter of Virginia expected of them. He was not the only person in the command to carry such feelings, and nearly all others expressed them openly, vocally, and at times violently. He actually started to pray that the British would return, and soon, for, if not, the army might very well rend itself apart.

And they had come, as if in answer to that prayer, and proved reality a curse.

In the first week of July the vanguard appeared; in the next weeks, more and yet more — ships of the line, frigates, fast sloops and brigs, supply ships — and then the transports brought regiment after regiment of England's finest. How ironic that with each passing day he could ride down to the narrows between Long Island and Staten Island and with telescope watch the ranks disembarking onto Staten Island. Regimental standards he remembered with such admiration from the last war floated on the breeze, and when the wind came from the west he could even hear their bands playing. And alongside men who were once old comrades were the blue uniforms of the regiments from Hesse and Hanover, men who at first were merely scorned, but soon would be feared by every man in his army.

The Howe brothers, Richard in command of the navy, William the army, had made their arrangements in a ponderous, leisurely fashion, the intent obvious, to overawe before the first shot was fired. There had even been diplomatic protocols observed, of offers of reconciliation if only Washington and his rabble would ground arms, renew allegiance to the king, and return peaceably to their homes.

The offers, of course, had been met with scorn and contempt. Officers around him had boasted that once swords were crossed, it would be the British who begged for mercy; before summer was out the entire lot of them would be sent packing to their humiliated master, George the Third.

Another gust of wind swept in from across the frozen plains of New Jersey, racing across the river, causing him to shiver again as the frigid rain lashed his face.

Few boasted now, few indeed.

This day, Christmas Day, had dawned clear and cold, the ground frozen, dusted with a light coating of snow. With a moon near full tonight, the weather at first appeared to be perfect for this move, roads frozen solid, light from the moon to guide them . . . and then by midday the harbingers of what was coming appeared. Glover's Marblehead men, checking their boats, would raise their heads and in their nearly incomprehensible New England dialect pronounce that a regular "nor'easter was comin'."

With John Glover, the taciturn fisherman from the tempestuous New England coast, there was not the personal bond of affection that he felt had evolved between himself and Knox, but here was a doughty man he knew he could rely upon.

He had seen such weather often enough back home at Mount Vernon, the wind backing around to the east, clouds rolling up from the south, the broad Potomac tossed with whitecaps, temperature at first rising and then plummeting, as it now was.

The plan for tonight had been that by sunset the army would be mustered and already moved by individual columns of battalions to the points of embarkation. That plan had collapsed as the last rays of the sun were blanketed by the lowering clouds already lashing out with icy rain driving in from the east. The army was to have made its first move to concealed positions

within a few minutes' walk from the riverbank while it was still light. Some of the
men were not yet out of their camps, and
all semblance of an orderly preparation,
which once darkness closed in was to have
been unleashed by a fast rush to the boats
and then across the river, was already falling apart. Now the far shore was an indis-
tinct blur, waves kicking up midstream, ice
floes crashing and bobbing as they swirled
by.

The plan had been threatened with collapse even before it was supposed to start.
Only now were troops beginning to move
toward the river, and boats that should have
been in place were still being maneuvered
out of concealment. His hopes of bringing
the boats alongshore at a dozen points for
loading and then off-loading on the far
shore were dashed by the rising of the river,
tossed now with waves and blanketed with
ice floes. Every single man, horse, and gun
would have to be funneled to one narrow
dock at the ferry and then off-loaded at an
equally small dock on the opposite shore.
Already it was obvious it would take twice,
three times as long to complete the crossing.

A shiver ran through him.

A company of riflemen and several compa-

41

nies of his trusted Virginians, who would be the first to cross and establish a picket line, sloshed past him, kicking up icy slush. The riflemen at least had some semblance of uniforms, their famed round hats and fringed hunting jackets, long ago white, now filth-encrusted and stained to gray, brown, and black, patched and repatched; a lucky few still had boots or shoes, but many had burlap strips wrapped around their feet, and more than a few were barefoot. They did not see him standing in the shadows and passed in loose order, complaining and cursing.

"Damn this, damn all of this," a voice echoed, and they staggered past, not recognizing their general in the shadows. "I tell you the captain said it's off, he heard from . . . Come next week I'm going for home . . ."

"Just shut up and keep moving," a deep voice boomed. "This is going to work."

He marked with his gaze the last man in the column, a sergeant from the looks of him, someone who still believed and was urging his men onward.

The sergeant fell out for a moment to retie the burlap around his feet; obviously an older man, for in the fading light Washington could see his gray beard. He had the look of a man who, in spite of all privations, was as tough as seasoned hickory. Looking up as he finished retying his foot wrappings, the sergeant saw who was watching. He merely stood up, gave a casual salute, and without comment or flourish turned and pressed on, disappearing into the shadows and mists.

He could not help but smile. A time perhaps, he thought, when I looked like that. I was too young for a graybeard, but the hunting smock, loose leggings, a lean, strongman, moving with a casual ease that spoke of experience in the woods — that was once me.

Was it really twenty years past that he had marched with Braddock to that ghastly defeat near Pittsburgh? The years prior to that surveying the valley of the Shenandoah, venturing even as far as the Ohio. So many nights like this one, but huddled under a lean-to in winter storms, a good fire going, the day's take of game roasting, there was no battle ahead to worry about, other than a concern that the natives might decide to change their views and pay a visit during the night. More than one of his comrades of those days had simply disappeared into the wilderness, a rumor perhaps drifting out later of a quick death in an ambush or a very slow and lingering death by torture.

Yet he had ventured westward as a young man, and at times still he dreamed of those days when he had gladly accepted the risks. That in part had been the thrill of it all. To explore land seen by only a handful of white men, to never know what he would experience around the next bend of the trail, to stake out more land in a day than an English baron could ever dream of owning.

Good days those, fine days. He could climb a ridge and see the unexplored world spread out before him, a vista stretching to eternity. Most of the English soldiers he knew in the last war had found the dark forests, the wilderness, disorienting, frightful even. They longed to return to England, its ordered fields, well-tended lanes, and teeming cities.

That was a difference between us so profound. Beyond the issues of the rights of free Englishmen, defined now as Americans, there was something deeper, harder to define, and the men who had just marched past him, echoing his own youth, perhaps symbolized it.

Beyond the Ohio he had explored in his youth there was the Mississippi. The few he knew who had seen it said the Ohio was merely a brook by comparison. And beyond that the Missouri, and beyond that river there were vague distant places that kings in Europe claimed were theirs but had never seen, and would trade back and forth as lines on a map, and mountains that supposedly dwarfed the Alps.

England could no longer rule this land; Englanders had no sense of it as we who were born to it did. They could never comprehend it unless they had trekked it for months at a time as he had. There was a time long ago when he had longed to travel to England, the motherland as some still called it, even invited there by comrades of old with whom he had served in the war against the French. But he knew now he never would, unless it was in chains to face a hanging. He grimaced at the thought, remembering what Ben Franklin had said about hanging together or hanging separately for what they now did. No, not the rope if we lose this night; they will not take me alive, and I will never surrender.

He turned to look back at the waters of the Delaware. Dark, foreboding. He knew those gathered nearby were waiting, most likely praying that he would end what they thought of as this mad venture. Knox had indeed said it outright earlier in the day with his booming voice, though his artillery chief did not know he was listening.

"It is one turn of the cards tonight, gentlemen," Knox had said solemnly when he thought his General was beyond earshot, "and if trumped, it is the end for all of us."

As the skies lowered and more and more men turned to look upward, muttering that it was going to be a blow, he could sense their wavering. But there was no turning back. The army was at a ragged end. Enlistments of all but a handful expired at the beginning of the new year, but six days off. An army once thirty thousand strong on the day independence was proclaimed had collapsed to a pitiful frozen few. He could muster five thousand tonight. In days it might only be five hundred.

That is why I cannot turn back, he thought, though common sense tells me that I should. My instinct tells me we have no choice. It is not for mere symbolism that I chose "victory or death" as our password for this night. It is a gamble, but it is the only gamble we can take.

The plan was well-nigh impossible to execute even by a professional fighting force trained to it for years, as were the English and even more so the Hessians, the finest professional soldiers to be had in Europe.

His army was to cross in three parts, his main force here, nine miles north of Trenton; a second, diversionary force at Bordentown, downriver from Trenton; and then, just before dawn, a third force directly below the town to block any escape by the garrison they planned to attack at first light. Even if, by some strange device, he could speak instantly to the commanders of his other two forces and monitor each step of their moves, even then such an attack at night was a challenge near to overwhelming, as he knew almost all of his staff believed.

The men were poorly fed, many having wolfed down the three days of so-called rations within minutes after receiving the leathery beef and hardtack. The march this night would be a hard one on ice-covered roads, which by the feel of this storm would soon turn to slush and semifrozen mud. Of the five thousand reported as present, the surgeon's report this day declared barely half fit for duty, and a night of hard marching would most likely mean hundreds of them collapsing before dawn. And that report had been given before this storm rolled in.

Dr. Benjamin Rush, an old friend, had come up from Philadelphia several days ago to visit and inspect the army. Congress as usual was looking over his shoulder even though in a proclamation of two weeks back, after fleeing Philadelphia for Baltimore, they had all but given him dictatorial powers to recruit a new army and command it. He trusted Rush, though, and welcomed him. Rush was a man of optimism and encouragement who swore that in spite of the unrelenting defeats a new spirit was beginning to rise up in defiance.

"Perhaps we Americans need a good thrashing now and again to wake us up," Rush had said.

He could not reply to that, for he was the commander who had been thrashed, and soundly. From Long Island all the way across New York and New Jersey to the Pennsylvania side of the Delaware, he had been beaten in every stand-up fight, and now, as his army lost morale and men, he was reduced to a final desperate act.

He had shared with Rush his plan to somehow strike back before the end of the year, to achieve some victory that would boost morale and in turn encourage at least some of the men to stay with the colors and renew their enlistments. The comment had been made that it would be "victory or death," and those three words, at that moment, had not in the least sounded like a line delivered by an actor upon the stage.

Of course, he loved plays.

Like all soldiers, he could not help but smile when the play was about war, and great heroics were enacted. When the first volley struck into Braddock's column in 1755, dropping scores of men instantly, there had been no pause in which Braddock could deliver a speech. That was no thimbleful of stage blood when a musket ball smashed into the face of the man next to him. It was easy enough for an actor to cry out, "Victory or death," but now, at this moment?

He had told Rush there would be no alternative on this night. If he flinched from the weather and the risks, from the difficulties and the enemy, the collapse in morale would lead his army to disintegrate. Within a week there would no longer be an American army. Then death would be his fate and the fate of every leader of the Revolution.

Victory or death. If the Hessians were forewarned, aroused, and awaiting them in full battle array, he would lose. Of that he had no doubt. His men hated, loathed the Hessians after the reports of their bayoneting of prisoners and wounded at Long Island and Manhattan. They feared them as well for their clocklike precision, discipline, and frightful ability to pour out four volleys a minute to the two ragged volleys of his "Continental line," and as for the militia, they barely knew how to load their weapons, let alone fire them in a disciplined manner. If the Hessians were waiting and deployed, what was left of his army would be pinned to the east bank of the Delaware and then overwhelmed by the British garrison, warm and well fed, pouring down from Princeton.

He looked up at the dark sky and found himself wondering if he would ever see home again.

Martha and Mount Vernon? What of them?

She would survive, he prayed. The English were not savages; in fact, it was tragic in a way that they faced each other now like this. For they were of the same blood. The Howe brothers were gentlemen and would not take vengeance on the widow of a slain enemy. But Mount Vernon? It would be confiscated as a prize of war, and Martha would be turned out to live off the charity of friends, at least those friends who had stayed Loyalist and thus still held their property.

He had written her that afternoon, confided in her how much he missed her and how he longed to be home in their wonderful place looking out over the Potomac. He had not confided that his men were cold and hungry, his army losing courage, their situation reduced to this last, desperate lunge. He had promised to write her on the morrow and reminded her of the love he felt in the depths of his being. He had said winning this war was vital to him, not only for America and freedom, but because it would let him go back home to the cherished companionship of the one whom he loved more than life itself. He thought briefly of Martha by the fire down in Virginia and shook his head. Time now only to decide, act, lead, arouse, and impose. Time now to show the Hessians and the British what kind of people they were trying to enslave.

Another gust of wind roared in across the river, coming more from the northeast, driving a gale of frozen rain. The moon was up, visible in the gaps that momentarily appeared in the scudding clouds. But the western horizon beyond the hills bordering the river was now obscured as well, and what little light there was seemed to be extinguished, like a candle snuffed out, and the world went dark.

The far bank disappeared from sight. The

wind howling across the river now was a steady blow, treetops swaying and crackling as the icy rain froze to branches and then shattered.

Damn, it was so damned cold.

He pulled his cape in tighter and turned to face Knox.

"Start them across," he announced.

He could barely make out the features of his chief of artillery, who was tasked this night with commanding the crossing of the river.

Knox was one of the few men in this world whom he actually had to look up to.

For a few seconds, Knox looked into his trusted friend's eyes. Nothing needed to be said; the time to debate was over. Knox saluted, turned, and started down to the ferry dock.

"We're going!" he bellowed. "Start loading up."

No one moved. He could sense their disbelief that he was pressing forward in an enterprise that most all of them believed to be a forlorn hope.

Washington forced a smile. "Just keep telling them the Hessians will be asleep. What awaits them in Trenton will be warm shelter, hot food, and dry boots for the taking."

Even the words sounded wooden to him.

Merciful God, are we so pathetic in this endeavor that I must motivate men by the promise of dry shoes taken from the enemy?

He could see the response in their eyes as they circled around him. Knox was aflame, as was Greene, but the others?

They would be facing the Hessians come dawn, and nearly all in the rank and file feared them.

"It is time to pay them back, gentlemen. Pay them back for the humiliations dealt to us. Tonight will be our night. Now to your duties."

The group slowly began to break up except for Knox, who stormed off, shouting orders, his voice booming above the thunder of the storm.

The Hessians. Mercenaries. My God, how could those who were once our own countrymen do this, hire a foreign army to trample down our liberties? Yes, they had aroused the ire of his army, when first sighted, but now all they did was arouse fear. For they were the best disciplined infantry in the world and the most relentless on the battlefield.

His spies had told him whom he would face. A Colonel Rall. He had glimpsed him on the battlefields at Fort Washington and White Plains. Fearless, and rumor was, one of their best.

Am I a fool to think that these frozen men around me, ragged, barefoot, already soaked through, will face and defeat Rall in the morning?

Or was all hope of surprise already lost? Rall was a professional, his intelligence reports saying he was a man with thirty years' experience in war. And at this moment he and his men were warm, well fed, and resting.

He felt a dark premonition and pushed it aside. By dawn, he would face Rall, and it would be the German commander who would take the sword from his dying hand.

He turned back to watch the men beginning to file past.

"Close up the ranks, boys, and keep moving. Remember, it is victory or death."

CHAPTER TWO

Trenton, New Jersey
6:00 P.M., December 25, 1776

Colonel Johann Rall leaned back in his chair, gazed at his host with a contented grin, and moved his black checker over his opponent's last survivor, thus winning the game.

There was a friendly laugh from his host, Mr. Potts, who had so graciously offered his home as headquarters for, as he put it, "our allies in the suppression of treasonous rebels." Shaking his head, Potts stood up, went to the sideboard, and held up a decanter filled with wine.

"You are too good an opponent," Potts announced, gesturing with the decanter as an offer to refill the colonel's glass.

"No, sir. Duty. I must not drink much," Rall replied with a smile.

He felt that his English was awkward, though he had been practicing ever since his prince had informed him, nearly a year ago, that his regiment would be sent to the Americas to help "our English cousins" against this peasant rebellion sweeping their colonies.

Potts, who could speak some German, made a second offer of just a bit more to celebrate this Christmas night, and Rall again refused, this time in German as well.

It did not stop Potts from refilling his own glass before returning to sit across from the colonel, motioning to the checkerboard, offering to set up another game.

Rall nodded and Potts began to reset the pieces.

Rall was glad to find a fairly decent competitor in this game. Like any gentleman he could play a good round of chess, but on a night like this he preferred a game that required far less concentration, that he could play casually while he dwelt on other concerns.

The wind outside continued to rise, windowpanes and closed shutters rattling. One of the shutters, breaking free and swinging out and then slamming back, sounded almost like a musket shot. Old soldier that he was, he tried not to show a reaction to the sharp sound, but it did cause him to look over with a start.

Potts caught the somewhat anxious glance, understood, and called for one of his African servants to go outside and secure the shutter. He apologized for the intrusion.

As the servant opened the door, a cold gust came rushing in, causing the crackling blaze in the fireplace to waver and flicker.

"A terrible night to be out and about," Potts said. "I will bet you a pound to a shilling, sir, those damn rebels will be hiding in their holes tonight."

Rall did not reply.

Yes, a terrible night, he thought. But would it be a night so terrible that he and his men might truly relax and enjoy a peaceful sleep?

He could recall that on more than one night such as this he had forced his men to march for a surprise attack at dawn.

And the bet? As a gentleman, of course, he would never make a wager with a civilian on such an issue. He had learned long ago that such bets could indeed be bad luck.

Potts began the game and Rall played along, absently losing three checkers rather quickly, Potts obviously delighted to have gained an advantage in the opening moves.

Thirty-five years! And now I find myself in this godforsaken land, Rall thought glumly. Yet it was what his prince had ordered, and like any good soldier he had obeyed his orders, though to more than a few in his ranks the orders seemed nothing short of insane.

What stake did he have in this fight? None, other than the honor of his regiment and the practical realization that, with Europe at peace, this expedition would at least provide some training for his men and keep them in fighting trim for when a real war ignited. Already there were rumors that the French just might intervene in America, and for him, as for most Germans, another chance at the French did have its appeal. But if the confidence of the English commanders was to be believed, this war was all but over. Come spring, he and his regiment would embark on the long and nauseating six-week sail homeward with their mission completed, though more than a hundred of his men would never return, having found a place to rest until the final trumpet in this strange land.

Was it worth the price?

Unlike the stereo type of some of his fellow officers, especially the officious and noisome division commander Colonel Donop, he truly did care for his men and took pride in knowing most of them by their family names. A good officer, he always said to his youngest and newest lieutenants, learned to take care of the feet of his men first, and from there their stomachs and hearts, and by that means he could motivate their souls. If such means did not work there was always the lash, but he always believed that to be the absolute last resource of a good officer and too often the first choice of a bad officer.

When the lowest of privates realized that, they would surely follow such an officer into the gates of hell if need be. Nor would the officer ever have to fear that death on the battlefield would come from a musket ball striking his back between the shoulder blades.

Unlike the British army, an officer gained his rank in the armies of Hesse-Cassel and even that of Prussia itself by merit and leadership, and not by how much they could pay for their commissions. How the English could run an army in such a manner was beyond him, and though he would never voice it publicly he felt that was the source of many of the problems this campaign had faced. He had respect, to a certain degree, for Lord Cornwallis, but as for the rest . . .

He stirred, looking over at the portly American merchant who was his host, the man studiously examining the checkerboard. He wondered, deep in his heart, what this man actually thought of the war. Potts had greeted them with open arms, loudly crying that he was delighted to be free at last of the rebel thieves. Had the man said the same thing five months back when independence was declared, or had he cheered along with the rest of the rabble, but now turned eager to make his peace?

Potts finally made his move. Rall nodded politely, quickly made his in reply and settled back, turning his gaze toward the crackling fire. Like his father before him, he had served his prince, entering service at the age of fourteen. At sixteen he had seen his first action when the great Frederick had led the north German states against Austria. During the Seven Years' War, which these strange Americans called the War of the French and Indians, he had seen a dozen pitched battles and scores of minor ones, and had even been presented to the King of Prussia and commended for bravery at the Battle of Luetzen.

The memory of that filled him with pride, so that his attention to the game wavered and he quickly lost two pieces to only one of Mr. Potts's.

Thus he had learned how to lead men. A true German officer led the charge from the front, regimental flag by his side, and if he retreated he had to be the last to leave the field. Such was expected of a true German officer, and so he insisted on with those whom he trained and led into battle. Oh, the British officers were certainly brave enough, but they seemed to lack that bond to their common soldiers that he demanded of his officers.

He had even fought against the Turks when his ruler had loaned some of his most trusted officers to his cousin Catherine, the czarina of Russia, and his portfolio of personal commendations swelled as the czarina herself praised his skill and bravery.

All of those years of service, and here I find myself in this godforsaken land on the edge of a dark and godforsaken wilderness. What the appeal was of this America was beyond him. The people were dirty and ill bred, their farmsteads lacking neatness and order. The taverns served awful beer and even worse wine. The beds more often than not were filled with bugs, and as for the roads . . . The memory of the march from Amboy to Trenton was one of unrelenting mud and slime.

He gazed at the checkerboard for a moment, at last offering a riposte, clipping off one of Potts's pieces, and settled back while the portly American merchant grunted with disapproval and would most likely spend the next five minutes contemplating a reply.

I should not even be here, he thought ruefully. If handled correctly, the war, if one could call it that, should already be over, my men at sea even now, returning home.

He held these Americans in contempt. Their pretension to what they called an army was truly a joke, but at times the British, or at least their officers, had proved to be little better.

Upon arrival at New York he had attended the briefing offered by one of Howe's aides on the disposition of forces, and the plan for the campaign to sweep the enemy off Long Island.

Folly.

If Frederick were in command, he would have laughed with derision and finished the rebellion in a week. The Hudson was a broad enough river that with the tide behind them and a wind from the south or southwest, the entire fleet could have simply sailed a few miles upriver without any fear of the enemy batteries and disembarked in the farmland in the middle of Manhattan Island. That move would have cut off most of Washington's army, which was deployed at the lower end of the island and across the

East River on the long island that some called Brook Land.

Digging in across the width of the island, the British would have cut off the rebel city from supplies and eventually forced the rabble to attack out of sheer desperation.

Once they were dispatched, a holding force would remain in the city, guarded by the fleet. Troops moved back down the river would disembark again below the village of Amboy, and two days of hard marching across the province of Jersey would bring them to the rebel capital of Philadelphia. The British had the fleet and one of the finest harbors in the world. Any attempt by the Americans to move from one bank of the river to the other would require days of marching; their crossing of rivers could easily be blocked. On the other hand, British ships could move entire armies back and forth in little more than a hour or two. Why the Howe brothers had not taken better advantage of this was beyond his understanding.

Once Washington and his scum were bottled up and destroyed, a quick march across Jersey, or if the British did not wish to muddy their feet, a day's sail around the southern cape of Jersey, could then have placed them within a quick short march of the enemy capital.

End of the war and home by Christmas. Instead I sit here.

That is how the great Frederick would have done it. It was a problem so elementary that even the newest of his sergeants could have figured it out, and most of them had, chaffing at the orders of their "cousins," who seemed to view this war, not so much as a snuffing out of a rebellion, but as an exercise in leisurely campaigning and at times what appeared almost to be a parent's coaxing of a wayward child.

Settle it sharply and quickly, with the bayonet if need be, and the hell with the coaxing. A recalcitrant child should always be whipped, and whipped soundly.

Instead, months had been wasted. The battle for Long Island, and allowing the enemy to escape to Manhattan — that in itself had filled him and the men of his command with disgust. One sharp day of battle and the damn rebels had run like rabbits; by the thousands they had huddled along the shore, literally under the guns of the British navy blocking their retreat across the East River. He had begged Donop to ignore the British orders, to close with the bayonet and finish it then and there, driving them into the river or forcing surrender, but that damnable Lord Howe had ordered them to hold until the morning, when they would finish it.

Under cover of night, and he had to admit grudgingly, in a masterful move, Washington had evacuated his entire army across the East River, literally between the bow of one British frigate and the stern of another. My God, was every man aboard those ships asleep that night? The entire crew of every ship, from captain to lowest seaman, should have been flogged for their failure to keep proper watch.

And so Washington and his rabble had escaped, and would escape again and again as summer ended and autumn settled on the land. And finally, in the last weeks of this year, they had fled across Jersey.

His men had been in the vanguard of that pursuit. Countless times he had begged for release, for one day, just one day, to be slipped free of the leash and lead his men forward relentlessly to finish this war so they could go home. Just one forced march by night to the flank and into the enemy rear before dawn, as he had so often done in Bohemia, Silesia, and on the Turkish border. One night of movement free of ponderous restraints. Or just one day of hot pursuit with bayonets leveled. But always the order was given by Howe to bring his men to rest.

If there was a kindred spirit in the British command it was their Lord Cornwallis. He, too, had bridled at the slow movements, the chances lost, as Washington and his rebellious scum, like oily serpents, escaped the traps laid, traps that any German officer would have ensured were indeed traps, and not nets with holes in them.

"I have my first king, sir," Potts announced grandly as he double-jumped two of Rall's black pieces.

Rall smiled graciously and said nothing. Couldn't the man see that his opponent was barely paying attention to the game?

The wind outside rose in pitch, howling under the eaves of the house, counterpointed by a thump, a second thump, and then several more.

"Jacob, that damn shutter is loose again!" Potts shouted, calling for his servant to go outside.

Rall sat bolt upright, head cocked slightly. Another thump.

"That was not your shutter, sir," Rall announced in German, standing up, straightbacked chair falling with a clatter behind him.

He headed for the door, which was flung open before he could reach it. One of his staff, young Münchasen, rivulets of icy water dripping from his cape, stood in the open doorway, breathing hard.

"Sir. The rebels, sir."

"I know, Münchasen. Where is my horse?"

Without taking time to put on a cape or overcoat, Rall was out the door. An orderly was leading his horse from the stable behind Potts's house, saddled and ready. He climbed up, Münchasen gaining his own horse as well.

Another thump followed by what sounded like a ragged volley of a dozen or more muskets, the sound distant, barely audible against the wind.

From the northwest, most likely the outpost on the River Road.

He raced down Queen Street. A drummer was standing outside the stone barracks in the center of town, beating assembly. His was the duty regiment for the garrison this evening, the men ordered to remain in full uniform, cartridge boxes strapped on at all times, muskets on hand even when resting in their bunks, and now they were filing out on the run. Some had overcoats on, many did not. He slowed for a few seconds to watch. These men knew their duty. They began to form up along the street with heads lowered, hats pulled low over their brows, ready for action, complete with musket locks wrapped in oiled cloth to keep them dry.

No need to stop here. He spurred his mount, turning on to the River Road, and after passing a block of houses and a church was out to the edge of town. Münchasen was struggling to keep up. *"Herr Oberst.* Please slow down. The rebels could be anywhere!"

Rall ignored him, pressing hard. In the darkness he saw movement. It was the guard company, posted in the center of town and kept under full arms, weapons loaded. They were running hard, struggling with the damnable mud as they advanced. He edged off to the side of the road, splashing through what passed as a drainage ditch and coming up to the head of the column of fifty men.

At the sight of their colonel in the lead, the men's pace quickened. Captain Metzger shouted for his command to press forward.

"That's it, my children!" Rall shouted. "Quickly now, quickly!"

The outpost in a farmhouse a hundred yards north of the village could be seen, windows illuminated. A musket flashed within.

"Comrades!" Metzger shouted. "Comrades!"

Several more flashes from outside the house, the sound of a musket ball whizzing close by Rall.

Just stay in place, damn you, he thought. Just stay in place a few seconds more!

"Charge, lads, charge!" he cried, saber out, pointing the way, urging his mount to a gallop, the nervous Münchasen pressing up by his side, trying as usual, against all etiquette, to place himself between his colonel and enemy fire.

They reached the open gate leading into the farmyard . . . and there was nothing.

The door to the outpost was flung open as Rall reined in a splatter of mud.

It took him a moment to register who it was.

"Sergeant Lindermann, where are they?" Rall cried.

The sergeant looked about, unable to reply.

"Where are they?"

"Sir, I believe they have fled."

"Damn them," Rall growled as he started to dismount.

"Sir, shall we pursue?" Metzger asked, breathing hard, coming up alongside the colonel.

Angrily, Rall shook his head. "The cowardly peasants have fled, as usual."

He looked to the sky. If the moon were out, he would have pursued them. But if the weather had been clear, the fields bright with moonlight on snow, the rebels would never have dared to creep in this close to town and to linger as long as they had.

"Useless, Captain Metzger. Post guards around the house, and keep them away from the light of the windows. The rest of the detachment, move into the barn for now and out of this storm."

Metzger saluted and began to shout orders, detailing off pickets as Rall, heart still racing, climbed the four steps to the broad porch of the farmhouse.

"Now, sergeant, your full report."

"Sir, I have wounded inside."

Rall brushed past him and into the house. He could hear cries of anguish from the back, and the kitchen looked like a slaughtering shed. One man was on the floor, gasping for air, foaming frothy blood with each breath. Two more were sitting on the floor, one with arterial blood pulsing from a gaping wound in his left forearm, a corporal kneeling by his side, already tightening a tourniquet around it as blood pooled and spread across the brick floor and splattered against the wall. This man, if he survived, would go home with that arm missing.

Two others were bleeding as well, one with a hole through his cheek, crying out as he spat blood and shattered teeth. It was an agonizing wound, and Rall paused for a moment, bending by his side, putting a hand on the young man's shoulder.

"Be brave, my lad, be brave."

The soldier looked up, saw who was addressing him, and his crying ceased.

"The damn cowardly dogs!" someone cried, coming down the stairs from the second floor. "They got Yeager in the face and Franz in shoulder —"

The corporal stopped his cursing as he stormed into the kitchen and saw his colonel. He snapped to attention.

Rall took it all in. There was food on the table, plates knocked over, some shattered on the floor. Several muskets, never used, were leaning against the wall behind the table. The room was heavy with the smell of gunpowder, a cold breeze racing in through broken windows and driving the smoke out. There were bullet holes in the wall, one with a splattering of blood around it.

He did not need to be told what had happened.

The outpost guards, with the onset of the storm, and this being Christmas night, had settled down to a feast. Following his

71

orders, they had not taken any spirits, which were banned for the entire army this night. But they had let their guard down. It was all so clearly evident. The raiders had literally crept beneath the eaves of the house and into every window fired a volley.

It was little better than murder. It was also a surprise that never should have happened.

He turned to face the sergeant, who stood before him, features pale.

"Did you have an outside guard posted at all four corners?" Rall snapped.

"Not exactly, sir."

"Did you, or did you not, sergeant?"

"No, sir."

"Why not?"

"Sir, Private Withers shot a deer this morning and we roasted it." He pointed woodenly toward the table where half-carved haunches of venison rested.

"I was changing the guard, sir, allowing the men coming in to dry off. Those about to go out took but a few minutes more to eat before going out into the storm." His voice trailed away.

"And the damn rebels were out there, watching, waiting for just such a mistake, were they not, sergeant?"

The sergeant could not reply.

"You are reduced in rank to private." He

gestured toward the man's uniform facings as if to tear them off.

He paused for a second, to look around the room.

"Corporal Steiner, you are now sergeant of this detachment. Your men are relieved of this position for the night. Escort your wounded back to the surgeon. I will pass the word for him to be ready to receive you."

"Yes, colonel."

"Both of you will appear before me after morning roll to explain your actions here."

Standing at rigid attention, they said nothing.

"Dismissed."

Rall turned and strode out of the kitchen and onto the porch.

Captain Metzger was waiting for orders.

"Your men are to take over the watch here. There is to be no repeat of this folly. I want guards posted at all four corners of the house throughout the night. Detail off a dozen men to help carry the wounded to town. Captain Yoder's company will replace your command as the guard company in town until relieved at midnight."

Metzger saluted and turned back to his men, shouting more orders.

"Münchasen, ride back to town. Order the men to stand down and to get out of this foul weather, but rest under arms to continue throughout the night. Inform the surgeon to prepare to receive casualties."

Münchasen did as ordered and galloped into the dark.

Still seething, Rall remounted, passed through the gate, and rode alone the few hundred yards to the center of town.

"Damn cowardly scum," he muttered. Raiders, the same ones most likely who had been harassing his command since they were posted to this pathetic village. Meanwhile Cornwallis kept headquarters thirty miles away in Amboy, and two full British regiments rested comfortably in the spacious village of Princeton, twelve miles away. They put us out here, to be harassed day and night, sometimes by a single shot from the woods, and on a night such as this, even bolder, actually catching the unfortunate fools within this house by surprise. To move a single message back to Cornwallis now required a full guard of dragoons and mounted jaegers.

Damn this country!

As he reached the center of town he saw the last of his men filing into their barracks. It had been this way nearly every night for the last two weeks, his men staggering with exhaustion as two and sometimes three alarms a night rousted them out of their warm quarters, and on this night into a howling gale.

He was aware now of his own folly in rushing out without a cape or overcoat. His heavy woolen uniform was already soaked at the shoulders. In his back and legs the chill was setting in.

If there was any comfort, it was knowing that he would be back in a warm house in a few minutes, whereas the damn rebels, if still out and about, were wet and freezing. He hoped that hell rather than being a place of fire, was instead of ice and eternal cold.

Now his men were soaked as well . . . and he sensed it was going to be a very long night.

CHAPTER THREE

McConkey's Ferry
6:00 P.M. December 25, 1776

General Washington followed Knox at a discreet distance, letting him run the operation. Delegating responsibilities was something he found difficult to do. He knew it was a common complaint by men under his command that he tried to do everything himself, and on this night they were right. He would have to delegate and then pray for the best, letting them do their jobs beyond his watchful gaze. That also was frustrating, for so much could go wrong, was already going wrong.

Torches were flickering to life on the ferry dock. Glover's men from Marblehead, as usual, manned the boats. The men who had saved the army at Long Island, carried the army across the Hudson, and once already across this same river as they retreated, would labor throughout the night again.

The first of the boats, a heavy bulk transport the locals called a Durham boat, after the maker — forty to sixty feet in length, flat bottomed, no seats except for the four to eight rowers — was tied to the dock. A company of the Pennsylvania riflemen was climbing aboard, cursing when they discovered the hull held several inches of slush and water.

He walked slowly toward the dock, mentally counting off the time, waiting as the boat filled, the men standing to make more room, boatmen already at the oars, stoic, as if the gale and the river were just another annoyance in a world filled with annoyances. There was confusion as one of the men, perhaps drunk, nearly went over the side, comrades grabbing him, the boat rocking violently, the Marblehead men cursing the Pennsylvanians soundly. There was a momentary debate as one of the men collapsed, sick, cold, or afraid, and was at last lifted out of the boat and deposited on the dock.

"Filled! Wait for the next un," someone shouted, and then the lines were cast off. With oars inverted for use as poles, the Marble-headers pushed off from the dock. Once clear of its scant protection, the boat pivoted in the strong current, floes banging against its broad-beamed side, the riflemen cursing, several shouting out that the boat was going over.

The crew dug in with their oars, pulling hard, broaching against the current and then the boat was gone from view, disappearing into the gale.

A second boat, tied off just below the dock, was pulled into position with much heaving and cursing, and Knox came to the General's side, shaking his head.

It had taken nearly ten minutes to load this one boat and get it off, and Glover had assured him they could do it in half that time. But that promise had been made when the weather was clear, there was no wind, and it was assumed moonlight would help them.

"I'm sorry, sir," Knox offered. "I know what you are thinking. It's taking too long."

"We're committed," Washington replied.

"This damn storm, it's like it was sent from hell, sir."

He forced a smile and shook his head. "Heaven-sent." He said the words loudly, wanting others to hear him and pass it along.

"Heaven-sent, I tell you. The enemy will think only madmen would be out on a night like this. And we are mad. Victory or death,

Knox. It's victory or death."

He clapped Knox on the shoulder and could see the trace of a smile.

"I'll be in the ferry house. Now keep them moving."

Knox saluted and returned to his work.

Washington returned to the riverbank. His personal detachment, orderlies, men of the Pennsylvania cavalry assigned as his guards, and the scouts who would lead the columns once the march started, stood by, waiting.

"We'll cross once most of the army is across. Find some shelter in the barn behind the ferry house and I'll send for you when the time comes."

The men saluted and left. He felt a wave of pity for them. The ferry house and attached outbuildings were already crammed to overflowing with staff, along with a couple of surgeons tending to men who had collapsed from illness and the cold. They'd have to wait in the unheated barn.

He caught the eye of one of the scouts. There were two assigned to his headquarters this night, local boys from the New Jersey militia who had stayed on with the army rather than desert, as had most of their comrades. These lads were called upon to act as guides. The youngest of them was looking straight at him, eyes wide, features pale, shivering uncontrollably.

He paused. "Try and find a dry place, son." He put a fatherly hand on his shoulder.

The boy didn't speak, could only nod, his teeth chattering.

"Are you well?"

The young man forced a nod. "I'm fine, sir."

"That's the spirit."

He squeezed his shoulder and, turning, walked away. At the dock, troops were lining up, heads bent against the wind, waiting for what he knew would most likely be hours before they would cross to what awaited them on the other side.

Private Jonathan van Dorn stood silent as the General walked off.

"You wooden fool, you missed your chance."

Peter Wellsley had joined the militia on the same day he had, five months back, when General Ewing marched into town, heading to New York to join the Continental Army, and promised each lad a ten-dollar bounty for joining.

Jonathan had needed no such encouragement. He was burning with desire to go, ignoring his parents' protestations. He had joined with Peter and half a dozen other men of the village of Trenton, alongside his brother James.

"You should have told him the truth, you ass," Peter said.

"What truth?"

"That you're sick, damn it. You're burning with fever. He'd have excused you."

Jonathan shook his head vehemently.

"Just a chill, that's all."

"Come on, lads. You heard the General. Let's get out of this storm."

It was one of the Pennsylvania cavalrymen pushing past the two. They followed the seasoned troopers into the barn behind the ferry house, light glowing from within. One of the troopers, opening the door, was greeted with howls of protest that it was too crowded, to shut the damn door and go someplace else, but the sergeant shoved his way in, ordering the others to follow. Those crammed within were men of "the line," Marylanders from the looks of the few who wore semblances of uniforms. Jonathan hesitated at the door, the disdain and barriers between militia and regulars were apparent now.

Peter followed the cavalrymen in, pushing Jonathan along.

"God damn militia, there's no more room."

"They're with us," the cavalry sergeant announced.

"I don't give a damn who they're with," one of the Marylanders snapped, pushing through the crowd. "Out now!"

Jonathan looked at the Maryland lieutenant and wondered how any of them could tell who was who. Everyone was ragged, filthy, the bright gray uniforms of summer long since reduced to threadbare and a nearly universal dingy brown. Few of them had shaved in weeks. It was just too damn cold. In the closed air of the barn, his head swam with the stench so that he actually was tempted to back up and retreat out the door.

The Pennsylvania sergeant stepped in front of the Marylander.

"General's orders. They're with us, and we are staying here waiting for orders."

"Which general? We got so damn many of them."

"Washington, that's who."

The Marylander hesitated.

"Oh," a long pause. "Him."

"What the hell does that mean?" the sergeant snapped. The lieutenant was looking at him with a cool gaze.

Jonathan felt trapped between the two, saying nothing.

"Were you at Brooklyn?" the lieutenant asked.

The sergeant nodded.

"Yes. I was there. And yes, I saw what happened to you."

Jonathan gazed at the lieutenant. He had not seen it. His unit was held in reserve that day, so long ago, back in August, but the entire army knew how the Maryland line had been cut off and then slashed to ribbons, overrun, scores of their wounded supposedly bayoneted by the Hessians even as they begged for mercy. And more than a few of them blamed the general from Virginia, General Washington, for the fiasco of that day.

The barn was silent as the two glared at each other.

"Save it for the bastards on the other side," someone from the back of the crowd snapped, and Jonathan could sense the tension breaking. The sergeant still held the Marylander's gaze but nodded in agreement.

The Maryland lieutenant stepped back slightly, giving a sidelong glance at Jonathan and Peter.

"You two. Militia?"

"Yes, sir," Peter replied, trying to sound defiant, but he was shaking nearly as hard as Jonathan, his voice breaking.

"And I say, damn all militia. Let me guess, New Jersey no less."

"So what if we are?" Peter replied. There was defiance in his voice.

"We got the last two from New Jersey with us, boys. So much for Jersey."

The lieutenant's disdainful gaze shifted to Jonathan, who would not lower his eyes.

"How fast can you run away, boy?"

"Not fast enough to keep up with you," he said, trying to suppress the rasping cough that had been tormenting him for days.

"You damn whelp." The lieutenant started to draw back a hand to strike him.

"He's game and I'm with him," the sergeant announced, shouldering forward several of the Pennsylvania troopers, who were crowding in as well. "We are all going back to New Jersey tonight, and it is nice to have some New Jersey men to help us in *their* home state."

For a moment Jonathan thought a brawl was about to erupt. The lieutenant stood silent.

"Lieutenant Elkins! Leave off it."

An officer, wearing the epaulette of a major pushed his way through the press.

The major glared at the sergeant and then at Jonathan.

"Just stay away from my men."

Jonathan and the sergeant said nothing. The order was rather absurd; they were crowded nearly shoulder to shoulder in the small barn.

The major looked back at his own men.

"Stand at ease, all of you. There'll be plenty of those damn Germans to take it out on tomorrow."

The lieutenant spared a final menacing glance for Jonathan and then pushed back in with his own men.

Jonathan started to cough, nearly choking for a moment as phlegm clogged his lungs and then broke loose. Bent double, gasping for breath, he spit it out and felt Peter's arm around him, helping him to stand up straight.

"Your friend is right," the sergeant said, his tone almost fatherly. "Lad, go to the surgeon. They'll excuse you."

Jonathan shook his head.

"I'm staying. The General said he needs guides who live in Trenton, and that means me and my friend here."

The sergeant smiled. "That's the spirit, boy." He produced a battered wooden canteen, uncorked it, and offered it to him.

"Take a pull on this. It'll warm you."

Jonathan did as ordered. He had never drunk rum before joining the army, except once when he and James had secretly filled a small bucket from a newly delivered barrel of rum behind a tavern, and then slipped off to Assunpink Creek to while away the afternoon fishing and drinking like men do when they fish. They had drained the bucket dry and staggered home roaring drunk. Two years ago — he was fifteen then, James seventeen, and their father had thrashed them soundly for their heathen behavior.

Two years, a lifetime ago. He had learned a lot in the last five months, though. Drinking rum was one of the things he had learned, and though he would die before admitting it, especially now, he had learned how to run with the best of them.

He took a deep swallow of the rum, its warmth bursting through him, stilling the trembling from the cold and fever. He handed the canteen to Peter, who took a swallow as well and handed it back to the sergeant.

"I'm Howard, Sergeant Howard." The three shook hands.

"You really Jersey militia?"

Jonathan braced slightly, wondering if the friend of the moment might turn.

He nodded.

"No bother," Howard replied. "At least you two lads have stuck with it."

"A lot more of us," Peter ventured. "We were down with General Ewing until yesterday on the other side of the river from Trenton. We got six hundred or more."

Howard said nothing, and Jonathan knew it was a bit of a cover. When the call had gone out in the summer, a thousand or more had answered just from Burlington and Salem Counties alone. What a time that had been, the march from Trenton up to New York. They had been feted at every village and town along the way. Cheered, even kissed by more than a few girls. No uniforms like the men of the regular line, but he had felt cocky enough in a fine dark gray linsey-woolsey hunting frock and broad brimmed hat, fowling piece on his shoulder. Though his parents had stood firmly against him and James going off to the war, they had at least made sure their boys were dressed for it, and each had a haversack packed with smoked ham, dried fruit, and even coffee beans.

Those had been wonderful, exciting days, even though, as they reached the broad Hudson and gazed in wonder at New York, the city across the river with well nigh on to thirty thousand living there, the British fleet already was at anchor in the outer harbor.

They had laughed then at the sight of the ships, pointing out to each other the fortifications that lined both banks of the inner harbor that would surely smash the fleet to pieces if it ever dared to venture in.

The laughter had soon died away and was stilled forever at Brooklyn. He had had his own moment of terror when a British column scaled the heights of the Palisades and maneuvered to take Fort Lee. He, along with the rest of his comrades, had fled before the enemy was even in sight and thus had started what some derisively called the Jersey Foot Races. The British light cavalry and Hessians had herded the demoralized army completely out of the state.

James. He did not like to think of his brother.

The rum had gone to his head. After the long cold day outside, the warmth within the barn suddenly felt hot, his knees going weak, and for a moment he feared he would faint.

Sighing, he leaned against Peter, who helped him a few feet to the corner of a stall. The floor was covered with a splattering of cow manure, but he didn't care. There was enough space to sit down. Sergeant Howard came over and squatted down beside them.

"So you boys are the guides?"

"We grew up in Trenton," Peter announced. "General Ewing asked for volunteers who lived there, so Jonathan and me stepped forward. We were told to come up here. It was a bit of a hike, and damned cold."

"You could've dodged off once out of sight," Howard said. "Good for you, sticking with it."

"We're not giving up," Jonathan announced, trying to sound manly even as he trembled.

"Your families live there? In Trenton?"

"My family owns a farm, a mile or so east, but I've hunted the fields all around there, along with Jonathan here. His family, they're regular merchants. Own a store and everything."

"What kind of store?"

"Dry goods and leather from a tannery we own," Jonathan said softly.

"So your family's there now?"

Jonathan nodded.

"You see 'em when we retreated through the town?"

He looked at the sergeant and shook his head.

"Haven't seen my family since I joined up."

There was more than a wistful tone in his voice. Looking closely, Jonathan could see that the sergeant was an older man, in his thirties at least, maybe forties.

"Wife and four children in Philadelphia," he sighed. "At least, last I heard."

He gazed off.

"Last I heard," he said again. "I don't know if they're still there or took off. Word is half the city emptied out when Congress fled. The ones that stayed, most of them are Tories just waiting for us to be finished off."

"Same in Trenton," Peter replied bitterly.

Jonathan shifted uncomfortably.

Peter gave him a sidelong glance. He fumbled a bit and lowered his head. "At least that's what I heard."

Howard gazed at them.

"Guess it will be hard on you two, guiding us in to the attack. I mean, friends, neighbors, kin in the way."

"It's what we volunteered for," Jonathan said. The bitterness in his voice was evident. "We have to beat the British to be free, and we are going to."

He slouched lower against the wall and pulled his damp cape, actually just a tattered worn blanket, in tight around his body. Sergeant Howard drew back, as if sensing that a raw nerve had been touched.

Sitting there Jonathan studied his feet. The shoes his parents had given him had disintegrated and rotted off long ago, even though as tanners his parents had made sure that James and he had shoes of the finest leather, with even an extra pair tucked into their packs. He had given the second pair to Peter, an act of pity, and now both of them were barefoot, feet encased in strips of burlap, toes sticking out, swollen, cracked, filthy.

He had given up trying to patch his trousers. The frayed ends rose over his ankles, both knees sticking out, the thighs of the pants no longer white but black. As to his backside he was ashamed that only the blanket covered that nakedness. His hat did little to keep out the rain, the heavy felt long since matted out, the crown split open for several inches along a crease.

This is what I volunteered for, he realized. The romance of it was long gone. The girls who had so eagerly kissed him as he proudly marched out of Trenton would most likely recoil with disgust if they saw and smelled him now. Or, worse yet, count him a fool. So many others had stayed, as his parents had begged him to do on the day when what

91

was left of the army passed through Trenton; they were safe at home, well fed, warm, and offered the protection of a forgiving and benevolent king.

"Damn my brothers," he whispered softly. "Damn all of them."

He thought again of what he might do when this army took Trenton back, as surely it must. He remembered far too clearly what James had done and what he suspected his other brother Allen might now be doing. When the army had retreated through Trenton three weeks ago, he deliberately avoided going to his house out of fear of what he might discover. But after this? After all this if we survive the night? He would not back down this time.

His parents? They had professed leanings for the patriots in the heady days of summer when the Declaration had been read from the steps of their church. But now? Hessians were most likely quartered in their home and store, and without a doubt his father, who had come to this land forty years ago and could still speak Dutch and even some German, was most likely drinking a Christmas toast with them at this very moment.

Another seizure of coughing took him. Leaning forward, he gasped for air, Peter bracing him, slapping him on the back as if that would actually help to clear his lungs.

He coughed up more phlegm and fell back against the wall of the stall, shivering, and then feeling hot. Peter, more a brother to him now than anyone else in this world, looked at him with concern.

"I'll be fine," he said, forcing a smile.

He closed his eyes, letting his thoughts drift back to summer, the warmth. Being the youngest and indulged by his mother he had been able to slip off from chores, most especially the noisome tasks at the tannery, his mother arguing that her boys were now of the upper class, as was she, and they did not need to stink of curing leather. She had dreams that he would have started this autumn at the college up in Princeton, for he could already read Latin and even some Greek. Even though it was a Presbyterian college and they were Lutherans, she had dreamed of her youngest being educated — a minister, perhaps, or a lawyer.

He smiled at the thought. Now I'm a private, dressed in rags. If we fail tonight and I'm taken alive, I'll rot in one of the prison hulks anchored in the East River off of Brooklyn. So much for my Latin and Greek.

And yet no regrets. If anything, his heart

was even more hardened to see it through.

The coughing spasm having passed, he opened his eyes. It was a bit brighter in the barn; someone had managed to strike a flame, lanterns had been found, a few men were fishing out stubs of candles. Sergeant Howard actually looked somewhat absurd, holding his cupped hands over a candle set atop the wall of the barn stall, rubbing them over the tiny flame, trying to get the chill out.

Jonathan fumbled under his blanket in what was left of the once smart-looking hunting frock; underneath he still had something of an actual linen shirt, not washed, though, in months, and, if washed, would most likely crumble into rags. He found his Bible, tucked down near his belt, and pulled it out. By the pale light of the candle he could have made out some of the words, the book easily opening to the Ninety-first Psalm. He didn't actually need to read it; he knew it by heart, could even say a few lines of it in Greek. Howard, watching him, moved his hands so as not to block the flickering candlelight.

Folded over and tucked into the Bible were a few sheets of paper, stitched together, that he was actually looking for, and he pulled them out. He held them close to his face, the words hard to see by the faint light and harder to read when a bout of shivering struck him, the pamphlet trembling like a leaf on a wind-swept tree.

Outside, the wind was howling, rattling some loose boards, the candle flame nearly going out. Howard cupped his hands around it again to protect it until the gust had passed. As the wind died away, Jonathan could hear the hard pelting of sleet and freezing rain against the side of the barn.

"What you got there?" Howard asked.

"Thomas Paine, he just wrote it."

At the mention of the name Thomas Paine, those around him looked in his direction.

"You got that new pamphlet by Paine?" someone asked. He looked up. It was one of the Marylanders.

"Yup. They passed out a few of them with my battalion yesterday."

"Major Bartlett got a copy, he read a bit of it to us earlier," the Marylander announced. "And that's the same thing?"

Jonathan nodded.

The Marylander turned.

"You men, let's have some quiet here."

"What the hell for?" came a reply.

"That boy from Jersey, he's got the new pamphlet by Tom Paine."

"Give it over here, Jersey."

It was the Maryland lieutenant.

Jonathan rose to his feet and shook his head.

"No, sir, it's mine."

The lieutenant gazed at him as if judging what to do with the defiance of this militiaman, from New Jersey no less, and then turned back.

"Barry, fetch that lantern over here."

A moment later the lieutenant was by Jonathan's side, holding the lantern high, its bright light illuminating the tattered and water-stained pamphlet.

"Go ahead, Jersey. Read it."

"These are . . ." Another coughing spasm hit. Embarrassed, he leaned over, gasping, coughing up more phlegm.

"Can you read it?" the lieutenant asked, as Jonathan stood up. There was no insult in his voice. It was a simple question.

"I was camped beside him up in Newark the night he started to write this," Jonathan announced, his voice filled with emotion. "I can read it."

The lieutenant fell silent. All around him were silent. The only thing that could keep him from being heard was the howling of the gale outside, sweeping across the ice-choked Delaware, carrying with it the distant sound of men laboring to load a cannon on one of the boats, other men struggling with the lead of a horse that had slipped off the dock into the freezing water and was now crying out pitifully.

He held the pamphlet tight, but strangely, he no longer even needed to read it. It was in his heart and soul.

"*The Crisis,* by Thomas Paine," he began, trying to hold back his emotions. "Number one."

"These are the times that try men's souls . . ."

CHAPTER FOUR

Newark, New Jersey
November 24, 1776

Rain. Blinding sheets of rain lashed down from an angry heaven.

A chilled river of it was coursing through the thin, worn fabric of his tent, trickling down his neck, and, even worse, splashing on the page of foolscap he was trying to write on, smearing the first lines.

"Damn it all to hell," he snapped, scooping up the soggy sheet of paper from the slab of wood he had been writing on, crumpling it and throwing it to the muddy ground.

Thomas Paine, more than a little drunk on this disgusting November evening, pushed his "writing desk," off his knees, stood up, and drove the sheet of paper into the mud with the heel of his boot.

His head brushed against the peak of his tent, triggering another cascade of water on his bare head and down his neck.

It didn't worsen his condition. Inside a tent or out, everyone was drenched on this miserable night. At least he had shoes on and wool socks. An adjutant to General Greene had insisted he accept them earlier in the day, along with the tent. He knew he was supposed to feel guilt for having these luxuries — shoes, socks, a tent — while the rest of the army was out in the open tonight, shivering around smoldering fires, nearly all of them barefoot, more than a few of them all but naked under a blanket cape. Even the best of those, including that worn by "His Excellency the General," were threadbare and worn.

At least I have this, he thought ruefully, reaching into his backpack and pulling out a leather sack, still half full of rum. He took a long pull on the flagon, resealed it, and stuck it under his jacket. At least it gave a momentary warmth, dulled the pain, the memories, and put off the problem of what he was supposed to write next.

Since coming to America, he had rarely indulged but tonight, in this miserable muck, he no longer cared, and besides, half the army was drunk, the other half wished they were.

The rain, the suffering, the fear — they

were almost secondary now. What in hell should I, can I, write?

The American Crisis. He already knew the title. He had written it twenty times on that sheet of paper now crushed into the mud, but beyond that?

He uncorked the flagon, took another drink, and sat back down on another luxury General Greene had provided for him, a field cot so that he didn't have to sleep in the mud, the way the men he claimed to be one of would try and sleep this night.

Why did they all look to me? Because they believe I can write? They were the ones who had faced fire at Long Island, Manhattan, White Plains, and still were with the army.

His own service? A joke, other than that he could write.

Common Sense had been in everyone's hands for nearly a year now. It had been easy enough to write last winter, safe and warm in Philadelphia, the argument for this war no longer being about Englishmen defending the rights of Englishmen; this was now a war about a new nation, a new concept, an ideal called America. We are Americans now and will die for the right to live free.

He had written it because he had to. It had flooded out of him in a dream, a burst

100

of energy pent up for nearly his entire life, a life of degradation, poverty, and tragedy. His pen had given him, at last, the means to lash back at the world, the Old World he had fled in disgrace and abject poverty, where he had left behind an embittered wife and the threat of debtor's prison.

Squatting on the wet cot, rubbing his hands against the cold, he could not help but smile at his current state. Poverty? At least in prison, if you had a few pence to bribe the turnkeys, you could get a dry room, even a fire and a cooked meal. Here? Hell, the only money the sullen citizens of Newark would take for food or a dry corner in a shed was British or Spanish silver. The wads of paper money being handed out as pay were all but worthless. More than one soldier had sarcastically used a five-dollar note as kindling or, in a more dramatic statement of crude humor, publicly wiped himself with it to the laughing taunts of his comrades.

Yet I would not trade being here rather than being back in England for a hundred pounds sterling. He was feeling more than a bit woozy as he took another pull on the flagon of rum. Despite his cynicism about all that life had handed him so far, he felt for the first time that he belonged to something. He had helped to start something. Now he was being asked to ensure that it survived, and that was exactly why he was drunk.

He was not sure what to write.

Two years ago he had been an utter failure, a stay and corset maker like his father. That had ended when his first wife, Mary, died trying to give birth to their child. He drank himself half to death after she and the baby were put into the ground. Friends helped to get him a job as an excise collector. My God, he thought ruefully, I actually collected taxes for that damned king. Finally lost that position, too, sinking the ship when, among other things, he had written a protest pamphlet demanding better conditions and pay for the excisemen who squeezed the taxes for the crown. It was hard to admit to another reason, that, more than once, rather than showing up for a day's work, he was passed out drunk. Even tried a tobacco shop. It failed. Tried a second marriage. It failed, and as he looked back upon it, he could not blame Elizabeth for pushing him out of her bed and life. Perhaps memories of Mary had haunted that second marriage and brought it to a rapid and untimely end.

He opened the flagon, looked at it, and

forced the cork back in. He knew where this was leading. Finish off the rum, collapse on the cot, shiver through the night, and, at dawn, fall back in with the troops, swarming southward, away from British-occupied New York, panic-stricken in retreat. And not a word on paper to explain why.

They want me to explain why. They look to me to give meaning to their sacrifice and pain. Their eyes look hauntingly in expectation.

"I'm cursed by my own success."

And penniless as well. That was the joke of it. He could picture his friend Dr. Benjamin Rush shaking his head at him and his self-inflicted poverty. It was Rush who had literally carried him off the boat two years earlier when it docked in Philadelphia, half the passengers near dead from typhoid, and nursed him back to health. It was Rush who had told him to write, that writing was his God-given mission for "the Cause."

Common Sense had sold over a hundred thousand copies so far, the most popular work ever written on this shore, and yet he had barely collected a pound for it. One evening Rush had run a calculation for him, how many hundreds of pounds he should have in his pocket this day, and he had given it all away, telling publishers to print it and be damned who made the money. In his passion for "the Cause" many another had freely published his work and he had pocketed only a few guineas, which he had quickly drunk away.

Rush called me a bloody idealistic fool and blessed me for it, he thought with a sad smile. Published it for "the Cause," and now I sit here penniless, half drunk, freezing. And they want me to write another uplifting, compelling, reassuring pamphlet. General Greene had openly begged him for it. Rush had sent him a dozen missives, each one with more pressure than the last, even "His Excellency" George Washington had sat him down and said, "You have to write something! Anything!"

"Damn them." He sighed and stood up, his head brushing the inside of the tent, the sodden canvas spilling more water onto his bare head.

He had given his hat away the day before to a piteous freezing scarecrow standing picket, shivering with fever. He took an old scarf, hanging on the inside of the tent pole where it was supposed to dry out a bit. The wool was wet, stinking of sweat and filth. He covered the top of his head, and tied it under his chin, pulled back the flap of his tent, and stepped out.

The rain was easing slightly, coming in fitful bursts, a cold edge to it. Snow by morning most likely, he thought. Maybe a blessing; maybe it will just make the suffering worse.

The vista before him was pathetic. The small village of Newark, a few hundred homes and shops huddled along the banks of the Passaic River, was packed to overflowing. It was shrouded in mist and the smoke from hundreds of sputtering, hissing campfires. Every house in the village had been requisitioned for the sick, staff, or officers; the citizens who had cheered them all so loudly in the summer, had withdrawn in silence, hiding their livestock and food in the nearby marshlands, demanding payment for dry firewood, howling with rage when desperate men told them to go to hell and took the wood anyhow. He hated this place, hated all of New Jersey for that matter, which, now that the army was in retreat, had, overnight, gone Tory. Even now he could imagine the citizens of this village pulling the Union Jacks out of hiding places in the attic, eager to hang them out their windows when this forlorn army decamped at dawn and continued its retreat toward Philadelphia. By this time tomorrow the pursuing British and Hessians will have marched in . . . with shining guineas and German coins in their pockets.

It was rumored that the British general Howe was preparing a proclamation for the citizens of New Jersey: If they would step forward and sign an oath of renewed allegiance to King George, all would be forgiven and hard currency paid for goods acquired and to any who would take up arms to suppress the traitorous rebels. It was a rumor he knew was most likely true. By tomorrow night the "citizens" of this town would be lining up to sign it, and to be paid for doing so.

The American army, or what was left of it, was encamped on the low hills above the town, if the site could be called a camp or the men an army anymore. When they abandoned Fort Lee six days back, the army had been forced to leave behind most of its artillery and rations, hundreds of wagons, even its tents. So fast was the retreat that even the food on the hoof, cattle and swine, had been abandoned as well. Now they starved, stood around smoldering fires, sodden, and tomorrow they would most likely freeze. Tomorrow, there might not be an American army at all. The Revolution would have frozen to death.

One hell of a cause I belong to, he

thought. Damn, why does it always seem to rain on armies in retreat?

Not even sure where I am going.

Looking, but for what? For the first powerful sentence that everyone needs and that I can't write.

He was tempted to turn back from this fool's venture, go inside the tent, and get drunk. No, not now! He pushed against the wind, the rain, and the biting cold.

"This is the time of crisis," he had written, then a few more lines. He had taken a drink, and froze, not just from the cold but from the lack of inspiration, not knowing what he was to write next. "The time of crisis is at hand," and then another drink. "This time of crisis will try us . . ."

Oh, the hell with it!

Twilight. The leaden overcast was disappearing into blackness. The choking smoke from campfires made of green wood, mixed with the mist rising from the river and fetid marshlands on the far side of the Passaic, made all seem like something out of Dante, a dark, foreboding Hades for the condemned souls of the Revolution he had helped to inspire.

He could easily turn to his right at this moment and head down the few hundred yards to the house where Nathanael Greene had set up his headquarters. He knew he'd be welcomed, honored, given a place by a fire, perhaps even some food, and always something to drink. Though Greene was a Quaker and held against liquor, he did not deny it to his staff, and as was typical of officers, he always seemed to have enough.

The thought was tempting, but then Greene would come and sit by his side, smile in his friendly fashion and give him "that look." The look so many gave him. That he was a conjurer, a minister of the soul of this Revolution, and could magically spin out of air the words that would somehow dispel the gloom, the cold, the mist and rain, the hunger. His words would warm, revive, and renew the fervor all had carried in the halcyon days of summer.

If I go there now, he will ask, "Have you written it yet?" Or far worse, "I've been thinking, maybe you should write this."

Damn all of them. He could not resist. Reaching into his torn jacket, he took out the leather sack of rum for one more pull. He recalled a nursery story about a goose and its golden eggs. In the end the greedy owners had cut its throat.

Well, maybe not a knife to my throat, but if it goes on much longer like this, most definitely a rope around my neck. If the

British capture me and find out who I am . . .

He pushed on through the mud and filth, angling away from the village.

He had pitched his tent with men of the First Continental. Pennsylvania. A rough-hewn lot, mostly from beyond the Susquehanna or down from the northern frontier of the Wyoming Valley. They seemed impervious to this suffering. Their whole lives had been suffering and they didn't even know it. Nearly all were riflemen, usually tasked during the retreat with covering the rear guard, to hold the pursuing Hessian dragoons and jaegers at bay.

He slipped past a group of frontiersmen standing around a green wood fire of hissing embers and dark coals. A few looked up.

"Mr. Paine," one of them said.

He hated that. Mister Sir. It is only "private" now, or as we called each other, not too long ago, "brother" or "citizen." He nodded an acknowledgment and pressed on.

A knot of men was gathered around. He caught a glimpse of flapping dirty wings. Someone had snatched a chicken, and lopped its head off. Soon he was gutting it, and another was helping by yanking out fistfuls of feathers. One chicken for a dozen hungry soldiers. The fire they planned to cook it on was barely alive, more smoke than heat. They would most likely eat it half raw rather than wait for it to cook through.

"The crisis is at hand." He watched as the chicken was neatly quartered and thrown into a pot, the water not yet at a boil. Several looked at him warily, not recognizing him in the deepening gloom, their looks conveying warning that another beggar around the pot was not welcome.

"For want of a chicken a revolution will be lost . . ."

Shakespeare was becoming popular once more. Steal a line or two from him. Few here had most likely ever read Shakespeare; no one would notice or care if he wrote about bands of brothers. Some brothers, he thought, looking hungrily at the chicken in the iron pot. He pressed on.

Shortly after the adoption of the Declaration, he had put down his pen and enlisted. It was all the rage of the moment, joining. Of all things, he had fallen in with the old elite unit of the City of Brotherly Love — the Philadelphia Associators they called themselves. Many had turned out in natty uniforms of blue with red trim, armed with roughly made muskets; they had been ferried across the Delaware with much fanfare and started north to the war. They never got north of Amboy. There they were ordered to hold against the threat of the huge British forces disembarking on the other side of the tidal waters that separated Staten Island and New Jersey. In the ensuing months they had collapsed into drunken idleness while the battles raged on Long Island and Manhattan. At times they would wander to water's edge and shout insults at their British counterparts on the other shore, even trade a few harmless shots and gestures.

That had been the war experience of his "brothers" among the Associators. As word came back of the unrelenting disasters on the far side of the Hudson, the ardor of his comrades had cooled. The welcome offered by the citizens of Amboy in July had turned to outright hostility by October. When food and liquor were no longer offered for free by grateful citizens, instead were charged for, and then refused, the Associators simply took them.

In the end they had broken up and gone home. One or two a night at first, then half a dozen, and finally the entire command; the men cursing the useless Continental Congress, the ungrateful louts of New Jersey, and even Washington, who they said had actually been bribed to divide his army up so it could be cut apart piecemeal. They had decided they would not be one of those pieces.

His brothers in days of sunshine and warmth had melted away in the autumn cold and gone home, leaving only a few like himself, without unit or command, to fend for themselves.

"We who were patriots in the sunshine?" He wondered. Start with that?

Leaving Amboy, he had walked to Fort Lee, just in time to come running back pell-mell like the others with the British and Hessians at their heels.

On the road north he had passed hundreds going the other way. Most of them were men from the New Jersey militias, but some came from as far away as Virginia, every one of them sick to death of it all. He had camped with a few, chanced meetings on the evening road, they curious as to why he was going the other way, calling him a damn fool until they heard him speak his name. A laughing few claimed he was a damn liar. Tom Paine most likely was safe and warm back in Philadelphia, eating roast goose, drinking fine port wine with all the money he had made deluding them. A few believed him; a few even drew out his pamphlet, torn and battered. One man wept, sitting by a campfire with him, holding *Common Sense,* starting to read it, and he had realized suddenly that the man could not read; he was illiterate. He had heard it read so many times that he had memorized the first few pages and kept the unreadable pamphlet as a talisman from a time when he believed.

They had fallen asleep side by side. When he awoke next morning, his comrade of the night was gone, slipped away, but he had left half a loaf of bread behind as an offering. It was one of the few times he had cried across all these long bitter months.

"Pangs of physical hunger must not deter us now, for we hunger for a greater prize, a prize our souls have longed for . . . and that is the prize of freedom . . ."

He shook his head. Damn, it just would not work.

He headed into the gloomy mist rising above the Passaic and skirted the edge of the town. If I go into the town I will go into a house, and they will recognize me if there are officers; they will lure me, and I'll get drunk. Something told him he could not afford that blessed oblivion this night. He would stay with those whom in his heart he still called comrades and fellow citizens.

What was left of the Jersey militias had

been posted as sentries along the bank of the Passaic. The logic of it was simple enough. In the hills around the town the rest of the army was camped. Any men from Jersey wanting to desert would have to cross through the ranks of these men from Pennsylvania, the more disciplined troops of Maryland and Virginia, and the soldiers of New England, for whom desertion was nearly impossible since the British blocked the way north.

In reality, though, few seemed to care if a knot of shivering, bedraggled militia staggered through their camp, heading south and west. There might be a few taunts and curses, but no one stopped them. For that matter, even for those who were staying, enlistments would be up either on the first of December or of January of the new year, and then nearly all who were still here could legally walk out. Not even "His Excellency General George Washington" would dare to stop them.

The gloom deepened, occasionally relieved by the dull orange flicker of a campfire some lucky souls had managed to stir to life. There was a flaring up of one nearby, and he wandered over. Another home owner in Newark would awake at dawn to find his well-made, whitewashed picket fence gone.

Yet the scene there was not of momentary celebration. Paine heard sobbing. A young boy squatting in the mud was cradling a prone form, an older man, beard gray, features pinched, by the firelight the face ashen, lips drawn back in that grimace the dead so often have. He thought for a moment of his Mary on the blood-soaked bed, the dead baby nestled in her arms, and forced it aside. No, that would break me. The others around the weeping boy were silent, heads bowed, one of the men kneeling down to hold the lad.

"It was his heart. It just must have gave out while you were getting the wood. We're sorry, Jamie."

The boy was inconsolable. Tom wanted to stop, to kneel down, to offer a word, but knew it would be a useless intrusion. After all, what could he ever say or write for this boy? Was this worth it to him now? If we lose, it will, of course, be meaningless. And even if we win? Could I ever write something to let him find meaning in the death of this old man, most likely his father?

Several looked up at him. He sensed they recognized him. Strange how so many seemed to know who he was. There were even a few nods, but he did not draw closer to the beckoning fire. It was touched at this moment by death that seemed without meaning. He backed away.

He turned into the gloom. Just go to your tent, get drunk, try to write something tomorrow — it did seem a reasonable thought. The flagon was still inside his jacket. He looked into the darkness. If another was close by, he would feel uncomfortable drinking and not offering to share. He saw no one, and he took a long swallow, feeling again the momentary blessing of warmth.

He walked on, nearly tripping into a shallow ditch and then retching. It was an open latrine, and in the shadows he could hear a man suffering the agonies of the flux, or dysentery or typhoid. Memories of the nightmare crossing from England, when the drinking water in the lower hold of the ship was discovered to be foul once out to sea and already too far along to turn back. Nearly everyone on board had come down with typhoid.

So much for the free passage that Benjamin Franklin had given him when the two met in England. He still wondered why. What had Franklin seen in him that others had not, recruiting him to venture to America and try his skills there, providing passage and even sending a letter ahead by fast packet to Dr. Rush, his friend, to take the corset maker, failed tax collector, and occasional writer under his wing once he landed in America?

He backed away from the foul sink, struggling not to vomit, edged around it, and pressed on toward the river. Why he headed there he was not sure. It was not the most pleasant of streams, banked on one side by marshlands, lined with a number of tannery mills on this side that dumped their refuse and filth into the waters, a filth to which the people of Newark seemed immune.

He caught sight of a flickering glow and angled toward it. Half a dozen men were gathered about a low fire that suddenly flared up high. As at the last one, these men had apparently slipped into the town to steal something dry and seasoned to burn on this rainy night. A fresh-faced boy, chin mottled with wisps of a scraggly beard, came to his side.

"Brother, can you help me?" he gasped.

The boy was staggering under a load of firewood. Thomas reached over, taking more than half of it, the boy groaning, thanking him. As they approached the fire, he saw two fish dangling from the boy's belt: carp, big ones.

"Our Jonathan, back from the hunt as

well" came a greeting. A couple of men rushed over to help him the last few feet, taking his armload of wood and, without thought of need an hour or two from now, tossed all of it on the fire. Within seconds the dried apple and cherry wood crackled, spreading warmth for the moment.

"Fish, no less!" The boy, obviously proud of his find, untied them from his belt and handed them over.

"You go fishing as well?"

He laughed softly. "No, they were hanging in the woodshed I visited, so I figured to bring them along."

"Fine bunch of thieves we're reduced to, stealing a few stinking carp!"

The others around the fire fell silent. Tom could see the resemblance between the forager and the young man complaining about the fish.

One of the men drew out a knife, a short, beefy man with hands like ham hocks. He spilled out the guts of the two fish, and without bothering to scrape off their scales, he drew the ramrod from his mud-splattered musket, impaled the carp, and bracing the ramrod with a log, put the fish out over the fire to roast.

Tom stood watching, still holding the heavy load of firewood. When the short, beefy man beckoned for him to dump his load by the side of the fire, he did so and found that the logs were a dry spot to park himself on, and so he sat down. Carp or not, there was enough food for all of them, and he felt something of an invitation for having carried the wood the last few feet.

"You look familiar," the young forager said, and extended his hand. "My name is Jonathan. Jonathan van Dorn."

"Tom," he replied quietly.

"Just Tom? What regiment you with?"

"Was with the Associators out of Philadelphia."

There were several snorts of derision. He took no offense.

"So what the hell are you doing here? Word was, all your friends ran for home a month ago."

"What unit are you?" Tom replied.

There was a pause.

"Jersey militia, out of Burlington County." There was a slight defensive tone in Jonathan's voice.

"Well, heard nearly all of you boys ran off as well."

He said the words lightly, as if offering a joke in reply, but an uncomfortable pause ensued.

"But you and me, we're still here," Tom

finally added, and that broke the tension.

"Stuck here for tonight," came a voice from the other side of the fire, "but tomorrow? Word is we're running again."

Tom looked over at the man who had spoken.

"That's my brother James," Jonathan announced. James nodded, and Jonathan introduced the others, Peter Wellsley, Elijah Hunt, their sergeant, Bartholomew Weiner, who was cooking the fish, and several others, all that was left of the Burlington militia. It was Bartholomew who broke the moment, not looking back as he tended the roasting carp.

"You're Tom Paine, ain't you?"

Tom nodded his head. "Yup."

"Thought so."

"You're Tom Paine?" Jonathan gasped and extended his hand. "An honor, sir."

Tom took it. It was an American custom he was still not quite used to, this shaking of hands. Every American seemed willing to shake every other American's hand. In England one only did so if the other was of the same class and station. He liked the custom. It was almost a symbol of what they were fighting for.

"So, why are you here?" Jonathan asked.

Tom shook his head. "Studying."

"Studying what? How to freeze? How to die from the shits?" Bartholomew quipped.

"You could say that."

"Why ain't you off with the officers down in the town? They'd let you in. I heard even that George Washington himself likes you, tells people to read what you write. He'd give you a warm bed for the night."

"Kind of prefer the company here."

No one spoke for a moment. It was embarrassing. He could see the open admiration in young Jonathan's eyes, the cynical glance from his brother James, the weary indifference of the sergeant.

A gust of wind whipped around them, sending up a shower of sparks. Turning away from the smoke, he caught a distant glimpse of glowing lights on the far side of the river.

"They over there?" he asked.

"Coming up thick as fleas on an old dog," Bartholomew snorted, and then, clearing his throat, he spat. "We'll most likely pack and be gone come dawn."

"Not soon enough for me," James announced.

Tom looked over at him and saw that a couple of the men to either side were nodding in agreement, heads lowered against the wind.

"Stow it," Bartholomew snapped.

"And I suppose you are going to make me?" James retorted. "I thought the Declaration was about our freedom. Well, damn it, I have the freedom to speak my mind."

"You flap your mouth too much, lad," Bartholomew retorted.

There were several glances now toward their guest, as if he had intruded on a family argument, wondering if he would intervene.

"Did you ever think it would turn to this?" James asked sharply, directing his ire at Tom. "I had to listen night after night to my brother there reading your pamphlet. Listened to it so much that I even volunteered for this army out of Bedlam. So what do I have now? Ask the sergeant there how many of our men have died? Barely a one from a bullet, but God knows dozens, scores from the flux, bad food, rotting food while those bastards in Congress eat off fine china, and you encourage us to sacrifice all. And I ask, for what?"

Eyes turned back toward Tom. Even the admiring glances of Jonathan had dulled a bit.

He had not wandered out to do this on this night. He was more than a little drunk, and tired, and plain exhausted with trying to think what he should write, for that was what all of them would want by next morning and the day after.

"We're here," he finally said. "Out of so many, we're the ones who are here. That says something about us, about what we believe in."

"Believed in," James replied. "Believed in, but now? This is beyond too much for any to endure. I'm sick to death of it, I tell you."

"Who the hell isn't," Jonathan snapped back. "You think we like it any more than you?"

Bartholomew cursed under his breath as he lowered the ramrod toward the fire to cook the fish faster. The smell of the burning flesh wafted over them, stilling the argument for a moment.

"Shad. Now if only we had some shad," Peter Wellsley said. "Where you from, Mr. Paine?"

"England, until two years ago. Trout there in the rivers, fat big ones. Would love to have a couple of them roasting now."

"When the shad run on the Delaware in the spring, you can almost walk across their backs to Pennsylvania," Peter sighed. "Stuff ourselves on them 'til we burst. Wish that was shad cooking, feel a mite better."

They were breaking a taboo that had fallen upon the army of late. Talking of food they could not have.

"It's carp, damned carp. Most likely sucked on the bodies of our men that drowned in that river," James replied with a cold laugh.

"You don't have to eat 'em if you don't want to," Jonathan snapped, coming to his feet.

James stood up, fists clenched. "You're still my younger brother. If you want a thrashing, Jonathan, I'm the man to give it to you."

"Both of you, shut up," Bartholomew roared, "or I'll knock both your heads together."

The two glared at each other but sat back down.

"Mr. Paine."

It was Jonathan.

"It's Thomas, or just Tom. Hell, I'm no different than you, son."

"You really meant what you wrote last year?" Reaching under his ragged blanket cloak and into his shirt he pulled out a tattered copy of *Common Sense.*

For a moment Tom couldn't speak. All had fallen silent, staring at him.

What do they want from me? he thought. They seem to want more, more than I can give. Yes, I wrote it. I wrote it. I knew the struggle ahead would be hard, but never did I dream that it would come to this, to this level of suffering, filth, pain, and death. He prided himself on a certain cynicism, a sense of realism, about the bitter offerings of this world, which life had taught him so well; but now, among these sunken-cheeked men squatting around the fire, he wondered to himself, had he ever thought it could be this ghastly?

These were the last of them. He had long ago stopped shedding tears over the tragedies of life. He looked over at Jonathan, who was still clutching the pamphlet. That boy will die for the cause I wrote about. He had seen it in the faces of some, a precious few. They believed so fervently that they would die to make it happen. He felt his throat tighten. If there is a God, do I bear responsibility for what they believe in and will die for?

"I meant it" was all he could say.

"And that is why you are here now?" Jonathan pressed.

He could only nod in reply.

"I think they're done," Peter announced.

Bartholomew grunted and pulled the ramrod and the scorched fish out of the fire. He looked around and then set them down on a split log by Tom's side. Pulling out his knife, he cut one into three pieces. He looked at Tom for a few seconds, and then without comment cut the other into four.

Now the old soldier's ritual was played out. Jonathan came around to Tom's side and squatted down as the sergeant turned his back on the fish.

"Who shall have this?" Jonathan asked, pointing at the midsection of the smaller carp.

"Peter," the sergeant replied, back turned so he could not see what piece had been selected.

Peter, smiling, picked up his piece, cursing softly and kissing his singed fingertips as he carried off his prize.

"Who shall have this?" Jonathan announced, pointing to the head of the larger fish.

"Myself."

Laughing, Jonathan handed him the head with a bit of meat to the gills. The sergeant cursed under his breath.

The rest was thus doled out, James cursing for getting the tail of the bigger fish, saying it was his luck, Thomas saying nothing when he got the head of the smaller one, though the sergeant had cut it in such a way that there was still some meat to be had from it.

"Watch the bones there, Tom," Bartholomew said. "These ain't no fancy English trout. Carp are nothing but fat and bones."

"Still fill you a bit, though," Tom replied.

Peter did momentarily choke on a bone, gasping until he coughed it out. Almost instinctively, Tom reached into his jacket and pulled out the half-empty sack of rum.

There was complete silence at the sight of it.

"Go on. Take a drink."

"What is it?"

"Rum."

Jonathan laughed.

"He don't hold with drinking liquor."

"I do now," Peter replied. He took the flagon, tilted his head back, and seconds later the others laughed as he gasped and choked even more.

He handed the leather sack back to Tom, who saw the others gaze longingly at it.

Oh, damn it all to hell, he thought, there goes a good drunk for tonight.

"Take a round, brothers. Take a round."

The sack did go around. He tried not to watch, only nodding as each of them gasped a thanks. The last of them, Sergeant Bartholomew, held it to his ear, shook it, looked over at Thomas, and then, to Tom's amazement, made a gesture of taking a swallow and handed it back.

"Last one's for you, sir. Drain it now."

Again that tightness in the throat hit him. He could see it in the man's eyes. How long since this sergeant had had a good drink, and yet he would be damned if he would take the last one from Tom Paine.

There was a strange sense of ceremony as he held the sack, feeling there was just enough inside for one more good pull.

He stood up, wiping the grease from the fishhead on his thighs, tossing what was left of it into the fire.

He held the sack up.

"To us, my brothers, to freedom, and to America."

"To America," most of them replied.

He tilted his head back and drank. Strangely, it was one of the sweetest he had ever tasted. I would rather have this moment, he thought, than dine with a king or even with the General. I would rather have this.

Then there was an awkward moment of silence. He had learned much in the short time he had been with this army. These soldiers were unlike any the world had ever seen. An army of farmers, shopkeepers, mechanics, sailors, fishermen, laborers, runaway slaves. And yet most were literate,

128

and nearly all, at least at the start, could debate for hours on end the intricacies of why they fought. In fact, the debating was something like a sport, an openness of dialogue no army of Europe would ever tolerate in the rank and file. If they felt the urge, they'd shout down an officer, call him a dog if he could not hold his own in a debate or a match of fisticuffs, but later that night share the last of their rum with him if they thought he was, nevertheless, a man of courage. Yet when it came to sentiment, to open expressions of patriotism, especially now, there was a hard edge. He sensed that somehow they saw he was the man who could write down the words burning in their hearts that their own scribblings could not capture. It was not the high-flown, educated language of men such as Washington or Rush or Jefferson. It was the new language of common men who stood defiant for the rights of other common men.

That is what they want of me, Thomas Paine realized. That is why I am here on this rainy night, and, by God, that is why I must figure out what to write for and about them.

At this moment, though, he felt himself an utter failure. For how could he ever find words to write about this.

"America, you say?"

It was James.

He looked back across the river. The rain had all but stopped, the cold wind now sweeping in, blowing clear some of the smoke and mist . . . and now the first flakes of snow were dancing down.

They could see the fires on the far shore, hundreds of them.

"They're warm over there tonight," James said. "They have tents, food. Tomorrow the people of this town will hang out their flags for England and cheer. Even for the Hessians they'll cheer.

"You talk of America? What in hell are you talking about? If we are America, then I say we are nothing but damn fools, and you, Tom Paine, are one of the bastards who talked us into this madness. When the end comes, Congress will run or cower and crawl back to save their own skins. And since so many of them are gentlemen, they will shake hands like gentlemen with Howe, while any of us dumb enough to still believe will be shoved into the prison ships or hanged.

"What will you do, Paine, when the end comes? For God's sake, man, can't you see that this is the end of it?"

"I'll die," Tom said quietly. "If it is the

end, I'll die, but I don't believe it is over yet, not with men like you here around this fire."

He paused.

"Or men even like me or men like Greene or General Washington."

James snorted derisively and spat into the fire.

"God damn all gentlemen like them! Especially that Washington, who led us into this mess."

And now Jonathan did spring, stepping around the fire, slamming into his brother, knocking him over.

Seconds later all had piled in, several trading punches, Bartholomew, Tom, and Peter struggling to separate them.

Tom got his arms around Jonathan and pulled him away from James, who tried to lunge for him, but the sergeant blocked him, shoving him back.

"You're nothing but a damned Tory," Jonathan screamed, his voice breaking.

"I should never have listened to you," James roared. "Our parents were right. We're fools. Our brother and parents are safe at home. No matter who wins, they'll be warm and prosper. We're all fools!"

"Then if that's how you feel," Bartholomew snapped. "Go, damn you! I've listened to your bellyaching for the last month. Just go. Get the hell out of here and go home to Trenton."

Bartholomew let go of James, shoving him away.

James glared at him.

"I'll go then, you fools. You're all madmen, and you, damn you" — he pointed, and Tom wasn't sure that it was straight at him or at Jonathan, whom he was still holding on to — "you're the worst of the lot."

James went over to where their packs were stacked, fished his out of the pile, and slung it over his shoulder.

He glanced at the others.

"Anyone else here with me?" He paused and grimaced sarcastically at Tom. "Anyone with some common sense?"

"I'm with you."

It was Elijah Hunt, who picked up his pack and stepped over to James's side.

"They could shoot you for desertion," Peter cried. "Elijah, not you, too."

"Why bother?" Bartholomew said coldly. "Let them go. Desert. Go ahead. You're not worth the effort of forcing you to stay."

He turned his back on the two.

"They'd run anyhow come the next fight."

James laughed in reply.

"Hell. Run? It's what we've all been doing

for months. At least I'm running back to something. While the rest of you, you'll just run away and keep running until you're all dead."

"I'd rather be dead than a coward," Jonathan retorted bitterly.

James bristled at the accusation, balling his fists, but the sergeant was now between the two, and he could easily hammer any and all into submission.

"Damn you! Just leave," the sergeant retorted, his voice suddenly grown weary.

James started to pick up a musket.

"The guns stay," Bartholomew snapped. "I'd rather throw them in the river than have you take them."

James, held the gun for a moment, looking down at it, and then let it fall into the mud.

"James."

It was Jonathan, his voice choked with emotion.

"What now?" and then James softened for a moment. "Little brother, can't you see it's over? Come with me. Mother and Father said it would come down to this. We can still go home."

There was a note of pleading in his voice, but Jonathan shook his head in reply.

"You were nothing but a patriot when the

sun was shining, but now that winter is here? My God, James, how you try my soul. Some day, when others give thanks for what we endure, your name will be forgotten. As I have already forgotten you."

James could not reply. Tom could see his anguish as well, for Jonathan's words had cut to his soul.

"To try one's soul. The sunshine patriot . . . to try one's soul . . ."

James turned away, Elijah following him.

"James."

He looked back.

"Tell Mother and Father I love them."

James nodded. "And our brother? What word for him?"

Jonathan hesitated.

"Tell him . . . ," he choked back a sob. Tom, who was still holding him, could feel him shudder.

"If Allen has gone over to the damn Loyalists as I suspect he has, tell him he is no longer my brother . . . nor are you."

James said nothing more, and with Elijah by his side, he disappeared into the darkness. Jonathan broke into sobs then, the others around him silent. Tom held him until the boy, as if embarrassed and shamed, broke away, wiping his face with the dirty sleeve of his blanket.

"To try one's soul," Tom thought again, looking at the lad, who stood shamed but defiant.

And he knew it was time to go.

"Thank you for the meal," he said softly, backing away from the fire.

The sergeant nodded curtly.

"Peter, you take picket down by the river. I'll relieve you in the middle of the night," Bartholomew announced. "Jonathan, why don't you try and get some sleep."

The boy did not reply.

"Write about this," Jonathan said to Tom. "Write about us."

Tom nodded. "I will, brother."

He turned and started up the mud-slick hill, the fire behind him disappearing into mist, smoke, and snow.

It took awhile of wandering to find his tent, staggering past groups of men huddled around their fires, the long cold night still ahead as they drew closer to the feeble heat that their green firewood gave out.

He was eager to write, afraid that what was forming would evaporate and slip away if he did not get back to his tent at once. At last he found it.

Curled up in the mud nearby was a drummer boy, wrapped in a soggy blanket, shivering in his sleep, drum by his side.

Tom picked the drum up and carried it into his tent. The candle he had left lit was still burning. Reaching into his pack, he pulled out two more, the last he had. He thought about it for a moment, cut one in half with his penknife, and lit the two pieces.

He sat down on his cot, the canvas wet as was the blanket atop it. He drew out a small ink pot. Thank God it wasn't frozen. He found a quill in the bottom of his pack, and used a penknife to sharpen the point. Carefully, he drew out a sheet of dry paper wrapped inside an oilskin, a gift as well from General Greene.

He spread the paper on the head of the drum and now, though he was still a bit drunk, there was no hesitation.

"These are the times that try men's souls. The summer soldier and the sunshine patriot will, in this crisis, shrink from the service of his country; but he that stands it NOW, deserves the love and thanks of every man and woman."

So he would write through the night.

McConkey's Ferry
7:00 P.M. December 25, 1776
The sleet against the windowpane sounded

136

like the tinkling of a shower of broken glass . . . and then an explosion.

George Washington, drifting on the edge of sleep sat up with a muffled cry, the others gathered around him by the fireplace in the ferry house were silent, giving him furtive glances but saying nothing. He suddenly felt embarrassed. In the warmth of the fire he had drifted off to sleep for a few minutes, and was awakened by a loose shutter slamming closed.

He had been dreaming. Back on the Monongahela River with Braddock. A strange dream had haunted his sleep for twenty years. In the dream he already knew the ambush by the French and Indians lay ahead. In some ways, though, it was not a dream, not a nightmare, at all. On that terrible day, on that Pennsylvania frontier near Pittsburgh, a column of more than two thousand British troops and colonial militia was all but annihilated. On that day, everyone familiar with life beyond the frontier had sensed the trap. Throughout the morning, as the lengthy column pushed through the forest, those who knew the land were reporting in, and Braddock was ignoring them. After all, they were only rabble, foul-smelling colonials who came bearing warnings, and he was a professional soldier from

Europe, immune to rumormongering and panic.

Scouts ranging around the advancing column of British and colonial militia reported signs, a low-hanging bough broken, sap from the white pine tree oozing from the break and not yet solidifying, leaves scuffed up to reveal the damp mulch underneath, mushrooms trampled by a human foot, a tree someone had urinated against. No Indian would be so stupid as to do that; it obviously had to be a Frenchman. There was even a particular scent in the air, that scent of unwashed human bodies that lingered long after men had moved on. Anyone who lived on the frontier could tell the difference between an Indian and a Frenchman a hundred yards off; some even claimed they could tell which tribe. Anyone, at such a moment, foolish enough to be smoking tobacco, could be sensed a hundred paces away if the wind was right, and more than a few claimed they had smelled the tobacco the French were fond of smoking, along with gobs of spittle from those who chewed it.

In the dream he was riding forward to try and convince Braddock to halt the column, form a defensive position, send scouts out to probe, and in the dream he already knew the haughty response. A British officer taking advice from a colonial officer? Impossible. "Why, thank you, my good man, I'll note your diligence," and the subtext, not spoken but revealed by a glance, a slight curl of the lips, "I'll remember you are a cowardly bumpkin and note it in my reports."

In that dream, that damned recurring dream, it was all so real, the frustration, the sense of impending doom . . . and the rage. He was as good a man as any British professional officer, and still they looked down on him. He did not quite know how the latest fashion in London dictated that one held a teacup in camp at the evening mess. His accent was pronounced, clear evidence of a colonial, even if he was an aristocrat, but only of the Virginia aristocracy and so lacking in that certain hauteur of London, Cambridge, and Oxford. He was not to be taken seriously, nor ever would be taken seriously, even at this moment, in his world, in these forests of the western frontier, when in a few seconds they would be slaughtered for their absurdities and arrogance.

In the dream he had just ridden to Braddock's side — and then the shutter had slammed. In that final confused second of the dream it was a musket firing . . . the ball striking his chest, not Braddock's, as it had while by his side. I am the one who is shot . . . and he just sits there, looking disdainfully at me.

He had all but jumped up with a start. His staff, silent, looked at him for an instant and averted their eyes.

A soldier's dream. A soldier's nightmare.

Of course, all soldiers had them, and none ever spoke of them. Across the long months of this bitter campaign, more than once the sleep of others was interrupted by a muffled cry, a sob as someone came awake, bolt upright, sweating. He wondered uncomfortably how many times his iron control had given way while he was asleep and he had cried out, as he apparently had at this moment.

No one spoke. There were a few nervous coughs. His servant, Billy Lee, squatting by the side of the fireplace, did not even bother to look back at him; he poked the fire with an iron and then threw a few more logs on it.

Through half-open eyes he looked at Billy's back. Such a strange mix of emotions he felt for this person. Billy had been his servant, his slave, for years. Billy could keep his seat on the wildest of rides; he always made sure that Billy was as well mounted as himself. He prided himself on being considered one of the finest horsemen in Virginia and most definitely in this army. Billy came a very close second, much to the chagrin of many a white landholder in Virginia when they rode to the hounds, or, in this last year, on the battlefields around New York.

Billy would die for him without hesitation. That had been proven often enough these last months. When the bullets and shot were whistling pretty, more than once he had snapped at Billy to go to the rear, because the man was obviously positioning himself and his horse to take the blow if a round, errant or aimed, came their way. Unusual for a slave, Billy rode with a brace of pistols strapped to his saddle, for the protection of his master, of course. But still . . . a slave armed?

He knew Billy would, without a second's hesitation, give his life to protect him. Would I do the same in that instance, he wondered?

The fact that "his" man did not look back in concern at his outcry when he awoke from the dream spoke volumes. This had happened before, the weakness when one was asleep. Billy made a studied effort to be indifferent, and the others in the room took their cue from him.

The gusts of wind outside caused a back draft in the fire Billy was tending, and for an instant smoke puffed into the room. The storm was increasing in fury.

Awake now, he fumbled at his breast pocket to draw out his pocket watch, clicked open the cover . . . seven ten in the evening.

No one spoke, and he did not want to ask. To ask implied nervousness; regardless of the dream he had to show outward calm. He mimicked a casual mood, trying to find a comfortable position in the straight-backed wooden chair, stretching out his long legs. His feet were still damp, but he did not want to ask Billy to help pull his boots off; he had to be ready in an instant to go outside if needed.

He heard the outer door to the house fling open and slam shut, the draft slipping in under the door to this inner room. By the heavy footballs he knew who it was. No one spoke as the cold draft came whisking in, but all heads turned.

Again he resisted. He would not anticipate and look back.

"How goes it, Colonel Knox?" he asked. Again a demonstration of calm and control. Everyone in that room was on edge, nervous, even frightened by the prospect before them. His role was to demonstrate complete calm and indifference.

Though acting was a profession detested by those of his class, he had to be an actor this night. His lines and every single gesture were well rehearsed, contemplated, and planned. He had to know, before the first shot was fired, every move he would make, for all eyes would be upon him. I must inculcate in all of them now, at this moment, the roles they, too, will have to play . . . and that is the role of confidence, strength, and belief that victory on this dawn is foreordained . . . even if I have my own inner doubts and worries.

"General."

There was a slight clicking of heels, far too British or Hessian a gesture, but then again, Knox the bookseller had first learned this trade of soldiering inside his bookstore in Boston, reading everything he could find on the military arts.

He had learned those lessons well. It was he who first ventured the idea of going nearly three hundred miles westward to Fort Ticonderoga to empty the captured fort of the heavy guns placed there during the war with France and then drag them overland, three hundred miles, on sleds in the depth of winter, and use them to displace the British and drive them and their fleet from Boston. Many now said the trek was the American equal of the anabasis of Xenophon. The feat had made Knox, transforming him from an oversize bookstore owner into an admired soldier.

Realizing the moment required formality, Washington came to his feet and returned Knox's salute.

"Sir, I beg to report that, regrettably, the crossing is not on schedule."

Again the sound of sleet and freezing rain slashing against the windowpane, followed a few seconds later by the banging of the shutter. This time he did not blanch at the explosive sound.

"The weather, Colonel Knox, is beyond your control, but do keep the men moving. We shall not recall this attack, whatever the weather."

"Sir, we've already lost one of our boats. Capsized when the horses aboard panicked. The Marblehead men have managed to drag it back to shore but it is stove in from a horse kick. The animals are half frozen from going in the river."

"To be expected," Washington replied, as if the loss was not of the slightest concern, though every boat was precious.

"The Pennsylvania riflemen and the advance scouts are across, though. The other bank is secured, and scouts are moving forward to secure the road toward Trenton and arrest any civilians moving about and keep them in place. I just returned from the other shore, and so far, at least, it seems we have complete surprise. No report of advance patrols that either the Hessians and British are about this evening. We have a report from several patriot families on the far shore that the Hessians are completely unaware of our movement and no one has anticipated it."

He nodded. That had been a great fear. That the scattering of dwellings and farmhouses along the road to Trenton might have along it a Tory family that at the first stirring would send a report galloping southward. It had been a balancing act, to be sure. On the one hand, he had counted on a nearly full moon and clear weather to facilitate the crossing. On the other, the storm was heaven-sent, for only madmen would be about on a night such as this, and most certainly not an army, no matter how desperate their straits.

"It is the loading of the artillery and horses, sir, that is proving difficult. The storm is shifting, temperature dropping; the approaches and the dock are slippery with ice and sleet. I wish I had thought of it, sir, to acquire sand, even dirt, to spread about so the men and animals had better footing. I'm sorry."

"It is not your fault, Colonel," and in a rather uncharacteristic gesture he approached Knox and gave him a friendly pat on the shoulder.

He knew the others were listening to every word.

"Knox, this storm is heaven-sent, I tell you. If prayers are indeed answered by Providence, then they have been answered this night.

"I should perhaps have warned you beforehand that my prayers would be answered," and he smiled at his weak attempt at humor.

Knox forced a smile in response.

"We never were sure of the loyalty of the families on the Jersey shore. I feared that if but one of them observed us and slipped off to send warning, we would have been met by a roused garrison of Hessian troops, the British garrison in Princeton then coming down to strike us on the flank.

"This storm is our Christmas miracle. Just keep the men moving, and when you feel the time is right for me to cross, come fetch me."

"Sir, that might not be until midnight at best."

He took that in. Midnight? The plan was that by midnight the army would already be on the march southward to Trenton, to deploy long before dawn and strike before first light. Midnight?

There was a moment of fear, an inner nagging voice whispering that it was not too late. Even now he could call this thing off, recall the men on the far shore, order the rest back to their camps. He could sense the eyes of the staff behind him, staring at him, more than a few silently praying that he would see reason, that rather than call the storm heaven-sent he would see the logic, the reality of it. Never in the history of war had an army attempted this, to cross a river at night, to then put that flooding river at their backs and attempt an assault in the dark against a vastly superior and well-rested foe.

Stop it now, they were silently begging.

He stood, staring at Knox, wondering if this man felt the same. He was in himself, with slush dripping off his uniform to puddle on the floor, His soaked, bedraggled appearance, a warning that nothing was going according to plan this night.

In the silence the memory of the dream,

of the bullet striking him, recurred. Was that dream a warning? Was it that the bullet struck, not him, but this last desperate enterprise, and that the British, in all their strength and arrogance would be awaiting them at dawn?

He shook his head.

No.

"Who crosses next?" he asked. He could actually hear the audible sighs of the others in the room. Like the disappointment, even exasperation, of children anticipating they were about to be relieved of some chore and told to go play or off to warm beds instead — and were not.

"The plan was for the Maryland line to cross, sir, to put up barricades and form a circle of defense on the other shore, supported by half a dozen four- and six-pounders of my artillery."

He smiled at the way Knox said "my artillery." Good, very good, the words bespoke possessiveness and pride. In an army so notoriously weak in the firepower of its infantry, especially now, on a night that would foul muskets, the guns of Knox could still be counted on.

"Then, Colonel Knox," he said with a slight crease of a smile lighting his features, "why are you here? Send them across!"

There was actually a moment of surprise on Knox's face, then a smile in return and a formal salute. It was evident that Knox had come here half expecting to be ordered to stop this movement, retrieve the men on the far shore, and call off the assault. His General's own response had renewed this man's confidence.

"Yes, sir!" Knox replied, and yet again the formal salute, which he returned, and an instant of a shared intensity, almost as if Knox were saying, "I was half hoping, sir, but, damn it, if you are game for this, so am I."

Knox left the room, trailing a river of slush. The door closed. Seconds later he could hear Knox's booming voice.

"Damn you. If need be, put a blinder on that damn horse and get him aboard the boat. Keep moving!"

Washington looked around at his staff. No one met his gaze. All affected a studied indifference. Some slouched down in their chairs, feet toward the roaring fire, hats pulled low over their eyes. One of the men stirred, went to a sideboard where a pot of tepid tea sat, poured himself a cup, looked his way with a gesture, and Washington shook his head in reply. The officer gulped the tea down and returned to his chair and settled in, making a show of acting as if he were about to relax and fall asleep.

Washington settled back into his chair. The only one to meet his gaze directly, Billy Lee, still squatting by the fire, absently poking at the logs, picked up another split log of slow-burning chestnut and tossed it in.

For several long seconds Billy held his gaze, and the man smiled at him, as if conveying approval.

He nodded in reply, then closed his eyes to hide his feelings.

I know what I am fighting for, he found himself thinking. But what of Billy? Loyalty to me, yes. But what of him? The thought was troubling. There were so many thoughts to trouble him this night, though, and he pushed it aside.

He kept his eyes closed, and like many a seasoned veteran at such a moment, he drifted off to sleep, to grab a few more precious minutes to gain energy before the crisis to come.

"Maryland line! Maryland line, fall in!"

The cry startled Jonathan van Dorn from his fitful slumber.

Like nearly all who awake in strange surroundings there was a moment of disorientation. Am I home? In my bed, a plush goose down pillow under my head? Feeling guilty as well, for he had been dreaming that Diana Mueller was actually alongside him. Dear, dear Diana, who had kissed him on the lips and flung her arms around him on the day the Burlington militia paraded down Queen and King Streets in Trenton and marched off to the war.

She had been half asleep beside him, her eyes greeting him in the dream he had been having, her arms going around him, pulling him in closer to her side . . . and then . . .

No. Embarrassed, he opened his eyes, wondering if any had heard or noticed what he had been dreaming.

Instead, he found himself curled up in the corner of a pig stall in a stinking filthy barn. The frozen manure of the pigs under his backside and thighs was thawed by his resting in the filth, and soaked through his threadbare trousers.

He stank, became aware of the hundred itching sores from the lice infesting his jacket. Like all soldiers of this forsaken army, he awoke to scratch, still half asleep but hoping he would find one of the little bastards so he could exact revenge and crush it with his cracked and dirty fingernails.

"Maryland line! Maryland line! Fall in,

we're crossing over!"

Jonathan opened his eyes.

The candle that someone had placed on the railing of the stall above him while he had read from Thomas Paine was still glowing but was slacked halfway down. He must have drifted off for an hour or two. The tattered pamphlet by Paine was still in his hands.

Confused, he looked about. Had he fallen asleep while reading?

Peter was by his side, not Diana, but there was a deep love there nevertheless, his friend's head resting on his shoulder. He was still asleep, shivering, muttering something undistinguishable. Not to disturb him, he did not move, struggling to suppress a spasm of coughing that was about to hit.

"Maryland line! Damn you all, fall in!"

A hundred or more men were standing up, cursing, rolling up tattered blankets, most draping them around their shoulders and with a bit of burlap or leather tying them on as capes.

Men were coughing, hawking, and spitting. Jonathan saw several passing around a bottle, draining off the last of the contents. A sergeant was kicking, but not too hard, a drummer boy who cursed him vehemently, to the delight of the men already standing, the sergeant then extending a hand to pull the boy to his feet, the boy still half asleep and leaning against the sergeant for support.

"Clean out your pans but don't put in fresh powder, boys. Wait till we get there," the sergeant announced.

The men did as ordered, opening the locks of their muskets, using a bit of rag or dirty fingers to wipe out the damp powder, that in most cases was a greasy paste that never would have fired. The few that had a brass or bronze wire with them used it to clean out the touchhole, then loaned the valuable tool to their neighbors, who did the same. They checked their flints, carefully wiping them clean, then they took a strip of oiled or grease-covered cloth and bound it back around the lock in what was most likely a vain attempt to keep it dry.

The door to the barn was wide open, admitting an icy blast of wind, bringing with it sleet and thick, heavy flakes of snow.

"Come on, you bastards! Move it!"

The sergeant led the way. The men, cursing, complaining, shuffled along after him, many pausing for a moment to check the bindings of the rags wrapped around their feet. A few, gazing out, seeing the futility of foot rags on such a night, pulled them off, tucking the damp rags under their jackets, and ventured out barefoot.

One of the last to leave was the officer of the Maryland line whom Jonathan had nearly come to blows with earlier, the officer shoving along the reluctant few who were holding back.

The lieutenant looked his way and their gazes locked. It was a long-drawn-out matter of but a few seconds. Protocol demanded that Jonathan come to his feet and offer some sort of salute, but he did not want to stir, to wake Peter from his deep slumber, and besides this man had insulted him.

The moment held, and then the lieutenant nodded.

"Luck to you, New Jersey."

Startled, he could not reply.

"You read that Paine like you know it by heart."

"Like I said, I met him once," Jonathan replied.

"I'll see you in Trenton, and we'll give them hell."

Startled even more, Jonathan offered a salute in reply, even as he remained seated so as not to disturb Peter.

"Luck to you, too, sir," he replied.

The lieutenant forced a smile, then shook his head, looking out through the door at the wintry blast.

"Ah, what the hell, chances are we'll all be dead come dawn anyhow. Frozen or shot. But what the hell."

Jonathan could not help but smile.

"Then I'll see you in hell, sir. At least it will be warm there."

The lieutenant shook his head and laughed softly.

"See you in hell, Jersey," he replied, and then went through the barn door, slamming it shut behind him.

Peter was still asleep, and though struggling to control his cough, Jonathan could not help but let a spasm overwhelm him. It did not wake his friend.

Peter was still shivering in his sleep, and Jonathan reached around, and pulled up his own frayed blanket around his friend. A loving gesture but also a pragmatic one, their body heat would help warm each other, and he held him closer. Not Diana to be certain, but at this moment he loved his friend just as intensely and cherished his warmth. Peter's shivering died away, and like a child his friend drifted deeper into slumber, again whispering something he could not quite understand, but it sounded as if he was saying something to his mother.

From outside the barn Jonathan could

hear orders being shouted for the men of the Maryland line to fall in and form ranks. Men were cursing the cold, the war, the weather, each other, cursing everything one could ever imagine. He could hear them sloshing off, drifting their way to the ferry dock.

Now that the barn was no longer packed to overflowing with men, there was at least one blessing. The wretched stench of a hundred or more soldiers packed tight together was gone. The stink of unwashed bodies, foul uniforms, of so many suffering from dysentery and every other damned illness imaginable was washed away as the icy wind shrieked through the cracks between the boards and eaves. The only men still inside were Peter, Jonathan, and the troopers of the General's personal guard. The one drawback to the Maryland line's leaving — the temperature inside the barn plummeted in a few minutes to well below freezing. He started to shiver.

The remaining troopers stretched out on the floor of the barn. Sergeant Howard, who had befriended him, walked by, looked down at the two of them, and reaching into his jacket he pulled out a leather sack of rum and offered it.

Jonathan gratefully took it, swallowed a

few gulps, the hot warmth of the rum coursing through him, hitting him hard so that
his head swam.

"You feeling better, son?"

"Yes." It was a lie. His chest felt like it
was on fire.

"That stuff will cure you right quick."

"It certainly does."

"Good for you, lad. Rest easy now. They'll
call us when the time comes. It might be
hours yet."

The sergeant, like a mother hen checking
her chicks, moved on, leaving the two of
them alone in the pig stall. If not for Peter
asleep in his arms he would have crawled
out of the stench and found some hay or
straw to rest upon, but he did not wish to
disturb his friend, and so, curled up with
him, he sat beneath the flickering candle.

Sleep would not come again.

He tried to conjure up the image of Diana
by his side but it would not come. Besides,
with Peter asleep in his arms, the thought
seemed strange and uncomfortable. What
would Diana say if one day he should tell
her of this moment and admit the secret
desires he harbored. That would never do,
for her father was a deacon of their church
and surely she would be repulsed by such
thoughts.

The cold crept in around him, icy tentacles that penetrated the thin, worn, damp blanket and threadbare uniform so that he began to shiver uncontrollably. He wished the sergeant would come back again and offer another drink, and then another. In the army he had learned to drink. At least for a few minutes a drink would ward off the cold that seemed part and parcel of this wretched existence, not just warding off the cold of the body, but also the cold of the soul.

But he could not bestir himself, and besides, it would break what dignity he still had to go and seek a drink from another.

His thoughts drifted to that night they camped before Newark. Not the memory of his brother James deserting. That was a memory he worked diligently to wash out of his soul forever. Instead, it was of his friend Thomas Paine.

I can call him my friend, he thought, for he called me brother. Thomas Paine called me brother, and he remembered how his friend so readily produced the sack of rum and shared it with him and the others around their campfire, and without complaint accepted the miserable head of a carp and ate it without protest. Jonathan had been more than eager to offer him the choice morsel that he had been allotted.

He remembered how, after Paine had left their company, he could not get to sleep thinking about it. A new custom was emerging in the army. Soldiers were asking the famous author to place his signature on copies of his pamphlet *Common Sense.* He had lacked the nerve to ask, and besides, on such a miserable night how could one do so without pen or quill? Perhaps when this is all over I'll seek him out. Perhaps he just might remember me and I will ask him to sign it and we will laugh together about our shared meal and forget how it ended with my brother James deserting. Perhaps, just perhaps, I somehow helped him, for he had written down what I said to James. "You try my soul!"

Could I have helped him to create that? Jonathan wondered. If so, then maybe all of this is worth it, he thought, as he held Peter closer to stop his own shivering.

After Mr. Paine had left their miserable fireside, Sergeant Bartholomew had acted so strangely. Gone was his gruffness and endless stream of obscenities. Bartholomew had sat by the fire, poking the coals with his bayonet, muttering to himself.

Poor Bartholomew. When they finally reached Trenton and from there retreated across the Delaware, the skiff Bartholomew was in upended crossing over to Pennsylvania. Powerful man that he was, Bartholomew could not swim a stroke and disappeared in the ice floes and swirling current.

He wished he could write to the poor man's wife to tell her of her husband's fate, to somehow, like Mr. Paine, find the words to explain. But he did not have paper or ink and pen to do so. Nor did he even know where his sergeant had come from, for the man rarely spoke of his family, his wife and the five children he had left behind to go and fight this war. He had joked that he had joined the army so he could have a night of peaceful sleep without squalling brats and a wife pestering him to help make another. All of them had seen through that. He loved them, he missed them, and now he was drowned, as dead as if struck down in battle, and his family would never know.

When this is over, I will seek them out and tell them, Jonathan resolved.

Peter sighed and nestled in closer by his side. Jonathan pulled their blankets in closer around Peter's shoulders and his own, settling back.

On the other side of the thin boards that separated him from the raging storm he could hear the wind howling, feeling the cold sweeping in, hear the distant sound of the men of the Maryland line loading aboard the boats to cross over to the Jersey shore.

"Get some sleep, boys." It was the sergeant whispering. "The General can't go over there without us. We got a few hours yet. Get some sleep."

Jonathan closed his eyes, but sleep would not come. Each breath was a labor, and with each breath he fought not to cough and awaken his friend.

His thoughts raced.

"These are the times that try men's souls," his friend had written.

But for this moment, the warmer thoughts of a girl who had kissed him but once made him smile, and for a few precious moments he did drift off to sleep.

McConkey's Ferry
7:30 P.M. December 25, 1776

Unable to conceal his impatience, Washington stood up, abandoning the warmth of the fireplace, and left the tight-packed room. Several of his staff prepared to follow, and he looked back at them, shaking his head.

He stepped out into the storm.

The troops waiting before the ferry house

were motionless, heads bent low against the storm, some muttering, some cursing, and mingled with the howling of the storm the sounds of incessant coughing, rattled breathing, men hawking and spitting and coughing again.

Benjamin Rush had warned him of this.

"One night out in bad weather now and I tell you, sir, half of the men will be down with inflammation of the lungs and die from it. Can you not find warm dry quarters anywhere and just give them a few days rest?"

No rest tonight, he thought grimly and felt a wave of pity as he walked along the side of the road, staying in the shadows, studying them intently.

Rush was right, most of them were indeed sick. Sick, emaciated, ragged, barefoot, shivering from the wet and cold. Even as he watched, one simply sat down in the mud and slush, head bent, shaking uncontrollably.

An officer standing near the collapsed soldier came to his side and knelt down, his words hard to hear.

"Come on, William, lad, back to your feet now."

The officer put his arms around the soldier and tried to lift him up, but the boy just leaned against him as a dead weight.

"Sergeant Compton," the officer sighed. "William here is finished. Find a dry place to put him and report back."

The sergeant nearly picked the boy up and staggered off into the dark.

The officer saw Washington in the shadows and came to attention.

"I'm sorry, sir," he announced nervously. "William is a good man, but his lungs have been really bad for days. We told him he could report sick, but he tried to come anyhow."

Washington nodded.

"He and you tried your best. Carry on."

The officer, obviously relieved that he would not face an upbraiding, turned away.

The unit was close-knit, perhaps the young soldier a nephew or neighbor before the war the way the officer had almost tenderly tried to rouse him.

Another boat was loaded and pushed off, and the suffering column staggered forward a dozen feet and then came to a stop again.

More muttering, cursing, and the incessant coughing the only sounds from those enduring agony and waiting.

He turned away, angling down to the riverbank, downstream from the ferry dock.

Yet another river. Across the years of peace

after the last war he had ordered many of the best works from England on the art of war and read them at his leisure. At a moment like this it is almost too painful to recall quiet evenings on the porch of Mount Vernon looking over the broad expanse of the Potomac, often with Martha by his side in the next chair, sometimes sewing, often reading or catching up on her correspondence. Other times, late at night on winter evenings, sitting by a warm fire, the only sounds were the crackling of the blazing logs of hickory and chestnut and the soft gentle tick-tock deliberation of the clock in the corner gradually luring him to a comfortable nap in his chair, book falling to the floor by his side.

Books describing the great battles of the past, the campaigns of Marlborough, Frederick of Germany, and, farther back, Caesar. How Caesar in little more than a week bridged the mighty Rhine, four times as broad as this river, flung his legions across on a raid, and then, when it was completed, actually tore the bridge down. To have but one legion of those troops on this night, he thought wistfully.

There was no bridge here, though. There had been one on the Raritan less than a month ago, he remembered, and that had been a near disaster . . .

They had been harried since the break of a fog-shrouded dawn. Ever since the retreat from Newark his worst fear had been that Howe would fling a blocking force across the narrow strait dividing Staten Island from Jersey and push forward to block the single bridge and ferry dock at the Raritan River. His advance guard, however, had reported the way ahead was clear, and Greene had pushed his exhausted command forward to seize the crossing and prepare for the rest of the army to follow.

The bridge was secured, but by dawn and the resumption of the exhausting march, Hessian troops were upon their rear and pressing in. He feared that, as the Romans were trapped by Hannibal against the Po, his army would bunch up, with their backs to a river having only one crossing, and disintegrate in panic. Such a position was often described in the books he had read as the last day of an army, and the river by evening would be running red and choked with the bodies of the slain.

The cold fog shifted over to lowering clouds out of which came a cold drizzle, mixed with occasional flakes of snow and driving sleet. Riding alongside the column, he saw the men pressed on, not as they once had, with élan, eyes afire, believing some "mischief" as they called it, awaited them ahead. They shuffled along woodenly, moving fast, to be sure, but doing so with fear in their eyes, faces drawn and pinched from exhaustion and hunger, nervously looking over their shoulders. Passing woodlots bordering the road he could see tracks where more than one man had broken from the column and dashed into the woods. Some most likely had offered the usual excuse, that with the bloody flux running rampant in the army they had to relieve themselves, even though he had given specific orders that proprieties and modesty were to be forgotten; if a man was seized with such needs he could fall out by the side of the road but no farther. From the tracks he could see that few had returned to the march. Cowering in the woods, scores of men — perhaps hundreds — were breaking off from the column, never to return. They would wait until the armies had passed and then slip off for homes in Massachusetts, Pennsylvania, or the faraway frontier of Virginia.

The Raritan was not a large river at all.

Though swollen by the early winter storms, it was still narrow enough that a bridge could span it and afford a dry crossing. Knox had arrayed a battery on the north side, guns dismounted, on a low rise just outside of the village of Brunswick. He rode up to him.

"Amazing, sir," Knox exclaimed. "Yesterday, they could have sent just a few boats up this river from Staten Island, seized the bridge, and destroyed it."

Washington said nothing, studying the narrow single-lane crossing, just wide enough for the artillery and the army's few remaining supply wagons to get across.

Greene came up to join them.

"Sir, half my command is across. Your orders?"

"Good work. Deploy on the south bank and be ready to defend the crossing as the rest of the men get across. Knox, be ready to pull your guns out quickly and find some good ground on the south shore."

There was the distant rattle of musketry. He turned about and headed north without waiting for a reply, followed only by Billy Lee.

Riding against the stream of the column he could see that the men were picking up their pace. As always, the mud, the dam-

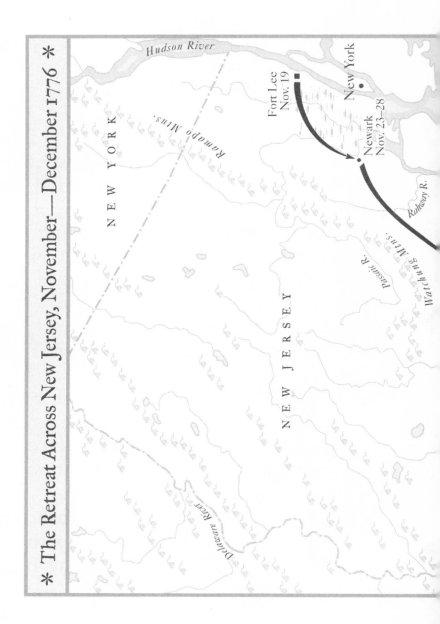

* The Retreat Across New Jersey, November—December 1776 *

Hudson River

New York

Fort Lee
Nov. 19

Newark
Nov. 23–28

Rahway R.

Ramapo Mtns.

NEW YORK

NEW JERSEY

Passaic R.

Watchung Mtns.

Delaware River

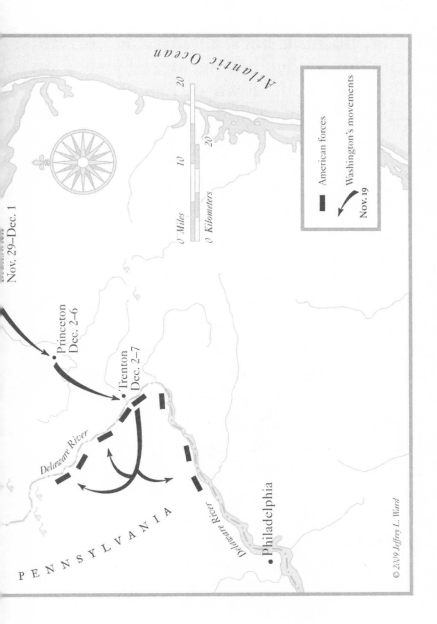

Nov. 29–Dec. 1

Princeton
Dec. 2–6

Trenton
Dec. 2–7

Delaware River

Delaware River

Philadelphia

P E N N S Y L V A N I A

Atlantic Ocean

0 Miles   10   20

0 Kilometers   20

American forces

Washington's movements

Nov. 19

© 2009 Jeffrey L. Ward

nable mud, clung to them, caking the rags wrapped about their feet. One man, lucky enough to have shoes, suddenly stopped, cursing, pushing back against the current, the clinging sludge having sucked a shoe off his foot. He went down on his knees, feeling about, trying to find that precious shoe, men stumbling over him, the column bunching up.

"You there!" Washington cried. "Fall in and keep moving!"

"My shoe, sir!"

"Fall in and keep moving."

The soldier shot him a defiant stare but then reluctantly gave up the search and fell in with the retreating ranks.

He felt a wave of pity for him in spite of the disruption he had caused, the knot of men who had been slowed untangling and resuming their pace. The loss of a shoe, if the temperature fell, might very well mean a frozen foot by tomorrow and amputation a week hence.

More musketry, and as he drew closer he could distinguish the sharp crackle of rifle fire. Our men or the Hessian's mounted jaegers?

He was approaching the rear of the column, now bunched up, any semblance of unit cohesion, of anyone in command, gone.

A wagon sat in the middle of the road, front axle snapped, sagging, team already cut loose, driver vanished. It was stacked with barrels stamped SALT BEEF, and his heart sank. There was no time to attempt to retrieve them. There were enough rations to feed a meal to a thousand men, but of so pitiful a condition the pursuing British troops most likely would scorn them and set them ablaze.

Men flowed around the wagon, not bothering to stop for a minute to bust a barrel open and fill their haversacks. With the enemy closing in from behind, they were too afraid.

"The bridge is just ahead, boys," he repeated again and again.

The retreating column began to thin out. Stragglers were staggering with exhaustion, struggling to escape, looking back over their shoulders, eyes wide with fear. A wounded man, lean, tough-looking, blood dripping from his hand, answered his unasked question. "Sons of bitches shot me, sir, but I got one of 'em, an officer from the looks of 'im" he announced coolly and pressed on.

Now a thin ragged line of riflemen, and in the center of the road a lone artillery piece, a four-pounder that suddenly fired, kicking back, mud spraying up under its wheels.

The gun was retreating by fire. A lone mule pulled the field piece by ropes attached to it, the crew working to reload as the driver urged the mule on with harsh prodding, several of the gunners pushing at the wheels.

He looked past the gun and could see the pursuers, jaegers, some mounted, others on foot. The flash from a rifle, a ball singing past, another flash, another bullet — they were obviously aiming at him. If musketmen, their aim would be a joke, but these jaegers were nearly as good as his own riflemen. On a calm dry day they were able to pick a man off at two hundred yards.

He ignored the threat.

The gunners finished with their work and shouted for the driver to halt the mule. The obedient animal was most likely glad to stop its labors, ears pressed down as if anticipating the explosion. The gun's sergeant squatted down, sighted along the barrel, stepped back, whipped the linstock with burning taper on the end around his head a few times to get it glowing hot and placed it on the touchhole.

The gesture was seen by the jaegers, now little more than a hundred yards off, and in spite of the muck they dived to the ground. The gun kicked back, sending out a spray of iron balls, nails, anything deemed lethal that could be jammed down the barrel.

The impact kicked up sprays of mud. One of the jaegers, obviously hit, half rose from the mud, mouth open, screaming, clutching at the stump of his arm. The impact and the damage done enraged the Hessians, who began to sprint forward, their curses audible. The riflemen escorting the field piece now systematically took aim, delivering measured shots, and another jaeger went down.

The charge slowed, rifles were raised in reply and shots winged in.

The scream of the mule was nearly deafening as the pathetic animal rose on its rear legs and collapsed on its side. Though its back was toward the enemy a rifle ball had shattered the creature's skull. Its driver stood there, stunned, looking down at the animal as it kicked feebly and then was still.

He raised his lash, looking back defiantly.

"You goddamn bastards, you killed my mule!"

He actually started to push his way forward, as if to take on the enemy single-handed. Several comrades grabbed hold, restraining him.

The gunnery sergeant looked up at Washington, as if awaiting orders.

The General sighed and shook his head.

"Abandon the gun. Now run for it, boys."

The men did not need any more urging, though the sergeant took a few precious seconds to pull open a box strapped to the side of the prolonge, pulled out a nail and mallet and with several sharp blows drove the nail into the touchhole at the breech, rendering the gun useless, at least for now.

The Hessians, seeing that the gun was being abandoned, came on the double.

It was humiliation, once again, utter humiliation!

"Run, men, run!" Washington urged as he turned, the ever-present Billy Lee moving to put himself between the General and the far-too-accurate rifle fire. Mud splattered around them, the sergeant struggling to keep up. Billy Lee reached down, offered a hand, half lifting the sergeant out of the mud, the artilleryman clinging to Lee's saddle. The riflemen had wisely moved off the road, sprinting through orchards, a woodlot where several paused to reload, turn, and fire. He caught a glimpse of one of them deciding the game was up, and rather than continue retreating toward the river, the man turned to the west and sprinted off. Perhaps he would come back later. More likely he would continue west, trudging the two hundred miles to his home on the edge of the frontier or beyond.

With the artillerymen and few riflemen still with him, he fell back onto the bridge. The last of his exhausted infantry was streaming over it. Two more wagons had been abandoned just short of safety, their precious contents, salt pork and beef, hard bread, dried corn, spilled out in the mud-clogged street and trampled under.

Knox and his gunners were across, the last among them, young Alexander Hamilton, moving his pieces to the east side of the road, across from a broken-down tavern.

"Move, boys, move," he kept chanting trying to stay calm, looking back at the relentlessly advancing enemy.

Humiliation.

"Boat away."

Stirred from his thoughts, he looked upstream. Another Durham boat was shoving off into the ice-choked Delaware.

River crossings.

He sighed.

It wasn't like the books he had read on summer evenings on the porch at Mount Vernon or during the pleasant chill of a winter night in his library.

Head lowered against the storm, he turned

to go back into the ferry house and continue the wait.

CHAPTER FIVE

Trenton, New Jersey
December 9, 1776

The cold cut through the clothing — the humidity made it all the colder — and every marching soldier was shivering. Night was settling, covering all with a freezing blanket of mist rising up from the Delaware River, a ghostly undulating mist engulfing the village ahead.

"There's Trenton, boys."

Thomas Paine raised his head as someone exclaimed that the village and the safety of the river was just ahead. There were no shouts of joy.

"There's Trenton, boys," and the wooden pace continued. Raise your foot, put it ahead of you, heavy mud caking thick on each boot. Put your foot forward, sink into the congealing glue nearly to the boot top, the chilled slop sometimes spilling inside. Pull your other foot up out of the slop, stag-

177

ger forward another step. There was no longer any semblance of a marching column, just an endlessly weaving line of men ahead, the last few stragglers of this broken army. Take a step, move forward another two feet, curl your toes inside your boot to hold tight to it so it isn't sucked off. Take another step.

Dusk was closing in, giving him a strange, distant feeling, as if his universe were collapsing in upon itself. He felt that in a few more minutes he would be totally alone and that this was his eternity, his hell, punishment for his sins. He wondered if there were a God who could so cruelly set a man upon such a road without end, an agony more painful than Sisyphus had ever endured, for at least the ground beneath his accursed feet had been firm . . . and the weather hot.

Raritan Crossing
December 1, 1776
Hot. It had been hot a few days back at least . . . hot for the blood, even though it was snowing . . . his first taste of combat.

South of Newark the army had reached the Raritan at Brunswick, and the dread many of them carried, that the British might jump the narrow channel between Jersey and Staten Island with a blocking force, thus pinning the army, had proven to be unfounded. The way south was still open, but Cornwallis was closing in fast from the north as the last of the army, using the ferry and a narrow bridge, struggled to reach the south shore.

It had been snowing intermittently for two days, temperature hovering near the freezing point, making life even more miserable. The road had not frozen solid enough, so it was churned into rivers of gluelike mud. It felt as if heaven itself had turned its back upon them.

On the north side of the river there was an air of panic, behind them there was the occasional rattle of musketry, the muffled thump of a field piece, and, most annoying in a way, bugle calls. The calls had set his blood to boiling, flash memories of childhood, the "gentlemen" of the countryside chasing their damn foxes, at times trampling down precious crops. Oh, there would be apologies, a "sorry, my good man," the flip of a half crown or a guinea from a purse to compensate before they rode on. It was their attitude, though, that rankled him when he stood there as a boy watching them. They were lords, lords and gentlemen, because that was the way of the world. And he was the son of a staymaker . . . and so it was —

unchangeable — unchallengeable — a fact of British life.

And now, laughingly, they were using the same foxhunting calls to herd the Americans along. The men waiting to cross the bridge were near to panic, just like a fox, cornered, panting, waiting for the hounds to close in for the kill, while the gentlemen smiled and shared a drink as their prey was literally torn apart.

He had crossed the wooden bridge, shuffling along with the others, one of the last. No orders kept him to his place; it was rather a kind of perverse curiosity. It was time to see if there was still at least some shred of a fight left in the army. He had to know this if he was to write about it, to add something more to the meager pages wrapped up in his pack.

On the south shore a few men were at work with axes, chopping away at several of the bridge piers and not making much progress. Others were dragging up brush, some siding from a barn, hoping to set the structure on fire. He knew that effort would be vain as well; everything was too wet.

The endless muddy track led on southward. It could no longer be called a road, though until the war it had been fairly well maintained, since it was the highway and post road linking Philadelphia and New York. The passing and repassing of armies across the months had churned it into mud, and now the weather had turned it into a glutinous river of slush.

It was snowing again, the view obscured for the moment. To his left he saw a section of four field pieces, mixed caliber; two of them looked to be four-pounders, the others heavier six-pounders. The gunners were standing ready, sergeants shielding the glowing tapers on the end of the linstocks, touchholes covered with oiled cloth to keep them dry. He recognized their commander, the lad from New York, only nineteen and, word was, already destined for bigger things, Alexander Hamilton.

He watched them for a moment. Hamilton had raised a small field glass, a bit of a vain gesture since the far shore was barely visible through the swirling snow. He was tempted to go over, stand by, watch, lend a hand, and so perhaps get a chance to fire a shot. It would be a pleasure. Surely if he dropped his name, the men would let him fire one round.

But on the other side of the road was shelter, what looked like a tavern. It had already been picked clean, its door gone, torn from its hinges, most likely part of the kindling meant to set the bridge afire, broken crockery scattered about on the porch. He chose momentary comfort over the thrill of defiance.

Inside the tavern was as cold as outside, the fireplace dark, the place looted, cupboards torn open. He poked around with the instincts of a poor man, and fate, for once, was kind. Two bottles of gin were tucked beneath a torn-up floorboard, most likely the remnants of a stash. These last bottles he claimed as the rightful property of the Revolution. Finding the two bottles he felt that fate was luring him into another losing fight with drink. Besides on a day like this who wouldn't drink? Returning to the porch, which was momentarily bathed in feeble sunlight by a break in the snowfall, he settled down, cracked open one of the bottles, and began to drink.

Stupid move.

A minute later, several of the artillerymen wandered over and he had to share, especially when their young officer came to herd the men back and recognized him, extending his hand. It was an honor to meet Tom Paine.

Damn fame. He sighed inwardly as he offered the bottle, but kept the other concealed. The artillerymen each took a drink, strangely polite now, one of the men offering the half-empty bottle to Hamilton, who took a quick sip. A scattering of musketry echoed from the far bank. Hamilton ordered his men back to their posts, thanking Paine and — again that strange custom of this land — shaking his hand and asking the same infernal question.

"What are you writing now?"

Tom forced a smile and shrugged, as Hamilton returned to his guns.

Thinking better of where he chose to drink, Paine slipped back into the looted tavern and sat on the floor, careful not to settle down on any broken glass. He finished off the bottle, pulled out the second, and set to work on it.

"Democracy be damned," he muttered, nursing his cheap gin alone.

More shots outside. The four cannons lit off, rattling the building. He looked out the open doorway. Smoke was whipping around the gunners as they reloaded.

A bad spot to be in, he suddenly thought, if the British rush the bridge and I'm sitting here half drunk.

The gunners will give me warning enough. When they run, I'll run. Besides, he had stayed to watch the fight for the river, and this was as good a spot as any.

"In here!"

He was startled when two men appeared at the doorway. They were lean, tough, dressed in brown fringed hunting frocks, long leggings, broad-brimmed hats tied down with strips of burlap to protect their ears from the cold, and in their hands they carried the famed instruments of their trade, Pennsylvania long rifles. Their long, rifled barrels could reach out far beyond any musket and deliver death with an accuracy that stunned men who had never seen them in use before.

After the two came to a halt, staring down at him, one of them smiled and, without asking, extended his hand. Sighing, Tom passed the bottle up and each took a liberal swig.

"Good a spot as any, I figure," one of them announced, and seconds later they had smashed out the lower panes and frame of a window facing the river and knelt down. The snow was abating, occasional flickers of sunlight as the low clouds scudded southeastward, then snow again, then another splash of sunlight.

Curious, he went over to stand behind them at the window.

The far shore, a hundred and fifty yards away, was now an enemy landscape. A few dragoons galloped along the riverbank; seconds later, a half dozen more, these men riding slowly, came out of a woodlot, herding several dozen prisoners before them with the flats of their swords. The ferry house on the north shore was in their hands, but the last men across had cut the tow cable. There were flickers of movement, then nothing. Several men in green uniforms were darting through a doorway of a warehouse and more into a nearby house.

Jaegers. Hessian riflemen, he realized.

"Now you just stand there a moment," one of the Pennsylvania riflemen announced, giving Tom a quick glance over his shoulder. "You're a good target. After they get you, we'll get the bastard that dropped you."

As if in fulfillment of prophecy a windowpane over the head of one of the riflemen shattered, the bullet singing by Tom's face before it slapped into the far wall. He ducked down, both of his comrades chuckling, one glancing back but the other still focused.

"His smoke, see it!"

There was a flash, a concussive crack, the shooter trying to peer through the smoke. He settled back down, leaning against the wall, drawing out his ramrod to start reloading while the other one stayed posted at the window.

"Missed the bastard, Joshua. Think he's laughing at you."

Joshua said nothing, looking at Tom, who had instinctively sprawled out on the floor.

"Made you shit yourself, didn't it?" Joshua asked.

"Nothing left inside to give," Tom replied, trying to sound just as laconic. Joshua grinned.

"Them's Hessian jaegers over there on the other shore. Not as good as us, but they got rifles, men from their forests. Think the word means hunter or something. Not as good as us, but close enough."

Joshua grinned as he continued to load, pouring a measure of powder down the barrel of his rifle, drawing out a greased patch, setting the ball atop it, pressing it into the muzzle with his thumb, then pressing down with the ramrod, pushing the charge home. A man armed with a smoothbore musket could load a couple of times a minute, a grenadier on the other side of the river was expected to load four times a minute, but an unaimed shot wasn't worth much after fifty yards. Joshua spent a good two minutes loading, but he could carry death out to two hundred and fifty yards.

"I'm just about ready," Joshua announced. "Would you mind getting up and standing by the window again?"

"You can kiss my ass," Tom retorted, and the two laughed.

Still feeling a bit shaken, he drew the bottle of gin out of his haversack, looked at the two, uncorked it, and made an offer.

Joshua shook his head.

"Workin' now. After we get one we'll celebrate, but go ahead, brother, don't let us stop ya. Looks like you need another drink."

Tom did not argue the point, his knees felt like jelly. He took a long pull. Crouching low, he went out the door and sat down on the porch.

It was a comfortable spot, facing southeast, protected from the cold wind, and when the sun did peek out, there was even a touch of warmth for a moment.

The crews trying to tear down the bridge or set it afire were now being peppered by harassing fire from the far shore, and one by one they broke away and ran for cover.

All we do is run, he thought. Another crack of a rifle from within, followed by Joshua's cursing.

He watched the two riflemen at work through the open door of the tavern.

"That one. See 'im?" Joshua announced, peeking up over the edge of the windowsill. "Upper window, the house with the green shutters and two chimneys. Yup, watch this!"

The flash of flint striking, a puff of smoke, the cracking recoil of the long-barreled rifle, the two peering through the smoke, one of them laughing.

"Ya missed the son of a bitch," his companion said. "Clipped his hat, though." A few seconds later both ducked as a bullet shattered another windowpane above them. Tom could imagine laughter on the other side. It was nearly a game to them.

The skirmish was spreading out, with dismounted jaegers on the far side of the river, Pennsylvania and Virginia riflemen on the near side running across a field behind the tavern, a couple sliding in behind an ancient oak.

He liked these men — tough, sinewy, self-confident — not the types to stand on the volley line. They were more at home in this kind of fight, loading carefully, working as a team, one man spotting, pointing out a likely target, providing cover while his comrade reloaded and then took careful aim.

"Paine? Thomas Paine, is that you? What are you doing here?"

Startled, he looked back to the road and there he was — General Washington, horse mud-splattered, cloak dripping with wet flakes of snow, and beside him his black servant, mounted on a horse every bit as good as the General's.

Tom stepped down from the porch, not sure what to do and offered a salute. That felt strange. There were few men in this world he would ever offer a salute, but somehow, with this man, it seemed the right thing to do.

A humming whistle cut the air between them. He flinched. Washington remained unmoved, except for a flicker of a smile. Behind him, though, the servant did react, nudging his horse, moving himself between the General, the river, and the far shore. The General looked peeved but said nothing.

A sharp crack erupted. On the far side of the road one of Hamilton's guns kicked back, yellow gray smoke boiling out, wind whipping it around the General, for an instant almost like a portrait of a war god in battle. He turned toward the far shore and saw a chimney collapse.

"A bit lower, Captain Hamilton, if you please," Washington called out, his voice almost cheery. "But try not to hit the houses. There are civilians inside." Then he whispered. "Even if they are Tories now."

Tom barely heard the words.

Young Hamilton, obviously proud to be noticed, saluted and turned to his section of gunners, shouting for them to adjust aim.

"Now, Mr. Paine, you have not responded to my query," the General said, a slight chiding to his voice.

"Ah, sir, don't you think we should move around this building, out of the way of fire?"

As he spoke, another bullet whistled close by, Washington's servant not flinching, but edging his horse closer in to act literally as a bodyguard.

Washington did not move.

"Your response to my question, Mr. Paine."

"Sir, I was with the army, felt I should come along with the rear guard and observe things a bit. And now I'm here."

Washington looked down at him.

"Have you been drinking again?"

No sense in lying, and he merely nodded his head. But what the hell, half the army was drunk, and the half that wasn't wished they were.

Washington sighed.

"Mr. Paine. I have some officers at least who know how to lead," and as if in reinforcement to his argument Hamilton behind them shouted the order for his crew to stand clear, a gunnery sergeant touching off one of the four-pounders. The two stopped their conversation to watch the effect. A second small group of dragoons, thinking they were well beyond the range of the harassing rifle fire, scattered, one of the horses going down, screaming, its rider jumping off, limping, obviously wounded.

"Better, Captain Hamilton!" Washington announced, then turned his attention back to Tom.

The flurry of snow increased in intensity, driven by the northwesterly wind, obscuring the far bank. Tom shivered as the cold blast cut through the thin blanket draped around his shoulders.

"Mr. Paine, as I was saying, I have some officers who can lead, and I still have some soldiers who can fight. But you, sir, how many do I have who can write as you do?"

Tom did not reply. Part of him was complimented beyond all measure that this man was taking the time to address him while a battle was obviously building. The snow cleared for a moment and he could see where two British field pieces were moving into position about three hundred yards off. Hamilton called for his two six-pounders to begin counterbattery fire.

The General and Tom watched as the two guns fired, the second shot so well aimed that it shattered the wheel of one of the British guns, its crew running for cover.

"Excellent, Captain Hamilton. Excellent. Now keep at it. I wish Colonel Knox were here to see your men at work like this!"

Hamilton, grinning like an excited schoolboy, stood there glowing and then turned to his guns.

"Have you been writing?" the General asked, shifting his attention to Tom.

Again he could not reply. A mere nod of the head.

Washington was silent, gazing at him for a moment, and he dreaded what would come next. The man would ask to see what he had done. His work was rolled up inside an oilcloth wrapping inside his pack, pages of it, poured out, starting in Newark, more added last night, the title now clearly *The American Crisis*, the words memorized in his heart and scribbled down on foolscap.

"Mr. Paine, what is your value to us, to this army, to me at this moment?"

He stood there, feeling a bit like a child being chastised but aware of a building defiance as well. God damn it all, he had been with this army now for months and not once fired a shot. All he had known was suffering, hunger, dysentery, watching others freeze, watching others die. At this moment he felt utterly useless. Perhaps the two backwoodsmen in the tavern behind him were right after all. At least he could be a decoy, a target, and he was drunk enough that he no longer gave a damn.

"What you're writing, do you have it with you?"

"Yes, sir."

Washington gazed at him. If he asks to see it, do I refuse? Tom wondered. He hated it when someone asked to see something before it was done. Would someone walk into a silversmith's shop, stare at a rounded lump of glowing metal, and exclaim that the work wasn't proper and explain what was wrong?

"Mr. Paine, suppose you get yourself killed out here? What then? What happens to what you write?"

Tom stood silent. If whoever took the time to bury him was literate, he might read it and wonder. If not, well, the paper was still of use for other things . . . and yes, it would be lost forever. "These are the times that try men's souls." His words, his words about these men, about all he had seen of them, all they were enduring.

"I'm sorry, sir," was all he could say. It was a damned rare day when he offered an apology.

"Mr. Paine, fall in with this army and head to the rear."

The General turned, and as he looked about for the last few stragglers heading south, Tom heard an audible sigh.

Army? A few days from now, enlistments for hundreds will expire and he doubted that even one would stay on. New England men would simply pack up at dawn, and since the way north to home was blocked by Cornwallis's advancing army, they would turn westward, heading for the Watchung Hills, with the intent of circling west around the enemy and then turning north. Men from the south would just walk off. As for the remainder of the Jersey militia, they had already melted away. If unarmed, they would be allowed by the British to pass back to their homes, and there, upon signing oaths of allegiance to the king, all would be forgiven.

What army? While waiting with the throng to cross over the bridge, he had heard a disgusted officer announce that barely three thousand men were still with them this morning. He had predicted not one would be left by the time they reached the Delaware.

Still he could not reply. Washington actually forced a smile.

"Your duty, sir. My orders to you are this. Fall in with the army, stay with it till Trenton. I'll make sure someone is there to get you across and carried to Philadelphia."

Washington could see the last of his men trudging southward on the half-frozen mud that was their road of agony.

"Just remember what you see here," the General said, his voice weary. "Remember it and write of it."

Paine could only nod, unable to speak.

The General turned his mount away and galloped off, his servant following by his side, forcing his way to keep himself between the General and the fire from the jaegers on the north shore of the Raritan.

"Paine, you Tom Paine?"

The call came from within the tavern, and he stepped up onto the porch. One of the riflemen, Joshua, was leaning against the wall inside.

"Yes, that's me."

"Well, I'll be damned. And here I was happy to use your head as bait for those damn Germans. I'll be damned!"

"There he is again." It was the other rifleman, still peering cautiously out the window.

"Where?"

"Same as before. Son of a bitch, second floor, window to the right."

"All right then," Joshua announced, stepping toward the window, leveling his rifle, aiming it through a broken windowpane.

He squeezed off the shot. There was the beginning of a laugh, "Got him," and then with a grunt he staggered back, dropping his rifle.

Tom could see the blood, arterial blood, spurting out of the man's left arm, just below the shoulder.

"We got each other, I think." Joshua grunted, sitting woodenly on the floor, looking at his arm with self-reproach, as if a part of his body had betrayed him.

Tom scurried to his side. The rifleman's comrade, knife out, was already cutting into Joshua's hunting shirt, ripping it open.

The bullet had slashed into flesh several inches below the armpit, and with every pulse blood welled out.

"You got a good one this time," Joshua's comrade muttered as he cut a long strip of cloth from the man's sleeve, wrapped it several times around his arm, just above the wound, looked around, finally picked up a wood fragment from the broken window frame, stuck it into the bandage and started to rotate it, Joshua clenching his teeth, hissing as the tourniquet clamped down and the pulsing of blood slowed to a trickle.

Tom reached into his haversack, pulled out the bottle of gin, uncorked it, and held it to Joshua's lips, the man taking a long gulp this time.

"You need a surgeon," Tom announced.

"Go to hell. Leave that on awhile, it'll clot up. Bullet went clean through. Had worse."

"You need a surgeon," Tom repeated forcefully, and Joshua's comrade nodded in agreement as the two half dragged him to the far doorway. They went out to the porch, Joshua regaining his footing, using his rifle for support. Tom darted down and across the muddy road to where Hamilton was working his guns. Two more pieces had been rolled up, the battery of six making good work of keeping the dragoons back, spraying the far shore with grapeshot, crews cursing as the long-distance harassing fire of the German riflemen whistled about their ears, while the two six-pounders continued to pin down the remaining British field piece.

Hamilton saw him approach, nodding as Tom saluted.

"A friend of mine over there" — he

pointed back to the porch of the tavern — "took a bullet in the arm. He needs a surgeon. Got any idea where I can find one?"

"Most likely set up down the road a bit," Hamilton replied and then turned back to his work.

Not much help.

Minutes later the three were on the muddy road, following the tracks of the army, the booming of Hamilton's guns and the occasional crack of rifle fire echoing behind them. A quarter of a mile on was a well-built house of brick, the porch crowded with exhausted men, injured men, dying men. Helping Joshua up the steps, he eased the man down. Though obviously someone tough from the backwoods, he was apparently not used to hard liquor; the half bottle of gin Tom had poured down his throat along the way had left him uproariously drunk and more than a little belligerent, cursing that no damn surgeon was going to take his arm away.

He left them there and returned to the road, half regretting his democratic leanings in sharing the last of his newfound liquor with a stranger, but feeling guilty as well for leaving him. He was glad to be moving south, the contents wrapped up in his backpack almost burning him with a sense of haste, yet he was reluctant to leave, wanting to take at least a few shots at the bastards on the other shore. What a pleasure it would be to shoot one of those damn aristocrat officers. Instead, some poor clod of a German had shot the man next to him and been shot by him in turn. Strange, war. More than a few of the Pennsylvania riflemen were of German stock; had they not crossed over here, they might be wearing jaeger green instead of hunting frocks and leather leggings.

Thus he had mused from Brunswick to Kingston, the weather turning colder, snow increasing, the road at last freezing over. This was a war about the freedom of the common man, and yet it was common men on the other side who were doing the killing for their officers and kings.

On occasion the General would ride by, harrying the rear of the column, urging them to keep moving. He no longer noticed Tom, who was as filthy, worn, and slump-shouldered as the rest, a part of the dark, herded mass crawling along a muddy road heading south and west. Some responded to the General, looking up and saluting or telling him they were still with him. A few looked at him sullenly, cursing under their breath. When no officer was in sight, these would turn off the road and head into a nearby wood to disappear from the war. Tom no longer had the spirit to raise even a feeble argument. No one knew him. He was just another soldier, his regiment long since gone, drifting with the wreckage of an army in retreat.

They slept in the open that night in Kingston, and on the following day marched on to Princeton. More snow, but at least there were dry quarters that night. He actually slept in the library of the college. What a strange war. To fall asleep reading Locke, with a couple of works by Defoe as a pillow. In the morning he was tempted to slip Locke into his haversack, but it weighed a few pounds, too much to carry, and he pushed on.

Now Trenton was in sight, and beyond it a temporary refuge across the river Delaware.

The outskirts of the town were typical of so many villages in this lush farmland of Jersey, well-made houses of stone and brick, barns even bigger than the houses, but all of them emptied, the farmers having taken their livestock into the woods or far from the line of march. Fences were gone from the roadside, the wood taken for campfires. Houses were shuttered. On one porch a father and three sons sat on the steps, watching them pass, all four of them cradling fowling pieces, the message obvious: Step foot on this land and someone dies. The men staggering along with him were too exhausted to offer a taunt.

The road was slightly better here, graveled in low spots. At a stone bridge crossing the creek that bordered the town, warm fires burned on either end, clearly fed by some looted fence rails.

"This is Trenton, boys." It was an officer wearing a semblance of a uniform. "No looting by order of the General. Find your regiments. Just find your regiments and be ready to cross. This is Trenton, boys. No looting by order of the General . . ."

Tom shuffled along, suddenly feeling hemmed in as the open countryside gave way to a narrow street, shops clustered together, sidewalks of wooden planks, the smell of a town suddenly engulfing him, wood fires, candle wax, a fetid drain, food cooking. My God, it was roasting pork!

The village wasn't much, maybe five hundred, a thousand souls, a dozen or so blocks of houses, shops, outbuildings. The vanguard of the army had obviously taken it over, after the straggling retreat from New-ark a week ago. Any semblance of organization had by now collapsed. Provost guards were here in abundance, some of them as bedraggled as those they shepherded along, asking men for their regiment and then pointing the way, armed, some with bayoneted rifles, others with pistols or a drawn sword.

One approached Tom, blocking his path, pistol half raised in his direction.

"Which regiment are ye?" The man sounded New England, and though Tom had been a Pennsylvanian for little more than two years, he felt a distrust.

"I have no regiment."

"What in hell do you mean, you got no regiment?"

"They ran off."

The guard looked at him, not sure how to respond.

"You Jersey militia?" There was a sarcastic edge to his voice.

Tom threw back his head and laughed.

"Look, damn it, all I want to do is get across the river."

"Which regiment?"

God damn, were all such men the same across history? he wondered. Given an order but unable to think beyond it.

"I have no regiment, as I told you. They all ran off. If I was thinking of deserting, wouldn't I have done it by now?" Tom replied sharply. "My orders are to cross the river and head to Philadelphia."

"Whose orders."

"Damn it all," Tom sighed. "George Washington."

"Come with me." The provost put a hand on his shoulder.

Tom stiffened. "Get your hands off me!"

"You're under arrest."

"I said, get your hands off of me," and Tom pulled back. He had no weapon other than his fists and he raised them, the provost now pointing his pistol at him.

Those who had silently dragged along with him throughout the day stood watching, a few muttering as if ready to join in the fray, but none moving to help.

The two stood frozen in place. He gazed at the pistol. Would this man actually dare to shoot him?

He looked into the haggard face and hollow eyes of the man, ghostlike in the drifting mist. The man was shivering from the cold. He almost felt a pity for him and yet he would not be ordered about by him.

"I told you," Tom said slowly. "I have orders to cross the river."

"Show them, or you're coming with me."

"The hell with you," one of the onlookers snapped. "Like the man said, if we was deserting would we be so stupid as to come into this godforsaken town?"

"I have my orders."

"There's always someone like you with their orders," Tom sighed. "Well, I have mine, damn you."

"Paine! Tom Paine! I'm looking for Paine!"

Tom looked past the provost. He didn't recognize who was calling his name. An elderly man, mounted, leading a horse.

"That's me," Tom announced loudly.

"You Tom Paine?" the provost asked, even as the elderly man approached.

"To hell with you," Tom snapped. "No, I'm not, and I'm a goddamn liar. Actually, I'm that son of a bitch, King George."

The small group gathered to watch the fight laughed raucously. At the calling of his name, they were now firmly on his side.

The mounted rider drew closer, and those standing nearby came to attention as he passed.

"It's Old Put," he heard someone exclaim.

The rider reined in and glared down at him and the provost guard.

"Are you Tom Paine?"

"You found him," he paused, looking up.

"And who the hell are you?"

"General Israel Putnam, damn your impudent mouth."

There was a momentary silence, then Putnam leaned down and extended his hand.

"The General said you were filthy, ugly, and foul-mouthed. I guess you fit the bill." He could see that Putnam, "Old Put" as the men called him, was grinning.

Tom shook his hand, the grip hard, leathery, not sure yet if he cared for this man or not. Putnam had a reputation as a fighter, to be sure, and was held in high regard at the start of the war, but was haunted by the debacle at Long Island, most of his command having deserted after the fight.

"You're to come with me," Putnam announced. "I've got a mount for you."

"Where?"

"To Philadelphia. General Washington orders you to go there with all possible haste and I'm to shepherd you along. So get mounted, Mr. Paine."

Tom looked at the gape-mouthed provost guard who but a minute before was ready to arrest him. He could not suppress a grin.

"Still want to arrest me as a deserter?" he asked. There was something about such officials, echoes of the country he had fled, self-important and officious, that made his skin crawl.

"That's it," one of the bystanders laughed. "The rights of man against asses like him."

The provost, glaring, turned and stalked off, looking for someone else to bully. The small crowd taunted him as he left.

"Time's awasting, Paine," Putnam announced, offering the reins of the horse he was leading.

Tom looked at the beast warily. For him, as for so many of his class, riding a horse was a rare experience. The poor animal gazed at him with rheumy eyes. He was old, swaybacked, with about as much life left in him as the army he had been drafted into.

As Tom gingerly mounted, the poor animal let out an audible sigh, and Tom pitied him. Following Putnam's lead, he turned about and headed down to the docks along streets lined with weary men. Mist was rising from the river, cold, bone chilling, wrapping all in a strange light.

He heard arguing, cursing, and had a momentary glimpse into an open doorway of a shop, a mud-caked soldier standing within, the shopkeeper and his wife shouting at the soldier, the young soldier shouting back. The boy looked familiar, the one with the carp back in Newark. Tom rode on.

Glimpsing a lone rifleman shuffling through the mists, Tom slowed and leaned over.

"Aren't you Joshua's friend?" he asked.

The rifleman looked up.

"I was his brother."

"Was?"

The rifleman gazed at him intently.

"The goddamn surgeon took his arm off. He didn't need to have done that. I told him just to tie the bleeding off, but no, he didn't have time for that, the bastard. Said the arm had to come off, and I, like a damn fool, held Joshua down. He bled out on the table while they hacked away at him and died an hour later."

The riflemen, so hard, tough-looking, stifled a sob.

"I should have cut the bastard's throat for killing him, but he was already gone. Ran off they said. If I ever find him again, I will. To hell with this damn war, I'm going home."

Tom was unable to reply, stunned. It had not seemed much of a wound.

"Paine!"

It was old Putnam, barely visible in the fog.

"Come on, damn you!"

Tom kicked the flanks of his horse and

the old nag stumbled forward, the rifleman gone from view.

Ahead there was a strange glow, diffused in the mist, glaring bright as he approached, a ghastly light illuminating a river dock. Men were gathered about, some trying to push their way forward, others just standing there, as if no longer caring. A large flatbed ferry was docked, a line of Maryland Infantry guarding the approach.

"Those with passes only!" an officer was shouting. "The rest of you stand back, find your regiments, and cross when they do."

Tom sensed that if the men gathered had but an ounce of fight left in them, they would storm the boat, but they no longer seemed to care.

Putnam pushed his mount through the crowd. Tom followed, passing between the bonfires lighting the approach, conjuring a literary allusion, as if he were passing down to the river Styx. But which bank was it? Was he leaving hell or crossing over to it?

Putnam handed down a slip of paper to the officer, who held it up to the light. He scanned it, nodded, and handed it back and motioned for him to pass through the cordon. Tom followed.

"That's right," someone cried. "Officers first."

Tom looked around, feeling guilty, almost tempted to announce who he was, that he was not an officer, that he was one of them, a citizen like them, and that he had been ordered to go to Philadelphia, that what he carried in his backpack was a weapon to help them, but he knew that such an appeal was of no use. Not here, not this night.

He dismounted with Putnam and led his old horse onto the ferry, which was nearly filled with some of the army's precious supply wagons. Their cargo was the sick and wounded, the air unwholesome with the fetid smell of death mingled with the cold damp of the river.

The ferryman shouted for them to push in closer, and a moment later the boat shoved off, bow angled upstream, unseen hands on the far shore laboring at the cable to pull the boat across.

Tom stood silent, looking back. The glare of the fires receded into the mists. The river rushing by but inches away was pitch-black, frightening. If the boat should roll over, he knew all aboard would die. As for himself, he could not swim a stroke. Old Put bit off a chew of tobacco, nudged him, and he took a bite and handed it back.

"Out of one hell and into another," Putnam grumbled.

"How's that?"

"Haven't you heard?"

"What?"

"Congress, the cowards. They're going to abandon Philadelphia and run for Baltimore. My orders are to find them, report on what is happening, and try to recruit more men."

"They're gonna run?"

"What the hell else do you think they would do? Hell, we're all running now."

"So why am I going with you?" Tom asked.

Putnam leaned over the railing and spat, the wind blowing most of the tobacco juice onto Tom's ragged trousers.

"Find a printer and get whatever you wrote published. The General thinks it might stop some from running. He thinks you may be our best weapon at sustaining the Revolution. We need your new pamphlet. That's your orders."

Tom said nothing. The fires on the east bank had faded from view. The far side of the river was dark as well.

CHAPTER SIX

McConkey's Ferry
11:00 P.M., December 25, 1776

A frigid wind blew in through the open doorway.

"General, I think it is time for you to cross the river."

Stirred from his thoughts, Washington looked up. If not for the terrible stress of the moment, he might have offered a gibe in reply. Colonel Knox, all three hundred pounds of him, stood in the doorway looking like a drowned rat. In the few seconds he had been standing there, water was already puddling around his feet. His tricornered hat was bent down by the weight of sleet and ice it had accumulated, his wool coat hanging heavy and limp.

Washington felt a sense of guilt. He had tasked Colonel Knox with direct command of the crossing earlier in the day before any hint of the intensity of the storm that was now upon them. While he had been waiting here in the comfort of the home of the ferry operator, Knox had been out in the driving storm, shouting, cursing, directing the loading of each boat.

Washington stood up, beckoning toward the fireplace.

"For heaven's sake man, take a few minutes to warm yourself." Knox accepted the offer without hesitation. He extended his hands to the glowing flames, rubbing them vigorously.

Washington came up to Knox's side and offered him the cup of coffee he had been sipping. Knox eagerly took it, draining it down in two short gulps. Washington took the cup back and handed it to Billy Lee, who went to refill it.

"I'm sorry, sir," Knox began. His voice was quavering a bit, not from nervousness, but from the cold. "We are far behind schedule."

"I know," Washington replied. There was no reproach in his voice though for the last hour, while waiting for word that he should cross, every few minutes he had checked the time. According to the elaborate schedule he had laid out in writing for this attack, they were now nearly three hours behind.

His staff sat silent. No one had dared to speak, to comment on how the plan was falling apart or offer any words to divert him as he kept opening and closing his gold pocket watch.

Billy Lee came back bearing a cup filled nearly to the brim with coffee, and as Washington took it he could feel the heat. He offered it over to Knox in a friendly gesture.

"Careful," he said. "This is hot."

Knox cradled the cup in both hands, spilling some of the contents on his bare hands, whispering an oath under his breath. Washington's men generally tended to control their "soldier's talk" around him, though in moments of stress he was known to curse with the best of them, or the worst. Now he acted if he had not heard his friend's words.

"The temperature is dropping," Knox said at last. "Can't seem to make up it's mind, though. Rain, sleet, snow, sometimes all of it together. A regular nor'easter."

He paused, taking another gulp.

The way Knox said "nor'easter" sounded almost alien. The dialects of New England and Boston seemed to come from a different world, at times as hard to understand as the words of a man fresh off the boat from Yorkshire or Scotland.

Americans. Strange how this war is making us all Americans, Washington thought.

"That's better," Knox sighed. The shivering abated as the fire and the syrupy drink warmed his body.

"As I was saying, sir," Knox continued, now slightly embarrassed for having forgotten that momentarily focusing on his physical discomfort and relief might be seen as an insult to the General.

"Go on."

"A regular nor'easter it is. The freezing rain is making the approach to the landing dock all but impossible for the horses and a nightmare for moving the guns. I have men spreading straw, manure, dirt, anything for footing. After every crossing we have to smash the ice off the gunwales of the boats else they become top-heavy. Several men have broken arms or legs falling, but, thank the Lord, no boats have gone under, and there are no reports of men falling overboard."

"The Jersey shore?"

"I've crossed twice since we've started. Our advance pickets have secured the road for more than two miles ahead. I've taken the liberty, therefore, of allowing fires to be built to warm the men while they form up."

Washington thought about that for a moment and then nodded in agreement.

"If the road is secured as far as you say, there is no sense in the men waiting in discomfort."

"Just about half the men and guns are across, so, as you originally planned, General, I think it time for you to cross and take command on the other shore."

"Then let us begin."

He looked back at his staff. All were ready. The tedium and the tension of waiting were over at last. They were committed.

Knox was reluctant to leave the comfort of the fire, but did not hesitate. He finished the last of his coffee, audibly sighing, and then put the cup on the mantel over the fireplace.

His staff was up now, a few having to be roused from their fitful slumber. As was always his practice when occupying a civilian's home or business place, he looked about to make sure that all was in order, nothing disturbed, broken, or taken.

Buttoning his cloak at his throat, he nodded to Knox.

"Lead the way, sir."

As he stepped out the door he understood instantly why Henry had so relished the few minutes of warmth and dryness to be found in the ferryman's house. The wind was

215

howling down from the northeast, icy pellets slashing into his face. Instinctively, he tucked his chin down into his chest and pulled his hat low over his brow, holding on to it lest it be blown into the darkness.

Two great bonfires were burning on either side of the approach to the ferry dock, and as he stepped out of the house he confronted a line of men, formed up, blankets, if they had them, pulled close to their emaciated bodies, more than a few barefoot, stamping their feet as they stood in place. If they were grumbling or cursing the weather, the British, the Hessians, or even their commander, he could not hear them, the howling of the wind encompassing all.

He walked alongside them, moving down to the dock, the men to his left all but oblivious of his passing as they waited to board the boats. By the great bonfires that lit the last few feet to the dock he saw that those feeding them were most definitely disobeying orders this night. Fence rails were being thrown in. He had given specific orders that a farmer's valuable fences were not to be touched. But they were dried and seasoned wood — chestnut, and hickory — and would burn with fury. He said nothing as two sergeants picked up several rails and heaved them onto one of the fires, sparks whipping away with the howling wind.

He drew closer. There were two officers. One kept endlessly chanting: "Wait your turn, men, wait your turn. Get in the boat assigned. Stand and move close together. Don't worry, boys, these boats are manned by Glover's men, they know their business . . .

"Wait your turn, men . . . Wait your turn . . ."

He walked past the officer, who was obviously wet through, shivering, near to breaking by the sound of his voice.

His attention was suddenly seized by a second officer on the far side of the shivering, frozen, miserable column of men waiting to board the boats.

"By order of the General, men, I'm going to read something. Listen now. Listen. This is what Tom Paine just wrote: 'These are the times that try men's souls.' "

Not normally given to emotion Washington stood silent for a moment, closing his eyes.

"Oh God," he whispered, "let this not be in vain, I beseech Thee. If we are doomed to die, Thy will be done. If it is Thy will that this night shall bring victory to our cause, may we never forget Thee and the blessing Thou has given us and give thanks to Thee daily, forever more. Those that fall on this night and in the day to come, I beg Thee to gather them peacefully into Thy arms and let their names not be forgotten."

He opened his eyes.

"Wait your turn, men. 'These are the times that try men's souls . . .' "

Henry Knox stood beside him. By the light of the fire he could see that his friend had been watching him. He had said nothing, and Washington wondered if the man had heard his whispered prayer.

Most likely not, given the demonic howling of the wind.

Knox struggled to clear his throat.

"Sir, your boat. It is that Durham boat on the left side."

"Thank you, Henry."

Even as they spoke he could hear some muttered cursing behind him. Looking back, the column was moving a bit to one side of the half-frozen mud-choked path. It was his guard and escort detail, rousted out to fall in and join their commander.

"General Washington! I'm looking for General Washington!"

From out of the darkness he saw a horse man approaching, the illumination of the fires at last making him visible.

"Over here!" Knox shouted. The man

drew closer and he recognized him. It was young Major Wilkinson, of General Gates's staff. The mere sight of the lad caused Washington's heart to constrict.

Wilkinson's mount nearly lost its footing on the icy pathway down to the ferry dock, the waiting soldiers cursing, jumping back. The horse regained its footing and Wilkinson dismounted.

"Sir, I bear a personal dispatch from General Gates," he announced, breathing hard and shivering, like all of them.

Wilkinson handed over a leather dispatch case and then, in an obvious gesture, stepped back several feet, as if by so doing he was disasociating himself from its contents.

Wilkinson's move was signal enough. Washington opened the case, drew out the letter, broke the seal and opened it up, holding it high so he could read it by the light of the fire, trying not to hold it too close and thereby revealing the fact that in private, of late, he had been forced to wear spectacles.

He scanned the contents of the letter. Paused, and then reread it, incredulous, disbelieving, as if by rereading the words they would somehow change. "Regret to inform you, sir, that . . . In my judgment this offensive action at this time is ill advised. Sir, since I have heard not to the contrary from you I shall this day order my men to remain upon the west bank of the Delaware and proceed to Baltimore where Congress has sought refuge, to seek their guidance . . . I pray, sir, that my movement is but a reflection of your own wishes at this moment which I would not otherwise do if I should hear the contrary from you . . ."

He reread it.

The plan had been for General Gates, based in Philadelphia, to move on this night as well, to cross to the eastern bank of the Delaware. The taking of Trenton was but a part of his overall plan. Gates, by crossing from Philadelphia to the New Jersey village of Camden, would trigger one of two results. Ideally, it might very well lure the British garrison based at Princeton to move in haste in that direction, thereby cutting them off as he seized Trenton, and with Gates as an anvil, he could be the hammer coming in from behind to finish them off. The other option would be of some benefit. The overwhelming effect of his column, that of Cadwalader crossing below Trenton, and Gates at Philadelphia would so catch the British and Hessians off guard, that after he seized Trenton, the enemy garrison at Princeton would retreat back to Brunswick or even to Staten Island.

He held the letter, this letter of betrayal, struggling to control his emotions. He could not let the rank and file, standing but a few feet away, see him thus unnerved. Armies were the same throughout history. A commander's every word and gesture could, within an hour, spread like wild fire to either hearten or to create panic.

And yet!

Struggling for control he stalked off, moving away from the fires.

Damn the man!

Gates's move was obvious, the words so carefully crafted. He was going to ask Congress's advice on his next action! Therefore, if I lose this night, this last remnant slaughtered and I with it, Gates will be in Baltimore, ready to have the title of commander in chief bestowed upon him! If, instead, I am victorious, he can claim prudence guided him because even at the very last instant he had not heard from me. This storm itself would be his excuse. Even if I move against him, should I survive this action, he will be firmly wrapped in the bosom of his friends in Congress and too well protected.

"Damn him," he gasped. "Can I not even trust my own officers anymore?" The fact that General Lee had recently so openly disobeyed him, and then, after being taken prisoner a week ago, was reportedly dining with General Howe and advising him. That was bad enough. But this?

"Bad news, sir?"

He looked up. Knox was silhouetted by the roaring fires that marked the dock.

He hesitated, looking down at the letter in his hand.

Knox was trembling again from the cold, the icy blasts that whipped around them changing, at least for this moment, from rain to sleet and snow.

He wanted to shout out a bitter reply, to send a dispatch rider back to Philadelphia, to order Gates's men to cross. To cross now!

Absurd. Eight to ten hours, and by then it will be decided anyhow.

He crumpled the letter. He stared at the dark waters of the Delaware, the reflections of the bonfires shimmering off the white-capped river. On impulse he threw the note into the swirling flow.

A momentary regret. He had just thrown away a bit of evidence for history. A bit of evidence, if dawn does bring us victory, with which I could bring Gates up on charges.

No, that was useless. Typical of so many of his ilk, Gates had his friends in the

Congress. He had written each word carefully, and victory or no, he could argue that he had taken the prudent path.

Prudence.

Prudence does not win battles . . . or wars.

"Sir, is it bad news?"

General George Washington forced a smile.

"Nothing, Knox. Nothing. A matter of the moment is all."

"Sir, your boat is waiting to cross."

"Fine then," he said softly. "Lead the way."

Though seething inside he had to make his expression show indifference, indicating to all that the contents of the note had been trivial, even though it meant that given the delay here, the entire plan was unraveling.

No. Don't let any of them know that a third of the force expected to cross this night would not do so. It would unnerve them.

It must not unnerve me.

He forced a look of quiet determination as he stepped back into the firelight.

He saw Major Wilkinson standing nervously at the edge of the dock. The lad stepped forward.

"Sir, is there any message I should bear back. My mount is tired, but I think I could return to Philadelphia by midmorning."

"No, major. No reply."

Wilkinson stared at him, and he could see what was in the boy's eyes. And it heartened him. There was a look of relief. Wilkinson, without doubt, knew every word of the dispatch.

"Major, I assume you know the contents of that letter."

"Yes, sir." He hesitated, obviously concerned that Washington might think he had somehow looked at it even though it was sealed or that he might face the legendary consequence of being the "Greek messenger."

Washington smiled and shook his head.

"It is our secret," he whispered, voice barely heard because of the rushing storm. "Not a word to anyone."

Wilkinson grinned, a young man now sharing a great secret with a commanding general.

"Sir, if I am not to return to Philadelphia, I beg you, sir, to let me have the honor of volunteering to cross with you."

He knew others were listening, and those who might suspect knew that Wilkinson was on Gates's staff.

"Why?" Washington asked.

"So I can tell my grandchildren I crossed with you this night," Wilkinson replied.

His words sounded far too melodramatic but in a gesture that was completely uncharacteristic, Washington clapped him on the shoulder.

"Then you must know the watchword for tonight, major," he replied.

He looked at the shivering men of the line awaiting their turn to cross.

"The watchword is: 'Victory or death.' "

Wilkinson repeated the words and then actually smiled.

Washington turned away and walked the last few feet to his boat. The men of his staff and personal escort were already aboard the forty-foot-long Durham boat. The vessel was eminently suited for this night. Broad of beam, flat-bottomed, it was designed to haul bulk freight on the Delaware, its crew using sweeps or long poles to guide it up and down the river. On this night, it was one of many craft, from the large Durhams, up to sixty feet and more to small scows and rowboats, laboriously moving back and forth against the current of the ice-choked Delaware.

The men of his personal guard, escorts, staff, and guides had already piled into the boat, only waiting for him. They were packed nearly shoulder to shoulder. Glover's men were ready, too, with sweeps raised, oars inverted to be used as poles to push off; other men, still on the dock and squatting down, held the boat firmly in place. The planking of the dock was slick with ice. Boarding was a difficult moment; fall now and far too many will see it as a portent.

He stepped onto the boat, a couple of his guards moving aside to make room, and he could feel several inches, perhaps half a foot, of icy water sloshing around his feet.

He looked back at Knox, now towering above him on the dock.

"Sir, I'll cross with the last boats," Knox shouted.

"Keep them moving" was all he could say.

He caught the eye of Colonel Glover, the man sitting at the tiller.

"Take us across."

Glover shouted for his men to cast off. The boat lay on the leeward side of the dock. They drifted clear and broadside to the river, the crew using the butts of their oars to brace it, push off, and then quickly turn the oars about, sitting down on the narrow rowing benches, and dig in hard. The bow turned, facing at a forty-five-degree angle into the flood current and, now clear of the dock, it began to rock, rattling booms shaking the boat as ice floes slammed against the upstream side. The rowers strained, grunting, heads bent over, backs and shoulders slumped over, then leaning back with each pull of the sweeps.

The boat began to rock, pivoting as a gust of wind caught it on the flank, threatening to turn them broadside, the hat of a man in front of the General whipping off, disappearing in an instant.

The boat drew only a couple of feet even when fully loaded with its usual bulk cargo of wheat, ore, and lumber. Still, as he looked over the side, it felt threatening, the dark frigid waters just a few feet away, the boat rocking. Some of the men around him were leaning against each other, trying to move back and forth to compensate.

"Damn all!" Glover shouted. "Don't move! Don't move!"

Washington looked back at him.

"Sorry, sir," the Marbleheader offered.

This was, of course, the same man who had saved the entire army after the Battle of Long Island, slipping them across the East River at night, under cover of fog, literally pushing between the blockading frigates of the British undetected. He had saved the Revolution that night, and now here he was again at another vital point performing an irreplaceable role.

"No offense, colonel. You are in command

of this boat now."

Glover nodded, eye turned upstream, as if in the darkness he could somehow detect what might be flowing their way.

There was a shout from their right and a glimpse of another Durham boat returning to the Pennsylvania side, seen only for a second and then lost in the darkness.

On the shore he had just left he could still mark the glow of the twin bonfires, and now, ahead, two more, marking their landing point.

He stood lost in thought. The slushy water was soaking through his already waterlogged boots. No one spoke. There were no heroic comments now, no posturing, no desire on his part to say something that might be remembered, to strike some sort of pose to inspire others, as he was wont to do on a battlefield. When mounted, he would often ride along the line, letting the men see him unperturbed by the musket balls and cannon shot screaming by.

Here, alone in the dark, packed in tight with the others, there was nothing he could do but be yet another man crossing a river to an unknown fate. The Jersey shore edged closer, the boat angled steeply against the flood current, rowers straining, groaning.

It was no wonder they were so far behind

schedule. When the plan had been contemplated it was thought it would be a matter of but several minutes to cross the river. It was taking twice and three times as long fighting against the current and floes. Not too much of a strain if the crew was doing it once or twice. But these men would be making the journey several dozen times this night, and already they were at the point of exhaustion, and the grinding effects of the storm were sapping their strength even more.

It was a miracle they had anything left at all, anything more than sheer willpower to keep the boats moving.

The dock on the Jersey side was illuminated clearly by the fires. Down close to the riverbank, the landing was somewhat sheltered from the northeasterly blow, but that now presented its own difficulties. Ice floes drifting in were not being driven clear by the wind, and were now piling up, the entire mass added to by the freezing rain, which was reflecting the firelight like sparkling diamonds.

Another boat was at the dock, off-loading a field piece, a nightmare task even in good weather. Its crew was moving the bulk of more than a ton up and out of the boat by manhandling it, men slipping and cursing on the icy dock. Their boat had to wait. Glover pointed their prow straight into the current, rowers again inverting oars, using the handles to plunge down into the river, digging into the bottom and leaning against the poles to keep the boat in place.

The gun was finally out, a couple of dozen men with ropes heaving it up the slope of the bank, shouting, cursing, slipping.

The empty boat cast off, its crew pushing out, pivoting on the current, its bow slamming into their boat, crews of both boats cursing, blaming each other. Finally, the other boat bobbed off into the night.

"Smartly now!" Glover shouted, and the oarsmen leaned into their inverted oars, pushing, inching their boat toward the dock. Then, twenty-five feet short, it ground to a stop.

"Damn you! Push, damn it, push!"

The boat moved a few more inches. Washington felt something scraping beneath his feet. They were snagging bottom, the way ahead blocked by the river ice piling up around the dock.

A man at the bow tossed a cable across to a hand on the dock, missed, the man on the dock slipping on the icy surface as he scrambled to catch it and nearly falling into the river. A second try, the rope falling just short.

Glover stood up at the helm.

"Damn all to hell," he roared. "I need volunteers. Someone carry that damn cable to the dock, three or four of you get off to lighten the load."

No one moved.

"Now!"

Washington looked back at him, tempted to volunteer to lead the way. No, I can't, I must stay focused on the hours ahead. If I drown or freeze out there . . . He inwardly detested the moment, the restraints that command placed upon his acting as he wished.

"I'll go."

One of the men farther forward edged to the bow, handing his musket to another, and then another followed.

"It's only a few feet deep!" Glover shouted. "You'll be fine. Take the cable and walk it in."

The two went over the side.

"You damn fool," Peter hissed.

Jonathan said nothing. Slipping over the side, he found that Glover was right, the water was barely above his knees. The way ahead was filling up with ice floes. Just push them aside.

"Careful now: Don't slip!"

It was the boatman forward, leaning over, handing him the end of the heavy cable. It was covered thick with ice. No wonder the men waiting on the dock were having a hard time snagging the end.

Peter fell in beside him, the two grasping the two-inch-thick rope. Now clear of the bow of the boat, the current all but knocked them over, ice banging against their thighs, the blows stinging, storm swirling about them. Only twenty feet to go.

He struggled forward, leaning against the current.

A dozen feet.

He took the next step, ready to hold the cable up for those leaning out from the edge of the dock.

Then he stepped into a hole, lost his footing, the current knocking his other foot out from under him. Jonathan went under.

In that instant he could only think that anyone who said that freezing to death was not as bad as fire . . . had not tried one or the other. It felt as if a thousand icy knives were being driven into his flesh, the wind knocked out of his lungs in a convulsive gasp. The world was pitch-black, terrifying. He could feel the cable slipping from his numbed grasp.

He surfaced. Peter, one hand holding the cable, was reaching out with the other to grab Jonathan as he floundered.

Someone was by his side, bracing him. Who, he didn't know.

He started to thrash, terrified. Strong arms were about his chest.

"Hold tight, boy, to the rope, boy! I got you!"

He couldn't see. He felt someone pull the cable from his hands and then, seconds later, lift him up.

Other hands grabbed him and tossed him onto the dock, gasping. He could not catch his breath.

His rescuer, one of the dock workers, was being pulled up by his comrades.

"You damn fool, you'll kill yourself," he could hear one exclaim.

"The General is on that boat!" the rescuer shouted. "Now pull, you bastards."

The boat cleared the snag and seconds later was up against the dock, Glover's men reaching out to grab and hold it as the men began to get off.

Someone was pulling Jonathan to his feet. It was Peter.

"Damn you, Jonathan! Damn you!"

Jonathan couldn't speak, he was shaking uncontrollably.

"Get the boy over to the fire and strip him down."

He looked into the face of a bearded, burly Marblehead man and sensed this was his rescuer.

"Thank you," Jonathan gasped.

"Boy, get to that fire or you'll be dead in minutes."

The man was soaked from the waist down, water was pouring off of him, and Jonathan, though his mind was clouded with shock, wondered about this man's strength.

"Thank you," he tried to say again. The Marbleheader offered a momentary smile and then went back to his work of holding the gunnel of the boat as men streamed off, a couple of them slipping and falling on the dock.

Peter dragged Jonathan up to the roaring bonfire. Like the fires on the Pennsylvania shore, it was fed with well-seasoned fence rails, the fire white hot. A knot of men was gathered around, some cursing as Peter elbowed his way closer, until they saw Jonathan, completely soaked, shaking violently.

"Someone help me!" Peter cried, as he struggled to keep Jonathan erect, while stripping off his blanket cape, the soaked jacket underneath. One of Washington's guards came up. The sergeant set their muskets down on a log.

"You're a damn fool, lad," the sergeant exclaimed and then, while Peter held his friend up, the sergeant unbuttoned Jonathan's trousers and began to pull them down.

Jonathan struggled.

"Stay still, boy. No shame in this. No lasses around to admire you here. Now stay still."

In an almost fatherly way, as if helping a small boy out of his clothes after a dunking, the sergeant pulled Peter's trousers off and laid them, along with his jacket and cape on a log facing the fire, then pushed Jonathan as close to the fire as they dared to approach. It was the wrong side, wind driving billows of smoke and hot gases around them, but there was no possible way to get to the other side, as other men were now packed in too tight.

Jonathan felt something dry go around his naked shoulders. The sergeant had given him his own blanket cape.

He was still shaking uncontrollably, and it was nearly impossible to breathe. Having taken in some water, a spasm of coughing consumed him, doubling him over. The sergeant slapped him on the back as he half coughed, half-vomited the water out.

"This lad's damn near drowned," the sergeant exclaimed. "For God's sake, does anyone have a drink on them."

No one moved.

"My God, men, have some pity."

A lone soldier wearing the tattered uniform of a New York regiment edged over to them, pulled out a flask, and offered it.

Peter held it to Jonathan's lips and he managed to get a gulp down before another spasm of coughing hit.

It was cheap gin, but the warmth hit his stomach and seconds later his head, making him feel light.

"Jersey, we're forming up there!" and the sergeant pointed to the low crest above the ferry dock. "Dry out and join us there. It'll be another hour or two before we move."

"For heaven's sake," Peter replied, "let him go back. He's finished."

The sergeant said nothing.

"I'll be fine," Jonathan gasped. "Just give me a few minutes to get warm."

"That's the spirit, son," the sergeant replied. He slapped him on the shoulder, then moved to fall in with his unit.

Jonathan watched him leave, with a rush of emotions. The Marbleheader who had jumped in to save him was still at work at the dock. The last few men were getting off the boat, the sergeant making his way up the slippery path. Even the New Yorker, taking the flask back, had returned to join his comrades. Strangers all and yet brothers, far more than my own blood brother.

Emotion flooded him, and hot tears came to his eyes. Shaking, he felt Peter actually embracing him, holding him closer.

"You'll get warm. My God, that fire is like a furnace."

Peter could not tell he was crying, and he was grateful for that. To be unmanned before these comrades?

The heat beat upon him like a furnace on one side, yet the other side of his body was freezing. He was suddenly embarrassed beyond all measure. He was completely naked except for the blanket cape loaned by the sergeant. But as he looked around, squinting against the hot air and sparks, he saw more than a few like him, men literally naked, some with bare backsides turned to the fire. There were no jokes, no ribald comments, all of them miserable beyond describing. If there would be any laughter, he thought, it would be from their enemies if they should storm upon them now. Enemies well dressed in heavy wool uniforms, heavy capes and cloaks to ward off the storm, dry boots, capturing naked scarecrows who, inspired by some mad dream, actually believed they could defy the greatest empire on earth.

Peter let go of his side and squatted down, turning Jonathan's trousers and jacket over against the side of a log so that the heat would strike the inside of it, and a least drive out some of the icy water.

"The book," Jonathan gasped.

"What book."

"Paine. In my haversack."

His haversack lay limp against the log, water dripping out of it.

"Get it out."

"Oh, forget about it."

"Get it out!"

Peter opened the haversack, inverting it. A few pathetic things within. A spoon, a folding pocketknife, a few pieces of hard bread and salt pork that were now soaked and useless. The extra ammunition issued out, thirty rounds, all the paper cartridges soaked and useless. A small bundle wrapped in oiled seal skin. Peter handed it up to Jonathan. Water was leaking out as he unwrapped it, to his dismay it, too, was wet, but at least not completely. The front of his pocket Bible, most of the Old Testament, was soaked, and the pamphlet tucked in behind it wet but not destroyed.

Now feeling scorched on one side, he turned, shifting his blanket cape around to his front to cover his nakedness, bare backside facing the fire. Again the moment could be taken as either absurd or pathetic. But as he looked over his shoulders "pathetic" was clearly the word. This was an army that was supposed to sweep the Hessians aside at dawn?

Pathetic.

Another coughing spasm, a bit more river water coming up, gasping again for breath.

"The General," he heard someone announce.

He looked up. Washington had been standing on the dock for some minutes watching as another boat came in, this one carrying several horses, one of them his. Now he was making his way up the icy slope, leading his white stallion by its bridle, stepping carefully, steadying the animal so it wouldn't slip, behind him his African servant leading his own horse.

Washington looked toward him and nodded.

"I saw what you did, son," the General said. "Thank you."

Jonathan could not reply, afraid that if he spoke his voice would break. He could not salute, afraid and ashamed that the blanket

might slip off, revealing his complete nakedness.

"Can you dry out and stay with us?"

"Of course, sir," Jonathan gasped.

Washington nodded and continued up the
slope.

"Now you are being a fool," Peter snapped
angrily. "He offered you a chance to get out
of this madness."

"Go to hell" was all Jonathan could whisper in reply.

Peter laughed.

"You escapee from Bedlam, we are in hell.
At least our bare asses facing the fire are
being roasted."

Several around them, hearing this, laughed
ruefully.

The General was gone. Fire roasting his
back to the point he could no longer stand
it, hot sparks peppering him, Jonathan
turned about, switching the blanket to cover
his back. Men pressed in around him, some
cursing, a few praying, most silent; more
than a few were so cold he could hear their
teeth chattering even as one side of them
roasted and the other froze. And all the time
the nor'easter continued to howl through
the treetops. Smoke, heat, freezing rain,
sleet, and snow — mixing, swirling, choking, blinding — warming for an instant,

240

then freezing again those who stood around the fire.

Jonathan looked down at the book and the pamphlet clutched in his numbed hands. The paper was soggy, but where it was not touching his hands, it was actually freezing together into a lump of pulp and ink.

"Out of the darkness I cry unto Thee, oh Lord," he whispered and then, removing the pamphlet from the back of the waterlogged Bible, he tried to separate the first leaves. It was useless, he would have to wait till later, to let it dry out . . . but there was no need to do so . . . the words were in his heart.

With Peter by his side, he stood by the fire, turning, then turning, then turning again, and the chill stayed, down deep in his bones. The wind continued to howl, driving its mixture of sleet and freezing rain, and one thing the fire could not help . . . the ground he was standing on was trampled into a churned-up glue of semifrozen mud. The pain in his feet was gone. He could no longer feel them. They had gone completely numb.

He thought of his brother James. Most likely at this very minute he was sitting by the fireplace of their home in Trenton, feet up, warmed by the fire, drink in hand, his older brother with him. If they saw me now, they would call me the fool.

Again he turned, facing back to the fire. Behind him another boatload of troops marched past. This time an artillery crew, groaning, pulling on two lengths of cable hooked to their heavy nine-pounder, toiled up the slope, the gun itself weighing more as mud and ice clung to the wheels, barrel, and carriage, and yet still they toiled, laboring past him.

"New York line! New York line! Fall in! Once on the road, column forming to the left, ahead of the Connecticut line."

Some of the men gathered around the fire, grumbling, shouldered muskets, those who had stripped down struggling to pull on trousers that though warmed were still damp, putting on jackets, damp blanket capes drawn back over shoulders that within seconds after being drawn back from the fire, would instantly turn chilled again. The men staggered off, the man who had given Jonathan a sip of gin, pausing, looking at him.

"Luck to you, boy," he sighed.

"You, too, and thank you."

The men scrambled up the slope, disappearing into the night. There was more room by the fire, but within a minute, soaking wet men coming off the boats staggered up to fill the empty spots.

He looked at these men, thought of his brothers in Trenton, and looked over at Peter. His friend stood by his shoulder, silent.

Jonathan van Dorn knew who his brothers were now and where he had to be, even as he turned, and turned again, roasting on one side, freezing on the other, as if caught somewhere between hell and some strange dark mystery that was building in the shadows beyond.

CHAPTER SEVEN

Philadelphia
December 9, 1776

The blustery wind cut through his thin jacket, knifelike, driving into his back.

Tom Paine pressed his chin down and held on to his hat to keep it from being swept away.

General Putnam, riding beside him, said nothing; he had said nothing for several hours. They had found little in common. Both were exhausted, and there really wasn't much to say. Putnam was in a mood to match Tom's. In a way Tom was grateful for the silence. At least Putnam had not pestered him about what he had written and was now carrying in his haversack or offered suggestions as to what he should write next.

After the numbing march across New Jersey to the eastern shore of the Delaware, the first hour or so of riding had been a blessing. Fear that at any minute British dragoons or mounted Hessian jaegers might close in was now on that far shore as well. But as they rode through the night, muscles began to protest. The swayback Putnam had rounded up for him had an uncomfortable gait and on occasion would stumble. Within two hours Tom's backside was rubbed raw. Putnam had refused to stop until just before dawn, when they reined in at a tavern in Bristol.

The food there had been his first decent meal in days. Strange how the army was starving to death, a few hours' ride away; but if you had a guinea or a Dutch or Spanish silver in your pocket — as Putnam did — smoked ham, eggs, and even a warm apple cobbler washed down with beer were there for the asking.

Few had been about as they rode up before dawn; most staying at the tavern overnight were still asleep, but the smell wafting from the kitchen chimney was signal enough that the inn was open. Tom had felt faint at the scent.

Many had been the maddening nights in the alleyways of London when, if the opportunity had arisen, he might very well have waylaid someone and knocked him senseless in order to steal a few farthings for a meal. At this moment he said nothing, for Putnam was a general, and though he had undying respect for Washington himself, he had noted, along with others in the ranks, that generals rarely starved. If Putnam wanted to eat, so would he, and that had indeed been the case.

The innkeeper, German or Dutch from the sound of his thick accent, had been wary when they first walked in, until Putnam laid a shilling on the counter and told him to fetch them both a meal and be quick about it and to see to their horses as well.

The innkeeper's wife, portly, face red, obviously well fed, had come protectively out of the kitchen, but at the sight of the coin in her husband's hands she was suddenly all smiles.

"Soldiers with money, a miracle this day," she exclaimed.

"Is that so unusual now?" Tom ventured, in spite of his exhaustion. The woman's fat round face triggered a vague memory of his company stopping here months back as they marched north to the wars. Then the innkeeper and his wife had greeted them gladly, even offering a small barrel of beer for free to their brave defenders and heroes.

But that was in the world of the sunshine patriots, and he thought again of the new pages rolled up in his backpack.

The husband shot her a stern glance, and she fell silent and returned to the kitchen.

The two ate their meal in silence, and that added to the strangeness. Innkeepers were usually a garrulous lot, always eager for news and gossip. This man said barely a word other than to announce that the oats and hay for the horses would cost an additional sixpence.

Finishing his meal first, and acting as if he were heading out to the privy, Tom managed to barter with a boy in the kitchen for a few long pulls on a bottle of rum, five dollars continental a shot. Tom wasn't quite sure who had gotten the better of the bargain.

"Soldiers been passing here now for a couple of weeks," the boy told him. "A whole company from Virginia going home. Said their enlistments were up and the war lost. A lot more by themselves or in twos and threes. Mr. Dorman took pity on them at first, would usually give them some bread or porridge and let them sleep in the barn, but the missus . . ."

The boy lowered his voice.

"Tory, she is. Oh, all patriot until the weather changed, and she says they better come out on the right side for when the

British march through. So she drives them away when they come begging. You're the first in a week with real money in your pockets."

"The old man in there's a general," Tom replied.

"General of what?" the boy asked, and for a moment Tom wasn't sure if the boy was being sarcastic or not.

"He's going to report to Congress."

"Then he better ride quick. A dispatch rider stopped here last night and said Congress is running south to Wilmington or Baltimore."

Telling Putnam that bit of intelligence cost Tom his rest. Cursing roundly, the general finished his meal, paid the extra sixpence the wife demanded for the oats and hay, and they were on their way.

Few were on the road from Bristol to Philadelphia except for occasional small knots of soldiers heading south. At their approach more than a few cleared the road and made off into a nearby woodlot or field, though twice a group of men glared at Putnam with defiance and muttered taunts about generals riding off now as well.

Farmhouses along the way were shuttered. If anyone was about, there were no longer shouts and waves or pretty girls by the fence smiling as the gallant boys marched by.

He became used to that reception on the retreat across Jersey, but here, so close to the capital, where there had been endless days of joyous celebrations and every hand had been open to anyone in uniform going north, it was unnerving.

War had brought devastation to New Jersey. On the retreat from Fort Lee to Trenton houses and inns were broken into, barns stripped clean of food, the road itself churned into a morass. Here in Pennsylvania the farms were still well tended, animals out in the fields, the land fat and rich, as if there had never been a war at all.

Finally they crested a low rise and the church spires of Philadelphia appeared in the distance, illuminated by the clear light of a morning sun. The wind at their backs was still cold, kicking up whitecaps across the broad Delaware, as yet devoid of traffic. Not a boat, barge, or punt appeared on its broad expanse. The dockyards were nearly empty of traffic as well, the oceangoing ships there bottled up by the British blockade at the mouth of Delaware Bay.

As they reached the outskirts of the city Tom could sense an indefinable "something," an instinctive awareness imprinted in any who had survived in the slums of a city, especially that greatest cesspool of them all, London. It was learned quickly, else one was quickly dead, or beaten senseless and left for dead, or snatched up for some petty crime and press-ganged into the fleet or dangled at the end of a rope. Learn and survive — and he had learned it well.

Houses were shuttered, businesses closed, except for one tavern, which was doing a roaring business, its patrons coming out to see the two ride by and offer taunts about heroes back from the war.

Putnam, as if made of stone, rode on stoically, Tom trailing in his wake and watching warily until they were around a bend in the road. Every step the horse took was a jolting agony. He had never liked riding. He could feel the animal beneath him flagging, ready to collapse from exhaustion. Yet another emaciated veteran of the army, he thought sadly, and there was a momentary pity for the beast as it stumbled, recovered, and slowly pushed on. Even Putnam's fine mount was ready to give in, but the general kept urging him forward.

"It's not the Sabbath, is it?" Putnam asked, breaking the silence.

"What?"

"Sabbath?"

"Sunday? No, I don't think so," Tom finally replied woodenly. "Monday, or is it Tuesday?"

"Damned if I know."

Nothing more was said for another mile. The buildings were now closer together, some warehouses lining the river to their left. They were well into the city.

"Putnam. You Putnam?"

Five men were standing on a street corner in front of a warehouse, its doors open, the interior dark and empty.

Putnam slowed and looked over.

"I am."

The group laughed.

"Looking for your Congress, are you?"

Putnam bristled.

Tom recognized one of the group, Elijah Bellows, an outspoken Tory. "Don't bother," he whispered.

The five stood silent, grinning.

"Go on then, damn you. What do you have to say?" Putnam snapped.

"Better ride quick, general, if you want to catch them," Bellows finally announced. "They're running like rats jumping off a plague ship. And that's what I say now — a plague on them, you, and all damn rebels."

"Damn your eyes," Putnam snapped and started toward them. They backed up, laughing, into the darkness of the warehouse.

"Don't," Tom snapped, as Putnam moved to follow them. "A damn stupid way to get yourself killed."

Putnam looked back at him, eyes blazing.

Tom could see the setup even if Putnam could not. Once into the building they'd be taken from behind, most likely by a dozen more waiting within, and Putnam's horse could fetch a fair price. He had left his musket behind in Trenton, the only weapon on him a small knife tucked into his belt.

Putnam was ready to wade in, and Tom reached out, grabbing the horse's reins.

Bellows stood in the open doorway. "Come on, you damn coward. All you rebels are nothing but damned cowards."

"Make your report and then find them afterward," Tom hissed. Putnam, aging features red with rage, yanked the reins away from Tom and turned his mount to ride on.

The knot of laughing men taunted them to come back. Putnam, shoulders back, face twisted with rage, rode on; Tom looked back warily to see if they might follow.

"God damn them," Putnam hissed. "To give my back to the likes of them."

"We'd both be dead," Tom replied. "It's

the way of things sometimes."

He had long ago lost count of the times he had turned his back and fled. Fled from the son of the local squire long ago, who along with his friends had waylaid him, beat him senseless for the fun of it. A complaint filed with the sheriff, would have been greeted with a laugh: "his lordship's son was just feeling his oats." Fled from the gangs that stalked the streets of London. More than once he had awakened in a gutter, not sure that he was lucky to be alive.

He had spent most of his life running, had in a way run clear across the broad ocean to this place, and now he was running again.

He thought of the pages in his pack. "He that stands it now . . ."

He had learned long ago how to survive by running. But now? When do we stop running?

They were near to the center of town and as they turned onto Market Street, Tom realized they presented a pathetic sight. Two veterans returning from the wars, covered with mud and fresh horse droppings thrown by Bellows and his rum-fed crowd. Putnam was at least wearing a semblance of a uniform, but Thomas Paine, soldier from Philadelphia, was returning in borrowed boots that did not fit, the soles of both all but gone, bare knees sticking out of trousers that had gone from white to filthy gray, and a black, threadbare blanket wrapped around his slumped shoulders. His tricornered hat was another joke. A few years back they would have been taken for some bizarre beggars or escapees from a Bedlam riding into town to beg or steal.

And then they turned the corner onto Market Street. They could hear before they got there the buzz of a crowd, not someone rousing the rabble with a speech or a ceremony, just a random noise that echoed, rising and falling, shouting, arguing, laughing, cursing. In the open plaza before the state house, where Congress gathered, a large crowd was milling about. Within seconds he knew the rumor that Putnam had been sent to evaluate and the gossip shared by the boy at the tavern was true. Congress was preparing to abandon the capital of the Revolution.

A wagon, stacked high with boxes of papers, rolled past, followed by another, and then a carriage, well appointed, drawn by a matched team, curtains within drawn shut. Someone picked up a fresh horse dropping and hurled it.

"Bloody cowards!"

The crowd lining the street roared its approval and joined in the fun, pelting the wagon with filth. Others cursed. Many stood sullen, silent. Only a few seemed distraught, heads lowered in shame.

Another wagon passed, this one with a couple of street urchins hanging on the back. They knew their business well, one diverting the soldier who was sitting atop small bales of papers, while the other grabbed one and jumped off. Half a dozen boys fell in about the thief, and laughing, they tore the package open. It contained continentals, five-dollar bills, and the boys started to pocket their find, a crowd swarming around. But this was not a mob falling on a rich man's purse dropped in the street, ready to tear each other apart for the guineas waiting to be taken by the strongest. It was more of a lark — money being tossed in the air, snatched by some, trampled by others — more than a few making obscene comments about what they intended to do with the paper.

Paine watched in silence. When the army had been paid last month at Fort Lee, just before it fell, men had lined up in a freezing rain to draw their ten dollars continental — pay for a month of agony, of brutality, of facing death — and now it was merely worthless paper lying in the street.

As they rode the few yards to the hall that had been the home of the grandly named Congress of the United States of America, Tom looked about at the disorganized, milling crowd. He recognized more than a few, clerks, dockyard workers, day laborers. Men he had first met and drunk with upon arriving in this city. A few merchants with cloaks drawn tight, as if not wanting to be recognized, were scurrying about on business. Lawyers dressed in finery who had pressed their cases and causes while a hundred miles away an army was bleeding to death. He noticed a few of his former comrades from the Associators with whom he had marched months before. None were in uniform, which had been shucked when the entire regiment deserted. Some stood silent; more than a few were gathered with obvious knots of Tories enjoying the spectacle of the rabble fleeing the city.

In the heady months after the publication of *Common Sense* he had been the toast of this town. For the first time in his life he actually owned a well-made coat of fine broadcloth, proper stockings, even shoes with pewter buckles, and a wig. Dr. Rush had insisted that he have at least some semblance of respectability, especially when asked to dine with the likes of Jefferson, Adams, and others to discuss the issues of the day.

After *Common Sense* was printed, how life had changed, at least in that springtime when the city was aswarm with troops from the southlands, and members of the Continental Congress debated in the state house, debated on street corners, and at night boasted in taverns as all quoted Paine and cried for independence.

Hats had been doffed to him as he walked the streets that remarkable spring, as a rebellion for the rights of Englishmen became instead a war for independence. More than a few said it was his pamphlet that had shifted the thinking of so many.

Then he could barely walk a block without handshakes and, whenever he wished, free drinks in any of the taverns in town, and not just the swill he had drowned himself in in London. Instead there were the finest wines, or the raw hot drink of this new land, whiskey made from corn, and sometimes dark-colored rums.

Now, as he rode in worn clothing up Market Street, no one noticed him. He rubbed the stubble on his chin, actually a matted beard now, his face chilblained and sore. He had lost weight, perhaps a stone or more. He was just another scarecrow soldier drifting back from the war.

"I'm not sure where to report," Putnam grumbled as they reined in before the city meeting hall, some stragglers dragging out more boxes of documents, more paper. Amazing how much paper they have, Tom thought, as he watched them heaving it aboard a wagon.

The wind was picking up, turning colder, the spectators beginning to disperse. The militia guard surrounding the building were relaxed, leaning on muskets, some sitting on the steps, others gathered around a small bonfire in the street, trying to warm themselves. The scene had the feel of an ending of things, not with a spectacular roaring explosion of a mob storming the building, fighting in the streets, a defiant stand, but a sputtering out, a dying away, a movement dying, and few seemed to care.

Such a contrast, he thought bitterly. But forty miles north of here Washington was struggling to get his army across the river to safety after a grueling two and a half weeks of fighting withdrawal across Jersey. For all he knew, at this minute the army might be pinned with its back to the river, dying. Here Congress was running, the once cheering crowds silent, more than a few slipping home to find a concealed Union

Jack, ready to hoist it in surrender or even celebration, when Cornwallis's columns marched into town, which surely all expected.

Barricaded street by street this city could hold off entire armies, but obviously none of these had the stomach for that. All he could feel was disgust.

Putnam dismounted, tethered his horse, and looked up at the meeting hall.

"Get it done, Paine. Lord knows, we need the power of your words at a time like this. But first of all, for God's sake, get something to eat," he sighed, then without another word started up the steps. No one among the guards bothered to offer a salute as the general passed by.

Paine turned his weary old mount, kicking its ribs hard to get it to move, and the animal plodded along. He rode another block, the world hazy, red-rimmed it seemed. When he stopped, the building in front of him was familiar. There was even a warm memory to it.

MCKINNEY & SONS the sign read above the door, PRINTER AND PURVEYOR OF FINE BOOKS. Like all the shops this day, its windows were shuttered. It took a moment to work up the strength to stand in the saddle, swing a leg over and dismount.

He tried the door. It was locked, and he pounded on it. No answer, and he pounded again and again.

He heard the bolt thrown back, and a face peeked out.

"And what do you want?"

"I have something for you," Tom said softly, throat so dry he felt as if it would crack apart when he spoke.

"Go away." McKinney started to close the door.

Tom put his foot in, blocking him. "I'm Paine."

McKinney's eyes widened. "The devil you say!"

More than a bit startled, the printer opened the door, looking about nervously as Tom shuffled in.

The smells that greeted him gave him a thrill. The smell of paper, of ink, raised a memory of another world.

McKinney closed the door and stepped away from Tom.

"My God, man, you look near dead."

"Could I have something to drink?"

McKinney hesitated, nodded. Not bothering to offer Tom a place to sit, he went into a back room and returned with a tepid cup of coffee. Tom drank it down, the brew rousing him slightly but leaving him feeling nauseous.

"Now best be on your way," McKinney announced. "I have no work for you, Thomas."

Tom shook his head and struggled to slip off his backpack. Untying the leather bindings, he drew out the rolled-up oilskin, untied the string holding it tight, and handed it to McKinney.

"Just take a moment," Tom asked.

McKinney went over to a table and unrolled the papers, picking up the first sheet. Adjusting his spectacles he scanned the page, and then shook his head.

"You think me daft?" McKinney announced.

"What?"

"To print this now?"

Tom could not reply.

"You're back from the war, aren't you?"

"Yes."

"Then you don't know what it is like here. Word is the British will come marching up Market Street by tomorrow."

"They're a week or more away."

"Oh really?" McKinney replied with a rueful laugh. "I heard that not an hour ago from a clerk from Congress. Put this on my press as they come marching in, and both of us will be dancing at the end of a rope."

"They're a week away."

"The army is gone, Paine. Finished."

"That's a damn lie. I was just with them this time yesterday."

"A lot's happened since yesterday, Paine."

"I can see that," Tom replied bitterly. "A lot since the last time I saw you."

McKinney tried to hold his gaze and then lowered his eyes.

"Thomas, my advice to you: Burn this devil's tract." He gestured toward the fireplace with the pages as if ready to do the deed.

Thomas leapt forward and snatched them from McKinney and stuffed them into his pack, not bothering to roll them up.

"Listen to me, Thomas. It is over. Leave now. They will hang you, you know that?"

"Let them try."

McKinney sadly shook his head.

"Leave, follow the damn fools to Baltimore if you must. Or just go west, where they can't find you. There'll be a price on your head. Take my advice."

"So you won't print it?"

McKinney laughed. "Even if I could, I can't. Paper is not to be found unless you have the money."

"So that's it?" Thomas retorted. "You're

afraid to print it, but if the price is right and I bring paper?"

"If I'm still here," McKinney replied. "I printed that last pamphlet of yours, so they have my name, too."

"Just crawl out when they do come and beg the king's pardon," Tom replied bitterly, "Hell, you might make money printing up pardons for them. They'll sell well."

The printer stood silent, and Tom went for the door.

"Paine."

Tom turned and looked back. McKinney was reaching into his vest pocket. He drew out a couple of shillings and came over, trying to put them in Tom's hand.

"For God's sake, man, toss out those stinking rags you have on and buy some clothes with this. The war is over."

Tom took the shillings, looking down at the image of the king stamped upon them. For the first time in his life he threw money aside.

His exhausted mount, it seemed the only friend he had in this city, stood patiently by the curb. He did not have the strength to mount, and taking the bridle he slowly led it away. He weaved along for a few blocks and then, as if driven by some instinct, turned down the lane that led to his first benefactor in this land.

He stopped in front of the home of Dr. Rush and found that for a long moment he could not even move.

The door to the smart three-story home cracked open, an elderly black servant looking out at him, finely dressed in dark broadcloth and hose. The man was dressed better than many a general.

"What do you want?"

"I'm here to see Dr. Rush," Tom gasped.

"He's busy."

Tom didn't respond. His mind was not functioning clearly anymore. Too much, far too much. This time yesterday he was staggering through the mud on the road from Princeton to Trenton; he had ridden all night, had only one greasy meal at dawn, and now this, a return to a city that seemed to be dying.

The servant stood onto the top step and looked down at him. "You sick? A patient of the doctor's?"

"Michael, isn't it?" Tom whispered.

The man came down the steps and stared at him.

"Mr. Paine?" His voice was quizzical, rich with the melodious inflection of the Indies.

"The same."

"Why didn't you say so, sir." Michael's

tone softened. "I'm certain the doctor will want to see you at once."

The servant turned, as if pointing the way, but Tom did not move. After so long a journey, the last few steps seemed insurmountable.

"I can't move."

The man came to his side. Tom was afraid he was going to collapse, his legs numb. The servant supported him and led the way up the steps, calling for someone to tend to the horse.

In the parlor Michael took Tom to a straight-backed chair by the fire, eased him into it, and left to fetch the doctor.

Tom sat in silence, the warmth of the fire making him suddenly light-headed, the room closing in, almost choking him.

"Tom Paine?"

Benjamin Rush swept into the room. Tom tried to stand, but Rush put his hand on his shoulder and forced him to remain seated. He stared down at Tom, then wrinkled his nose.

"My heaven's, man, but you stink."

Tom tried to smile. "You should smell the rest of the army. I fit right in there."

Rush sat down beside him. Suddenly he was transformed; a doctor, not a member of Congress. He put a hand to Tom's forehead, the other feeling for his pulse, as he leaned to look into his eyes.

He removed his hand from Tom's forehead and shook it in disgust.

"You are lousy, man, absolutely lousy." With the heel of his shoe he crushed a louse that had sought the warmth of the doctor's hand.

"You're a bit feverish as well. How is your stomach?"

"Empty."

Rush drew back slightly.

"Michael!"

The servant was already returning, carrying a tray with a decanter of wine, two glasses, and some pastries.

"Put that down, Michael. Have one of the girls draw a bath out in the kitchen for Mr. Paine. The man is filthy with lice, so just strip him down." He turned to Tom. "Burn those rags and find him something clean to wear."

"I already got the water heating over the fire," Michael announced. He left the tray on a small table by Rush's side and hurried back to the kitchen shouting orders.

"I don't hold with the notion some have against bathing in winter," Rush announced. "Bathe first. Let Michael cut and comb out your hair to get rid of the lice. And that beard will have to go as well. I think I should bleed you later and draw out some of the bad humors."

Paine looked at him sullenly.

"Some rum inside of me would be better."

Rush smiled, filled a thick crystal glass with wine, and handed it to him.

"Drink slowly, my friend. It is just about the last of my port. Blockade and all, it's running short."

Tom drained the glass in a single gulp.

Rush shook his head. "I have to go to the state house but will be back later and we can talk then."

"Is it true Congress is running?"

"Damn cowards. Yes, at least most of them are. They're going to Baltimore, and it's triggering a panic. A few of us are staying on, though."

Tom liked the edge in the man's voice.

"My God, man, your breath is as fetid as a sewer. You do need bleeding, but first the bath."

He took the glass from Tom and offered a pastry, which Tom wolfed down in two gulps.

"Now tell me before I leave. Are the British truly marching on Philadelphia?"

"I don't know," Tom sighed. "I don't think

267

so, though. Their pursuit slowed once we got south of the Raritan River. I heard some say they are going into winter quarters. Others say Howe is going to sail around Jersey and come up the Delaware instead. It would only take one day of good weather to do so. I just don't know." His voice trailed off.

"Well, Congress is all in a panic," Rush replied. "The last of the fearful are leaving now, taking lock, stock, and barrel."

"And you, sir?"

"Damned if I'll run. I volunteered to stay behind as a special observer. They want me to investigate General Washington."

"What the hell does that mean?"

"I think you know as well as I do. Some want his head. They talk of Lee or Gates being put in command instead.

Rush patted his knee and then withdrew his hand, looking at it carefully first.

"We'll talk more later. I'd best be off."

Rush left him to sit by the fire. Once Rush was out of the room Tom forgot all decorum and gulped down the sweet cakes and drained the decanter. As the effect of the wine took hold, he heard Rush shouting some orders to Michael about getting Mr. Paine into the bath, burning all his clothes, and then putting him to bed.

The mention of burning set off a momentary panic. He fumbled into his backpack and drew out the sheets of paper, some of them crumpled by McKinney, placed them on a side table, and carefully flattened them out. As Rush headed out the front door, slamming it shut, Tom was unfolding toward the floor.

When Michael came in a few minutes later to help him to his bath in the kitchen, he found Tom Paine lying on the floor by the fireplace, drunk and fast asleep. The servant debated what to do and then noticed the sheets of paper on the table. Picking them up he scanned the first page and, for the moment, the man snoring by his feet was forgotten as Michael stood riveted, reading the words.

Born a slave in Barbados, Michael was now a free man, and he could read.

What he read cut into his soul like lightning.

Chapter Eight

East Shore of the Delaware, Nine Miles North of Trenton

2:45 A.M., December 26, 1776

Fuming with impatience, Washington snapped open his watch. It was becoming a nervous gesture, he knew, one that could only annoy the men observing him, but he could not help it. Shielding it against the storm, he held it to reflect the firelight off the face. Seeing the time, he snapped it shut again.

Lord, help us move faster, he prayed under his breath.

"Grab hold there, damn it!"

He looked back to the dock. It was Glover, angrily pacing back and forth on the icy planks, directing his men.

They were exhausted, chilled, moving woodenly after nearly ten hours out in this blow. Their pace was slowing. All could sense that, but Glover was still driving his company to their tasks. A hard man.

Though Washington doubted he would ever completely shed his mistrust of most New Englanders, his admiration for Glover was complete.

If ever there was a night of total humiliation in his life, in this war of unrelenting humiliations, Long Island transcended all on the night of August 29. Others had counseled that his deployment was folly, splitting his numerous forces between fortifications along the Jersey side of the Hudson, the island of Manhattan, and his main force on Long Island, dug in beyond the village of Brooklyn.

Though outnumbered at the point of battle, his men had spent the last two months digging in, ringing their positions with bastions, moats, trenches, deadfalls, and revetments.

It had taken only minutes for the disciplined lines of British and the dreaded Hessians to roust them out.

Monongahela had been an utter disaster, but this was different. Monongahela had been a surprise, at least for the general and the troops of the line fighting in an alien land. Brooklyn was supposed to be free men, defending their land, in an open fight

— and they had fled, all of them. Briefly, the Maryland line blocked the way, gaining time for thousands to escape while sacrificing themselves. When they were surrounded and attempted to honorably surrender, the Hessians had shown their true mettle and slaughtered prisoners and wounded by the score.

The memory of that slaughter would never leave this army, he thought, these shivering ranks deployed along the road, waiting for the last of their comrades to cross. Would the memory at dawn drive them forward with a fury, or cause them to turn in panic when the first shots were fired? He hoped for the former, but feared it might very well be the latter, especially if the Hessians were forewarned and aroused, as it seemed they must be after all the hours of delay. If the enemy was deployed for battle and waiting for his exhausted men to stagger into the fighting ground, then another disaster and slaughter would ensue.

"Clear this damn boat away!"

Glover, nearly losing his footing as he leaned over perilously, was helping to push a boat off. Its cargo, a single artillery piece, had been lifted by a couple of dozen men and manhandled out of the boat and was now being rolled up the icy slope. Its crew and some infantry drafted to help were slipping in the mud, cursing, one man yelling out loudly as his foot went under a wheel. Fortunately for him the ground was so soft that as the wheel passed over him he was able to stand up, hop about, then gingerly try to put weight on the injured member. From the looks of it, the bones were not broken as he limped off. Normally such an event would have triggered some laughter among the soldiers, but not now. Everyone was too cold, too miserable to take much notice of the suffering of another.

"Bring the next one in. Hurry now, you sons of Massachusetts!"

Glover again. God bless him.

As darkness descended on the night of August 29, the army on Long Island appeared to be lost . . . except he still had Glover and his men.

The Maryland line had gone down to bloody defeat, barely a third of its men escaping the trap; the rest of the troops had been routed. Much to his shame, some of the best from Virginia had cast aside their muskets and run. There had been barely a corporal's guard left that would stand and fight.

As twilight deepened, he had stood defiant, expecting death, but it had not come.

Either the British were incompetent, or, as so often happened in war, they had not realized how close they were to true and total victory. Howe had not advanced the last mile to crush the rebel troops huddled along the banks of the East River. The trap seemed sealed, and the Revolution would die at dawn.

He had skipped all courtesies and small talk and took up the issue at hand, going straight to the point with the Marblehead fisherman.

"Glover, can you get us out of here tonight?"

It had been raining hard for the better part of a day, what Glover and his men called a "nor'easter" and the Marblehead man smiled that the plan they had considered as a final act of desperation was about to be played out.

Glover turned to face into the wind sweeping down the East River.

"Better tonight than tomorrow," was his laconic reply.

"Why, sir?"

"This storm will pass, wind back around to the southwest, and they'll be behind us, that's for certain."

And as he spoke he gestured down toward the vast anchorage below Manhattan where dozens of Royal Ships could at times be seen through the curtains of rain.

"Surprised they haven't run up already," Glover continued, "wind, tide, that's all that's holding 'em back."

"Or Providence," Washington replied, voice barely heard.

"It'll take more than a night though," Glover continued. "Can get the wounded out, maybe some of the officers before dawn, but then . . ."

His voice had trailed off, gaze fixed, impassive.

An oath had nearly exploded at the implication of Glover's words, but he had held himself in check.

"My staff and I will take the last boat out, sir, the very last boat, after the entire army has been seen to first."

Glover did not flinch.

"Well, sir. Like I said, the first wave of boats across, I take the wounded. If you insist, sir, on staying, that is your wish," he paused for a moment, "your Excellency. But when they finally figure out that we're slipping the noose and if my men and I are on the far side of the river . . . Well, sir, after it is all over, I guess I'll see you in hell when my end finally comes, because there is no way that I will be able to venture back to you here on this side of earth if the Royal Navy decides to stop us."

There was something about the tone of the man that had made him smile and, uncharacteristically extend his hand.

"Then I'll see you in hell. The wounded and the troops go first."

Glover nodded and started to turn away.

"Pray for fog, sir."

"What?"

"Storm like this, sometimes when it breaks, it comes with wind and if it backs around to a westerly, it'll fill their sails and the frigates will come up this river to make sure the back door is bolted shut and we are dead if caught on the water."

As he spoke he pointed southward, to where the armada of the English laid at anchor. Why they had not sent ships up to bottle the East River was a mystery, though with what little he knew of sea-going affairs, the vicious tides that swept the waterway between Brooklyn and Manhattan, combined with this driving storm most likely played a factor.

"Sometimes though," and Glover spoke softly, as if he was a superstitious mariner and was afraid he'd "jink the weather," by uttering a hope. "Well sometimes, sir, after a blow like this the wind settles and we get a regular pea soup fog, If so, they won't venture their ships of war in this treacherous stretch of river in the dark. They might put out patrol boats, but not the frigates if a fog sets in."

"Then we pray for that," Washington replied softly.

The storm continued to rage even as the first of the wounded were carried aboard the absurd "fleet" of Glover, made up of every scow, rowboat, and piece of wood that Glover could scrounge up. The more grievously wounded were bluntly told that if they could not stifle their cries they would be gagged or left behind. Aware of the fate that awaited them from the Hessians if left behind, none complained. The knives of the surgeons on the farther shore held far less terror for them.

The boats had set out in single file, Glover leading the way, oars dipping silently, men pulling slowly, angling them against the racing tide once clear of the dock. A hundred feet out they were lost to view, swallowed up by the storm.

Washington nodded to Greene, who with a stage whisper passed the word for the first regiment of his command to come down to the dock. As the men passed, sergeants with hooded lanterns checked to ensure that

weapons were not loaded, tin cups dis-
carded, anything that could make a noise
secured. The men were told again and again
not even to whisper once aboard the boats.

Long minutes passed. He had stood at the
dock, heart racing, expecting at any second
for an alarm to be raised, shouts, signal guns
of the frigates firing off, and then the
screams of men dying as the small flotilla of
flimsy boats was torn apart by the concen-
trated fire of a hundred or more of the
ships' guns arrayed to block escape.

He tried to judge the time needed for
them to row across to Manhattan, a distance
of four hundred yards or so, disembark, and
then come back through the storm.

How men such as Glover could navigate
it was beyond his understanding. He had
sought solace in the thought that if roles
were reversed and he was guiding the fisherman through a trackless forest at night, then
all the signs he knew and registered, the
direction of the wind, moss on the side of
trees, scents on the air, the fact that one
could actually smell another man concealed
dozens of yards away if the wind was right,
would be lost on a man from Marblehead.

The thought fled. They were not in the
Ohio Valley, but trapped on the shore of
Long Island, and a watchful enemy on the

water was blocking their way.

"Is that him?" Greene hissed softly.

Something moved in the shadows, emerged, taking form. Glover was standing in the bow of a boat holding a coil of rope, a dozen rowers working slow but steady, barely a sound as oars dropped, pulled, were lifted, and then pulled again.

The end of the rope snaked out, one of Glover's dockmen taking it, helping to guide him in.

"My God, he did it," one of the waiting infantry announced. Greene turned on him. "And by God, I'll personally run through the next man that speaks or even breaks wind," he hissed.

Glover leapt from the bow of the boat to the dock, more boats emerging behind him.

"Can't promise we'll be so lucky next time," he announced laconically, turning a watchful eye as one boat after another materialized out of the fog. Greene silently urged his men to board each boat as it slipped up to the dock. Once filled, each cast off, turned about, and disappeared into the fog.

Glover had stood by Washington's side, neither of them saying a word for long minutes as the next wave went across. They had stood silent as more men filed down to the long dock. Orders were given to cast aside anything that might make a noise, weapons to be cleared; if a man spoke or cried out he was to be gagged or run through.

The orders did not need to be given now. An hour ago most had assumed themselves to be dead or prisoners by dawn. There was a faint glimmer of hope and none had needed to be told that the folly of a single man could dash the hopes of the entire army.

Unable to hide his anxiety, he had opened and closed his watch half a dozen times before the lead boat reappeared. Nearly thirty minutes for one trip across and back. He ran the numbers and calculations in his head as he counted off the men loading up.

"At least twenty crossings to get them all out," Washington had whispered to Glover. "There won't be enough time. Dawn will be upon us long before then. You must pick up the pace."

"I'd best get back into it," Glover replied. He jumped onto the lead boat, which was preparing to cast off.

"Since you're the last to go, I guess it will be in hell next time I see you, sir."

He said nothing. Glover, standing in the bow, disappeared into the storm.

It was a short hike back to his headquarters atop the Brooklyn Heights, where an anxious staff awaited him.

Orders had already been passed. Wounded first, then all those huddled behind the lines. All artillery to be abandoned, guns spiked, even horses to be left behind. Frustratingly, tragically, those men still holding the forward picket lines, the men with the stomach to stand it, would be the next to last to go. Ordered to hold position, keep fires burning, act as though they were five times or more than their actual numbers. If there were enough time left to get them out, they were to stoke up the campfires, and then quickly slip off and race for the dock.

Their chances had been slim at best.

He had gone forward, walking part of the line, forcing a smile, offering the pickets reassurance that all was going smoothly and they would soon be relieved and safe across the river, resolving that the moment the ships in the harbor did raise the alarm he would stay with these gallant few to face the charge that Howe would surely unleash once he learned of the attempt to escape.

For that matter, he still had not quite accepted that Howe had proved so passive on this night. Surely the British would attack long before dawn to vanquish the Americans.

He was certain that luck, or the "will of Providence" did turn, the wind abating, stars beginning to appear in the midnight heavens.

By two in the morning the storm was definitely on the wane, clouds scudding by overhead, the world around him becoming clear, picket fires of the enemy line visible. And then he had sensed it, the approach of first twilight.

At home, or even on the Ohio, the first indication of it would be the song of birds, a lone voice waking, followed by another and another. The sky would still be dark but one could sense the ever so gradual shift into light, a peaceful interlude when perhaps half awake one could sigh and decide to lie abed for a few more minutes. But not now. The pickets around him looked to the fog-shrouded sky, a few whispering nervously or gazing over at him, but none daring to speak. One man had opened the lock of his musket, dusted out the powder, torn open a new cartridge, and put fresh powder in and closed the frizzen, grasping his weapon tightly.

Standing on the bluffs looking down to dock, he could clearly see the long serpentine column, waiting to board, the men growing anxious. He stood silent, looking up at the heavens, silently praying with fervor . . . and the prayer was answered. Fog began to drift up, mist clinging to the ground, the howling of the wind but an hour earlier replaced by silence. With each passing minute the mist grew, rising, a sea-like fog that enveloped the bluffs of Brooklyn, and then seemed to spill down the slopes, greeting a fog forming on the waters.

And there was no wind . . . just a deep autumnal chill, the cold air touching the waters and the rain-soaked land. The dawn came, not with a sunrise that revealed all, and brought annihilation, with only half his army across, but in a gray creeping blanket.

More and yet more men were pulled from the line. So tight had been the secrecy that those who had stood on the front line did not even know they were being evacuated until they were sent to the dock, told to be silent and toss aside anything that made noise.

It was finally an hour past dawn, and if anything the world was darker, a uniform dull gray and still he stood, waiting; his cap, soaked clean through from the rain, now hung heavy, chilling him.

"General Washington?" One of his young

283

adjutants, breathing hard, had came up behind him.

"Sir, the last of the troops are crossing now. Word is being passed along the line for the pickets to fall back to the dock."

"Thank God" was all he could say.

The men standing about him needed no urging. Several ran to the smoldering campfires, throwing on the last of the wood, stoking them up.

A distant voice had echoed . . . from the British camp. "Damn rebels, better warm up now. We'll be putting you in the ground this dawn."

To not reply might cause alarm. Taunts between the lines at night were part of war.

A sergeant had looked to Washington, who nodded.

"It'll be you in the ground, you damn lobsterback. The only place I'll be lying is next to your wife, after you're dead."

"You son of a bitch."

The sergeant had laughed, several around him joining in, even as they turned and, with heads lowered, began to run down the slope toward the river.

He had forced himself to walk slowly, even as the men raced by. They had stood gallantly throughout the night, but now, with rescue so near, there was an edge of panic to them. And the fog was beginning to lift. What had been indistinguishable shadows but ten feet away, only minutes before, now could be seen as men thirty or fifty feet away.

The dock had been packed with men, and yet more were streaming down the hill.

Boats were pushing off, moving faster, others coming in; order was beginning to break down, with men beginning to shove to get to the fore.

"All of you," Washington had hissed. "Stand easy!"

They had turned to look back at him.

"Show your courage, lads. Mr. Glover will not leave a one of you behind. Now show your courage."

The panic was stilled, though the men continued to look about anxiously, some toward the river, others toward the heights, expecting at any second to see the advancing enemy.

More boats appeared. They could be seen from fifty or more yards away now, emerging out of the fog. Men piled in. He caught a glimpse of Knox, head lowered, obviously crestfallen over the abandonment of so many of his precious guns.

Boats were cast off, and then, suddenly, the dock was nearly empty. He had gazed about. Abandoned equipment — knapsacks, canteens, cups, more than a few muskets, an overturned artillery piece — littered the shore. Dozens of horses had milled about looking forlorn as if sensing they were being abandoned. Someone had suggested that their throats be cut so as not to leave them to the enemy, but that suggestion had met with no reply; he could never have given such an order. The enemy had more than enough horses anyhow, and such wanton killing was repugnant to any who loved them. He was leaving his own mount behind, and hoping that a proper gentlemen would get him.

Two boats then had emerged out of the fog. As he gazed at them, his heart stilled. Above the mist he could see a ship's mast in the river.

Glover had been in the lead boat.

"Quickly!" Glover had hissed. "They can see us, by God."

He had needed no urging, climbing into the boat, Billy Lee and the last few stragglers joining him, and the boat cast off.

"Pull hard," Glover said.

He realized at this instant that though the night had been for him nerve-wracking, for Glover and his men it had been utterly exhausting. He could see the fatigue in their drawn faces, straining with each pull of the oar. A man slipped, an oar splashed, Glover hissed a curse. The exhausted rower did not bother to look back as he hunched over and resumed the beat.

They were nearly to midstream river when he saw it — and could barely suppress a gasp of surprise. The stern of a British patrol boat clearly silhouetted in the gray mist of dawn, a lantern hanging over the aft railing, and what appeared to be the outline of a man who was resting against the steering oar. To the other side, the bowsprit of another boat jutted out; voices echoed; someone was relieving himself in the river. A bell rang, startling him; then others rang, up and down the river.

They had slipped past the two small patrol boats. The shoreline of Manhattan, and a church spire, were visible.

"Surely they saw us?" Washington whispered.

Glover chuckled softly, exhaling noisily. "Fog plays queer tricks, it does. Easier to see up than down at times. Another ten minutes, though, and with the tide changing . . ."

He fell silent, cocking his head, looking back, pointing.

Someone on the stern of the boat they had

passed was pointing straight at them, another man joining him, disappearing. Seconds passed, and the distinct long roll of a drum began. A bell began to ring.

"Five minutes more," Glover whispered. "I'll be damned, I'll be damned."

He looked over at Glover and shook his head. "We're not damned yet." Washington forced a smile as he slapped Glover on the back. "I think we are blessed instead."

He had nearly lost his footing as the boat slammed in hard against the Manhattan dock. Those waiting for them urged all to get the hell out before the frigate opened fire.

He had taken his time, though, getting out, making a show of stretching, and with hands clasped behind his back gazing defiantly back at the British Fleet out in the bay as its crew was beat to quarters.

Whoever was captain of that ship would have a lot to answer for this day, he had thought with smile.

"I think our appointment in hell will have to wait, Mr. Glover," he said, extending his hand.

"Sir, it might come sooner than you think if you don't get off this dock right now. It's going to be hot here in another minute."

■ ■ ■ ■

"You there, damn it, get that damn horse off this dock!"

Stirred from his thoughts Washington looked back to where Glover, storming about and cursing, was helping to shove a skittish horse ashore.

He opened his watch again, memories of Long Island gone and the challenge of the Delaware getting all his attention once again.

It was nearly three now.

He sighed and closed the watch.

Surely the Hessians would be aroused by now. Merciful God, dare I ask for yet another miracle?

Trenton, New Jersey
2:55 A.M., December 26, 1776
"My colonel!"

"Enter."

He had actually managed to doze off for a few minutes. Münchasen was again at the open door. He sat up. The room was cold, his damp uniform clammy. He had stretched out, not even daring to take his boots off. Mrs. Potts would say nothing, of course, though he feared he had ruined the bed coverings, smearing them with mud and filth.

"Another alarm?"

"Yes, sir. Raiders on the Pennington road."

"I'm coming."

With a groan he sat up, Münchasen coming over to help him get to his feet with one hand while holding a lantern with the other.

He followed Münchasen down the steps and out to the street. The guard company was ready, deployed in column.

He gasped as he stepped out the door. The storm had increased in fury in the short time he had been dozing. It was a mad, insane mix of freezing rain, sleet, heavy snow, all of it driven into his face by the gale-force wind.

The men ready to advance as a relief force were huddled over, shivering, teeth chattering, all of them soaked. He could see they had oiled rags wrapped around their musket locks, but doubted that would do any good now, so intense was the fury of the storm.

An anxious courier, mounted on a horse, saluted.

"Your report."

"Sir. Rebel raiders struck along the Pennington road. Report is that some looked like jaegers. They are armed with rifles."

He took that in. The cowardly band that

had been harassing them for days, led by someone named Ewing or Wing were apparently local rabble, militia armed with fowling pieces and an occasional musket.

"How do you know they were riflemen?" As he spoke he gestured up toward the sky.

"Did you see them yourself?"

The messenger hesitated, then shook his head.

"No, sir. The sergeant of the guard said he thought they were riflemen."

He took that in.

It would have meant they were literally face to face on a night such as this.

"Any killed or wounded?"

"No, sir. Just some shots fired at the house on the road to Pen Town," the courier announced, not sure of the name of the village north of Trenton, "and then they fled."

"Any prisoners taken?"

"No, sir."

"Then how is it that the sergeant is sure of his report?"

The courier did not reply.

Rall considered — the intensity of the storm, the men waiting to be ordered out to provide relief, the young courier with a confused report.

Damn this country.

"Return to your sergeant and tell him next

time, if he thinks he is fighting riflemen, to bring one to me as proof. You have dragged these men out on a miserable soaking night with this alarm about an attack which is obviously over, and roused nearly every man in this town."

As he spoke, his voice rose with exasperation. He gestured down the street, to houses where lights were lit, men coming out, forming up, as was the routine when an alarm sounded during the night. The lead company was already formed, and now freezing with the cold.

"Go back and tell your sergeant what he has accomplished."

"Yes, sir."

The courier, obviously crestfallen, turned his horse about, the animal slipping on the ice, losing its footing, falling, nearly knocking the colonel over as the rider struggled to stay mounted. Münchasen leapt forward to grab the bridle and steady the panicky animal, which kicked and thrashed as it fought to stay up.

The young soldier, now thoroughly shaken, blurted apologies as he rode off.

Rall watched him disappear, then turned to the officer of the watch.

"Get your men back inside. Have them strip down and put on something warm.

Have Captain von Carl's company relieve yours for the rest of the night."

"Sir, it is still an hour before changing of the watch."

"Just follow my orders, captain. Your men are frozen and now useless in a fight. Do as you are told."

"Thank you, sir." He could hear the relief in the young officer's voice.

The company, ordered to turn about, tried to make some show of marching off, even as more than one of the men, wearing hobnailed boots, slipped and fell on the ice, muskets clattering. Rall held his breath expecting at least one to fire off, but then again, the powder in their pans was most likely wet by now.

He stepped into the foyer of Potts's house, pulled out his watch and muttered a curse.

Water had seeped into the works; the watch had stopped.

"The time, Münchasen?"

Münchasen carefully unbuttoned his overcoat, uniform jacket, and vest, drew his watch out from underneath all the layers of clothing, and snapped it open.

"Just after three, sir."

Four hours to first light. If indeed it had been raiders in any kind of force, they had struck to annoy, to rouse the garrison, and cause it to fall out, as they had, and the scum were most likely settling down now into some tavern miles away, laughing about their heroics and the discomfort they'd caused.

Damn cowardly rebels.

Four hours till dawn. Few in his command had slept at all; most were cold and wet. The alarms for the night were likely over. Any rebels out in this weather would be far wetter and colder, and just as frozen as his own men. It would be midmorning at the earliest before they were dried out, sobered up, for surely they were all drunkards to be running about on such a night.

"Münchasen. Get some rest. Let the men stay inside until this storm is passed. Morning parade is canceled."

"Are you certain of that, sir?" Münchasen asked.

That caught him by surprise. How dare this young man question his thirty-five years of experience.

He paused for an instant, trying to gather his thoughts. Even as he did so a shiver ran through him. His heavy woolen uniform was soaked, weighing twice as much as usual with all the water in it. He was cold, had not slept right in days, longed for a damn good drink but dared not take one.

This godforsaken country was worse than Russia.

If it was Austrians he was facing, or French, even those damn Turks he had fought while serving the czarina, he might heed Münchasen's questioning. But here, against this cowardly rabble? Washington might send out his worthless militia to run about with false heroics on a winter night and play at harassing decent men out of their sleep. But Washington himself? Damn him, he was abed, and in the morning would without doubt laugh when Wing, Ewing, whoever it was, came in to report.

"You heard my orders," he snapped, and without waiting for a reply he went back up to his bed. He debated the issue for a moment and then with a struggle pulled his boots off. He didn't need some hausfrau glaring at him and muttering about her ruined sheets.

CHAPTER NINE

McConkey's Ferry
3:15 A.M., December 26, 1776

The storm increased in fury. Wind tore at cloaks and coats. Frozen rain mixed with snow drove into men's faces. Horses huddled from the storm and moved reluctantly.

General Washington edged his way down to the landing dock, staying to the side of the path as infantry staggered up the icy, mud-churned path to the main road.

To his right he saw his headquarters guard gathered, several of them stripped naked, around a flickering fire. He caught the eye of one of their officers, and gestured.

"Form up!" the sergeant cried. "Come on, men! It's time to move."

One of them, naked, moved woodenly, two men helping him to slip his tattered trousers on, then pull on a jacket and a blanket cape. The boy held up two long strips of burlap, looked down at his bare feet as if debating, and then let them drop and fell in with the last of the men heading up the slope to the road.

The scent of wood smoke was heavy on the wind. Watching his headquarters detachment move, Washington could see where, at regular intervals along the road, fires were burning. Men were gathered around them, but orders were now being shouted for the column to fall in and form ranks.

He guided his mount the last few feet to the dock. Colonel Knox stood there, waiting. A line of empty boats was drawn up along the riverbank.

"We still have at least six more boatloads coming across," Knox reported. "Stragglers, and one last gun."

Washington drew out his pocket watch, heavy in his hand, and, turning his back to the wind to shield it from the driving storm, he clicked open the lid. It was past three in the morning. The plan had called for the column to move out at midnight.

He closed the watch and slipped it into his vest pocket.

"I'm moving them out now," Washington announced. "We cannot wait any longer. Get the last of them across, then move up the column and join me. Two men to be left behind with each boat. They know their orders."

Knox nodded.

"If attacked, get the boats back across the river."

Knox turned and looked to the west. There was a momentary break in the storm, pale moonlight shining through, illuminating the white-capped river and its ice floes.

Neither needed to say more. If while the army was on the move, a flanking force, perhaps an alerted British garrison in Princeton, sent a raiding force over here, then the army would be truly cut off and pinned against the river. Saving the boats would be an act of futility, for there would no longer be an army to rescue.

"Sir, I am sorry about the delays," Knox offered, head a bit lowered, as if ashamed that he had somehow failed.

"Hannibal crossing the Alps could not have asked for a better man to lead the way," Washington replied.

He knew the line smacked of the stage, but it worked. Knox looked up at him and smiled.

"I will see you at the head of the column once you get the last boat off-loaded, Henry."

"Yes, sir."

"Remember the password."

"Victory or death," Henry repeated firmly, voice suddenly thick with emotion.

The General saluted, turned, and guided his mount up the slope. The column was nearly formed up. Men were slinging on packs and haversacks, shouldering muskets, stepping away from the fires.

As he rode alongside of the column, by the light of the flickering fires, he gazed intently at them. It was hard to see faces. Hats were pulled down over eyebrows, most of them using strips of cloth wrapped around the hat and tied off under their chins to keep them on, and also to provide some protection, however scant, for exposed ears and faces.

A few looked up at him, nodded. An occasional officer offered a formal salute. Few words were spoken; one man shouted "Victory or death!" as he trotted past, while those around him remained silent.

Nearly all of them stood facing to the south, keeping their backs to the storm as long as possible, shoulders hunched over against the blast, stamping their feet up and down to keep circulation going. Many of them were barefoot.

He had learned long ago that an officer, a good officer, could sense something about his troops. Nothing needed saying. It was an instinct, developed so long ago, out on the frontier, as a young man traveling with others of more experience. He had learned to watch every movement, gesture, and word, the way men walked, paused, sniffed at the air even, how they waited silently, sometimes for minutes, before moving again. There would be times when he would be with a small party, ambling along, talking, and then, suddenly, one of them would stop, frozen in place . . . for something was different. At first, he could not tell that difference, but a seasoned man of the frontier had better learn it, for those who did not died.

It might be a change in a background sound, or the opposite, a strange silence. It might be a scent drifting on a breeze — more than a few claimed they could tell whether it was a white man or Indian, and if Indian even which tribe by that scent. Or it might be the way a bit of moss on a rock in the pathway was scuffed, leaving the trace of a footprint, the moss not yet springing back.

He had learned from them, and he had survived. To survive an officer had to learn to sense what his men were feeling, and he felt he had that ability. An officer had to know when a line of men would go into battle, regardless of odds, and if need be die, and go down fighting. And know, on another day, that the same regiment might very well break and run before the first shot was fired.

He had learned, and as he rode along the shivering column now, he sensed many things.

A casual observer would have captured only the utter misery of the moment. All were soaked to the skin. The temperature was steadily dropping; the limbs of trees overarching the road were drooping with heavy loads of ice. Strange how the light from the dozens of fires almost made the moment look beautiful, firelight reflecting off the ice so that the road seemed like a glowing flickering tunnel, the light shifting and changing with each gust of wind.

What he sensed in them, in addition to exhaustion and absolute abject misery, was a certain defiance. Such suffering as they endured could push a man in one of two ways. For many, in fact most, it would be a collapse, a giving in, a feeling that the elements of heaven had turned against them and any further effort would be futile.

Men like that, however, were gone, long gone. He found himself thinking of what

Paine had written about sunshine patriots. Those men had gone. He had watched them leave by the thousands, even as he argued, told them to stay, and then, as he stood utterly humiliated, begged them. But they had fled.

But these here, on this road, on this night? These were all that were left. Again, a memory of the frontier. You learned quickly how to spot those new to the world beyond the Alleghenies who would survive and those who would not. The survivors had a certain "something" to their cast . . . they were lean, sinewy, tough, usually laconic, for a man who talked too much might not hear the quiet sounds that carried death. And around these there was almost a certain light that told you, here is a man you can trust, he will not abandon you. This is a man you want by your side, and at your back.

That was his army, this bitter, freezing night.

They were what was left, the final few who indeed were willing to choose victory or death. And if death came, they would face it and not turn away. The trust, he sensed, was mutual, they trusted him as he trusted that they would indeed follow him, this desperate night, to either victory or death.

As he gazed at them it was hard in a way to believe that this was the same army of but twenty-five days past.

December the first, he thought, head lowered, was in his heart a day of complete personal humiliation, not just because of the defeat at the bridge but because of what transpired that evening.

It was after the rout at the Raritan, the army staggering on a muddy road, their personal Calvary, and on that day the enlistments of hundreds had run out. These were men who had signed on for six months, back in the heady days of June, when word had raced across the colonies of the triumph at Boston, when talk of independence was in the air, when the juggernaut of an angry king's reply had yet to appear off New York Harbor.

Enlistments were up for a fair part of the army. The men that morning, honorable men who had stayed throughout the debacles, defeats, and numbing retreats, were now legally free to ground arms, turn themselves toward warm homes and firesides in Pennsylvania, Maryland, upstate New York. They had served their time and were free to leave without recourse or restraint. They had believed in their independence, had fought for it, had seen it totter to the edge of final defeat while he led them. There was nothing he could do but offer one final appeal to those free to go.

Those in question were paraded, arrayed in ranks, to shiver in tattered uniforms as the cold wind blew from the north. Men who knew that the war was all but lost anyhow, and, an ultimate irony, men who he could not even honorably give their six months of pay to, since the coffers of the nation were empty. He could sense the mood of these proud men, who had given all, felt their duty complete, honor fulfilled.

Their officers rode with him. As he approached the lines he could see it in their eyes as they looked up at him. They were finished with it.

One of the officers, riding slightly ahead, turned his mount and trotted up and down the line. His was the usual appeal, attempting to sound as if he were one of them in every way, the dialect of a Yankee farmer, taunting the damn lobsterbacks, praising them as stout men of proud lineage who surely would not turn their backs to the enemy and run away like cowards.

The words hit like a slashing blow, and

features hardened. Muttering arose from the ranks. "Who the hell does he think he is?" "We ain't cowards, damn him." "Son of a bitch, don't remember seeing him in a fight, but plenty of damn talk now."

Crestfallen, the officer turned away.

A second officer tried, invoking images of hearth and home, how they were all that stood between the Hessians and their wives and daughters: Would their wives greet them as heroes one day, or would they stand by and watch the ravishing to come. Again a cold response. One of the men dared now to step forward to shout a taunt: When the war stopped the Hessians would be gone anyhow, and where the hell was their back pay. The officer appealed for any who were men of courage to step forward and thereby pledge themselves to but one more month of service.

"Our pay, our pay, damn you, our pay!"

It became a chant. Washington had stayed back slightly, watching, listening, throat constricting. One of the men held his musket up, tossed it onto the ground, turned his back, and began to walk off in the other direction. Others around him seemed ready to follow his lead.

He had led, but he had never begged. But now?

He nudged his mount forward, the taunts continuing, and each word was like a lash to his soul. He turned his mount half a dozen paces in front of the line and slowly rode in front of the assembled ranks, saying nothing, not attempting to silence them with a harsh command, just looking at them, trying to gaze into the eyes of each man as he passed.

The taunting continued for several agonizing minutes, as if the pent-up rage of months of bitter defeat was now being poured out and heaped upon him.

He said nothing. They had their say. A man stepped forward, pointing to his bare, bloody feet, features red as he cursed a Congress that could not even provide shoes as he fought, while they huddled warm and fat in Philadelphia. He looked down at the man, unable to speak, for so many of them were barefoot, and money which had been promised them and shoes that any soldier had the right to expect, had never appeared. They were sick of it, exhausted, dying. The war was lost. They were going home.

If they went home, the war might indeed be lost, for with their departure, those who remained, with but thirty more days left on their own enlistments, would ask why they should stay. He knew that hundreds of these were standing in a loose circle around the formation, watching, listening, some joining in the protest.

He could sense that the army was on the verge of falling apart, never to reassemble.

He turned about and rode down the line. Gradually the shouting died away. They had made their statement, their protest. Their intentions were clear. All that was left now was the last ceremony, their dismissal, and it was ended, for no force could keep them.

At last they fell silent, awaiting the order of dismissal.

He drew in a deep breath, overwhelmed with humiliation for what he now had to do.

"Men," he began, "I have heard your protests, and they are just."

No one spoke, though he could see it in their eyes that they would listen and then leave.

"They are just. I am humiliated that I stand before you now, unable even to give you the pay you so rightly deserve. You have fought and bled. You have seen comrades die, and now in reply I cannot even give you a shilling of what you so richly deserve and have so honorably earned.

"I am not a man of orations, as you know. I have not the words for it. Nor shall I make any base appeal to sentiment, for that is beneath your dignity and mine.

"Yet you know I must now make this one final appeal."

He could see some of them shifting uncomfortably. Some held his gaze, others lowered their eyes, as if humiliated, not for themselves, but for him, and that cut to his soul.

He fell silent for a moment, unable to continue, fearing his voice would break. He drew in a deep breath of the frigid air.

"It shall be noted and written of some day, that here, at this place, our last home of freedom, the hope for a nation of free men died."

He lowered his head for a moment, then raised it again, saw more than a few looking at him.

"That is my appeal to you, my men. You have every right to turn away now. You have fulfilled your pledge with honor, and I thank you for that."

He hesitated.

"But I beg you now to think upon this. That if you turn away now, with the task unfinished, that on this day America may die.

"It has come down to this. To you few hundred. You have every right to turn away and go to your homes and I shall not stop you. No one shall stop you. All that can turn you back is the voice within your own souls.

"Yes, you have every reason to protest. As we stand here, we who endured so much, tens of thousands are at this moment warm in their houses. Men, who if we should win, will reap the bounty but will never have known the pain and anguish of the labor for our freedom.

"Thus it has always been. The labor is done by the few, and later many can lay claim to the bounty. Thus it has always been. But I for one will not let my heart be turned by such as they. For in my heart, as I am certain in yours, will be the proud realization that while others might scorn us now, and then one day say they were with us all along, we few will know the truth and that truth will warm our souls.

"The choice is yours. It is in your hands now, not mine. If it is your wish to leave, I will not hinder you. Some of us will stay, some at least will stay and tomorrow will face the final end, and die with pride in our hearts that we died in defense of a just cause and face God with that knowledge which He surely sees as well.

"It rests now solely with you as to whether the deaths of those who stay will be a final act of futility or something far greater. If you stay I can promise you nothing. I will not attempt to beguile you with promises of glory, for we have seen how hollow promises of glory can ring. I cannot even offer to you the promise of warmth, of shelter, food, or shoes. All I can offer you is a promise of what will rest in your soul if you stay.

"And that promise is honor."

He paused again.

"So I now ask you for but thirty more days. If at the end of those thirty days we do not see a change in our fortunes, then free you shall be to go. That is my pledge to you. Can you not find it in your hearts to make that pledge to me?"

He fell silent again, gathering his thoughts, gazing at them, the men silent.

He turned his mount and silently trotted down the line, trying to find the eyes of each man and look into them.

There were no more appeals to be made. It was finished.

"Those men who will pledge but thirty more days. Take three steps forward. Those who will not . . ."

His voice did indeed begin to break, and he was filled with humiliation that his emotions now so basely were betraying him.

"Those who will not . . . you are free to go."

He turned away and slowly rode back to where his staff waited. There was silence for a long moment, and finally he turned, praying that the gesture would not be seen as some futile begging appeal.

And then a lone man stepped forward, looking straight at him, not much more than a boy. He was not sure if the tears in the boy's eyes were produced by emotion or the frigid wind.

Long seconds passed. Another stepped forward, then another, and then just a score of men and no more.

A score of men, and the rest stood silent with heads lowered. Twenty out of more than a thousand followed him, falling back on the road toward Trenton, the others standing silent and then turning aside, heading westward, toward the hills of the Watchung and out of the war.

He had lost more in those five minutes than in the battle for Brooklyn Heights. A score followed him back to the assembled ranks and humiliated he had marched on.

He continued to ride down the line of men who were waiting for the command to begin the march on Trenton, met eyes with one of those waiting. Their gazes held for only a second.

"Victory or death, general," the soldier announced.

He could not reply. He nodded and rode on, returning the salute of a young Hamilton with his guns.

He knew that these men, freezing to death, upon this night, would march straight into hell if he asked them now. Their months of suffering, of humiliating defeat after defeat, had hardened them, and now, finally, they would stand, look death in the face, and strike back.

They were ready.

Now for just a little bit of luck with the Hessians, he thought. Let us pray the storm has lulled them into warmth and off their guard. Then we will have caught the fox. The hunt is on, and for the first time in months I am the hunter and my opponents are the prey. He felt warmed inside at the thought, even as his body felt chilled.

Twin bonfires marked the head of the column. There the men of his headquarters unit, who had been gathered around the fire by the ferry landing, were scrambling to fall into ranks.

A delegation awaited him, a local militia man and one of his Virginia riflemen, the militia man holding a sputtering torch.

"Sir, we've been sent back to report," the rifleman announced.

"Go on."

"Sir, the road is secured clear to the ford at Jacob's Creek."

"We know who the Tories are that live along the road," the militia man interjected, "and we have a guard posted in each of their houses."

"Well done."

"But, sir," the rifleman announced, "the road, sir, it is nothing but a sheet of ice and that creek . . . what's its name . . ."

"Jacob's Creek," the Jerseyman interjected.

"It's a bad un, sir. Steep approach, flooding up."

"This army moves as planned."

"Just thought you should know, sir."

He did not reply.

Looking over his shoulder he could see for only a few dozen yards. A swirling cloud of snow was whipping out of the northeast, trees shaking, ice cracking and tinkling down.

He caught the gaze of the colonel of his lead brigade, Stephens's Virginia Brigade, though on this night it was led by the second in command, Colonel Charles Scott.

He had chosen this unit deliberately. They were tough, seasoned, and — an important factor in his mind — Virginians. Though he had struggled to weave the fabric of this army from thirteen different states, at a moment like this he felt most comfortable that fellow Virginians were leading the way.

"You may begin the advance," he said to Scott, who stood expectant, trembling, as if with excitement, though obviously from the frightful cold.

Scott drew his sword and raised it in salute.

"Virginia! Virginia!" His voice was high-pitched, nearly lost in the thunder of the storm. "Forward march!"

The column lurched forward.

As it did so he drew out his pocket watch again, flicking open the lid. It was twenty minutes past three.

"We're moving!"

"Thank God," Jonathan gasped.

The hours before the fire had lulled him into a strange, nearly dreamlike state, as he slowly turned and turned again, warming one side of his body while the other side froze . . . and all the time his feet were going from anguished pain to numbness.

When the call had come that it was time

to form ranks, he had been snapped out of his near-comatose state, but then found he couldn't move. It had taken the joint efforts of his friend Peter and one of the corporals from the headquarters unit to help dress him. It was humiliating, Peter talking to him almost as if he were a child as he knelt down and helped pull his trousers on.

The hours his clothes had been laid out to dry had not done them much good. At least they were not soaking wet, but within a minute or so after he had struggled back into pants, shirt, and jacket, what warmth that had been imparted by the fire had fled, and the filthy rags clung again to him with the same clammy feel.

Holding up the two wet rags he had used as foot wraps, he realized that, after but a few dozen steps, they would be soaked clean through again, and in a hundred yards weighed down with mud. He tossed them aside. Marching barefoot would be better.

Slinging on his haversack, he fumbled inside it for a moment, making sure his Bible and the copy of Paine were secured, the oilskin wrappings having saved them from destruction when he fell into the river. Next his backpack and blanket cape went on, and then musket. He left his cartridge box behind, the ammunition inside useless from the dunking. When the time came, he could always borrow a few rounds from Peter.

The first few steps away from the fire were agony. Peter reached out to offer a hand.

"Can you walk?" Peter asked.

"What do you mean?"

"Your legs. They're all swollen from the cold."

Jonathan said nothing, but was glad to have his friend to lean on. Gasping for air, lungs burning, he made it up to the roadway. It was packed with troops, and he was forced to move along the side. Though his feet were numb he suddenly felt sharp stabs of pain as he stumbled over rocks and gravel. If not for Peter he would have gone sprawling. He hit one rock hard, knees buckling as he tripped, legs moving on their own without any ability on his part to control them.

It was hard to see where they were supposed to be. The troops on the road were an undistinguishable mass of huddled men, looking like lumps of stone covered with snow and ice.

"Jersey!"

Peter looked up. It was the sergeant calling to them. The two staggered back onto the road, for a moment the congealing and freezing mud beneath Jonathan's feet a balm to the sharp shooting pains. He wondered if, stumbling over the rock, he had broken a toe.

They stood silent for a moment, nothing happening, the only sound the wind howling through the trees, the tinkling fall of ice from the branches tumbling down on them.

The shadows ahead of them began to move forward, the sergeant of the detachment calling out for the company to march. Jonathan shuffled forward. If a toe was broken, at least for the moment it did not feel too bad. The road ahead had been churned to slop, but he still had to lean on Peter to steady himself.

For the first few hundred yards, the road moving along the east bank of the river followed the contour of the Delaware. He passed between two bonfires set to either side of the road which then turned right . . . straight up a long slope through the woods.

Then he felt as if he were in hell. The wet soothing mud gave way to hard, rocky ground, deeply rutted in places, ruts impossible to see as they tripped and staggered up the slope.

Any semblance of marching order broke down within a hundred yards, the ground so slippery in places that Peter gave up on the road, moving into the edge of the woods, grabbing hold of branches for bracing with one hand, and pulling Jonathan along with the other. Already a man was down, sitting against a tree, cursing.

"God damn arm. Broke my damn arm . . ."

Jonathan could barely see the man in the darkness, the storm was blowing full into his face, blinding him. He tucked his chin down low into his chest, hanging on to Peter, legs wooden, still barely functioning, as he willed himself forward one step at a time.

Pain was returning to his feet. Farther up the slope, which had been openly exposed to the full fury of the storm for hours, the ice was heaped an inch or more thick in places, jagged and as sharp as knives.

Peter slipped and fell, bringing Jonathan down with him, the two tumbling together with a clattering of muskets. Lying there panting for breath, Jonathan pulled himself back up.

"I can make it," he gasped. "Come on."

Letting go of Peter he reached to the next tree, pulling himself forward. The men to either side of him were strangers. The accents sounded like Virginia, but then the headquarters guard were Virginians as well. These men were carrying muskets. Most of the headquarters guard were cavalry, dismounted for this march, armed with sabers and pistols.

"Peter?"

"Here."

He looked back, his friend a shadow coming up beside him. He reached out and grasped Peter's hand. Not because he wanted to admit that he still needed bracing, though he was regaining some feeling in his legs due to the exertion, but because at this moment, pushing up a slope in the face of a gale, heading into some dark unknown, he needed to feel the touch of someone, anyone.

He felt foolish for a moment as Peter grabbed his hand and squeezed it tight, the two standing there for a moment, Jonathan gasping for breath.

"Come on," Peter hissed, but before letting go of Jonathan he squeezed his hand again.

If ever he felt love for another man it was at this moment, Jonathan realized. If Peter can make this climb, then I can, too. I must.

He started forward, gaining another few dozen yards until a man in front of them slipped and fell so heavily that he slid backward into them, nearly bowling them over.

They helped him to his feet.

"I swear to God Almighty," the man gasped. "If anyone ever talks to me again about my duty and loving my country . . ."

There was almost a rueful chuckle.

"I'll shoot the son of a bitch. Thanks, boys." Regaining his footing, he continued on.

The clouds above nearly parted for a moment, the feeble light spreading across the slope leading up from the Delaware. Grabbing hold of a tree, Jonathan turned to look back.

Behind him the woods to either side of the road were swarming with hunched-over men, leaning into the storm, struggling for footing, climbing upward, slipping, falling, getting back up again, gaining a few more yards. It seemed as if the forest itself had come alive, as though hundreds of stumps of trees of man size were coming to life and were now doggedly clawing their way forward.

He could barely see an artillery team coming onto the road. The horses had been shod with cleats that gave them some purchase, cracking through the ice to gain footing on the ground below, but still the going for them was slow, labored. Artillerymen leaned into the wheels of their pieces, slipping and sliding as they pushed the one-ton monsters up the long hill.

"Press on, men! Come on! Press on, men!"

He recognized the voice, looked up. It was the General, moving back down the middle of the road, his white horse standing out, ghostlike, in the moonlight, followed by his ever-present servant.

The General looked toward him and Peter.

"Come on, boys. You can do it. Press on! Press on! Just a few hundred more yards to the top!"

The General turned, his horse nearly losing footing for a moment, until his hooves cracked through the ice. The General, apparently without effort, remained mounted as the horse pawed for footing, gained it, then broke into a slow trot back up the slope.

The General's servant looked directly at Jonathan.

"The road flattens out at the top," he said. "You with the headquarters company?"

Jonathan nodded.

"Then, sir, you better move. They're already up there."

The clouds closed back over the moon, and seconds later all were enveloped again in a burst of snow and sleet. The servant and his General were lost to view.

With each step pain shot up from his feet. He could tell they were lacerated, wishing now for the cold numbness of an hour before. With each step he drew in another wheezing breath of frozen air, which cut into his lungs, burning them.

The only way he could sense direction was by the slope itself. Without that, he feared he might very well have staggered off and wandered into the woods until he collapsed and died.

Peter was again by his side, coaxing him along, arm now around his waist.

He found himself dwelling on a thought that he knew his preacher would say bordered on blasphemy. This hill was his own personal Calvary. He wondered if this was how Christ must have felt. But at least Christ knew what was coming, that in a few more hours the suffering would be over.

He was no longer sure if he was standing or collapsing, only Peter kept him upright.

"Jersey? You the Jersey boys?"

He opened his eyes. It was the company sergeant. Behind him a house, lights in the window.

"That's us," Peter gasped.

"Come on, boys, the company's already

322

heading south. Come on."

The sergeant pointed the way. The building looked to be a tavern. There was a vague memory for Jonathan of having hiked far up here as a boy, a long Saturday of wandering afield, playing at being Indians with Peter and his brother James, stalking travelers on the road, waiting for the mail stagecoach from New York to Philadelphia to come flying by, its four horses breaking into a run as they crested the slope up from the river, sparks flying from their ironshod hooves.

Bear Tavern — that was this place. The innkeeper's wife, Sue Keeler, playfully mimicking fright at the painted "Indians" who were lurking outside waiting to ambush and scalp all within, and then giving them each a mug of cold buttermilk as payment to spare their inn from pillage before sending them on the road back home to Trenton.

An inner voice whispered to him to simply fall out of the column, go to the tavern, and ask the innkeeper's wife if she remembered him from years past as a painted Indian waiting to pounce and might he have some buttermilk, or better yet hot tea.

He pressed on.

The column of troops, now on level ground, struggled to form into ranks even as their officers pushed them forward. There was no time for a break after the grueling climb. If they stopped here, within minutes they would block the advancing army to a standstill clear back to the river.

One mile . . . they had gained a mile, still eight miles to go. At this moment it was hard to recollect what was next . . . the ground flat and open ahead for a mile or so . . . but then . . . he remembered . . . there was still Jacob's Creek to cross.

"Easy going now?" the sergeant announced, looking over at the two. It was more a hopeful question than a statement of fact.

"Yes, easy going," was all Jonathan could say as they turned south, regaining the companionship of the unit they were assigned to.

At least the storm was at their back, the wind so strong he suddenly had a childlike fantasy that if he just opened his blanket cape and held it outstretched, perhaps it would be a sail that would effortlessly push him along.

The wind was at his back . . . and Jacob's Creek was ahead.

"Press on! You can't stop now, boys! Press on!"

For every step his men had taken in the last hour General Washington had ridden a dozen, constantly in motion, moving up and down the strung-out line shuffling through the night.

For Washington it all now had a maddening feel to it, a nightmare-like quality, a terrible dream where one was wading through mud, or deep water, trying to run as something horrifying approached or was waiting just ahead.

He had ridden back to the tavern again, and with relief saw that Knox had come up from the river at last, indicating that the rear of the column was across and moving. Knox was overseeing the movement of the lead section of guns, as they inched up the long slope from the river, the horses pulling the pieces and limber wagons, blowing out great billows of steaming breath, panting hard against the weight of the guns, ice crunching beneath their feet. Alexander Hamilton was in the lead as the first two guns turned and moved south at a faster pace as the ground gently sloped away, artillerymen trotting alongside the guns, calling for the infantry ahead to clear to either side of the road so that the artillery could take advantage of the slope to move at a trot.

Washington wheeled about and moved ahead of the pieces, riding hard, all the time chanting the same refrain over and over.

"Press on. Clear the way for the artillery. Press on."

The storm continued to rage, the ground slippery, but on this more gentle downward slope manageable, the land to either side mostly cleared fields, open farmland. The disadvantage was that the open fields were allowing the wind to sweep in, unbroken, but at least lashing into the men's backs almost as if it were helping to drive his army forward. And then ahead he saw it, a line of trees bisecting the road, knots of men gathered, not moving.

He had studied the maps hour upon hour as he plotted out this night, but in that plotting he had never considered a turn of the cards that would draw him this storm of ice.

He reined in, his advance column of Virginians bunched up, moving slowly.

"What is the holdup?"

"Sir."

He looked down, not recognizing the soldier, then a vague memory, one of the Jersey militia, the guide who had gone over the side to help haul the boat in and had nearly disappeared into the icy river.

"What is it?"

"Jacob's Creek," the boy announced. "Two ravines, one after the other."

"So why the holdup?" he snapped.

The boy could not reply, just looking up at him, shivering in the cold.

"Ice, sir," someone announced. "It's all ice-covered now."

Without replying Washington pushed his mount forward, into the treeline, the roadway narrowing. He could feel his mount becoming nervous, gingerly putting each foot down, the ice cracking underfoot so it still had some grip. The road turned and then turned again, following the contour of the slope downward, and in occasional flashes of moonlight he saw what made his heart sink.

The drop was steep, far too steep. Billy Lee was up by his side, his horse's rear hooves losing grip, the animal nearly sitting down. Lee was cursing under his breath as he hung on, the animal slipping, letting out a whinny of fear as it slid for a dozen feet down the road. Lee, a superb rider, kept his seat, hung on, reins loose because if he sawed at the horse's mouth, the animal would surely rear back and roll. He held his breath, Lee invisible in the shadows of the deep ravine. And then ever so calmly his voice echoed back out of the darkness.

"Sir, I think it best that you dismount."

In another time he might have smiled, but not now. He ignored his servant's advice, carefully maneuvering his mount down the ice-covered path, as he went into the deep ravine, a sharp drop of nearly fifty feet to the rushing creek, its thunderous passage outhowled by the storm, the roar all-encompassing, and his heart sank.

In the days before this march, he had been told the creek did not have a bridge, but not to worry, it was barely ankle-deep at the ford. As he came alongside Billy, who was still mounted, he could make out flashes of movement in the darkness. The creek was flooding, perhaps thigh deep. A couple of infantry pickets were looking up at him, and at the sight of their General one simply shook his head.

"Sir, it ain't good at all. Stephen and I been here now since before dark. Ya could have skipped across this twelve hours ago, and it's still rising."

"Anyone beyond you?" he asked sharply.

"Yes, sir. We picketed here just at dark as ordered. The advance company came through, I'd calculate a couple hours ago at least."

Did no news mean there were no problems

and the advance company was deployed and waiting for the rest of the army to come up? Or could it be that the advance company had run into something and might not even exist anymore, the Hessians just waiting for this army to get tangled in the ravine before launching a counterattack?

"Then go across. Find them. Let them know we are crossing and report back to me."

"If you say so, sir," and he wondered if there was reluctance in the man's voice.

He glared down at him, but in the shadows of the ravine, he could not distinguish any features.

Without further comment the man held his rifle up high, slid down the few feet to the creek, and splashed into it, cursing as he did so.

In the darkness he was hard to spot, but Washington could see the man struggling to maintain his footing, nearly falling over, water up to midthigh and then, gaining the other shore, lost to view.

He reined his horse around and started up the steep incline, Billy behind him, his mount so skittish that he loosened the reins, letting the animal pick its own way. His regret was that he had not actually come over here to look about a day or two ago, but to do that might have meant some Tory spotting him, reporting it, and that being taken as a sign of his intent.

At the top of the ravine troops were beginning to move down, staying off the road since it was so slippery, inching down the steep slope, again into the trees for handholds, more than one falling, a voice cursing that he had broken his ankle.

He could hear horses approaching, the creaking of wheels crushing ice. It was Hamilton with the lead battery of six-pounders.

"Over here!" Washington shouted.

Hamilton was up by his side, saluting.

"The slope ahead is impossible for horses," Washington announced. "They'll lose their footing on that ice and be crushed by the guns."

"You're not going to leave us behind?" Hamilton replied, the distress in his voice obvious.

"No."

As he spoke he could see Knox approaching.

He had already made his decision as he rode up the steep incline. Leave the artillery behind, and order the infantry alone to press ahead? Do that, we will run into the Hessians arrayed out in open field, undoubtedly with their artillery, and we will be torn to shreds. But if I wait to move these guns the plan of attack, already three or more hours behind will be even more behind. How much longer? Four hours, perhaps five? It will mean attacking Trenton in broad daylight, the garrison without doubt forewarned, deployed, and ready for battle. His men drenched, frozen, exhausted, the Hessians stepping out of heated barracks, well fed, in dry, warm clothes.

He drew his watch out, snapped it open, but it was so dark he could not see the face.

Knox was by his side, gazing down into the ravine and then back to his General.

"Sir," Knox announced. "It can be done, but it will take time."

Washington thanked God for a man like this. No questions at a moment of crisis, only the forming of a plan and a will to act on it.

"I recommend we unhitch the teams, lead them across to the opposite slope. Secure ropes to the guns, wrap the ropes around a tree, and play them out. I did it a hundred times or more with each of the guns we moved from Ticonderoga."

The matter-of-fact way he said it gave Washington heart. Knox made it sound almost casual, an everyday thing, not an operation performed in the middle of a maddening storm, in the dark, by men barefoot on raw ice and suffering.

"Then let's do it!" He was trying to sound firm and commanding and keep frustration out of his voice.

Knox was in his element now. He was moving guns across bad ground in bad weather. This is what had made him famous in the first place.

The horses were unhitched from the two lead guns, Hamilton ordering several men to take them across and get them up the slope on the far side. They started off, disappearing into the shadows of the ravine.

Knox was already shouting for some of the infantry of the Virginia brigade to fall out and stack muskets, while from the limber boxes of the first two guns, Hamilton and his men pulled out hundred-foot lengths of rope.

Though they worked swiftly under the guidance of the two officers, still it seemed forever before the first of the guns, barrel pointed down slope, was manhandled to the edge of the road and dropped into the ravine, two lengths of rope secured to it. Ten men on each rope coiled it around stout trees to give them control and better leverage. Knox stood behind the gun, shouting orders, the piece slowly rolling down the slope, ice cracking underneath it. Washington started to follow but realized if he did so mounted, and his horse slipped, they could easily crash into Knox and the gun.

He dismounted, tossing the reins to Billy and on foot followed down, watching the way Knox worked, the artilleryman bellowing orders for one team to play out more rope, then the other. It was hard to judge how long this was going to take. Five minutes . . . ten minutes?

Twice he nearly lost his own footing, boots sliding so that he had to reach out and grab a tree to keep balance, a shower of ice crystals cascading down on him.

"Damn it all to hell!"

It was Knox. Losing the struggle to preserve his dignity, Washington slid down to join him in a semisquat.

"We're still fifty or so feet short of the bottom of the ravine," Knox announced. The last of the rope had been played out. "Two more cables now!" Henry roared. "And twenty men!"

It took another five minutes for the men to get down in the gorge and, following Henry's orders, tie the ropes to the gun, make sure the ropes were around trees, and cinch tight. Then the piece was pulled back up the slope a couple of feet to put slack onto the ropes from the team farther up the hill, Henry personally untying each of the cables.

Without bothering to look to the General, Knox turned to Hamilton. "This is how we do it!" he shouted triumphantly, raising his voice to be heard above the roar of the flooded creek.

"Hamilton, you supervise the first team at the top of the slope, secure each gun, lowering them as you just saw us do it. Second team here takes over and gets it the rest of the way down to the water's edge."

"Why not just splice the ropes together into one long length?" Hamilton offered.

"Rope, Colonel Hamilton. Using two teams like this, we can lower two guns at a time with four hundred-foot lengths of rope. Spliced together, we need eight hundred feet for the same job, and we can only have one gun coming down at a time."

Washington said nothing. He marveled that Knox could so quickly calculate the advantage.

"Two sets of rope, four teams — we can keep two guns moving along. Get extra lengths of rope and while two guns are being lowered, the next one in line is prepared to speed things along. Have additional teams ready as well to relieve the ex-hausted."

He paused.

"Or in case something goes wrong and we lose some men."

"God save the lower group if the upper gun breaks loose," Hamilton said softly.

Knox did not reply.

"Gun crews move with their pieces. Once at the bottom here, they will have to man-handle them through the torrent. We must make sure the ammunition chests and the powder inside stay dry. We'll get more men across to move the guns out of the ravine. I'll get two more teams working the upslope on the far side; that should be easier because we can use horses for the upper part . . . then once up there, hitch 'em back up and then move like hell. Infantry stays off the road, they go down through the woods, pick anyplace but the road, cross, and reform on the far side."

"Sirs."

It was the lone sentry still posted at what, twelve hours earlier, had been an ankle-deep ford and a steep but still manageable road for a wagon or even an artillery piece.

"What is it?" Knox snapped.

"Uh, well, sir. Hate to tell you this, but this is just the first ravine. There's a second one, a fork of this here creek once you get up over yonder to the top."

"What?" Knox asked.

"Just that, sir. This here is the first of two ravines, and that second one, I think, is worse than this one."

Washington said nothing. With all his evaluating and managing here, the man had forgotten the map exercise and briefings of the day before. For some perverse reason, this road, rather than crossing the creek once a few hundred feet farther downstream, instead descended and crossed over the main creek and rose, then descended into a small tributary branch before rising again to level ground.

"Damn all to hell!" Henry roared. He stalked to the side of the road and slammed his fist against the trunk of a tree. Washington went to his side.

"Sir, it will take an hour at the very least, perhaps two or more," Knox hissed.

"And?"

"Sir," he paused, his voice thick, "we can still . . ."

He fell silent.

"You're suggesting?" Washington asked, voice pitched low so the men would not hear.

"I think you know," Knox replied. "It will

be dawn by the time we get the guns out of these ravines, if at all. One of them breaks loose, and smashes up, it will make a tangle of everything."

He threw up his arms in a gesture of exasperation.

"Sir, I moved guns over three hundred miles, in the dead of winter, and faced worse than this. But it was not a race against dawn then, with a storm howling around us, an unknown enemy ahead, our men already exhausted, and a flooding ice-choked river at our backs."

Silence again as Knox stood by his side.

"Go on."

"Sir, it is not my place to go on." Henry's face turned up to look at him, a momentary flash of moonlight revealing his features, drawn, exhausted. Directly behind him at the edge of the raging creek, men at the ropes looked in their direction, knowing that something was going on.

Knox was right. Everything he had said was correct. According to the plan he, his men, the artillery, should already be moving into final position around Trenton, with two other columns, one of them Gates's. Of the middle column, he had not heard a word. Gates, he already knew, was not coming.

It would be close on to dawn before he

could even hope to get the first of these guns clear of the ravines, infantry formed up . . . and Trenton would still be seven miles off. The storm howling through the trees above showed no sign of abating; if anything, it was increasing in intensity.

He stared at Knox, taking it all in. Infantry, hundreds of them, were already moving down the slope, grasping at trees to steady themselves, officers and sergeants urging them on. Men of his headquarters guards were filtering down along the side of the road, trying to stay closer to their commander, moving slowly, woodenly, more than one slipping, cursing as he crashed down.

He recognized two of the men holding on to each other, one of them staggering — the New Jersey scouts assigned to his personal guard. They passed but a few feet away, pushing on toward the creek. One hesitated for a moment, but then plunged into the torrent; he could hear the boy gasping as he did so. The two forded across and disappeared into the darkness.

He took it all in, stepped back, cupped his hands, and faced upslope.

"Billy Lee, get down here!"

No one spoke as his servant appeared out of the shadows, afoot, leading his own horse and the General's.

Washington mounted and looked down at Knox.

"Colonel Knox," he replied, voice raised so that it would carry.

"Sir."

"You have just told me it is impossible."

Knox did not reply.

"Sir. What is the watchword for this night?"

"Victory or death, sir."

"Those are the only alternatives left to us."

He raised his voice so that it echoed against the thunder of the creek, the howling of the storm.

"Victory or death, Colonel Knox. There is no other alternative, sir! We move on. Get your guns across, and I will see you in Trenton! Remember, this storm may help mask us from the Hessians as it makes our journey more miserable. Better a blizzard of snow than a blizzard of lead. This is *our* night to win."

Pulling on the reins of his mount, he set off, plunging into the creek.

Knox stood as if dumbstruck. All eyes had followed the General, and now were turning to him.

"I'd follow him to hell itself," Knox said softly, and then realized that no one was moving.

"You heard the General," he shouted in a commanding voice. "It is victory or death. Now move these damn guns!"

CHAPTER TEN

The Ford at Jacob's Creek
5:45 A.M., December 26, 1776

The narrow ravine was cloaked in frozen mist, tossed up by the roaring current.

He knew exhaustion was taking hold of his soul: exhaustion, complete and utter frustration, and an ever-growing thought, clawing at his willpower, that everything was going tragically wrong.

In all of the planning, contemplating, and final decision to make this bold night maneuver, he had tried to plan for every contingency. These ruinous ravines had never seriously figured in that planning.

Scouts and locals he had interrogated about the line of march had marked on a map every home and farm along the way that harbored known or suspected Tories, and even as the first contingent of his army crossed, his advance scouts had raced to each of those dwellings, placing those within

341

under guard. He had known that the first stretch of the road up to Bear Tavern would be steep and hard as an uphill march from the river valley, but the ravines?

No one had suggested the ravines might be this steep, the ice might be this hard, the water this cold, or the men this exhausted.

I never thought about what it could be like on a night such as this.

The storm continued in its fury. He could sense the wind was backing around more to the north, meaning that perhaps the worst of it was nearly over, but with that change in the wind, temperatures would most likely plummet, the sleet change over to snow.

"Tobias! Watch it!"

He heard screaming, cursing. Turning, he rode back to the edge of the second ravine and dismounted, tossing the reins of his horse to Billy Lee. Invisible men, down in the hollow, were shouting, a horse neighing in anguish. Staying clear of the road, he slid down the sharp face of the ravine, hanging on to trees, sliding a dozen feet, grabbing another and then another. In the shadowy mist to either side of him, infantrymen were still climbing upward, gasping, cursing, not even knowing who was going past them on the way down. More than one was damning all officers and the madman who had conceived this hellish ordeal.

Fires had finally been built at the bottom of the hollow. Whoever had managed to strike flint and get the blaze going was truly skilled in forest survival, most likely one of his Virginia or Pennsylvania riflemen from the frontier. They knew how to use bark peeled from birch trees and dead twigs from pines for kindling.

By the glow of the fire he caught glimpses of the tumbling creek. At the ford just above him, several artillery pieces had been lowered down the opposite face and were waiting to be hitched to cables for the final pull up by their exhausted crews.

The commotion was caused by half a dozen men, several of them in the stream, struggling with a panicked horse that had most likely slipped on the rocks and tumbled downstream. The poor animal was shrieking with terror, flailing; men were cursing, trying to avoid being kicked.

A burly man, an African, by what was left of his uniform a New York artilleryman, had hold of the horse's bridle and was holding on, not letting go, shouting for the others to back away.

The animal was half up, and the man holding the bridle moved closer, his voice loud but calming in the confusion, and the animal finally was still, both of them in the creek that flooded around them.

The animal's left foreleg was broken, the beast holding it up, limb dangling.

"Tobias, she's a goner," one of the others announced, squatting down to look, but keeping well back.

The black man kept his attention focused on the horse, both hands now holding the bridle tight, with the horse's rapid, labored exhalations, wreathing him in mist.

"No, sirra, no," Tobias replied, voice husky. "No, sirra."

"Get him out of the stream," Washington announced, and paused. "And then you have to finish him."

All looked at him, not realizing he was watching from only a few feet away.

"Sir?" Tobias started.

No one responded. Tobias looked at Washington, then nodded assent.

The animal fought for a moment, then with a hobbling limp moved the few feet up to the bank of the stream. One of the men started to draw a pistol.

"No gunfire," Washington exclaimed. A single shot could trigger confusion, even panic.

"Everything's soaked anyhow," another man announced. With a quick sure movement he had a knife out, came up alongside the horse, and cut its throat.

The horse gasped, screamed, thrashed, Tobias still holding on, getting splattered by blood spurting from the gash in the horse's throat.

"Sleep, friend, sleep now, sleep," he chanted, almost a singsong quality to his voice, an echo of the Caribbean isles.

Washington had to turn away, unable to watch. In such a harsh world, still there was something about putting down a horse or a beloved hunting dog that raised an anguish that cut into the heart. Holding on to tree limbs he made his way back the few dozen feet to the ford.

Knox was still at it. Someone motioned and Henry turned to offer a salute.

"These are the last of them, sir," he said, his voice heavy, rasping.

Even as he spoke a shout came from up the slope, the ropes secured to the gun going taut, the unseen crew above renewing their labors, a voice calling out, "Pull . . . pull . . . pull, lads . . . That's it, pull!" It sounded like Hamilton.

"The going's getting a bit easier," Knox reported. "Moving all the guns finally broke up the ice on the trail, but it's mud underneath."

He looked up.

"Feels like it's getting colder."

"It is."

"Good. It'll change to snow rather than this sleet."

And the colder wind will increase the suffering of the men, he realized. Even with his well-tailored uniform, heavy woolen cape, and tanned boots, he was soaked through. As long as he kept moving, it did not bother him much, but standing still, or when mounted, he could feel the chill setting in.

"Last of the infantry is just about across as well," Knox announced.

He didn't reply. The column was formed up on the road above the ravines where he had held them until all the guns were across. Otherwise they might be strung out on the road for several miles. If the Hessians were aroused and waiting . . . he needed everything together for that final fight . . . for surely it would be the final fight if the enemy was waiting . . . and he wanted his artillery at the front, and not straggling, to be devoured one piece at a time.

"I'd say ten more minutes, sir, and we'll have the last of these guns out of the ravine."

Washington reached into his vest pocket, for his watch. The cover was damp and he hoped moisture had not seeped into the

346

watch's delicate works. He snapped it open and held it so he could see the face by the smoky fire.

"Six by my watch," he announced.

He looked up. Sunrise was an hour and a half off. Even though they were in a mist-shrouded ravine, the storm still raging, he wondered if he could already sense the first faint trace of rising light, able to discern the tracery of ice-covered trees arching over their heads. Or was it just the occasional glimpse of moonlight above the racing clouds? It reminded him of the night crossing of the East River, that same sensing but not yet seeing that dawn was approaching. A silent, desperate appeal to God to somehow make the world freeze in place, to give but one extra hour of darkness. But he was not Joshua before Jericho; the sun would not remain motionless, and dawn would soon come.

The attack should have gone on more than an hour ago. There was no way of knowing what fate might already have befallen the thousand militiamen who were positioned below the falls at Trenton. They were supposed to have crossed by now and taken up position to block any retreat of the enemy south out of Trenton, and to then take the small enemy garrison of a hundred or so men in the village of Bordentown. If they were across the river, they were unsupported, with his column still six miles away. If discovered, the alarm would have already been sounded, the enemy aroused. Fifteen hundred of the king's toughest mercenaries against our militia would make short work, and then they could turn and be waiting in ambush for us.

He closed the watch and put it into his pocket. He felt a pang of hunger but far worse was the fear, the indecision that threatened to cut into him.

Another piece started up the slope.

The die is cast. We can't turn back now, not here. Not with this behind us. If I order a retreat, it will take two or more hours just to turn everything around again. The enemy will catch us here and the slaughter will be complete.

By my will alone I have forced the army this far, and they have done their duty. If I turn back now I doubt that but one in ten would ever follow me again — if they even manage to get back to the Delaware. They will endure this cold and exhaustion for a chance at victory. They will not tolerate it if their leader is indecisive or confused. Certainty is the key to everything now.

"We've lost half a dozen horses and several

dozen men," Knox said. "Broken limbs. Damn the ice."

Washington looked down the ravine. The death throes of the horse were nearly at an end. It was lying on its side, kicking feebly, Tobias cradling its head. Neither of the generals spoke for a moment. A soldier leaned over to pat Tobias on the shoulder and then helped to pull him up and away.

The small knot of artillerymen came up the ravine, passing the generals, Tobias struggling to hold back his sobs. They paused for a moment and then without orders fell in behind the last gun to push it along and up the slope.

"With such men," Washington said softly.

Letting his emotion show was rare. He had spent a lifetime mastering it, to avoid letting emotion, passion, rage, or sentiment show, to be a stoic, as any man of his birth should be.

And yet . . .

"I'm ordering the column to resume the march," he announced. "Bring these last guns up sharply."

He did not wait for a reply from Knox, and he followed one of the artillery pieces up the path.

The climb was short, less than a hundred feet, but the ravines had cost him more than a precious hour and a half to negotiate.

He reached the top of the ravine. With the ice broken on the road he sank halfway to his knees at times with every step. In the gloom he could see the wheels of the artillery pieces thick with congealing mud, men casting off ropes from the carriages, teamsters moving to hook the gun to its limber and team of horses.

Washington passed the black artilleryman, his tears stilled as he labored to hook the piece to its limber, the General noticing how one of the artilleryman's comrades comforted him, saying words inaudible to him.

Now Billy Lee was up by his side, leading his horse. Washington mounted. "With such men," he found himself thinking again as he watched the artillerymen swing their piece around.

As the column moved out, he heard whispered snatches of conversation. "About time, damn it . . ." "First damn Hessian I get, off comes his shoes once I kill him, I swear it by God . . ." "Let's get on with it."

They were grim, angry, yet not a word about turning back now. Perhaps Jacob's Creek was a blessing. With it at their backs, the prospect ahead was the only alternative; going back, melting into the woods, no longer was even a remote thought.

So unlike the retreat from Fort Lee.

That had truly been a debacle. The position atop the Jersey Palisades were deemed by all to be impregnable. The cliffs along the Hudson soared up from the river a hundred and fifty feet or more. It was a rise even more difficult than the one the legendary Wolfe had scaled seventeen years before to take Quebec, an action that had won universal awe and acclaim.

Four thousand men were garrisoned at Fort Lee, the fortifications containing within them his reserve supplies, thousands of rations, tentage to shelter an entire army, tons of powder, tens of thousands of flints and shot, fodder for horses and mules. It was a redoubt deemed to be solid, absolute, a barrier the British could never storm.

Cornwallis had achieved it without losing a man.

He had trusted Greene, and still did. But on that day, not much more than a month ago, someone had failed, and Greene had to shoulder the blame. Under cover of a moonless night Cornwallis, leading the advance, crossed the Hudson from the New York side and landed his men on a narrow spit of land below the Palisades, their first landfall so tenuous that a score of boys armed only with rocks, standing atop the cliffs, could have slain hundreds.

The guard on the spit of land had not been relieved when his watch was done. The guard who was supposed to keep an eye on the barely visible trail leading to the top of the cliffs was gone as well, no doubt drunk and assuming after months of tedious watching without action, nothing was amiss.

Cornwallis gained the heights, not only with his infantry, but according to reports that crossed through the lines, had even disassembled his artillery pieces and had them manhandled up the rocky cliff. He did have to admit to a grudging admiration of that feat. It was worthy of another Wolfe, and if someday this Revolution was lost, Cornwallis would return to England a hero, a peerage most likely awaiting him as reward.

It was the same Cornwallis who now commanded the far-flung garrisons spread across New Jersey this night. The Cornwallis he prayed he would humble this dawn was not a foe to be taken lightly. The man had proved that at Fort Lee.

Word had come at dawn that there the army was trumped, that thousands of British and Hessian troops were atop the Palisades and storming down upon the flanks and rear of the fort, about to cut off any hope of retreat.

He had also lost Fort Washington, on the northern tip of Manhattan in a bloody debacle. There was nothing he could possibly have done at that moment. To stand and fight would be folly, putting what was left of his army in a closed sack. All Cornwallis then needed to do was surround them, sit back, go to siege, and within days capture what was left of his army.

Humiliated, he ordered the abandonment of Fort Lee and full retreat. Any supplies that could not be carried out were to be torched.

He stood by helplessly as a mad frenzy of despair seized the army. Men racing about in panic, gathering up what they thought they should carry off, and within minutes bonfires erupted across the encampment area as everything else was put to the torch. In the panic, items that could have been saved burned as well, including three wagonloads of precious shoes newly arrived from up the Hudson, hundreds of trousers and winter jackets, men snatching just what they needed for themselves and then burning the rest with no thought of tomorrow.

There was no semblance of an army left as by the thousands they poured on to the road west, away from the accursed battlefields around New York, fleeing down from the heights toward the marshy open ground that was the only route to safety, the bridge across the Passaic River at Hackensack.

Throughout the day they had run — he riding at the back of the column; the side of the road littered with cast-off equipment, tents, food, muskets, empty bottles drained by men who were now drunk; and more than a few simply turning off the road, heading into the marshes to hide until all had passed, so that they could then slip away toward home.

All the time he raged inwardly at the utter folly, the waste, and could see in the eyes of the men he rode past increasing despair, and in more than a few, contempt for him, after yet another defeat.

His only hope was to gain the bridge ahead of the pursuers. In the distance he could hear their trumpet calls, some of them no longer even military, but instead the mocking, disdainful call of the fox hunt.

That had been almost too much to bear. He had struggled against the impulse to turn about, ride straight back with drawn saber, and make an end to it all. He could see from the way Billy Lee watched him throughout the day, as if reading his mind, that he was ready to stop him.

They had yet to seize the Hackensack bridge. A corporal's guard could have ended the war right there with a single volley into the mob that seethed about, pushing, shoving, fighting with one another to get across the narrow plank bridge.

He did not even bother to try to reestablish order, to ride through the mob. Instead, he had waited, resolved as always to be the last to cross, looking back anxiously up the road, seeing in the distance the enemy leisurely coming on, stopped only by a few skirmishers, as usual the undaunted men of the frontier, armed with their long rifles, trading shots with the Hessian jaegers, firing, falling back a few hundred paces as they reloaded, turning to fire again.

The last of the line infantry, militia, and two dozen precious field pieces were finally across. The ground on the east side of the bridge was a sickening field of litter and refuse, enough rations to feed the army for days tossed on the ground as men shed the few extra pounds of food in their exhausted state so as to lighten their loads, muskets by the hundreds, cartridge boxes, canteens, more than a few horses some dead, others just collapsed from exhaustion, cut from the traces of the guns and the few precious surviving supply wagons just left behind.

The refuse of an army in panicked retreat is a sight which he had become all too familiar with during the last three months.

They had marched into New York from Boston with such exuberant confidence in the spring, and, as winter closed in, fled in such ignominious terror and despair.

He could not imagine then that the despair could ever deepen and become worse. But it had.

And now, at this moment, a voice whispered within him that they were marching to their final fight. As he watched the men passing, staggering toward Trenton, he had a different sense of it all. Despair yes, but also defiance. If this was indeed the last day, they would die facing the enemy rather than running away.

He turned his mount and urged him forward. The road was packed with his troops, artillery pieces interspersed, men standing, huddled together for warmth. Waiting in the darkness . . . freezing in the darkness . . . a darkness which was beginning to shift to the first pale shadows of a stormy dawn.

"Forward, men. Forward!" he cried. "Victory or death. Now forward!"

"Thank God," Jonathan gasped.

He had been shaking so hard he felt that he was about to break apart at the joints. Each breath was an agony. The men of the headquarters company, at the head of the column, stood together in a tight knot. Peter had positioned himself to the windward side of Jonathan and without embarrassment had his arms tight around him, the two standing together, shivering, shaking. All around them men were bowed over, the heavy snow gathering on their battered hats and turned backs so that they looked almost like frozen lumps or snow-covered rocks firmly affixed to the road.

"Forward, men! Forward!"

They could hear his command, and the company captain repeated it. There were no drums to set the marching pace, no flags to mark the head of the column. The men began to shuffle forward. Several horsemen trotted past, one of them nearly pitching over as his mount stumbled on the ice, gaining the front of the column. A moment later Washington himself trotted past.

"Advance scouts?" Washington shouted. "Any reports?"

"Nothing, sir," the captain replied.

Jonathan barely noticed Washington's passage. Head bent, he pressed forward. In places the road was frozen solid; in others the ice was broken by the passage of the advance company sent to probe ahead of the main column. Lost in silent misery, he staggered on, step by labored step. Lift one foot out of the freezing mud, move it forward, for an instant test whether the ground beneath was solid and slippery, waiting to pitch him over, or solid enough that his numb bare feet could get a grasp; set that foot down, pull the other out of the sludge, move it forward. Step by step. He had run the calculation in his head while waiting for the previous hour, to think of anything to make the agonizing minutes pass. Six miles to Trenton. A man makes a step of two and a half feet. About two thousand steps per mile. Six miles equals . . . He couldn't quite sum the numbers; he didn't want to, the thought was too overwhelming.

"Jersey!"

He was shaken out of his misery and contemplation. It was the sergeant.

"General wants you two up forward with him. Let's go!"

The sergeant led the way, running as best he could, nearly pitching over, stumbling, regaining his feet. Jonathan ran as if in a nightmare. Strange thoughts surfaced. He remembered when he and James had stolen the rum from behind the tavern and gotten drunk for the first time in their lives. How his legs no longer obeyed what his brain commanded, and at the time how hysterically funny it had seemed to him.

It felt the same now, but there was nothing to laugh about. He could not feel his legs. It was as if he were removed from his own body and trying to will it to move. The weight of his water-soaked cape, bore down on him, as did the musket on his back, slung inverted to prevent the sleet and snow from lodging in the barrel . . . as if it mattered, since he did not have a single dry cartridge.

He followed the sergeant and then saw the General's white horse, in the lead, his servant riding beside him.

The sergeant came up by the General's side.

"Here are the local boys, sir."

Washington nodded and looked down.

Jonathan struggled to keep alongside of him, moving at a slow jog. The General, mounted, was forcing a fast pace now. The near jog was beginning to restore sensation to his legs and feet, and he wished it would not, for each step produced a stinging pain.

"Do you boys recognize this road?"

Jonathan, breathing hard, turned his attention forward.

Merciful God, he realized with a start,

dawn was coming.

We were supposed to attack in the dark, while the Hessians were asleep.

Now he could see a split rail fence by the side of the road bedecked with an inch or more of snow. And beyond it the shape of a house, well made of brick, a light within. And apple orchards on either side of the road.

It was the Gaines's farm, with acres of apples, pears, and even peaches on the southern slopes of the land.

Gay and Stanley Gaines had no children. All had died in a smallpox epidemic before Jonathan had been born, and they had always been indulgent of the boys, letting them take an apple or two as they passed by, the old woman sometimes giving them a hot apple turnover on a winter's day when he and his friends were afield hunting or exploring. She would smile at them, that wistful smile of a mother bereaved of her own children and thus embracing any child who might wander by. On occasion the elderly couple would come all the way into town to attend church and then, after services, linger for a while in the cemetery by the row of five small headstones.

He could see someone coming from the house now, holding a lantern.

"Gaines's farm," Peter announced, and motioned toward the house. "Yes, sir, we know where we are now."

"Good. Then stay close by."

"Yes, sir," Peter replied.

The elderly couple stood by the gate leading into their farm.

"General Washington?" It was a woman's voice.

The General wordlessly touched the brim of his hat as he passed.

"Morning, Mrs. Gaines," Peter announced. There was an almost boyish tone in his voice, prideful, even though without doubt she would not know who he was.

"Here, my lads," and she stepped through the gate, holding something out for Peter and Jonathan.

Shaking with the cold, Jonathan took the offering, feeling the warmth, smelling it. A warm apple turnover. The woman had a basket under her arm, filled with her offering.

"God bless you, my boys. God bless you."

She fell away from their side. He looked back. She and her husband were handing out the turnovers, to hands reaching out from the passing column. "Thank you, ma'am, oh, bless ya, ma'am . . . ," and her repeated refrain, breaking down into tears.

"God bless you, boys. God be with you."

She drifted away into the predawn mist, her voice first an echo, and then lost.

"Aren't you going to eat it?" Peter cried.

Jonathan looked down at the turnover, actually wanting to keep it in his hands for another minute. The warmth was a gift as well.

He raised the offering as if it were a communion host and took a bite. It was painful to work his jaws after the hours of chattering from the cold. He devoured the rest in several bites, feeling the warmth, a small ember of hope within, tears in his eyes from this simple act of charity, the tears now freezing.

"Keep moving! Keep up the pace, boys!"

It was the General, moving toward to the head of the column at a trot, the two boys having to all but run to keep up. Behind them they could hear the familiar sounds of an army on the move, the clatter of muskets banging against tin cups, the low undertone of voices, men gasping, cursing, the sound of the wind rising and falling in the trees as they passed through a tunnel-like woodlot, the slippery road dipping into a hollow and rising again, the going tough for a moment. Washington's horse nearly lost its footing more than once. One farm after another passed by and he could not recall their names.

And with each step the light was changing. There was no color to it at all, just darker shades of gray shifting to lighter, deep shadows of darkness in the woods, reflecting dully off the ice and snow that carpeted fields where corn had been harvested and shucked, orderly apple, pear, and peach orchards, the trees bent low, off glistening farmhouses, outbuildings, and barns. At each farmhouse there was a light, smoke from chimneys. Some had shutters bolted, sentries posted around the building; a few had doors open, those within watching the army pass.

How easy it would be to say he could not take another step, to go to an open door and pass within to find warmth by a fire.

"The sunshine patriot . . ."

That drove him onward. I am not one of them. I am not like James . . . I am not one of them . . . I am not like James . . .

And always there was the refrain, the General turning to ride back for several hundred yards, standing in his stirrups, shouting: "Forward! Keep moving, men! Forward!"

And then he would return to the front of the column, ensuring that the sharp pace of the march was maintained.

Keeping pace with the General, Peter rattled off the names of places passed, distances to go. The General looked down, nodding and now with the rising light they could distinguish his face, drawn with exhaustion, but filled, it seemed, by some inner light, a passion to his eyes.

"There, sir," Peter announced, pointing to his left. "It's a lane up to a wood lot. The Kindermans', I think. The lane, though, it continues from the northeast side of the woodlot, links up to the road that comes down from Princeton a mile or so farther on."

Washington turned, snapped an order to one of the men riding nearby. He reined about, calling for several of the infantrymen marching behind the headquarters company to follow him, and started up the lane.

Washington looked down at Jonathan.

"You, lad?" he asked. "You're the one who jumped into the river, aren't you?"

Peter had been doing most of the talking while Jonathan struggled to keep pace. Feeling had most definitely returned to his legs and the agony was nearly overwhelming. He had looked down only once, and in the early morning light the sight had frightened him. He had just stepped into a puddle of slush, which had washed the mud off, but there was something dark oozing out even as he pressed on . . . His feet were bleeding. He saw bloodstains in the snow. He looked back at the men pushing behind them, the way their feet were moving, the men staggering. Would the road be paved with blood? he wondered.

But it was breathing that he was most focused on. Each gasp of the damp air took effort. The faint warm glow of the offering of the Gaineses had long ago been extinguished. He just pushed on. He could not give in, but he had let Peter do the talking.

"Son, did you hear me?"

"Ah, yes, sir," he replied haltingly. "Yes, sir."

"Lad, are you feeling fit to continue?"

He wondered if this was an offer for him to fall out.

How far back to the Gaineses? Surely they would take him in. Surely they might remember him from years past.

The sunshine patriot . . .

No, damn it.

"Yes, sir. I'm with you, sir. I feel fine now, sir," he lied.

"How much farther to where the road forks?"

Did he detect something in the General's

voice. Almost like it was about to break?

"It should just be ahead, sir," Jonathan offered.

Washington turned to one of his staff.

"Tell General Sullivan to come up." He pressed on, the courier turning back and minutes later returning with Sullivan by his side.

Jonathan looked up at the famed officer who was considered one of the backbones of the army. His face was grim, and he was shivering from the cold, riding without a cape or cloak, his uniform clearly visible.

In the rising light Jonathan could resolve the shadows ahead into a small knot of men standing in the middle of the road, the advance scouts. He recognized the place, the hamlet of Birmingham. It was now just four miles or so to Trenton.

Washington slowed to engage Jonathan again. "Is this Birmingham and the Scotch Road?" he asked.

"Yes, sir."

The crossroad was marked by half a dozen homes, one of them an inn, another owned by a cabinetmaker of local renown. The crossroads had obviously been occupied by the advance guard, who were posted in front of each house, guides waiting in the middle of the road.

Washington rode forward at a trot, stopped for a moment to ask a hurried question, then turned back.

"General Sullivan, here is where our column divides," Washington announced. "Your troops will continue straight ahead. Deploy as close to the town as you dare, then drive straight in the moment you hear our guns open up. Do you understand?"

"Yes, sir."

"Then God be with you, sir," and he leaned over to shake Sullivan's hand.

"Victory or death, sir," Sullivan replied loudly.

Jonathan could see the General force a smile.

"I will see you after the battle, sir."

Though not privy to the plan of march Jonathan understood what was now happening. The road straight ahead was the one he had usually tramped along as a boy when venturing northward out of Trenton. Some called it the River Road, for in another mile it would drop down toward the Delaware and then run close to its banks for the rest of the way into Trenton. The General would turn his horse east, to lead the column on another line of march, swinging out and away from Trenton for a mile or so before turning south again, the road then taking them into Trenton on the eastern side of town.

Jonathan knew enough of strategy to grasp that Sullivan was to close the approach from the north side of town while the column led by General Washington with men mostly of General Greene's command would close from the northeast and east. It was the longer route, and he was shaken to realize he was nowhere near as familiar with this road as the one that Sullivan would take.

He looked over nervously at Peter.

"Do you know this way," he hissed.

"Of course I do. Remember when I got that deer two years ago? It was over near the Whitman farm. That's on this road."

It was hard to hold on to his thoughts, to remember the roads, lanes, and narrow paths he had explored as a boy. It was all becoming even more confusing, but he said nothing as the column led by the General turned left and pressed on, while Sullivan waited for his men, farther back in the line of march, to come up and then press straight in toward the town.

The march to the east was anguishing, for they were facing into the wind. The General had also quickened the pace, in spite of the condition of the road. In places it was frozen almost solid, and it was nearly impossible to keep one's footing. They turned down into a gentle hollow, crossing a marshy stretch that was flooding calf deep with icy water, then back up again.

Another crossroad appeared ahead, a few more advance scouts marking the way, and the column turned south.

All the time daylight was approaching. Its coming drove the General forward, as if goading him along. Peter and he had to run at a steady trot to keep up now. His lungs felt like a bellows drawing in fire.

And then they heard the sound of horses approaching, a movement in the mists ahead.

The sergeant behind them snapped a command and the headquarters company, moving at a flat-out run, two men spilling on the ice-covered ground, raced to either side of the road and began to form into a semblance of a line, men unslinging muskets from shoulders. All Jonathan could think of at that moment was the utter absurdity of the gesture. If there were Hessians ahead, chances were that few men in the entire army behind him or now deploying had a weapon with dry powder that could fire.

As Washington heard the sounds ahead there were a few seconds of tension, a coiling up, a quick thought that his horse pistol

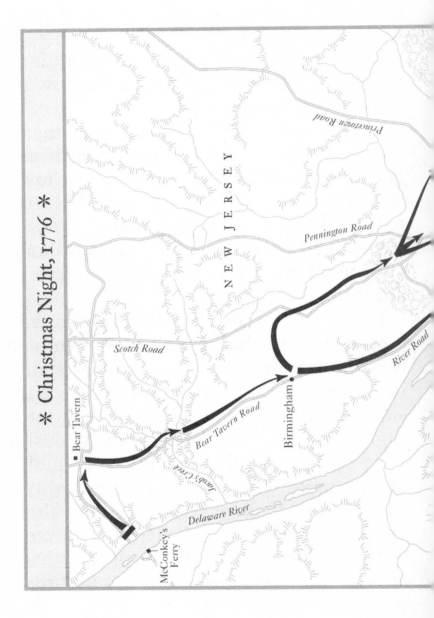

Princeton Road

N E W   J E R S E Y

Pennington Road

Scotch Road

Bear Tavern

Bear Tavern Road

Birmingham

River Road

Jacob's Creek

Delaware River

McConkey's Ferry

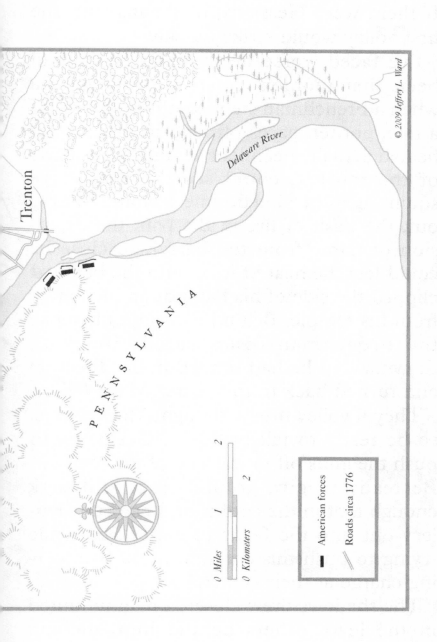

Trenton

Delaware River

PENNSYLVANIA

© 2009 Jeffrey L. Ward

0 Miles   1   2

0 Kilometers   2

■   American forces

╱╱   Roads circa 1776

in the saddle holster was most likely soaked. If there were Hessians, deploying out, the first volley would strike quickly.

I've faced worse he thought. There had been that moment on the Monongahela when a Frenchman stepped out from behind a tree, not ten paces off, and in that instant he had actually been looking into the muzzle of the musket, could see the man's eye squinting as he aimed, time seeming to drag out, the flash of fire in the pan, the explosion of flame from the barrel, so close he could feel the heat of it . . . and the ball had clipped the side of his hat, not an inch away from his temple. Behind a curtain of smoke the Frenchman disappeared, and with drawn sword he had saluted in his direction and turned back to the center of the fight.

They'll volley fire he thought, then charge, so be ready to fall back . . . Get Knox to push the guns off to the side of the road . . . Be ready to give ground. It is still dark enough that in the confusion I can run artillery out into the fields to either side while trying to push this column into a hammering charge at their center.

The shadows drew closer, a man mounted in the lead, others behind him, moving swiftly. They appeared to be Virginia troops, a captain of rifles leading the way.

They slowed at the sight of him. His heart still pounding, he assumed the role of actor upon the stage, knowing others were watching. He nudged his mount forward, as if expecting this encounter all along.

"Sir!"

The captain, breathing hard, stopped before him.

"Do you have something to report?" Washington asked, and then he could not contain himself. "The Hessians, are they coming?" he asked. "Are they behind you?"

He knew his questions were too hurried, his thought now being that these men were falling back to the main column with the enemy in hot pursuit.

"I don't think so, sir."

More men were coming out of the snow and fog, traversing an open field to the right that was covered with ice, corn stubble sticking up out of the frozen ground, hard going for some of the men who were barefoot and moving slowly.

"Your report then?"

"Sir, I must say it's a surprise to see you here."

The captain looked up at him excitedly, actually smiling.

"Who are you?"

"Captain Anderson, sir. Third Virginia, sir."

Third Virginia? He felt a moment of confusion. No advance scouts had been detached from that regiment.

"Yes, sir, Third Virginia. General Stephens, sir, we were talking to him yesterday and said that it was a shame, its being Christmas and all, and given how those damn Germans like to celebrate, that maybe we could come over and stir their party up a bit."

The captain actually chuckled at what he obviously thought was a delightful, boyish prank.

"So, General Stephens, he told me to take some men, get across the Delaware, poke around a bit and go ahead and have some fun. Up until yesterday it was only some militia with Ewing that were having all the fun, and the honor of Virginia was at stake if we didn't join in."

Washington felt that his heart was about to stop. Stephens had not been briefed until late yesterday afternoon on the plans for an attack. During that briefing Stephens had not said a word about this impromptu raid. He wondered if the man had forgotten or had decided simply not to say anything.

"And what happened?" Washington asked slowly, sick at heart with what he expected to be the reply, the excitement of the young captain answer enough.

"Sir, we hit them good. Waited until about four hours ago, got to the edge of the town and fired a few volleys right into the house where some of those damn Germans were keeping warm. We made it warm for them all right! Think we even got a few and, sir, we certainly stirred them up! Must've woke up the whole town, it did. We could hear drums rolling and men running about.

"Ruined their night of precious sleep, I'm certain of it. It was like hitting a hornet's nest with a rock. You should have heard them buzzing, but we was gone and nothing for them to sting! I bet they are still running around in circles."

The young captain was beaming with pride. The rest of his command, coming in from the nearby field, were gathering around, nodding their heads, obviously delighted with themselves.

"Well, that kicked up a stir, sir. We just headed back up into these fields. Got comfortable in a house and barn owned by some good patriot who, forgive us, sir, gave us some buttered rum to take away the chill, and we're just coming back out now when someone said you were on the road, so we came down to find out. We were thinking of maybe kicking 'em up again before heading back across the river and —"

"Damn you! Damn you, sir!"

The words exploded out of him with thunderous rage.

"You damn fools. You damnable fools!"

Washington's explosive outcry startled his mount, causing the horse to rear up slightly.

Turning, he looked to the troops behind him, struggling to keep the pace, were coming forward, still several dozen yards off.

"General Stephens!" he cried. "Up here now!"

He gazed angrily at the column of infantry that was slowing at the sight of their General stopped in the middle of the road, the headquarters company deploying as if for a fight. In the snow and mist it was impossible to see if Stephens was close by or not.

"You say you stirred them up after dark?" Washington shouted at the now thoroughly confused and frightened captain.

"Sir. I'm sorry, sir, but General Stephens told us we could do it, sir."

Washington could feel his temper about to descend on this man, to curse him, berate him. All was now in ruins, absolute ruins. Gates had not crossed. It was already well past dawn, and the plan had been to attack nearly three hours before dawn and catch

376

the enemy while still fast asleep. He had no word whatsoever whether the blocking force south of the town had crossed the river, and if it had done so undetected. And now this. Stephens had allowed some overeager men to cross the river to "stir things up a bit," and then had not admitted it or had conveniently forgotten to tell him.

The plan might well be in ruins. These men surely had aroused the Hessian garrison, most likely just before the watch was about to change. Any officer expecting further raids or suspecting that the evening sortie was the beginning of a full-scale attack would have now doubled his watch and kept most of the men under arms until dawn. He would have sent out probing parties to patrol the surrounding countryside.

The plan was ruined.

He glared down at the captain, and he could see the fear in the man's eyes.

The look disarmed him. The young man and his comrades had crossed over the river the day before, an act few would undertake, and was most likely returning expecting praise, and now he towered above him, filled with rage.

Washington closed his eyes and took a deep breath.

If Providence, in His wisdom has willed

all this so, then what more can I do? Gates, the storm, the maddening delay at Jacob's Creek, and now this. Is this the will of Providence?

We cannot turn back now, and to rage at this man will solve nothing. His heart told him the assault was truly doomed. But if that indeed was his fate, and of the men who had trusted in him, he would face it . . . and not curse an innocent man who believed he had been doing his duty.

He opened his eyes and shook his head wearily. "Captain, it is not your fault. Do you still have some fight in you?"

The captain was, startled, having expected something far different.

"Well, do you still have some fight in you?"

"Well, sir, we were planning to try and raid one of their outposts just down the road and then you came along, sir, and, well, I thought, sir —"

"Good then," Washington replied softly. "Fall in behind me, captain, and I will lead you into a bigger fight."

The captain, almost like an eager boy, saluted and shouted for his men to follow.

Washington's headquarters company had gathered around behind him, most likely hearing a fair part of the exchange. He could only hope that word of it did not race

back up the column, for it would surely unnerve men already staggering with exhaustion and cold to realize that any hope
whatsoever of surprise was gone. This attack, advancing against an enemy rested,
warm, and already aroused, was doomed.

Indeed it was a time to try a man's soul.

"Forward, men. Forward," he announced
to his headquarters company. The men of
the raiding party were falling in with him.

"Anyone got any dry powder?" he heard
someone ask.

"If your powder is wet, use cold steel,"
Washington called to him. "Pass the word
back. Fix bayonets if your powder is wet."

He could hear his order picked up,
shouted back to the marching column.

He caught a glimpse of the two boys from
Jersey. Both had unslung their muskets and
advanced with them leveled. Neither had a
bayonet.

He drew his sword and spurred his mount
forward, picking the pace up again. In the
early light of a stormy dawn, he saw a scattering of houses ahead.

CHAPTER ELEVEN

Philadelphia
December 13, 1776

A cold wind rattled the windowpanes of the bedroom.

Tom Paine woke up, confused, not sure for a moment where he was. The room was semidark, curtains drawn. It felt stifling, confining, and chokingly hot, with heat radiating from one of Franklin's stoves. Pulling back the covers, still not sure where he was, he was startled to discover he was naked. The room was elegant in its simplicity, candlesticks of fine pewter, sideboard of well-polished cherry wood, bed with a wool-stuffed mattress and down comforter.

Memory finally came back. His army uniform, which but a few months before he had worn so proudly, was gone, burned in the fireplace of Rush's kitchen. He remembered now the exclamations of disgust of the old woman who had picked it off the floor, holding the rags between forefinger and thumb before hurling them into the roaring fire. Michael had bathed him in the tin tub set by the fireplace, the old woman pouring gallons of warm water over him. In his exhaustion he had not even been embarrassed by her ministrations as she helped Michael to clip off his beard and shave him clean.

Several times she had drawn back in horror as one of the surviving lice still clinging to his body tried to make a dash for a new haven. She would vigorously slap her hands, then peer at the floor to make sure the pest had fallen to the brick paving where she could crush it.

In exasperation they had cut his hair short, picking out the nits with a fine-toothed comb. Then he had dozed off, having drunk the whole tankard of hot buttered rum that Michael had given him.

He stepped close to the mirror mounted in a dark mahogany frame over the sideboard. Leaning forward, he peered into it.

It was the first time he had looked at himself in weeks, and the reflection startled him. His features were gaunt, pale in the soft light. Was it dusk or dawn streaming in that gave his features a sickly tinge of gray? His leathery skin was deeply lined, as if several months at war had aged him ten years or more. Gray eyes peering back at him showed a weariness of body and soul.

His nearly shaved head was covered with red welts from the lice and flea bites. In fact, his entire body itched with the small pin-prick sores. When living on the streets of London he had been lousy, too; everyone was. But this time the infestation had been especially acute, and it felt strange now to be standing naked, in a warm room, looking at himself.

He felt aged, bowed down by weight and by guilt. He remembered how he must have looked six months past. After *Common Sense* had been published, he was "the Thomas Paine," and had never had to buy a meal for months. He had merely to walk into any inn and someone would call out his name; sometimes it would be one of the workers he had known from the docks and warehouses before his fame; or if he chose the right place at a convenient time when Congress was not in meeting, it would be one of the hangers-on seeking favor or appointment and believing that buying a meal and rum for "Mr. Thomas Paine" might help his cause. And he had been more than happy to accept that largess. At times it might even be a member of Congress. He had dined with Jefferson and Stockton off fine china with a servant at his shoulder. Or late at night in a back room, he had drained tankard after tankard of the finest rum while debating the meaning of this thing called Revolution.

And he had grown fat.

He remembered now how he had looked in those heady days of July and August. A man of some renown at a time when all toasted the Revolution, General George Washington, God bless him, and these United States. And always the drinks had been free. The roast beef thick with fat, the pies covered with cream, the sausages and fresh lamb chops brought in from the countryside by German farmers — all of it free for Mr. Paine.

Now what am I?

He was again a skeletal scarecrow, pinched sallow cheeks making his hook nose even more pronounced.

Laid out on a chair by the side of the bed were breeches and a jacket of brown broad cloth, soft cotton shirt, hose, and shoes . . . actual shoes. The sight of them flashed memory to a few days before, the struggling march from Princeton to Trenton, men sliding calf deep into the churned-up mud, most of them barefoot. How much would these shoes have fetched then in trade?

No, the thought was absurd. With an army they were useless; the mud would suck them off your feet within a few hundred paces. If you managed to somehow keep them on, they would be disintegrating from the mud and slush by the end of the day, the leather gone soggy and useless.

He sat down on the edge of the bed and picked the shoes up, examining them, the fine stitching, blackened tanned tops and leather bottoms, and pewter buckles. Such simple things, and how many men were dying for lack of proper boots. Yet here these waited for him.

My papers?

There was a flash of panic. Frantic, he looked around the room. Where are the papers?

"So the dead have arisen!" Benjamin Rush stood at the open door.

He felt a flash of embarrassment as he sat there naked.

Rush came into the room, Michael his servant following, carrying a tray covered with a cloth.

Tom let the shoes drop and reached around, pulling the comforter around his naked waist.

"Now, no false modesty, Thomas," Rush

announced. "I was a doctor before I got swept into all this revolutionary madness."

Michael put the tray down on the sideboard, left the room, and returned a moment later with a smaller tray, this one with a steaming cup of coffee and a plump roll slathered with melted butter.

"Breakfast, sir," Michael announced.

"Breakfast?"

"My good man, you've been sick and sleeping for days. It's dawn. We wanted you to sleep as long as you could."

Days? What a luxury. There had been days over the last month when he had actually dozed off while marching, leaning on some unnamed comrade. Twenty minutes of sleep was a blessing.

"Go ahead, a light repast first, then more later downstairs," Rush said cheerfully.

Tom did not wait for formalities. He gulped the brew down after devouring the roll and sighed, the coffee helping to jolt him awake.

"Now let me look you over."

The ministrations of a doctor, one who many claimed was the finest in the Americas, was still something of a shock to him, for, after all, only a few years ago he was one of the nameless poor of London, where from womb to grave visit with an actual doctor was as rare as an audience with the king.

"Stand now and let me look you over."

He nervously stood up, staring past Rush as if he were not there. Again he felt nervousness and shame over his spindly, emaciated body, sagging with an exhaustion that no amount of sleep could wash away.

Rush looked at his scalp, poking at a couple of the bites, muttering to himself, then asked him to open his mouth and stick out his tongue.

Next his eyes, peeling a lid down and staring closely.

"Jaundice, for starters," he muttered.

He drew a silver stick from his jacket pocket, and poked around inside Tom's mouth. There were flashes of real pain.

"Your breath is as fetid as a goat's. I think a couple of those teeth will have to go. I'll arrange for a man who is quick and nearly painless."

Tom shuddered at the thought of that.

Rush thumped at his chest, putting an ear to his sunken ribs, poked hard just below his ribs at the right side.

"Liver swollen. Bile is backed up for certain. And your bowels?"

"What the hell do you think?" Tom retorted, feeling embarrassed.

"Dysentery perhaps, bloody fluxes, definitely worms."

Tom sighed, saying nothing.

Rush drew out his pocket watch. Gold, of the finest, one of the newer ones with a second hand, and taking his wrist he counted off the beats, then put his head to Tom's chest, listening.

"Pulse is quick and reedy. Your blood is thick, my friend, your heart labored, lungs rattling."

"What does that mean?"

"In a moment, Thomas."

He looked back at Michael and rattled off a few sentences in Latin, Michael nodding.

"What was that about," Tom asked testily as Michael went out of the room.

"I believe sleep to always be the best of cures and thus I have not attempted to physic you until now," Rush proclaimed.

"First step is a good purging, my friend. That army food has filled your gut with worms, and I propose we get them out now."

Michael returned a moment later carrying a beaker and offered it to Tom. He sniffed it and wrinkled his nose.

"What in hell?"

"Chamomile, some other herbs, my own special formula, a good strong purgative, for starters. You'll be on the chamber pot for a day or two and will feel better for it, I promise you. A good purging now, so drink it quickly!"

The doctor almost seemed happy with his diagnosis and what was to come.

"I already have the fluxes and the trots," Tom exclaimed, "and you propose to have me sit on a chamber pot for the next day after drinking that?"

"Must worm you. The entire army is wormy. And you certainly came back with your fair share."

He shook his head emphatically.

"No."

"I'm your doctor."

"I have no time to be squatting here for the next day, sir," Tom argued. "No."

Rush sighed.

"Feared you might try and postpone the inevitable. I'll let you go for a day or two, but not for longer."

Rush sighed, shaking his head, and went to the sideboard. There was the clatter of metal and he turned. Tom blanched.

"Oh God, not that," he sighed.

"No helping it Tom. I'll let you ignore my professional judgment with the worming, at least for the moment, but this treatment you cannot escape, nor will I let you. Agree to this and we will skip the deworming for now."

He suddenly felt weak, light-headed, and sat down on the edge of the bed.

"Just a few cups of bleeding, my good man, and you will feel like a new man. Your humors are all out of balance. Your blood is too thick and needs to be tapped off so that new blood will emerge and thin it out. It will also help to drain the fluid out of your lungs. Agree to that and I will not force you to be dewormed . . . for now."

Tom looked at the instrument half concealed in Rush's hand. A spring-loaded lancet, a palm-size brass metal box. Using a small key, like the type used to wind up a child's music box, Rush wound up the spring-loaded mechanism inside.

"Come now, my friend. A quick flick, hardly a pinch of pain, and in minutes I promise you, you'll feel like a new man."

He felt overwhelmed. There was no escape. Woodenly he watched as Michael stepped closer, half concealing a porcelain bowl. Rush already had hold of his arm, pressing up a dark blue vein, just below the inside of his elbow, thumb pressing above the vein, causing it to swell and distend.

"Ah, now, that's a good one."

With a deft swift motion, so fast that Tom

barely had time to react, Rush pushed the lancet box down hard against Tom's arm and flicked the release button on the side.

Tom flinched, but it was too late, Rush had him in a firm grip. The half dozen spring driven blades slashed down, cutting into his arm, opening the vein and then snicked back into the brass box.

Rush withdrew the torture device from Tom's arm. Already a rivulet of blood was welling up.

"There! See!" Rush exclaimed proudly. "Dark, slow-flowing, thick, and discolored, exactly my diagnosis."

"Michael."

His servant, sitting down by Tom's arm, took hold with strong calloused hands, turning the arm so that the blood, running thick and slow, dripped into the porcelain bowl.

"A good cut, sir," Michael exclaimed.

"Of course." Rush held the lancet box up for Thomas to see. "Finest instrument, imported from Germany. They make exceptional scientific instruments there, those Germans. Cost me six guineas, but worth it. No more clumsy stabbing with a scalpel that makes a mess of things. Good clean cuts from half a dozen blades that flash out like lightning, cut and withdraw until next time. Very fine workmanship."

Rush held it up proudly, examining it as if it was a treasured jewel.

"You know what I say to it," Paine retorted angrily.

"My friend, once this war is over and I am back to my regular profession, a new medicine will flourish here in America, free of the superstitions of the old world, and, I tell you, in our lifetimes we will see the banishment of most diseases. Instruments such as these . . ."

Rush put the mechanical lancet on the tray and patted Tom on the shoulder.

"Let's see now."

The porcelain cup was already half full with several ounces of blood. Rush took a second cup from the tray, deftly put it under the first that Michael was still holding and transferred them. Holding the first cup up, he sniffed it; using his silver probe he stirred the blood, then held the probe up and peered closely as droplets of blood fell away into the bowl. He stuck his fingers into the liquid, withdrew them, and rubbed his bloody fingers together, and to Tom's disbelief tasted it.

"Exactly as I expected," he announced cheerfully.

"Your humors are indeed out of balance. The blood is thick, dark, and filled with bile, which we all know is poisonous."

"Of course," Tom replied sarcastically.

"Michael, twelve ounces."

"Yes, sir."

"In Europe, most still hold that bleeding is the realm of the barber surgeon. But those prejudices are dying in this new world of ours. The doctor takes no shame in being the surgeon. If time permitted and you let me purge, I'd use some leeches as well. At your nodes, on your neck, under your arms and groin. They would do the trick. That and some cupping on your back. Just a day, Thomas, and you'll feel like a new man."

"No!" Tom snapped emphatically.

"Tom Paine, you are too valuable to all of us to take this lightly. You are on the edge of physical collapse from your humors, worms, and a clogged liver. We lose you and we lose much. You are worth your weight in gold to us at the moment."

Tom said nothing, staring at Michael, who was squeezing and kneading his arm to draw out a continual flow of blood.

"Worth your weight in gold," Rush said again.

Tom looked at him quizzically.

"I read the first chapter of your new work. It is safely in my office."

Tom felt a flash of anger. It was not yet

ready for others to read. It was a draft only, written in the field. He still wanted a few more days, now that he was here, to polish his thoughts, to rewrite freshly and cleanly so there would be no mistakes with the printers. It still needed work.

"How did you find it?"

Rush blushed slightly.

"You left it on the table in the parlor. Michael here saw it, and placed it where I could read it. I pray you do not object."

Tom thought about the breach of etiquette and then shook his head. When he first came to these shores Dr. Rush was the man who had personally ordered him taken off the ship anchored out in the harbor, crew and passengers dying of the typhoid. This was the man, who, based solely on one letter from Benjamin Franklin, had opened his house, given him comfort, and literally saved his life. He could begrudge him nothing . . . not even this intrusion into his work.

"Michael will finish your bleeding," Rush announced. "I have more than a few letters to write in the meantime. Congress, as you must know, has fled."

"I saw that when I arrived in town."

"Michael will finish your treatment," and he looked over at his servant. "I would prefer a full sixteen ounces but if you can coax out twelve, that will be sufficient for today."

Michael nodded, not replying, attention focused on the steady flow of blood from Paine's arm.

"Once done here, Michael will help you dress, then Emily will set out breakfast for you. There is much to talk about, Tom Paine."

Rush patted him on the shoulder.

"In an hour, with those humors at least partially driven out, you will feel like a new man."

Rush left the room.

"Just a bit more, sir," Michael announced.

"Take your time," Paine replied, the sarcasm in his voice obvious. He could not help but recall the leeches who had attended his first wife, draining every shilling he had as they bled her and bled her again, and still she had died.

"Sir?"

"Yes, Michael."

"I read your words."

"And?"

"Well, sir," and beneath his dusky complexion Thomas could see the man redden.

"I only wish I could hoist a musket after reading that."

"You read, Michael?"

"Of course, sir," Michael replied, a tone of pride in his voice. "I was born in Barbados. My mistress, she married a man from Maryland, and I and my wife were brought here along with her. She died along with her first baby. Guess us being around was too much a reminder, and her husband freed us, said it was his wife's dying wish. I came here and Dr. Rush gave me a job. Local Quaker folk taught me to read, and the doctor, well, he made me his assistant for things like this."

Michael nodded down to Tom's arm, which he still held tightly, rubbing the vein with his thumbs, helping to push the blood out.

Thomas looked down at the stream of blood dripping from his arm.

"May I ask a question, sir?"

"Anything, Michael."

"Those words. Do they apply to me as well?"

"What?"

"All the words I've been hearing, about us being created equal and what you wrote. General George Washington himself sat in this house more than once last year talking of such things, while his slave sat in the kitchen with me, listening through the open door. Do such things mean all men, or just some men?"

Thomas gazed at him, unable to reply. He had seen the occasional black man in London but never actually spoken to one until he took ship to America. Until then they were an abstract concept, defined in his mind as sufferers in this world the same as he and so many others who suffered under the rule of kings and those born to aristocracy.

Here in America, though? The city teemed with them, some slaves, some free. When the armies came up from the South and passed through the city on the way to the war, many in the ranks were black men, or men who looked to have some African blood, some obviously servants, more than a few, though, with muskets on their shoulders. Others labored at the docks, in the taverns, again some slaves, others free men.

He did not know how to answer. All logic told him that this man who was holding his arm would bleed the same as he; Michael breathed air, loved, hated, dreamed, and would die the same as he. But equal as well? It was fine for them to stand on the volley line, to lean their backs into moving artillery, to cook what little food the army had, but did that mean they were equal?

He did not know what to say. He knew

what was in his heart, but in this strange country of thirteen different nations, some were more than emphatic that slavery would always exist here and to press otherwise would cause the alliance to shatter.

"Your wife?" Thomas asked, now uncomfortable.

"Dead."

Michael said the word coldly, clearly to cut the conversation short, a subject he did not wish to take further.

There was a long uneasy silence between the two as Michael kneaded his arm. The cup was now filled, and he nodded. "That should do it."

He put the cup on the tray and bound Tom's arm tight.

"Now, sir, let's get you dressed."

The tone of minutes before, of two men talking, was gone. Michael was again the servant, kneeling to help Tom put on his breeches, hose, shoes. Bracing him when Tom first stood up and felt for a moment as if he were going to faint.

Jacket on, Michael brushed him down and stepped back.

"Now, sir, you look a gentleman again."

Tom shot him a cold glance.

"Gentleman be damned, but at least I feel warm."

Michael stepped back and opened the door.

"I believe the doctor awaits you for breakfast, sir."

"Michael, my name is Thomas."

Michael did not reply.

"Michael, I am sorry. I did not know how to answer you," he paused. "Yet. In a way I was a slave, too."

"I know that. But no one could ever guess that now." Michael fell silent and turned slightly to look at the mirror.

The action struck Thomas like a bolt. I can be cleaned up, shaved, clothed in new broadcloth and look a gentleman. No matter what this man does in his life, others just merely need to see his color, as he himself now saw it as he gazed into the mirror.

Michael led the way downstairs into the dining room. Rush was at the end of the table, leaning back in his chair, documents piled high. He was holding one up so that the morning light shone on it, gazing intently until Tom approached.

Sighing, Rush tossed the document on the pile.

"Somehow it was easier when it was all just talk in the taverns," Rush sighed. "Now this! Paper and more paper. Bills, appeals, pleas for office, claims and counterclaims."

He pushed the pile back. "Damn them all." He motioned for Tom to sit by his side.

Even as Tom sat, the door into the kitchen opened and a serving girl came out carrying a tray with steaming coffee, followed by another bearing plates weighed down with thin slices of fried ham, and, of all things, omelets, actual omelets from eggs, stuffed with mushrooms, thin slices of bacon, and even chopped green peppers.

The sight of it almost made Tom weep. His thoughts flashed back to the night in Newark, to the boy who had brought in a couple of greasy carp, and how all had drooled in anticipation as the fish was divided, each man getting a piece. He had been grateful to receive the head.

Strangely, his stomach rebelled at the sight and scent of the food; the room too confining and warm after months in the field. He felt light-headed, nauseous.

"It will pass," Rush announced, leaning over, taking Tom's wrist and feeling for his pulse. "The humors of your body are readjusting after the bleeding. Now eat slowly and you will feel better."

Tom did as ordered, the two eating in silence while Rush returned to scanning the papers beside his plate. Meal finished, he personally refilled Thomas's cup with coffee.

"Now tell me all," Rush announced. "Start with the day you left here."

Thomas sat back, staring off, sipping his coffee, recounting what he had seen. The high hopes of late summer, then defeat after defeat and his regiment disintegrating and finally just running off. Wandering northward to fall in with General Greene. The debacles he had witnessed, the nightmare of the retreat across Jersey and then, finally, back to Philadelphia.

The clock in the parlor chimed through two hours as he spoke, Rush asking pointed questions at times.

Several times he focused on Washington. Did he make a mistake in his deployment along the Palisades of New Jersey? Why had they been given up without a fight? How did the men in the ranks feel about him? Then finally to General Charles Lee.

"More than a few say Lee is a pissant," Tom replied. "Rumor has it that he is loitering in the north, waiting for Washington to be crushed so he can take command."

"He won't now," and Rush pointed to the pile of paperwork. "A dispatch has come in that Lee was captured early this morning."

"And his army? Thomas exclaimed.

"Good God, that's several thousand men."

"Oh, they are well. Lee decided to bed down in some tavern miles away from the army and was surprised and captured by a British patrol. So he is no longer in the fight."

"Fine with me," Thomas replied. "In fact, I think his removal will improve our chances of winning. He was a troublemaker and a conspirator who wanted General Washington to fail. Without him we can focus on the British and not worry so much about plots in our own lines."

Rush said nothing for a moment.

"I've been asked by Congress to stay on here, to be a liaison to the army. I'm to observe and report."

"Craven of them to run like that," Thomas snapped.

Rush smiled. "I don't think it appropriate to reply to you about that, Thomas Paine. Heaven knows what you might write next."

"A free press, isn't it?"

"If we can find anyone to print you."

"I tried McKinney. He threatened to burn it."

"Half this town is just waiting to hang out the Union Jack. Every day there are rumors that Cornwallis will be across the river or Howe will sail up the Delaware. And if that is true, my friend, we'd better pack quickly, for we are on their list. When you passed through Princeton, did you happen to see my father-in-law?"

"Who, sir?"

"My wife's father. Witherspoon. His mansion is just outside of the village."

"I don't recall."

"He went over to the British," Rush announced.

"Didn't he sign the Declaration?"

"He did and now he is with them. I've been told he was fearful they would burn his home and hang him. Damn him. The first of the signers to change his coat. So far, the only one."

As he spoke he lowered his voice, obviously concerned that others in the house might hear.

"Your wife, sir?"

"She is safe here, but too ashamed to appear before others for the moment. But if we are forced to flee, her father's actions will assure her safety."

Tom could not reply.

"Now to work!" Rush announced. He pushed his chair back and led Thomas into his office. There, resting on a desk, were the tattered, water-stained pages Thomas had carried across New Jersey. He raced to them to pick them up, almost embracing them like a lover. They were safe.

"You have written with a pen of fire," Rush announced.

Tom looked back at him gratefully.

"But the scribbling, my man, is hard to read in places."

"Try writing in the middle of the night in a driving storm with only a candle and a half-frozen bottle of ink."

Rush gestured toward the desk. "I've laid out fresh paper for you. May I suggest you rewrite clearly. If you are too tired, I can call in Michael, and you can dictate."

Thomas shook his head. "The work is mine."

"Fine then."

Feeling uncomfortable when Rush did not continue, Tom sat down in his chair. The desk was neat, an ink pot of silver, quills cut and laid out, paper of good quality. He sat and stared at the tools of his new trade, and was aware that Rush was standing behind him. Watching.

"Go ahead, my friend. Go to work."

"Not with you here," Thomas said sharply. "I can't write with you staring over my shoulder like this. Everyone seems to think they can . . ."

A bit crestfallen, Rush nodded. "I'll go

see to some details. It might take awhile, but I think we can find someone with the courage to print this."

"And paper. We'll need paper. McKinney said nearly every printer in Philadelphia is out of stock."

Rush took the order as if he were the servant. He left the room, closing the door.

Thomas looked down at the fresh sheets of paper, and at the tattered first copy, water stains having blurred some of the words. But he did not need to be reminded.

He began to write.

Styner and Matthews, Philadelphia
December 19, 1776

A printer's office was familiar territory to Tom. It was where he had first found his new profession in America, as one of the editors of the *Pennsylvania Journal.* It was here that the first copies of *Common Sense* had been printed. Styner and Matthews, at least, still had some nerve left to them, and after days of cajoling by Rush, who had finally sent out Michael and others to scour the city and nearby villages for paper of good stock. Rush had purchased the paper at a fair price with his own money, not with continentals but with silver Dutch dollars.

All was now ready and Thomas felt a

quivering inside. He had taken off his fine jacket, put on a printer's smock, and sat at the proofing table, reading the type as it was set, a rare skill he had mastered, to read the raised letters backward as they were set into the chase, properly blocked and locked in place. To miss a letter or space meant having to take the entire page out, unlock the chase, move type to replace the mistake, and avoid creating new mistakes. A good typesetter and reader was a man worth much, and he had mastered the skill.

Rush stood behind him, and Thomas did not object to his watching him.

There was a feeling of nervous anticipation in the room. Thomas finally leaned back, nodding. "It's ready." There was a choke to his voice.

A printer's apprentice carefully lifted the heavy form, carried it to the press, and set it in place; Chris Matthews, the co-owner of the firm, himself ensuring that it was locked in firmly. With his own hand he ran the ink roller over the type, stepped back while the apprentice placed a sheet of paper atop it and another boy leaned into the lever that lowered the platen. Too light and the imprint would not take. Too hard and the paper would warp, the raised letters punching through.

Tom watched with rapt attention, Rush by his side, as Chris Matthews leaned on the press handle for a moment and then released it, plate with paper atop it sliding out from under the press. Tom stepped forward and peeled the sheet back, lifting it off swiftly but carefully so that the fresh ink would not smear and held it up to the light streaming in through the large windows all printers tried to have in their press room to make reading easier.

The imprint was dark, always the case with the very first sheet. He scanned the lines swiftly. A couple of lines were slightly off, drifting a few fractions of an inch downward, not braced in tight enough, one typo, but not enough to stop now. Rush tried to edge closer in, but Thomas did not release the sheet. For a minute this was his and his alone — the journal of suffering, of agony, of the dying of a cause before it was even properly born. This page spoke of all that, and more: perhaps he could breathe life back into it.

He finished the last line, looked at Chris Matthews, and nodded. "Print it" was all he could say.

He reached up and clipped the sheet to one of dozens of strings that ran the length of the room, from just below the ceiling, drying lines where the fresh sheets would hang until the ink set.

Until this moment he had been consumed with a deep fear that had been with him since the first night in Newark. That he might be killed. In itself that was almost inconsequential now, for he had seen so much of death these last few months that he had come to reason that if such were his fate, he could not choose better company. His fear was that, if they did roll him into a grave, those precious sheets of paper would molder with him.

Some inner voice told him that maybe this now was truly the one moment in his life that he had lived for. Whatever he had written before, or would ever write, would never match what he had written *here,* the first sheet now hanging on the drying line, a second sheet going up beside the first, and then a third.

They cannot kill me now, he thought. One can throw a single sheet into a flame and it is lost. In the days when he and Rush had wandered the streets, arguing with printers, struggling to find paper, he would obsessively dwell on the only two copies extant, the original stained sheets and the more neatly printed version resting on the typesetter's table.

Philadelphia had turned. Men like those who had tried to lure Putnam into a dark corner and murder him now openly wandered the streets, taunting and spreading rumors and threats. Houses were shuttered, shops closed. There was the inexpressible sense, like the feeling one had on a hot summer day, of a storm approaching. But which way would this storm break?

Might he and Rush have returned to find the house looted, the papers gone? That had so haunted him, when at night he retired to the room Rush had given him, he took the original with him, rolled up in his pack, ready at hand if he needed to flee.

Sleep had come hard. When it did, again the nightmares, the mud, snow, and staggering forward, step by step, as if in hell, and this was his fate forever, with his mouth sealed, his hands gone, unable to write and then speak aloud what he had written.

Now the nightmare was dissolving into print before his eyes.

Ten sheets now hung from the drying line, then fifteen and twenty.

Chris Matthews, unable to contain himself any longer, went to the first sheet and reached up to unclip it from the line. He looked over at Thomas as if seeking permission.

It no longer belongs to me, Thomas realized. I did not write it for me. I must let it go.

He nodded approval.

Matthews took the page down and walked over the window and held it up to the light. His eyes scanned back and forth, and Thomas could see a brightness to them.

Matthews cleared his throat: "*The American Crisis,*" he announced.

"These are the times that try men's souls: The summer soldier and the sunshine patriot will, in this crisis, shrink from the service of his country; but he that stands it NOW, deserves the love and thanks of man and woman."

Matthews's voice began to rise. The workers in the room fell silent, looking over at him. Matthews holding the sheet up high, cleared his voice and spoke as if delivering an oration.

"Tyranny, like hell, is not easily conquered; yet we have this consolation with us, that the harder the conflict, the more glorious the triumph. What we obtain too cheap, we esteem too lightly: — 'Tis dearness only that gives every thing its value. Heaven knows how to set a proper price upon its goods; and it would be strange indeed, if so celestial an article as FREEDOM should not be highly rated."

He looked over at Thomas, eyes wet. Thomas stood silent.

"Merciful God," Matthews whispered. "We'll hang for this, but the hell with the bloody bastards."

Thomas looked over at the printer, who gazed at him fiercely for an instant, and turned back to his typesetting. Printer's assistants at the press were rolling on ink, laying down paper, sliding the form under the press, printed sheet emerging, an apprentice peeling the sheet off and taking it to a drying line, passing it to another boy on a ladder who clipped it up.

Twenty sheets had doubled, and were doubling again.

Rush, silent, scanned down through the rest of the chapter, lips moving silently.

Another sheet was taken down, and then another, Matthews looking over his work, commenting on the need to reset because several of the lines were slipping, but not to do it until the next form was ready to be printed.

At a break in his work, he came over to Thomas and clasped his hand, both of them with hands blackened by printer's ink.

"Thank you," Matthews said softly. "See you in hell once those bloody lobsterbacks march in. If they're going to burn this shop, they'll have to kill me first."

"I'll stand with you when the time comes, my friend."

Matthews shook his head. "I just print this. You're the one who thinks it out, Tom Paine. No, I want you out of this city so you can keep on writing."

He saw the others were looking at him, nodding. He swallowed his emotions. He couldn't speak.

Rush went over to the drying lines and pulled down a dozen copies and rolled them up.

"I'm going north to inspect the army," Rush announced. "I'm taking these with me."

He looked around the room.

"The first copy goes directly into the hands of General Washington. I want it read to every man who is under arms and enduring hell this day. I want it read. Keep at it, Matthews. Keep at it."

He reached into his pocket and drew out a small purse.

"When you run out of paper, use this to buy more. I don't care how much. Just find the paper and keep at it."

Matthews took the purse but seemed almost reluctant to do so. He tossed it onto

411

a table and returned to supervising the press as another sheet came off, and then another and another.

Rush came up close to Paine and extended his hand. Thomas looked down at his own blackened fingers and palm. Rush laughed and grasped it anyhow.

"Thomas Paine. I think your words just might save a country," Rush announced, and, turning, he left the shop. As he departed Thomas noticed Michael standing in the corner, opening the door for Rush as he left. Their gazes locked for a moment. Michael nodded, as if in salute as he followed Rush out the door.

The printers hardly noticed Rush's departure. A hundred or more sheets were now up, one of the apprentices beginning to take the first ones down, stacking them up, ready to be bundled and carted out to street corners to be sold for a penny . . . or for five dollars continental.

Paine took one of the sheets and wandered to a far corner of the room, placing the sheet on a table. He knew Matthews's habits and went into a storage room, moved a few crates, found what he wanted and came out. He sat down at the table, gazing at the sheet of paper.

Matthews looked over at him, and for

once did not complain as Thomas Paine uncorked the bottle of rum, held it up, and took several long swallows.

He looked down at his words. No, not his words, the words of the men he had marched with, the words of men he had seen die, the words of a few, a gallant few who still believed.

He drained the bottle in minutes, lowered his head onto the sheet of paper, rich with the scent of fresh ink, filled with the dreams of his soul, and went to sleep.

Thomas Paine slept through the day, while a hundred sheets became a thousand, and then a thousand more. Boys raced out of the shop shouting that they carried Paine's new work, as crowds gathered together at street corners to read his words aloud, and men looked one to another, men who but days before felt defeated and beaten, and asked within their hearts, What shall I do now?

What must I do now that I have read these truths?

CHAPTER TWELVE

Trenton, New Jersey
8:10 A.M. December 26, 1776

The sleet all but concealed the column of men rushing down the slope.

Consumed with the passion of the moment, General George Washington could hardly contain himself. The advance company, a commingling of Virginians, the unfortunate and misguided scouts who had raided the day before, and his own headquarters company, started to run ahead of him, disappearing into the storm.

Behind him the advance regiments of Greene's men began to surge ahead as well, spreading out from the road.

It was as if the storm itself was driving them. Something long pent up, like a hunting pack unleashed for the kill, had been cut loose.

He spurred his horse, which nearly lost its footing on the ice-covered road, regained its feet, and broke into a fast trot. He caught up with his men in the advance guard. The storm with its varied pattern of eddies and swirls of snow, sleet and freezing rain, parted for a moment, granting a glimpse of a farmhouse several hundred yards ahead. Smoke whipped from the chimneys in the unrelenting gale.

"Hessian outpost!" one of the men from Anderson's raiding party shouted. "They got twenty or more men inside!"

As if the outburst could be heard, the front door of the house swung open, a blue uniform appearing, walking out onto the porch. Even from a distance Washington could sense that the man was looking toward them.

The lone Hessian stood for long seconds, gazing in their direction, not sure whether he was seeing ghosts or men, wondering if they were friends, enemies, or merely an illusion created by the storm.

At last he realized it was what had seemed impossible in this weather. These were the Americans. The man turned and darted back into the house.

Washington felt a wild surge of hope. If the enemy had already been aroused and on guard, it would not have been a lone man gazing at them and then turning to spread the alarm. Out of the snow, sleet, and wind-driven mist, a solid battle line would have been astride the road, ready to deliver a volley and then break his column apart before it could deploy for battle. Now one lone man had seen them and run into the outpost.

Could it possibly be? How could it be after such a night of mishaps, disasters, and follies? Had God preserved the surprise despite everything? All the anxiety, the pent-up fear that had torn at his soul throughout this longest of nights, began to melt away.

Would he meet his own death this morning? He had weighed that long ago and found it next to wholly unimportant. Surely Martha would suffer, and for that he would feel infinite regret. But, as for himself, victory or death was no mere watchword. It was his code of honor for this day. Either victory or death. Paine was right. This is the trial of my soul and of America's soul, and I am resolved to face it.

If the Revolution, this country, is destined to die this morning, my own death will be a fitting end, and a fitting reward for failure. His fear, his anguish, was for all those who had trusted in him, and had followed him throughout this endless night of agony.

"Merciful God," he whispered. "Can it be true?"

He was now up alongside the men in the advance; they were running full out, some falling on the ice-slick road, muskets clattering.

"Take them!" Washington roared. "Don't let a man escape! Take them!"

For an instant he was tempted to charge forward with sword leveled. He had let similar passion seize him in the past.

I am in command of this army. I must see to my duty. The men charging know now what is to be done.

He looked over his shoulder. The storm concealed the head of Greene's column.

There could still be a fight here. This forward sentry might be only a lure to bring him in on the rush, a trap still hidden in the swirling snow. I must get the artillery forward, must see to Greene's men.

Slowly, he reined in so his mount would not slip, turning to start up the slope to get Greene and Knox. He caught a glimpse of Billy Lee gazing at him, his servant nodding his head in agreement, without comment.

The advance company continued its charge toward the lone house. From the open doorway he saw men spilling out, blue uniforms. Definitely Hessians, but they came out in confused order, some trying to pull on overcoats, a man falling over on the slick steps, one waving a sword, his commands swept away by the howling wind.

His own men, at the sight of the enemy, let loose a wild cry. It was not a measured cheer, not the usual "huzzah"; instead it carried with it a spine-chilling effect, like the mad raging of wolves at the scent of blood.

The head of his attacking column slowed, spreading out into a ragged line. He wanted to turn back to order them to press the charge in, but going back would waste precious seconds. He continued up the slope while looking over his shoulder.

Puffs of smoke, a volley by his men. Range too long at seventy-five yards or more, especially in this storm, more than a few of the muskets misfiring. Others fell into the volley line, shouldering past men reloading or clearing out of their pans wet powder that had misfired, wiping off flints and the facing of frizzens to try to trigger a hot spark, then fumbling for fresh cartridges, tearing them open to prime their pans and try again.

A second volley, this one stronger than the first. The smoke and the sleet and the snow made it hard to see whether it had done any damage to the score or so of the enemy who had piled out of the house.

Muskets of the Hessians were leveled in reply, flashes of fire, Washington thought he heard a musket ball whiz past, but none of his men dropped. In the past, often just one volley would stall a line of his men, riveting them in place. But not this time. Seeing the enemy had fired without effect, the advance company charged without orders to do so. They knew the cruel formula: the Hessians could reload in fifteen seconds. Fifteen seconds, but if in those fifteen seconds they could close in, the fighting would be hand to hand. And in their frenzy and anger, they sought, indeed relished and needed, such a contest.

He reined to a full stop to watch, half expecting that a column of Hessian infantry would suddenly emerge out of the storm, the confusion of the enemy coming out of the farmhouse a ruse to lure him in, that Hessian artillery would be rolled out from behind the home or barn, slashing his men with a deadly blast . . .

Not today! There were no such cunning traps waiting for his arrival.

The Hessians in front of the house, to a man, turned and ran, several of them throwing aside their muskets. One man, breeches only half up, as if caught so by surprise, while relieving himself, fell to his knees and held hands up high, imploringly, for mercy.

He watched, incredulous at the sight of it. Never had he witnessed this. Not at Long Island, Manhattan, Harlem . . . Never had he seen the back of a Hessian . . . and now they were running. The panic of the Hessians was real. God in Heaven, the surprise, so unexpected, so unbelievable minutes ago, just might be true!

He looked up the road, straight into the eye of the storm, and out of it rode generals Greene and Knox. Behind them the column was advancing at the double. Men bent over, running as best they could on the ice-blanketed road, an unstoppable juggernaut racing down the slope of a mountain.

"The surprise is complete! We have them!" Washington roared. "Their advance outpost has fled. We have them by the grace of God! Advance at the run, boys!"

"By column or line?" Greene cried.

"Keep them moving! No time to deploy," Washington cried. "General Greene, keep your men moving!"

He turned to Henry. "Now's your time, Knox. Bring your guns up at the gallop and stay with me!"

The head of the column swept past him, and he edged to the side of the road, standing tall in the stirrups, sword raised high.

"Victory or death! We have them! Stay with your officers! Forward now, forward!"

Turning, astride his horse, the tallest man on the field, he led them into the battle for Trenton.

"Peter, a cartridge! Give me a damn cartridge!"

Jonathan looked down at his musket, frizzen flipped up. He had forgotten to change the powder. The sight that greeted him was a black oozing puddle of wet powder and ice. Frantically he tried to wipe it clean with trembling hands.

At last a chance to shoot, to actually fight back, and his damn musket misfires!

Peter had successfully fired off a round and was screamingly wildly, so caught up in the frenzy of the moment he ignored Jonathan's pleas.

Men shoved in around them, elbowing Jonathan aside.

"Take aim, boys!"

He couldn't see who was giving the command.

"Fire!"

A couple of dozen muskets rattled off, and the sound heightened his frustration and rage.

A flash thought. Strange. Fifty years from now my grandchildren will ask me about this. I will not be able to claim I fired the first shots of the Battle of Trenton. "I stood there with a soaking wet musket and did nothing."

"Charge them! Charge the bastards!"

Men shoved against him, pushing him forward. He abandoned trying to clear his flint and pan, moving blindly, unable to see Peter, following the back of a man; it looked like the friendly sergeant. Men around him pushed forward as if possessed, and he joined them. The hours of agony of this endless night, in fact the days, weeks, and months of agony, had turned at last. They were striking back!

"Here it comes!"

A second later he heard the volley and flinched, but no one fell, and those around him truly began to scream with a wild, animal-like roar.

Jonathan tried to give voice. He couldn't. His lungs were afire. It was hard enough even to keep his footing as he ran with the others. They reached the house the Hessians had occupied but a few minutes before. Through the open door Jonathan saw a roaring fire and a table set with food. The temptation was to go inside, grab a biscuit, a piece of bacon, and collapse by the fire, but someone was shouting for them to press forward.

"Come on lads! Drive the bastards. Drive 'em!"

The chase was on, and leaving the house behind, he joined in.

The ragged line, with men from several different units, raced down the road. He saw Peter, angled in to be at his side, and wanted to ask again for a dry cartridge but didn't have the breath to do so as he struggled to keep up. Sensation was returning to his feet, which had gone numb again after crossing Jacob's Creek, so that each step was an agony. Someone ahead of him fell. He thought for an instant the man was shot, but even as he ran past him the soldier was half up, cursing the ice.

He was aware again of the storm. It seemed as if rain, sleet, and snow were all falling at the same time, driven nearly horizontal by the wind out of the north, now at their backs.

Another flash of thought; in the eyes of the Hessians, it would be our advantage. In his lessons on ancient battles, the Greeks and Romans always had wanted the wind and the sun at their back in a fight.

Occasionally he glimpsed the retreating

Hessians. He had never faced them directly in battle, but he had seen their handiwork, the bayoneting and clubbing of prisoners, had heard of their arrogance, their mocking disdain. And now they were running. The sight filled him with glee, driving him forward in spite of his burning lungs, which labored like tattered bellows for each ragged breath.

For a few precious minutes he forgot his own ills. The enemy was running hard, disappearing for an instant behind a curtain of snow, then visible again.

The ground was familiar — the Vanderhaven farm, the front door open, no one visible. The road took a slight curve to the right.

"The town, it's just ahead!" Peter cried. "Not a hundred yards!"

Peter was right. The ground sloped off sharply here, and in the gloom Jonathan could see the outline of the houses and buildings where this road split into King and Queen streets.

And his home was one of those houses.

The Hessians they had been pursuing were turning, an officer trying to form them into some semblance of a line. A trickle of men were coming up the street, some of them trying to pull on overcoats, several still in their underbreeches and barefoot.

"Volley fire, boys!"

It sounded like the sergeant.

Men slowed, reaching into cartridge boxes, bringing out cartridges, several of them cursing, throwing the sodden mass to the ground. Jonathan came to Peter's side.

"A cartridge, just give me a damn cartridge!"

Peter, working his ramrod, paused, cursed Jonathan, but reached down and pulled one out. It felt solid and dry in Jonathan's hand. He placed one end in his mouth, holding it thus while flipping the lock of his musket open, wiping away the gummy mess of wet powder with his thumb. He tried to wipe the flint clean with his forefinger, his hand so numb that he didn't even realize it when the sharpened flint cut the finger nearly to the bone and blood spilled out.

Tearing the cartridge open, he filled the pan.

"Take aim!"

He tried to keep up, to close the lock, hoping the charge inside the barrel was still dry.

"Fire!"

The volley rang out, startling him. The men around him were screaming curses, shouting their defiance, their hatred, and their rage at the enemy, who had turned at the edge of the village.

He snapped his own frizzen shut and shouldered his musket while others around him were still reloading.

He was shaking so hard . . . He would never admit it was fear, but he could not even hope to aim properly. Besides, the storm was kicking up snow and sleet around him. The enemy was again like shadows. He pointed his weapon toward the Hessians arrayed not fifty yards off and squeezed the trigger.

There was a flash of fire and then smoke in the pan of his musket . . . and then nothing.

Blind rage filled him. His musket was useless. The ball would have to be extracted, powder cleaned out. Impossible in this fight.

The Hessians fired a ragged volley back. In the confusion, the panic, and the gusting storm, not a single round hit anyone, and that triggered jeers from the men around him. So much for the feared Hessian volley fire! Men to either side of Jonathan finished loading, leveled their weapons, and fired again, and he saw men in the Hessian line going down.

"Again, boys. Hit them again!"

Unable to fire, Jonathan stood there, having to double over for a moment as a coughing seized him.

Coming back upright, he saw where several of the enemy had reloaded. One of them was pointing his musket straight at him.

At least I can do something, Jonathan thought. "He that stands it now . . . ," and he stood defiant, not cringing as the enemy musket, from a range of less than forty yards, ignited.

For Colonel Rall remembering home as he lay half awake was a rare indulgence. His custom across so many decades of service was to be up an hour before dawn. This day he had drifted off after deciding to shed the damp weight of his jacket. Potts's servant had come in and piled more wood on the fire to take the chill out of the room and hung the jacket by the fire to dry.

So he had drifted off, half awake, half asleep, the first light of dawn rousing him for a moment. It was time to be up, to have his men fall out for morning parade, but the storm still raged outside, slashing against the windowpanes. He knew that barely a man had slept, having been repeatedly rousted out by the alarms. In his own exhausted state, he decided to let them, and himself, have an hour more of rest. Unlike proper Christians, many of those in this wretched land did not hold to the custom of celebrating Christmas; some, such as the hard-shelled peasants of New England, even asserted it was a pagan holiday and did not observe it at all. His men, however, had stood to arms throughout Christmas Day.

He had half assumed it would be like these people to disrupt a day that most held sacred, and thus he had ordered the men to stand at arms, nothing to drink other than the standard issue, which in this land was not even proper brandy but instead a vile brew made from their corn, and some rum at least halfway decent that had been seized in New York and brought down by supply wagons with his troops.

He thought of that city, settled by the Dutch. They were almost German, and thus a fairly decent sort who were more than glad to be shed of the rebels.

Most of the British army was back there, and their Christmas had been, without a doubt, a time of pleasure, filled with toasts, good food, and warmth, with admiring young ladies of the town joining in.

And we are stuck here, at the edge of the wilderness, in this squalid little village, harassed by damn cowards.

It was some thanks for loyal service. He

wondered for the hundredth time why it was that the German troops were sent to the forward edge while the British, whose war this really was, garrisoned the towns at the rear. At least Princeton, where several regiments were now lodged, boasted a semblance of a college and what in this country passed for a library, with several mansions to serve as proper headquarters. Cornwallis rested in Amboy and word had come that he had been granted leave to return to England in thanks for his service. His headquarters had undoubtedly enjoyed Christmas Day as well, for as always British headquarters were well stocked with the best of food, wine even, and ladies, some of dubious virtue, others perhaps of more refinement who could be seen in company at a social occasion without inspiring degrading rumors afterward. He half suspected that, when the time came, it would be the British who went home first, while his own prince hired his unit out for another year of service as garrison troops, unless, with luck, another war began with the Austrians or the French, or, better yet, the great Frederick decided to go on campaign again and rallied some of the various German states to his side.

That thought bothered him. It would be

our luck that, even so, we would be stuck here and miss the chance for glory on a proper battlefield, and gone, too, would be his opportunity to rise to the rank of general before retiring. But we are here, the British are safe and secure, and so my prince has ordered it, and I have always obeyed.

It triggered a memory of boyhood, when his father was an officer, garrisoned in a town he could not remember, a memory of another Christmas dinner, the men about the table recalling a battle of the war of the Spanish Succession in which his father had distinguished himself as a young lieutenant. He retained a warm memory of that snowy night, filled with anticipation of the ceremonial parade of Christmas Day for the pleasure of the Prussian king, with sweet-meats and candy for the children afterward.

He had drifted in thought too long, a sense of duty telling him it was time to rise, to call for poor overworked Münchasen to send word down the street for the men to finish their breakfasts, don uniforms, and muster. But after such a damn miserable night of alarms and false alarms triggered by such maddening cowards, it could wait for a few more minutes.

He closed his eyes.

A distant rattle. Was it the storm?

He half opened his eyes.

A shout of alarm?

Then another rattle. It was musketry. Close.

Damn them! Damn all of them. Another infuriating raid.

He threw back the comforter, bare feet hitting the cold floor, and rubbed the sleep from his eyes.

And then the door was flung open, a wide-eyed Münchasen rushing in.

"The rebels."

"Yes, I know, damn it. How many?"

"Their army, sir! It looks like their entire army!"

"Colonel Knox! Bring your guns up here!"

Knox was at the lead, pointing the way to a fair rise of ground that Washington was indicating, the ground sloping up from the center of Trenton a hundred yards away.

It was ideal for a gun position. Washington reined in by Knox's side, incredulous at the folly, the utter folly, of the enemy he faced. Such a rise of ground should have a redoubt. A simple fortification here, properly made with moat and wall, garrisoned by fifty men and two guns, would have stopped this attack in its tracks. Instead, it was wide-open ground offering a prospect of the entire village.

The sight of it left him with mixed feelings — absolute delight and more confidence in his agents, who had so craftily scouted the ground and reported it to be unguarded, and increased rage that his enemies held him in such contempt that they could not bother to make an effort to take so basic a precaution.

In a few minutes they would learn the folly of that contempt.

The first two guns came on, horses slipping, breaking through the crust of ice, gaining footing; gun crews urged them on, some actually risking a crushed foot or leg as they leaned into the wheels to help the animals up the last dozen feet of the slope.

There was a crackling roar off to the right. Washington turned, facing the sound. A definite volley. Whose?

Then he saw them. Again he wondered if somehow God's hand was in play at this moment. For the wind had shifted more to the north-west, bringing with it a momentary clearing.

Sullivan's men!

Deployed into a regiment-wide front, they were sweeping down either side of the River Road, driving a scattering of panicked Hessian pickets and guards before them.

"Load solid shot!" It was Knox. "Make sure your linstocks are lit and glowing!"

Washington turned back.

The first two guns, six-pounders, were being unlimbered. Two gunnery sergeants were swinging their linstocks over their heads. The linstocks were nothing more than short poles with slow-burning match tapers attached to them. The ends of the saltpeter-encrusted tapers on the brass cross trees at the end of the linstocks glowed red hot when whirled about, in spite of the storm. The sergeants had done their jobs well, protecting the precious flames, stowing burning tapers throughout the long march. They were ready. The men turned their backs to the storm, holding the linstocks close in against their bodies to protect the glowing tapers.

Loading crews were tearing open the limber chests, pulling out wooden containers, each one sealed tight, then breaking them open to grab at one-pound powder charges wrapped in a serge bag. With the sergeants hovering over them they ran the powder charges to the bores of their guns.

Slamming them in, they stepped back, and rammers pushed the charges home. Boys, bringing up the six-pound shot, placed them in the barrels to be rammed down in turn, everything now topped with wadding to keep all in place.

Horns filled with fine-grain powder were uncorked and upended at the touchholes in the breeches of the guns. Behind the guns, Knox paced, then squatted, sighting along the barrels, and shouting for one crew to drop their elevation.

Washington gave a quick glance toward the town when for a moment it was clearly visible. Sullivan was pushing down from the northwest, trading volleys with a thin line of Hessians at the very edge of the village. The enemy was already giving back.

Trenton was not a big town. The two main streets, King and Queen, starting at the end of the road his army had struggled along, spread out at slightly divergent angles, and swept down toward the Delaware. Other streets intersected them at right angles. Just above the river there was a small open square with several side streets radiating out. The distance from where he stood to the river was not much more than six hundred yards, and for a few moments he could almost see it.

He remembered it well from having just marched through it three weeks past, seeking the refuge of the far bank of the Delaware. A barracks from the French and

Indian wars loomed high on one of the side streets down near the river and was capable of housing several hundred men. Along the main streets there were several churches, shops, and homes, some of them prosperous three-storied affairs. Beyond them, several wharves lined the river.

In the center of the town, visible for the moment, he could see men stirring, some beginning to emerge from the stone barracks, others pouring out of houses, barns, and warehouses. A knot of soldiers was trying to form into ranks while moving up King Street, and there was a flag being uncased. No semblance of order yet, but these were Hessians. If they were given a few minutes of breathing room, they would most certainly form up.

He looked back at Knox, but no order needed to be given.

"Ready! Stand clear!" Knox cried.

Gunners jumped back from their pieces.

"Number one, fire!"

One of the sergeants, turned about, arm extended, linstock with burning taper coming down. The burning rope touched the mound of powder over the touchhole of the six-pounder and instantly ignited.

The gun leapt back with a roar even as Knox screamed for the second gun to fire.

The roar of the two guns even overcame the howling of the wind. There was a momentary glimpse of a partial line of Hessians forming and, a second later, scattering, several men going down near the flag.

"That's it!" Washington roared. "Feed it to them!"

So much was unfolding at once. He scanned the rise of ground and the open fields rimming the town.

Greene's column was coming up. He was standing tall in the stirrups, sword raised, breaking the column in half, sending a regiment directly toward the town, the men spreading out as they ran, to try to form on the left of Sullivan's line, which was nearly in the village.

The rest of Greene's men raced straight toward the low hill where the first guns had deployed, then moved along the hillside to come in behind the artillery and extend the line of attack and envelop the town from the southeast.

The left?

He looked in that direction, south of the town. If the plan had been followed, the fifteen hundred Jersey militia men who were supposed to cross south of Trenton should now charge in. Nothing.

Did they make it across and were they

now ready to fall in on his left? He didn't know.

This was not the time to stop and think about it. Looking down at the village he sensed that now, without doubt, the miracle was real. The way the Hessians were dribbling out of barracks, homes, and shops, many of them milling about in confusion, showed that, for whatever reason, they had been caught completely off guard.

"Knox!"

"Here, sir!"

Knox came running even as the first two guns were reloading.

"Down there!" Washington pointed to the edge of the village where the road split into King and Queen Streets. "I want guns literally on the streets. Sweep them with grapeshot. Bottle them up inside the houses while your guns up here hit the rest of the town!"

Knox grinned like a child who had been told to play a game that would create havoc. He was at last unleashed.

Without taking time to reply, he was off, a giant of man, running full out, waving to the next section of guns to swing down toward the edge of the town.

Meanwhile the two six-pounders fired again, solid shot streaking into the center of town, scattering the Hessians as they tried to form. Several more guns came up to the top of the slope, howitzers, the heavy pieces so laboriously brought across the Delaware and manhandled over Jacob's Creek. In a few minutes their heavy five-and-a-half-inch shells would be bursting in the village square.

And down in that village he could see two Hessian guns, pulled by teams of horses, trying to move up King Street in order to block the attack, but Knox was already on them, shouting for his gunners to tear the enemy pieces apart.

Hundreds of men were running past him, the men of Greene's command, shouting, hollering, some heading southward to bottle up the far side of the village, others deploying to support Knox's guns, which were swinging into position to fire down King and Queen Streets. His heart nearly broke at the sight of the men.

Their passage was marked by blood. Not blood from any wound by bullet or sword. Nearly all were barefoot, and after nine miles of marching and running toward the fight, their frozen, lacerated feet left splattered trails of blood.

George Washington stood up in his stirrups, sword raised. "Forward, men!" he cried. "Forward!"

■ ■ ■ ■

Münchasen struggled to help Rall get his wet boots on, Potts's servant kneeling beside him to help with the other foot. The sharp clap of artillery fire rattled the windows.

Startled, Rall stood up, his left foot not fully into his boot. The artillery could not be his, for the guns were stowed in sheds against the storm. No matter how well drilled his men, it would take long minutes to deploy them.

Merciful God, they have artillery!

"My jacket!"

Münchasen pulled it off the peg by the fireplace and helped him slip into it. It was cold, clammy.

Rall headed for the door, limping slightly until his left foot settled into the counter of the boot, then raced down the stairs. Potts was up, his rotund wife clinging to his arm.

"Is it the rebels?" she cried.

He ignored her as he headed toward the door.

"Oh God, they'll think we're Tories," she exclaimed. He did not understand her words, but he sensed the meaning of it. In another minute she most likely would be calculating which side would win this day

439

and how to react.

He was out the door, ignoring her, and a second later was against the side of the house, nearly hit by a shot that howled past, decapitating one of his men a few feet away.

He had seen thousands die on battlefields. This body collapsing, though, limbs twitching spasmodically for a few seconds, was one of his own men, and the sight filled him with rage.

The dead man's comrades, preparing to pour out of the house and form ranks, had pulled back in terror. Up and down the street he could see his men, some in doorways, half-dressed, peering out in confusion, some just emerging, donning jackets, some only in underbreeches and shirts, all caught by surprise.

Another shot howled past. He turned and looked up the street.

The wind whipped the smoke away, and he caught a glimpse of two rebel guns, crews working feverishly to reload, infantry lines moving behind and around the pieces.

His own men, trapped in the narrow streets, had no semblance of order. At the top of the street an officer was attempting to form a line but already the unit was melting away, men turning and, running. He tried to stop them in their panic, but they dodged to either side of him and fled.

To form a line in the face of artillery but a few dozen paces away was folly. They needed a rallying point out of range for a few minutes, and once rallied, secure in their ranks, knowing their comrades were in their proper place to either side, his men would show their nerve.

He stepped into the middle of the street and started to run down its length, Münchasen appearing by his side. Both headed toward the center of town and the stone barracks.

"Rally, men! Rally in the square. Follow me!"

And yet, even as he passed, only a handful of confused men emerged, as another blast, this time of grapeshot, thundered down the narrow street, the score of iron balls by some miracle passing to either side of the colonel, sparing him.

Jonathan, raging with frustration, stood impotent, unable to fire his musket while those around him blazed away at the thin line of Hessians attempting to form at the edge of his village. With the storm closing in again, it was hard to see, but obviously their volleys were hitting hard, for the enemy was dropping, windows of houses shattering.

"Clear the way!"

Over his shoulder Jonathan saw an artillery crew running alongside a four-pounder being pulled by a horse, the driver lashing the animal. Four more guns were behind them.

Peter was so intent on loading and shooting that Jonathan had to shove him to one side as the first gun skidded across the ice. The crew struggled to turn it about and unlimber the piece.

"Lend a hand!"

Jonathan, glad at last to be able to do something, anything, tossed his useless musket aside and grabbed hold of a wheel, putting his shoulder into it.

"Grapeshot! Load! Load!"

Even before the gun was in place a boy was slamming a powder bag into the breech, followed seconds later by a bag filled with lead balls, topped off with a liberal mix of nails and iron fragments.

Jonathan continued to brace the gun, leaning into it as it was turned about.

He glanced up for a second. The Hessians they had been facing were turning, running, retreating down King Street, stumbling, a confused mass of men. Some were trying to surge forward, led by an officer. He caught a glimpse of a flag being held up at the head of a column. Others were scattering, dodging into alleyways or going in the opposite direction.

"Stand clear, you damn fool!"

Someone grabbed Jonathan by the shoulder and pulled him away.

He was barely clear of the piece as it leapt back several feet, the explosion jarring Jonathan. The tongue of flame snapped out brightly, snow and sleet eddying and swirling as the shot howled down King Street, cutting into the Hessians, dropping several men, who cried out in pain and terror.

A second gun fired, windowpanes of the first house on the street blowing out, several balls tearing along the side planking and sheering back into the crowded street.

The gun he had been helping with was already being rolled forward, another charge rammed in. He tried to help, but so many eager hands were at work that he was shoved back, Peter grabbing hold of him, pulling him away.

"You damn near got crushed, you fool!" Peter cried.

"I don't care!"

Another gun fired, and then another, these aimed down Queen Street. This time it was impossible to see the effect.

Another salvo from the guns, more men going down in the street, snow closing in, again impossible to see.

Something screamed over their heads, men ducking. At least one Hessian field piece was firing back.

Men were piling in around Jonathan, far too many to help the gunners, in fact starting to get in their way. The artillerymen were roaring for them to stand clear and let them do their work.

Jonathan caught a glimpse of Knox, riding just a few feet behind them, hat off, shouting for the artillery to keep pouring it in.

All around him was confusion, shouts, orders, huzzahs; moments when it was impossible to see more than a few feet because of the smoke and the storm.

Though not moving he felt strangely hot, his body trembling, each breath an agony. But that did not matter.

There was a coiling up within, a rising tension, a frenzy. Men were shouting, cheering as each of the guns cut loose, their target now unseen in the storm, but knowing without doubt they were hitting something, for cries could be heard even above the storm.

They were like some primal force, which after month upon month of defeat, abuse, and scorn was lashing back.

At that moment he felt no pity, only a fierce, deadly rage as the cries of the enemy reached him. After all the long months of humiliation, of defeat, at last their moment had come.

"He that stands it now . . ."

I will stand it, he thought.

"Virginians! Who is with me!"

Knox, still mounted, was leaning over, pointing down the street. The storm had lifted for a moment, two enemy guns visible in the middle of the street. The men gathered around Knox had, to Jonathan's eyes, the appearance of hunting dogs about to be unleashed, eyes wide, hands tightly clenched on muskets and rifles.

"Take those guns!"

The Virginians leapt forward, and the moment swept through his soul.

"Come on, Peter!" Jonathan cried.

He fell in with the swarm of men charging down King Street and into the village. Men of Massachusetts and Virginia mingled together as one, truly American in their unity against the common enemy. A wild howling roar erupted from them, some shouting obscenities, others laughing with a mad hysterical edge, others just screaming.

This street . . . the street where he had

played for countless hours as a boy, watching in awe as the mail coach galloped through, stepping back as some wealthy personage came by with a matched pair of horses, the street he had walked down so many times on the way to church, to school, to go fishing in the river, this place of childhood dreams.

The ice-covered thoroughfare was slick with fresh blood, turning to slushy pink as the snow continued to fall.

From an upper window a Hessian leaned out, aiming a musket. A rifle cracked beside Jonathan, startling him, and the Hessian fell back.

Windowpanes to either side shattered. They could hear screaming from within. He passed a narrow alleyway, packed with Hessians, cowering. To his right several more of the enemy emerged, obviously caught by surprise, as if running from some other threat. A Virginian swung his musket like a club and Jonathan could hear the sickening sound of the man's skull being crushed. The other fleeing Hessians fell to their knees screaming.

"Ich ergebe mich!" [*I surrender!*]

Jonathan slowed to look at one of them. Not much older than himself, face clean shaven, long mustache, thin and scraggly, a boyish attempt at being a man.

He slowed, unarmed, Peter by his side, musket leveled.

He looked into the Hessian's eyes and saw the terror. Peter was there, still with a weapon in his hands, also not sure how to react.

Part of him, at that instant, wanted to kill this enemy, and he realized if he had held a loaded musket in his hand he just might have done that. And yet . . . He saw the terror in his enemy's eyes. That was victory enough for now.

Jonathan grabbed the Hessian's musket, tearing it from his grasp.

"Lie down!"

He pointed to the ground, and the young soldier fell on his face, sobbing with fear. Jonathan looked over at Peter, clenching the captured musket, grinning at him.

"Come on!"

The Virginians were still charging toward the enemy guns, now half a block away. Men were still falling, but not from enemy fire. The street was coated with ice and splattered with blood. They went in and over the enemy dead and wounded. A Hessian lay nearly decapitated, blood and brains oozing out onto the ice. Another, with arm torn off, was sitting against the side of the house, blood pouring from the stump. Others were holding up their hands begging for mercy. One man, small book in hand, obviously a Bible, was holding it up as if it were a talisman that could save his life, even as life drained out of a body riddled with grapeshot and nails.

The guns. They were nearly to the guns!

Half a dozen dead and dying horses were sprawled out behind the guns. In the lead was a young Virginia lieutenant who suddenly staggered backward nearly collapsing, clutching his shoulder, arterial blood spurting out, the young man trying to regain his footing and continue with the charge.

Jonathan reached out to help him. The wounded officer took Jonathan's hand, regaining his feet. There was a momentary glance, a nod of thanks, the officer pressing his hand tight against his torn shoulder in an attempt to stanch the flow of blood, but not willing to give up, weaving forward with the charge.

A lone Hessian, an officer, stood by one of the pieces as if ready to defend it, until the lead man in the charge came up, raising a sword on high. Then the Hessian turned and fled into the smoke, snow, and mist.

Wild cheers broke out. Men were slapping their hands against the gun, slapping each other on the back. Even in those seconds of celebration, panic-stricken enemy soldiers darted around and through them, pouring out of side alleys from the northwest side of town. Several were clubbed down; others dropped their weapons and pleaded for mercy. Some tried to turn back and then turned again, for seconds later it was men of Sullivan's command pushing through, triumphantly driving the enemy clear of King Street.

"Turn their own guns on them!" someone shouted. A dozen willing hands pitched in, swinging the Hessian guns about and pointing them toward the center of town. The enemy gunners had fled with their rammers and sponges; a cry went up to fetch replacements, but somehow, in their mad enthusiasm, the amateur gunners, in an act that in other times would be considered pure and utter madness, pushed powder bags down the hot barrels using the barrels of their own muskets, loaded in bags of grapeshot from the abandoned limbers, tore musket cartridges open to provide powder for the touchholes and set the field pieces alight by firing a pistol at the powder heaped on the touchholes. Amazingly, instead of blowing up, the guns sent blasts of fire and grapeshot the length of the street and into the village square where the enemy was attempting to rally.

Jonathan watched, incredulous. It was as if all of them were drunk with some wild frenzy. The sound of battle roared up from the south, Mercer's and Sullivan's men pushing up alleyways, yielding for a few minutes with shouts that the enemy was trying to rally but then charging forward again.

But Jonathan did not join them. He stood there, wooden, as if stricken, barely focused on the captured artillery pieces tearing apart any who tried to rally in the center of the town.

He clenched his captured musket tight. Occasional shots rang out from upper-story windows, desperate men firing down on their attackers. All up and down King Street the advancing infantry were turning their attention to any of the enemy still holding out on the upper floors of homes and shops, kicking in doors, gunshots echoing, the shouts of men now commingled with screams of women and children cowering within.

Jonathan stood before a doorway a few paces back from the artillery pieces that were pounding the center of the town and advanced toward the door, Peter by his side.

Jonathan slowed and then actually reached

out for the door handle and tried it. It was locked.

Somehow that filled him with a mad fury. Using the butt of his captured musket he slammed it against the door like a battering ram. The effort drained the last of his strength.

The mad frenzy of a minute before was pouring out of him, like the last rivulet from a broken dam. His knees were trembling, his entire body shaking with shock, exhilaration, exhaustion — and rage.

The brass doorknob broke, and Peter threw his weight into the door. It cracked open.

Jonathan, musket already turned, had his weapon up, cocked, and aimed. He kicked the door open the rest of the way.

On the far side of the door stood his father, eyes wide with fear.

"My horse!" Rall yelled.

He looked about, frantic. His men must see him mounted and in command. Several hundred or more were forming ranks in front of the stone barracks. A section of guns was out of the shed, the artillerymen pushing the pieces forward and onto Queen Street. The hope was forlorn, but they might buy a few minutes of the time he needed.

An orderly came up to his side, leading his mount, and he climbed into the saddle, for the moment feeling more secure, able at least to see over the heads of his men.

Few were in full uniform, many were without jackets, some even without muskets or boots. Companies were jumbled together, sergeants frantically racing about, some shouting for the men to form into column, others to shake out into volley line.

He tried to take it all in. Several company commanders, able to see him at last now that he was mounted, were running to his side for orders.

He had to calm himself, to display no confusion, no alarm. In the war against the Turks, while serving in the army of the czarina, the enemy had infilitrated their camp at night. With the Russian officers in a panic, he had taken command, forming a square, the formation rallying their courage so that at last they were able to leap forward and drive the enemy off.

Form a square now?

The town square was too small, and even as he contemplated the action, a volley swept in from the north side of town. He turned, facing into the wind, squinting, and saw the shadowy forms emerging, racing forward, his own men on that side of the square giving back, some turning to run.

Looking up the street that he had just come from, he could see it packed with rebel infantry, overrunning a gun. Send a column up to drive them back?

Do that and we are flanked from the north, he realized.

He felt a tug at his shoulder. A musket ball had clipped his uniform jacket. He turned and could actually see the man who had fired at him, shaking his fist, shouting some incoherent curse.

We're flanked either way we turn.

He looked south and knew it was their only recourse.

"Follow me, men!" he shouted, and with drawn saber pointed toward the open field south of town. Surely the rebels had not yet surrounded the town. But five minutes to form ranks, restore order out in an open field free of the confines of this miserable town, and he would charge back and retrieve the day, and the tattered shreds of his honor.

Chapter Thirteen

Trenton, New Jersey
9:05 A.M., December 26, 1776
The cold wind swept in through the open door, causing the glowing embers in the fireplace to flare upward.

Jonathan stood disbelieving, musket leveled at his father, who faced him defiantly in the middle of the room. Behind him were half a dozen men, Hessians. He scanned them quickly, realizing with sudden panic that his own weapon was not loaded. The Hessians gazed at him wide-eyed, near panic, uniforms dripping ice and water on the floor. Several held muskets, one of them half raised.

He swung his musket toward the Hessian, shouldering it.

"Surrender!" he shouted, as he struggled for a breath of air, his lungs feeling as if they were on fire.

Peter pushed in beside him, musket raised as well.

"Damn you!" Peter shouted. "Surrender or you're dead men! *Geben Sie auf! Oder sterben!*"

The Hessians seemed to be frozen in place.

The soldier with his weapon half raised slowly bent to place his weapon on the floor, the others following.

Jonathan stepped away from the door and gestured for them to get out.

"Out in the street! Keep your hands over your heads."

One of them turned to Jonathan's father. *"Bringen sie uns um?"* he asked. [Will they kill us?]

"Tün sie was sie sagen." Jonathan's father replied. [Do as they order].

The way the two spoke struck Jonathan like a bolt. These men had fled here because they were quartered here. They were living in *his* home.

The six raised their hands. Frightened, they started for the door, Jonathan and Peter backing away several feet, keeping their weapons pointed at them.

As they left, Jonathan tipped his head at Peter, who nodded and without comment followed the six out the door. There was

455

shouting outside, someone laughing that "Jersey militia" had bagged six more.

Jonathan turned to face his father.

"You won't kill them, will you?"

"We're not like them," Jonathan announced with proud assertiveness.

And then he had another shock. His own father did not know who he was. It was the way his father was looking at him, with outright fear, not even a glimmer of recognition.

The moment was like a tableau. The prodigal son returned. This prodigal son barefoot, trousers nothing but tattered rags, blanket cape pulled in tight, hat tied down under his chin with a strip of burlap.

"My family is in the back," his father said. "Do you promise them safety?"

"All your family?"

His father hesitated.

"Jonathan? My God, Jonathan, is that you?"

His son said nothing.

There was such a strange flood of emotion. He had stumbled through the village during the retreat and could not bring himself to stop, but this now was different. The goods of their store were intact, neatly arranged on shelves, tanned leather in bales, shoes and boots arrayed along a wall, belts, gloves. The fact that they were out on display meant that there had been some arrangement with the occupying Hessians. He glanced at his father, who stood silent.

"I suggest you hide all this now," Jonathan announced, gesturing toward the shelves

The old man gazed at him, shocked, confused by the exhausted skeletal apparition of his son standing thus.

Jonathan turned and pushed the door open leading to the family living quarters, a short corridor going straight to the kitchen.

And he could see them now. His mother was standing by the fireplace.

"Mother! It's Jonathan!" his father shouted behind him.

The woman stepped away from the fireplace and started slowly toward him, and then he saw, his brother.

James, how a month had changed him! Gone was the ragged beard and tattered clothes. He was clean shaven, dressed in a comfortable shirt and doeskin breeches, obviously well fed. His mother started to run toward Jonathan and then slowed as she drew closer, as if not sure.

"My boy?"

"Yes, Mother."

And her arms were around him, head buried against his chest, a shuddering sob escaping her.

He still held his musket in one hand, but his arm came around her and his gaze was fixed on James.

"I'm glad to see you are safe," James said woodenly.

"I'll bet you are."

"Don't start on this now, Jonathan," James replied sharply. "You have to protect this house."

"Protect it from what?"

"What's going on out there?" Jonathan could see that James was afraid.

The sound of battle outside continued unabated, the windowpanes in the kitchen rattling from the thump of artillery. He caught a glimpse through the kitchen window of men running down an alleyway, Hessians, shouting in terror, followed scant seconds later by his own comrades. One slowed, looked in the window, saw Jonathan, waved, and then ran on.

"What's going on out there?" James asked again.

Jonathan began to cough, struggling for breath. The room was hot and confining, and even though he was shaking, he felt as if he were on fire.

"We're winning a battle, damn you. That's what's going on."

"Don't take that tone with me," James announced.

"I'll take any damn tone I want with you from now on."

James took a step closer. Jonathan started to pull away from his mother, half bringing his musket up.

She clutched him even tighter.

"Jonathan, Jonathan, don't!"

He felt a hand on his shoulder. He tried to pull away from his mother and looked back. It was his father.

"Son . . ."

"William, he's burning up," his mother gasped, still holding him tight, her hand going to his forehead.

"Sit down, son," his father said, pointing to the bench at the kitchen table.

He could not resist for the moment, as his parents guided him the few feet to the bench. He collapsed on it, but still held on to his musket with one hand, gaze fixed on James, who stood silent by the other side of the table.

The table. It was spread with food, nearly a dozen plates, bacon, eggs, ham, fresh-baked bread, a wooden tub of butter. Some of the meals were half consumed, several of them spilled over, a number of broken plates on the floor, food trampled underneath.

For a few seconds he found himself looking at the food on the brick floor, actually wondering what might be worth saving, and then he looked back to the table.

"A regular feast you've set out here," he whispered to his mother, who hovered over him protectively, tears streaming down her face.

She didn't reply. She ran her hands over his face, again feeling his forehead, as she slipped off the strip of cloth under his chin and removed his hat. She looked at the hat with disgust, the look of a mother whose boy had just come in after a day of play and was covered with muck, and let it fall to the floor.

"Who is the meal for?" he asked again. "For us, perhaps?"

"The Hessians quartered twelve men here," his father interjected.

"I see. And you clearly were feeding them well."

"Jonathan, we had to!"

"Obviously."

The room began to swim before his eyes. It was warm, far too warm.

"William, he's burning with fever," his mother gasped.

His father stepped closer, putting a hand on his forehead.

"Let's get some dry clothes on you first, my boy," and as he spoke he took hold of the muzzle of the musket, as if to take it away.

"No!" Jonathan snapped, and clenched the weapon tight, gaze still fixed on James.

"Where's Allen?" he asked sharply.

James looked at his father.

"Where is he?"

No one spoke.

"Allen. Where is he?"

There eyes, shifting back and forth, told him everything. He motioned to the trapdoor that led down to the basement larder.

"Tell him to come up. He has nothing to fear."

"You'll give him protection?" his mother asked.

Jonathan sat back against the wall and actually laughed softly.

"My oldest brother? My protector? Tell him to come up."

James did not move, and Jonathan felt a momentary burst of pity.

"You know, James, deserters have been shot in our army. And you deserted."

"My God, Jonathan," his father cried. "You wouldn't —"

Jonathan shook his head wearily. "The fact that my brother is a coward is safe with me. I won't tell and bring shame upon our name. He has to live with it now, not me."

James bristled at the word "coward," but said nothing.

"Now get Allen out of that damn larder room."

The sound of battle outside was rising in intensity, and he wondered if he should leave this place and get back into the fight, but all his strength had drained out of him. All he could do was sit and stare as his brother went to the far end of the room, opened the trapdoor, and called out Allen's name.

As the head and shoulders of his oldest brother appeared, Jonathan felt a deep sickness welling up in him, and for a few seconds he feared he might vomit.

Allen was wearing a Loyalist uniform.

The freezing storm was peaking, as was the battle being fought in its murky confusion.

The Americans charging down into the village pressed forward with a wild fury. The road was wreathed in smoke. There were flashes of light from guns firing, the wind at Washington's right shoulder and back whipping the smoke and the noise away so that the drama was played out in near silence.

Sullivan's men were halfway into the town, disappearing into alleyways, reappearing again, relentlessly pushing forward, driving the blue-clad Hessians, who ran before them in mad panic. Storming in from the east end of the town, a jumbled mix of men, Mercer's Virginians, and his own headquarters company charged down King and Queen Streets. Never had General George Washington seen his men go forward like this. Never. They charged like men possessed. "To take on the aspect of a tiger . . ." He wasn't sure who had written that, but at this moment it fit. His men did indeed race into the battle like tigers.

Throughout the long cold night of confusion, agony, and doubts, his heart had been burdened with the great fear, that at dawn, upon approaching this village, arrayed to greet him would be three elite, well-drilled, warm, and rested regiments of the enemy, waiting and ready.

They were among the most feared troops in the world, some of them veterans of the armies of Frederick of Prussia. Men who regardless of losses, if given but a few minutes to form ranks, would rally into their precise lines and with clocklike precision lash out at any who dared to approach sending four terrible volleys a minute crashing into any troops who ventured into range.

He had worried that these formidable professionals would be waiting and that at the sight of them his men — frozen, hungry, numbed beyond exhaustion, hearts filled with memories of so many defeats — would be paralyzed by fear, indecision, and hopelessness. Then, with the first shattering volleys, they would turn about and run, as they had run so many times before, not because they were cowards, but because so much had been asked of them. And once they began to run, the Revolution would indeed be finished, for there would be no place to run to, other than toward the ferry where relentless pursuers would run them down and slaughter them mercilessly.

He had led his army to this place, fully resolved that if fate decreed it thus, he would die this day. There would be no ignominious capture such as General Lee seemed so ready to accept. No, never that. To be paraded before his captors, to be mocked and scorned, then taken to General Howe. Howe was, of course, a gentleman. He would prevent public humiliation once in British hands, but there would be humiliation, nevertheless, with demands to sign a final article of surrender. After his refusal, perhaps at least the offer of protection for Martha, also perhaps for some of his men if they now laid down arms, then on to England and the gallows.

When he had contemplated that [and the thoughts had haunted him throughout the long night], he had made his decision. If all was indeed lost, he would ride straight at the enemy line and seek a death befitting a soldier. The pagan practices of the Romans, no matter how honorable, of falling upon one's own sword no longer fit this world, but a well-aimed volley by a Hessian line would achieve the same end — death with honor.

"Sir, they're trying to break out."

Stirred from his thoughts, he looked up to see General Greene riding up the slope, coming from the south side of the town, pointing toward the village.

He did not need to be told twice. In the center of the town a knot of troops was attempting to array into column on the narrow streets, several flags among them, standing out stiffly in the tempest, the column heading south.

A six-pounder fired by his side, the flight of the ball impossible to trace. Three other guns fired seconds later, dropping solid shot and howitzer shells into the far end of the town. Behind him Greene's men continued to run past at the double, with little semblance of order, a surging mass of men, leaning forward, slipping on the icy ground, faces drawn, eyes afire, summoning up one last burst of strength, their passage marked by their bloody footprints on the ice.

"Then we shall stop them!"

He reined about, the ever-present Billy Lee by his side. A momentary glance, and he could see his servant, his companion of years, smiling, pistol in his hand, as eager as any of the others to get into the fray.

He turned to look for Knox. He had been down at the edge of the village when last he saw him. No time to find him now and pass orders, nor any need to at this moment, for Knox knew what to do. He would keep pounding with his artillery and driving men in from the east end of the town to close the vise.

Washington urged his mount to a gallop, shards of ice flying from under his horse's hooves, maneuvering down the gentle slope, swinging to one side to avoid trampling a knot of men who had slipped and fallen and were now tangled up with each other.

He rode past them, half standing in his stirrups, sword raised.

"Forward, boys! We've got them now. Forward!"

An orchard was before him. There a regiment of troops, lining up under a Massachusetts flag, was forming a volley line on the east side of bare apple trees.

At the sight of their General riding by, a ragged cheer arose.

He saluted. "We've got them now, lads. Get ready and give it to them!"

Behind the Massachusetts men the rest of Greene's division continued at the run, deploying across the open field that curved around the south end of town down toward Assunpink Creek.

It was so clearly evident now that yet another part of his plan had not worked. The men of Cadwalader's New Jersey militia were supposed to have crossed before dawn and deployed on the far side of the creek to block escape and to prevent the small enemy garrison in the village of Bordentown, five miles further south, from coming up to bring relief to Trenton. There was not a single man in position. Why, he did not know. Now was not the time to worry about it. Greene, so reliable this morning, as if redeeming himself for his failure at Fort Lee, was already seeing to this gap, pushing his thousand men out and around in an arc.

An advance guard of Greene's men were plunging into the creek, waist deep, holding muskets and cartridge boxes over their heads, braving ice-choked water again to get to the far side and set up a blocking force.

He slowed for a moment, watching them, emotion all but overwhelming him at the sight.

They had braved the Delaware, staggered through Jacob's Creek, endured a night march of freezing hell, and now, again, driven forward by this fury, were wading another freezing stream, in places having to break through a crust of ice. Several men were slipping and falling, floundering, comrades reaching out to pull numbed companions back up. Some of the men simply collapsed as they reached the far shore, unable to move. But others staggered on, deploying, getting in among bushes and trees on the bank of the stream, leveling muskets.

"Here they come!"

He looked to his right, the blast of the storm now in his face. The advantage Sullivan's men had coming down from the north, with the storm at their back and in their enemies' faces was reversed here, and he had to squint, leaning forward slightly.

Hard to see for a few seconds. Shadowy figures were emerging, but with no clear color to their uniforms. All was shrouded in tones of gray — snow, sleet, and smoke.

He turned about to move in behind a volley line, a single rank deep, men spaced several feet apart. Other troops, running hard, continued to move behind this line, Greene shouting for it to be extended.

More shadows appeared, moving like ghosts flying toward them.

There was a momentary fear: Were these his own men? Had some debacle unfolded in the village in the last few minutes? Had the Hessians, ever so precise and disciplined, re-formed? Were they now driving his men out? Would he in a few more seconds see the enemy emerge and advance inexorably, ready to return volley for volley?

More shadows appeared . . . uniforms . . . blue! They were running blindly.

"Make ready!"

The Massachusetts men raised their muskets high.

"Take aim!"

A hundred or more muskets were leveled. And at that instant the shadows before them began to slow, men sliding to a stop. Guttural cries drifted on the wind . . . in German.

"Fire!"

A volley rang out, half a dozen Hessians dropping.

There were cries of confusion, rage. Several raised muskets and fired back, shots going wide in the confusion.

The Massachusetts line was already reloading. More shots rang out. The men falling in to the left of the Massachusetts men were hurrying to join the fray.

Allen stepped away from the trapdoor, looking defiantly at Jonathan for a few seconds, and Jonathan slowly stood up. Seeing James again, warm, well dressed, and obviously well fed, had been bad enough.

But this?

There was shouting outside in the alleyway, triumphal cries, more men running past the window.

"For God's sake," Jonathan hissed, "take that goddamn jacket off now!"

Allen did as ordered, letting it fall to the floor.

As the oldest child Allen had always been the protective brother, pulling Jonathan out of so many childhood scrapes with James. It was Allen whom he had idealized, and it was Allen who so often said that it was Jonathan, though the "runt of the litter," as he would jokingly call him, was the one who was born with the brains and destined to attend college. It was Allen who, when Jonathan slipped away from his chores to play or wandered afield, would so often cover for him, quietly doing the chores himself and never saying a word. It was Allen who, when he went down to Philadelphia on family business, would always return with some small present for him, such as a book from Mr. Franklin's shop, and then tell him all the news of the wide world beyond.

"Jonathan," Allen sighed, and he came toward him, eyes filled with obvious relief.

Jonathan held his hand up in a gesture as if to ward him off.

"No, don't."

"My God, Jonathan, we've been worried sick for you."

"Obviously." He gestured toward the food spread on the table. "Even as you fed them."

"Jonathan, we had to," Allen replied.

"At least they didn't loot us," James interjected, speaking up at last. "The way your army wanted to when it ran through here three weeks ago."

"We did not," Jonathan retorted. "What we took we paid for."

James snorted derisively. "The money made good kindling." He gestured toward the blazing fire. "That's all it was worth."

"And from what I saw in the shop, you made certain most of the goods were well hidden."

"Son, do you want us reduced to poverty because of this damn war?" his father interjected.

"You know what I wanted."

"All of you, stop it," his mother snapped. The men fell silent.

"William, go fetch some dry clothes for our boy."

His father nodded and left the room.

She folded her arms and gazed at her sons. "All of you, sit down. I will have no fighting or profane words in my kitchen."

Jonathan could not help but chuckle sadly. Did she not know that a battle was literally raging outside her home? A war that months before seemed so distant when he had marched off to join it — with James by his side — had literally come to their doorstep. And one of the enemy stood before him.

Allen came to sit across from Jonathan, but as he pulled the bench back, Jonathan stood and backed away.

"I will not sit with you, Brother."

"For heaven's sake, Jonathan! Stop it."

"Why did you do it?" Jonathan asked, and was ashamed that his voice began to break with emotion.

"Jonathan."

Allen was up and by his side, arms going around him, and for a moment Jonathan did indeed break. He began to weep, Allen holding him as he had so often in the past when he lost a scrap or fell into trouble with his parents.

He wept and Allen held him.

"Jonathan, I had to."

"If not for Allen, they would have looted us clean," James interjected.

"Is that it? Is that what the price of your soul is worth?" Jonathan snapped, pulling away from Allen.

He glared at James.

"You I figured out, at last, to be a coward."

"You can go to hell, Jonathan."

"Sunshine patriot, that's all you ever were, James," Jonathan cried. "But you, Allen? You?"

"Do you actually believe in that rot?" James retorted.

"What rot?"

"Reverend White showed us a copy of what that fool Paine just wrote."

"And you call it rot?" Jonathan cried.

"Yes, the ravings of a drunken fool, and

you actually believe it."

"Yes, I do!"

He felt light-headed and in spite of himself collapsed back onto the bench, emotion all but overwhelming him. Outside the storm, the battle, continued to rage.

"Listen to that! There are good men, my comrades out there. Fighting, dying, for what you call rot."

James replied with a sarcastic sneer.

"Damn you. Don't you believe in anything?"

He nodded toward Allen, who looked down at him with a sad and weary expression.

"At least he believes in something, even if I now call him my enemy."

"Jonathan, you could never be my enemy," Allen whispered.

"Then why are you wearing that damn traitor's uniform?"

"Traitor? I am loyal to our king. Little Brother, which of us is the traitor?"

"All of you, stop it!"

There was a time when a mere whisper from his mother, far more effective than any shouted commands from his father, would have sent Jonathan scurrying, but not now.

"Mother," he sighed, "I will always respect you as my mother, but please don't try and stop me now."

"You are sick, my boy." Again her tone was that of a mother hovering over an ill child.

There was an instant when he did want to give way, to be led to bed, to be under warm covers with her sitting by his side, as she had so often done when he was sick as a boy.

James stalked out of the room and turned into a side room that was the office for their business. Jonathan could hear a desk drawer being opened, and seconds later James returned, holding up a newspaper.

"Reverend White gave this to us yesterday. Do you see it?"

He held it up before Jonathan. He could barely focus on it, but he knew what it was.

"And you actually believe the ravings of this madman? All of those damn madmen. Do you know that while you froze, that Congress of cowards ran away? While all this madness goes on, they are safe, warm, and fat in Baltimore?"

He pointed toward the window, the sound of battle rising in volume.

"For all you know, your army is on the run, and in a few more minutes those Hessians that were here will be back, looking for your hide, and Allen will of course try to save you, even though you don't deserve it."

The blow nearly lifted Colonel Rall from the saddle, knocking the breath out of him.

There was no pain. That had always struck him as strange. He had heard it in the garrison talk around the table when as a boy he was allowed to listen to the stories of old soldiers. Then there were his own memories of Luetzen, when he had nearly lost his arm, the slash of a Turkish saber across his thigh on the Romanian border. At first no pain, just a numbed blow. The pain would always come later.

"Sir!"

It was Münchasen, up by his side, offering a steadying hand. He waved the man off and actually forced a smile.

"Nothing, Münchasen. Now rally the men, please."

Münchasen looked at him, wide-eyed, another volley ringing out, his adjutant flinching.

"Never show fear Münchasen," he gasped. "Now help rally them!"

Münchasen drew away.

Rall could see the rebel lines. My God what was happening? This was not as before. They moved like ghosts in the storm, relentless, coming forward, swinging in to block him in. Behind the infantry he could see several guns being manhandled into position.

This could not be the damned rebels. Always they had run, always.

And in spite of his order to Münchasen, he felt fear for the first time. Not for his own life, though from the numbness in his side he did wonder if the blow was fatal. It was so hard to breathe now. But what of his honor? What of his men?

He looked down at them. To the column that had fled out of the town, he had passed the order that once clear of the village they were to form a square. But no square was forming. These men were milling about, some just gazing in shock at the ghostlike enemy, who now poured in volley after volley, a blast of grape sweeping in, bowling over half a dozen men. Those to either side were edging back in terror, a few tossing aside their weapons, falling to the ground.

He looked toward the stream, strangely named Assunpink, some savage name most likely. The bridge was blocked, again by ghostlike enemies standing on the far shore, firing toward him.

"Colonel!"

He didn't recognize the man. Someone

from the other regiment under his command.

"What are you orders, colonel?"

The wound was beginning to stab with a painful agony. He struggled for a breath of the frigid storm-driven air. He couldn't draw the air in.

Out in the open? Without artillery to suppress theirs, they will pound us to pieces.

He looked toward the village. Head there? Try to take the barracks. It's a stone building. Hole up in there, make a defense. Try to get word to Cornwallis. Ask the damn British to come rescue us after putting us here?

He caught a glimpse of his flag. My flag. The bearer went down, a sergeant snatching the colors and holding them back up as a rally point.

I must at least save my colors. Merciful God, how can I ever go back home without my flag?

My God, what will I say to my prince?

"Colonel! Your orders?"

"Back to the town. Rally at the barracks."

And then the second blow hit, this one knocking him to the ground and, for the moment, oblivion.

Washington caught glimpses of faces. Men

wide-eyed, but not with terror and panic this time.

A fury of battle was being unleashed as more and more men fell in, extending the battle line southward around the town. As each man came into place, with Greene shouting for them to "get into it, boys," more and more men raised their muskets, leveled, and fired.

Wild shouts, curses, huzzahs, guttural screams of long-pent-up fury greeted each shot.

Before them was confusion. No military formation, just random knots of Hessians. Some milling about in panic. One formation was emerging, perhaps company strength, led by an officer waving a sword. Before they could level and fire, a volley from his own men dropped the officer and the enemy line disintegrated, turned, and ran back toward the village.

A flag could be glimpsed in the smoke and snow, more of the enemy coming up. His men did not flinch; instead, the sight was greeted with curses, shouts to get that "damn, bloody flag!"

The enemy charge surging toward the orchard disintegrated before it had really started. Greene was riding up and down behind his line, shouting encouragement, yelling for his men to hold and deliver disciplined volleys, but his encouragement was not needed, not this day.

Washington saw the flag go down, come up again, and a few seconds later a mounted officer riding alongside of it collapsing.

Washington watched in silence, heart swelling, awed by what he was seeing unleashed, at last.

The shadows in the smoke and snow fell back.

"Close in on them, men!" Washington roared. "Close in!"

They needed no urging. Without a single officer present these men would have pushed forward. At this moment they were filled with a mad passion, a passion for war, driven by the most primal of urges.

The line, ragged and disordered, pushed to the edge of the orchard, and as they came upon some of the fallen enemy, several of the men dashed forward, knelt down, and began to try to pull off their boots and jackets.

Officers shouted for the men to keep moving and reluctantly the looters, feet trailing smears of blood, fell back in and pressed on.

"Look there, sir!"

It was Greene, eyes afire, filled with fierce

delight, pointing farther south to the far side of Assunpink Creek.

A column on the move, pushing several artillery pieces along. Another moment of doubt: Why was Greene filled with such delight? And then he realized why. It was Continentals pouring out of the south side of the village, in orderly fashion, running at the double . . . Sullivan!

They were through the village, crossing the bridge, deploying to seal the gap that should have been filled by the Jersey militia, having enough presence of mind to bring up several cannon for support.

The two elements of the trap were closing tight.

A cone of fire was now slashing into the enemy from all directions, the jaws of the vise inexorably closing tighter and tighter.

He caught glimpses of a Hessian column that had advanced toward the orchard heading back into the town, perhaps trying to break through to the north, or rallying to make a final stand in the village. If they became organized, the battle would turn into a vicious house-by-house. Or if they could hole up in the stone barracks, it might take hours to dislodge them, and in the interim enemy reinforcements might arrive. This victory might still degenerate into a bloody killing match if they were allowed to still their panic and regain a semblance of command.

He knew that the scope of the battle was, at this instant, beyond his ability to control, with his own forces formed in a circle more than a quarter mile across. But his heart told him that though beyond his control, his men, this morning, knew what they must do and would not hesitate now that they were tasting this long-hoped-for victory.

The enemy column had disappeared, except for occasional glimpses of their flags. From the hill where he had first watched the battle begin, he could hear the thumping of the artillery, well-placed shots plowing into the flank of the enemy column, shredding it.

Some of Sullivan's men were deployed on the far side of the creek and at the bridge, others in buildings at the edge of the town were leaning out from windows to fire at their enemy in the open.

The Hessian retreat to the edge of the village was lost to view, fire increasing, while in the orchard the Massachusetts men came to a stop, dressed their line, and reloaded, some of the men casting aside weapons that had misfired, picking up muskets dropped by the Hessians.

"Here they come again, boys!"

It was Greene, who seemed to be everywhere at once, riding up and down the line, sword drawn, pointing toward the field below the orchard.

He was right. Another enemy surge was pouring out, in some vague semblance of order, the storm clearing enough for the moment that this time he could see them clearly. A ragged column, colors at the center, was attempting to deploy into volley line, to batter its way through their tormentors.

What unfolded was slaughter.

His artillery up on the hill plowed solid shot into the enemy ranks, one officer and his mount going down in a tangled mass. From out of the village, pursuit by his own soldiers followed, men firing, hurriedly reloading, pressing forward a few dozen feet, firing again. Men with wet muskets advanced with bayonets leveled, and if without bayonets, their muskets held high like clubs, waving them, screaming defiance.

From the south, Sullivan's men pressed in as well.

An enemy surge headed toward the bridge, but the artillery Sullivan had so brilliantly moved to the far side of the Assunpink opened on them with a salvo, dropping a dozen or so. That one salvo showed clearly enough that escape that way was impossible.

A milling knot of the enemy broke into a run, heading for the gap that was still in his line between the far left of Greene's command and the right flank of Sullivan's, the enemy tossing aside muskets, plunging into the creek. Some appeared to make it across, others were shot down before reaching the far bank. It was hard to see, but in the confusion it looked to be a hundred or more who were escaping.

All was happening so quickly he knew he could not react to fill this momentary breach in the circle. Sullivan would have to contain the enemy alone. To order Greene to try to push his line farther south might leave this barrier by the orchard too thin to block any renewed surge.

The advancing enemy numbered in the hundreds, clustered around their flags. Yet with every step, more and more of them fell, fire ringing them in. He heard musket balls and then a solid shot screech by overhead. The enemy was not firing in their confusion. The ring was now so tight around them that the bullets and artillery rounds must be coming from Sullivan and his men pressing out now from the town.

Another volley came from the men deployed at the edge of the orchard. Solid shot was plowing into the confusion, knocking Hessians over like ninepins, ghastly cries rising up.

"For God's sake," he whispered, "give up."

It was changing from a battle into a massacre.

There was the slightest ripple of fear. Not for himself, but for the battle itself. Might it have shifted after all, the Hessians rallying? Jonathan turned his attention away from James, looking out the window as if he could catch a glimpse beyond the alleyway.

The artillery fire had reached a crescendo. There was distant cheering, but by which side?

"At least Congress won't have to worry about printing more money to pay you fools at the end of the month," James taunted, even as Jonathan faced the window trying to discern what was happening outside, wondering now if he should just leave this damned house and rejoin his comrades for what might be their final stand.

"Though I bet Paine is still making his money. He's warm, well fed, and safe in Philadelphia, writing this drivel while you fools freeze and die at his bidding."

James turned to the fireplace, balling up

the paper as if about to throw it in.

Jonathan was out of his seat, and before Allen or his mother could stop him, he flung himself on James, the two bowling over. James let go of the paper, and it rolled into the fireplace. Reaching in, Jonathan grabbed it, cursing, scorching his hand as he pulled it out. With a feeble effort he grasped the paper tight and then stuck it in under his jacket to keep it safe.

He could barely hear his mother screaming, or feel the strength of Allen as he separated the two of them, the way he so often had when as boys they had fallen into yet another fight.

Jonathan, gasping for air, came to his feet. Without Allen's support he knew he'd collapse. He leaned against his brother.

"You better hold on to him," James sneered. "In a few minutes our old lodgers will be back, ready to run him through."

"At least I'll die for something I believe in," Jonathan said coldly. "You have no soul, you have nothing but yourself and your selfishness. God help you."

"Will they hurt him?" his mother asked, looking up at Allen.

"No, Mother. He's just a very sick boy. They know me. I won't let them hurt him."

"I don't need your pity," Jonathan gasped.

"Do you think they won?"

Jonathan's father was in the doorway to the kitchen holding a bundle of clothes. There was something about him, at this moment, for Jonathan, that was heartbreaking. He saw the old man so differently now. A merchant, a scared merchant, once portly with success, now shaken and uncertain.

"I think, Father," Jonathan whispered, "either way, you will lose."

He tried to pull away from Allen's grasp.

"Jonathan, you better stay close to me," Allen said. "They're not a bad sort once you get to know them."

"I can see you have."

He looked into his brother's eyes. Allen lowered his gaze.

"Someday, you might understand."

"I doubt it."

He looked back at James.

"You at least have the courage of your convictions, Allen."

The roar of battle echoed from outside, reaching a new peak and then, suddenly, began to die away, a strange eerie silence enveloping the room, punctuated only by the occasional musket shot and counterpointed by the ever-present howling of the window.

"It is finished," James said coldly. "You've lost."

CHAPTER FOURTEEN

"For God's sake," Washington cried out. "End it! Surrender!"

As if his thoughts had been picked up by the men around him, he heard shouts from his own line, in German.

Startled, he looked about. Some of his men were actually lowering their muskets, cupping hands to their mouths, shouting in German. *"Geben sie auf! Leben sie noch!"* [Surrender, damn you! Surrender! Quarter if you surrender!]

It caught his heart. The men shouting were riflemen from Pennsylvania and the Maryland line, men fully as German as their Hessian opponents. In a different world they, too, might have been in Hessian uniforms, but having chosen America were now loyal to their new home and their new dream.

The cry was picked up, others shouting in English.

Again there had been no order to do this, and his heart filled. He wondered, if all were reversed, would these Hessians be doing the same? Or would they be as merciless as they had been at Long Island and Harlem? There when his men were defeated, fleeing and pleading for mercy, the Hessians had advanced with the bayonet and slaughtered.

God, this is what we are, after all. But minutes ago these same men had fought with a demonlike fury, and now they were offering mercy.

"Surrender, you damn fools! It's over!"

The Hessians, pushed together into a confused mass, were not fifty yards away, ringed in tight on all sides, the storm lifting enough so that all was visible.

One of Washington's staff looked over at him, and he nodded, gesturing toward the Hessians.

"Tell them to surrender" — he pointed toward several guns that were being wheeled down the hill — "or it will be grapeshot at fifty paces."

The orderly nodded, sheathed his sword, and went forward, holding his hand up high. Washington could feel the tension of the moment. His men, unbidden, were offering mercy, but if an errant shot struck down this man, it would unleash hell. Now, at this moment, he was beginning to sense a crowning victory, a victory that as Americans we would wish to end this way, and not in an orgy of bloodletting that would sully all they had gained this miraculous morning.

"Kameraden!" the orderly shouted, hand still held high.

A Hessian officer stepped out of the ranks of his men.

Lying on the frozen ground Colonel Rall was not sure who was calling for surrender. Münchasen perhaps? He wanted to tell him no. Honor demanded that they fight to the end. But he could not speak. Someone was cradling him. He looked up. A drummer boy. The lad was crying. Terrified.

"Don't be afraid," he whispered to the sobbing boy. "You are a soldier of Hesse. Do not be afraid, my child."

He could hear someone shouting. It was Münchasen, and at that moment the pain in his soul overcame the agony he knew heralded death.

Münchasen was surrendering the command; asking, pleading for quarter.

He wanted to countermand him but could not as he looked around at his men. They were beaten, terrified. They had fought a hard war, and in the passion of that war, at times, they had shown no mercy to the rebels, for, after all, the enemy were not really soldiers to be treated with honor as one would the Austrian or French uniformed regiments of the line. They were peasant rebels and to be treated as such.

And now the rebels had the upper hand, and as was usually the case, slaughter would be their retribution.

Better to die fighting, but he could not draw the breath to countermand Münchasen.

If they were indeed spared, what honor was left? But from the appearance of his terrified men he could see that honor did not matter to them at this moment. They would not have to face their prince. Perhaps Münchasen would have to someday, but I will not, and he thanked God at least for that blessing.

My name will be disgraced forever.

Though the distance was but a few dozen paces it was hard to hear what was being said with the wind still howling about them. Washington turned to the gunners wheeling their pieces about, dropping the elevation on their guns.

"Grapeshot, if they do not yield," Washington announced, voice tight. The battery commander nodded and passed the order to his crew.

The mad passion of minutes before seemed already to be draining away. The order was passed as if reluctantly.

"My God, they're striking colors!" an officer near him gasped.

Washington turned to see.

The flags were being lowered; Hessian infantry were already dropping muskets, some taking hats off and holding them high as a gesture of surrender.

His orderly was running back across the narrow ground, waving his arms excitedly.

"They've struck! Hold your fire, men! They've surrendered!"

At that instant it was as if all passion, all energy and fire, drained out of his men. There were a few cheers; an officer with the Marylanders called for three huzzahs, but only a few joined in. Most of the men stood in silence, muskets clenched tightly. A few slapped each other on the back, several men actually went to their knees and lowered their heads in prayerful thanks. A pale-faced boy swayed and then with a clatter of a dropped musket simply collapsed, creating a momentary fear that the gun might discharge and shatter the silence and perhaps unleash mad confusion.

Washington rode forward, sheathing his sword.

"Ground your weapons, men, but stand ready," he shouted, moving out into the killing ground between the two forces. There was scattered firing still coming from the south, down by the bridge and inside the town. He inclined his head toward Greene no order needing to be given. Greene shouted for his staff to ride like hell and pass the word that the enemy had struck.

A Hessian officer, the one his orderly had spoken to, came forward, snapped to attention, and saluted.

"General Washington?"

His English had but a slight trace of an accent.

"I am he."

"Sir, on behalf of my colonel, who lies wounded, I beg to offer the surrender of his command," and with a flourish he reversed his sword and held it up, hilt first.

For the first time in this war, for the first time in all his years of soldiering, an enemy officer was offering his sword in surrender. The gesture caught him so by surprise that for on instant he did not know how to react. Then the years of breeding, of old ways, of a code of behavior as a gentleman and leader took hold. The hundreds of enemy were watching, not sure of their fate, perhaps more than a few remembering the treatment they had given to these conquerors during the fighting around New York, and most likely expecting the same.

"You have fought with honor," Washington replied. "You may keep your sword, sir."

The Hessian officer looked at him, astonished.

"Gather your fallen and get them into shelter. Have your men stack arms here. Your officers to keep their swords and sidearms."

"Sir, you are generous."

There was a momentary flaring-up, a desire to snap back a reply that such was far better than he might have been offered had positions been reversed.

"We're Americans, sir," he said coldly. "Not savages."

The Hessian lowered his head at the reproach.

Even as they spoke, men from the Pennsylvania and Maryland regiments were cautiously moving down, approaching their foes, some of them calling out in German that the fighting was over.

The moment seemed to be frozen as the storm whipped around them. Somewhere someone was crying. A young Hessian was kneeling beside an elderly sergeant who had lost his left leg below the knee, the boy frantically trying to stop the bleeding. A Pennsylvania rifleman was down beside him, taking off his belt, already helping to put on a tourniquet, while others stood about, gazing at one another, the fight having gone out of both sides now, some conversing in German, too.

"With such men . . . ," Washington reflected again.

The firing to the south was continuing. He caught Greene's attention. "See to escorting these men back into the village. Secure them in the barracks or churches."

Without waiting for a reply, he rode off, escorted only by Billy Lee. He saw ahead another milling crowd of Hessians pressed in near the creek, some still trying to cross, but this fight was tapering off, and then it stopped. From out of the smoke a lone officer approached. It was Major Wilkinson, the young officer who had been the bearer of the message from General Gates.

Was that really less than twelve hours ago, he thought, the word that Gates would not move in support. At the time he had thought it the harbinger of the unraveling of all his hopes, a betrayal that could foredoom this attack.

Wilkinson, at the sight of his General, stood in his stirrups, waving his sword overhead.

"Sir, they've struck. General Sullivan begs to report the enemy regiment he faced by the bridge has been repulsed and is surrendering!"

The last of the gunfire was dying away, and the scene behind Wilkinson was similar to that he had just left. Hessians were laying down their muskets, lowering flags, his men circling in around them.

Wilkinson reined in by his side, and for a moment all formality was put aside.

Grinning, Washington extended his hand to Wilkinson, the young major proudly taking it.

"Major Wilkinson. This is a glorious day for our country!" Washington stated formally.

Wilkinson grinned at him with boyish delight.

"Sir, I am honored . . ." The young officer paused, his face full of joy. "I am honored, sir."

"General Washington!"

It was Sullivan, followed by some of his staff, as filled with delight as Wilkinson.

"Excellent work, General Sullivan. Indeed excellent!"

"Thank you, sir. Sir, I regret to report that some of the enemy did escape, fleeing across the bridge before we could seize it. Several hundred at least. They are retreating toward Bordentown. Should I order pursuit?"

Men of Sullivan's command were breaking away from the surrendering Hessians, coming up to watch the exchange. He scanned their faces. There was joy to be sure, but exhaustion as well. The fury of battle was passing. The flame within, after such a bitter, hellish night, was flickering out. The features of these soldiers were drawn, numbed. All of them were wet, trembling with cold, exhausted, fatigued beyond describing, having borne more than any man should ever be asked to bear.

It was now clearly evident that for all his elaborate planning, of three crossings from north of Trenton down to Philadelphia, these men, this force alone, had reached the eastern shore of the Delaware.

If the other columns had crossed, Bordentown would already be seized, that escape route blocked for those Hessians who had managed to slip out of Trenton.

The men waited, saying nothing, and he realized with wonder that, if ordered to do so, they would in fact pursue the enemy until they dropped in their tracks.

"Post a picket to hold the bridge. Send out scouts to shadow those who escaped."

He looked again at his freezing men.

"I want these brave lads sent to the village. Warm houses, dry clothes, and food is what these men deserve now, General Sullivan."

Sullivan accepted the order with obvious relief, those gathered around him offering a ragged cheer.

"You are brave lads, all of you," Washington cried. "God bless you for what you've done this day for our country!"

He turned about, the men cheering him again, and started for the town; Wilkinson, Billy Lee, and several staff falling in beside him.

It was only a few hundred yards to the village. As he approached the edge of town he came upon a knot of Hessian soldiers carrying an officer who was bleeding profusely, blood dripping on the ground.

He slowed, the men looking up.

"General Washington?" one of them asked.

"It is the General," Wilkinson announced.

The wounded Hessian, carried in a blanket litter stirred, trying to sit up, groaning, laying back.

"This is Colonel Rall," a Hessian lieutenant announced.

Washington stopped. He had heard much of this man. Of his boasts, of his disdain for the "peasant rabble," of his men despoiling the countryside as they marched through New Jersey, and of how he did not react when prisoners taken by his command had been stripped naked and paraded about to the jeers of his men.

Rall's features were already going gray with the pallor of approaching death. "General Washington?" Rall gasped.

"I am, sir."

He spoke in German. The lieutenant translated. "General, do I have your pledge to spare my men?"

There was a moment when he was tempted to offer an angry reply, but pity stayed him. The man was dying, and he knew that if this situation was reversed, that would be his first question, his plea as well.

"Your men shall be treated justly, according to the rules of war," Washington replied. "They have nothing to fear from us now," he added. "That is how we Americans fight, sir, and how we treat those who have surrendered."

He almost regretted saying it, for he could see the look in Rall's eyes. Was it shame?

Shame over his defeat at the hands of this peasant rabble, or it was it something more? Shame for what he himself had done over the last six months, now to be met by this victorious foe, who was offering civilized compassion to an enemy?

"Thank you, General Washington," Rall gasped as he lay back, obviously wracked with pain.

"Do you have a competent surgeon with your command?" Washington asked the lieutenant.

"We do, sir. Thank you."

"Take him to his quarters. If you should need assistance, send a messenger to me. My surgeons will help with your wounded, of course."

The lieutenant looked up at him with wonder and saluted.

"You are most generous, sir. Again, thank you. My colonel thanks you."

Washington did not reply and rode on, back into the town of Trenton, which was American territory again.

So that is Washington, Rall thought, mind clear for a moment.

He had pictured him as being molded on the model of most British officers, diffident, haughty, almost disdainful.

Not like that.

He had pledged that his men would be spared. Something told him that this man would keep his word. And the reproach offered had cut into his heart.

For the first time since this war began he realized he was not fighting a rabble. He was fighting an army. An army that had, in spite of his thirty-five years as a soldier, bested him . . . and killed him.

Colonel Johann Rall lay back in the blanket litter and prayed that death would come soon, without too much pain, and that his God would not blame him too much for the sins he and his men had committed in service to their land and prince.

Jonathan felt stronger and broke away from his brother's grasp. There was shouting coming from Queen Street, and as he stepped to the kitchen door he saw that the door to the street was still open. He slowly walked toward it. Men were outside, moving slowly.

Several Hessians were standing outside as if about to come in, and he braced himself, ready to meet their rush.

How ironic, to march off to war, hundreds of miles, and wind up dying here in the front of my family at the end of it all.

He stepped out into the area of the family

store and his heart swelled.

One of the Hessians was pointing in, as if gesturing toward Jonathan, turning to say something.

"Move along there, you." The voice was thick with a New England twang. "Move along."

The Hessians turned away from the door, others falling in with the first three and continued down Queen Street, heads lowered, one cradling a bleeding arm, escorted by a lone soldier who was prodding them with leveled bayonet. Peter appeared in the open doorway, breathing hard, as if he had been running, looking in, features alight with a childlike grin.

"They've struck their colors!" Peter cried. "We've won!"

Jonathan could not react; he stood there. He felt Allen's hand on his shoulder slipping away.

"Allen, it looks like you're my prisoner after all."

"Allen. A Tory?"

It was Peter stepping into the room.

"How are you, Peter?"

"A lot better than you are now," Peter replied. "We've won, damn it. We've won. They're surrendering out in the fields south of town and coming back in now!"

503

Peter then fell silent, gazing coldly at Allen. As Jonathan's childhood friend, he had held Allen in high esteem as well.

"Allen, why?" Peter whispered.

Allen sadly shook his head.

"Peter, little Peter. You, Jonathan, and James ran off. Someone had to stay behind."

"But as a damn Tory!" Peter cried.

Jonathan looked to his friend and then back to his brother.

"Yes, Peter, he's a Tory."

"You two," Allen replied, his voice distant, "you may have won this battle today, for this moment. Before the day is out the British garrison at Princeton will be swarming down here to finish you off. This is but a victory of the moment."

"And you wanted to come out on the winning side, is that it?" Jonathan whispered.

Allen shook his head. "Mother and father worked for years to build this business. Our grandfather before them. When you and James ran off like that on your half-crazed dream, it almost destroyed them and risked destroying two generations of work."

"So you decided to play the other side, is that it?"

"Jonathan, you've been led into this risk by nothing but a band of either idealists or cynics. I see little difference between the two. Men like you and Peter will certainly do the dying. And when you are dead and all is lost, they will strike their deals and save their own skins."

Jonathan shook his head, trying to form a rebuttal, but the fever that was wracking him made any coherent thought difficult.

"As for the idealists, they're fools as well. Do you honestly think men like Jefferson, that wild fanatic Samuel Adams, or Hancock can run things better than the king and his ministers?"

"Washington?"

"Another Caesar in the making. Come on, Jonathan. You're the learned one among us. You know your history. Caesar, Cromwell. Washington will be the next dictator if he should ever win, which he won't. They're all of the same cloth."

"You're wrong on that count," Peter interjected. "We marched with him. We know his measure."

"Little Peter," Allen chuckled sadly. "Always the child who wanted to play at war."

Peter glared at him.

"And you, Allen van Dorn, are a traitor on the losing side."

The two armies were commingled now, all moving slowly as they faced into the storm.

Hessians walked as if in shock. Little more than an hour earlier they had been fast asleep or sitting down to warm breakfasts in the barracks or houses where they were quartered. Now they were a shattered, defeated rabble, defeated by a force they had, until an hour ago, viewed with contempt.

His own men? As Washington rode past them he could see the looks they gave him. How different those looks were now. Days before, those looks had showed dejection, despair, and, in the eyes of more than a few, smoldering anger. Twelve hours earlier, their faces were drawn, the faces of men who would try one more time, and face a death most expected would greet them at dawn. They had been willing to die, and most had expected they would die.

What had driven them? The crossing had been, for many, a final act of defiance of fate. They had wagered all for their country. Many believed their country had forgotten them, but they had not forgotten their country, and they were willing to die for it, even if that death was a futile gesture, a final farewell to a world they had dreamed of shaping, but was not yet ready for that shaping.

He thought of Thomas Paine. What he had

written had come from the souls of these men. Paine had shaped the thoughts, vague and unspoken by so many of these taciturn men from Massachusetts farms, Pennsylvania frontiers, the rich lowlands of Maryland and Virginia. Shaped the thoughts into words that would be associated from this day until the ending of the world with these frozen, staggering, exhausted men who now trudged toward the village of Trenton.

What did they think now? What did they feel? Victory? A revolution saved? Perhaps. But he knew other thoughts were far closer to their hearts at this moment.

Dry shoes and socks. A warm fireplace where they could strip off their filthy rags to dry them out. Maybe, just maybe, something warm to put in their stomachs. Of all that they fought for, those most simple of things, shoes, a dry blanket, a fire, food, for such things a revolution had been saved as well.

He was into the streets of the village. The carnage of battle was a sight he was long used to, but in these narrow confines the horror was somehow worse. The pavement was carpeted with frozen blood, cries of the Hessian wounded echoed, bodies of men and horses lying in the frozen muck.

"General Washington, sir!"

Knox's booming voice greeted him, and the colonel came running up on foot, nearly slipping on the ice, hand outstretched.

"I thank God you are safe, sir," Knox cried.

"And you, too, colonel," Washington said, grasping Knox's hand warmly.

"The town is secured, sir. Did you stop them as they fled?"

"Nearly all are rounded up," Washington replied. "We are bringing them in now."

"Glorious!" Knox shouted, "By Jove, sir, you did it!"

Washington smiled. "Our thanks this day must be to God and to these young, courageous Americans," he said softly.

Knox nodded. "Sir, I think the home over there is appropriate for our headquarters. I already have my staff in there." He pointed down Queen Street, the flag of Knox's command hanging from a windowsill.

Washington's mind was elsewhere. "As you see the other generals, tell them to report. Staff meeting as soon as we can get everyone gathered. Prisoners are to be secured in the barracks and churches. Any abuse of them will be dealt with harshly by me personally. Do I make myself clear, colonel?"

"Yes, sir."

He hesitated. "How bad are our losses?"

"Sir, I count only two wounded and one dead so far."

"What? Are you certain?"

"Yes, sir."

He could not believe what he was hearing. Knox must be carried away with the moment. When the reports finally came in from the other commands, surely it would number in the hundreds, for evidence in the street was clear enough that the fighting had been vicious.

"Sir, trust me. They were in such a blind panic with our surprise attack that those few who did fire upon us had worse aim than any green militia. A miracle it is, sir."

"Indeed it is," he whispered.

He rode on toward the house Knox had pointed out.

An abandoned Hessian gun was in the middle of the street. A dozen or so of his men had gathered around it and now, grinning up at him with delight, their faces begrimed with powder smoke.

"We hit 'em good, sir, with their own gun no less! Should have seen the way they scattered!"

He returned their salute and rode on, men behind him exclaiming, "See the way he saluted us. Did you see that!"

He saw one of his men, in a blood-soaked Virginia uniform, sitting in an open doorway. Jacket torn open, grimacing as a surgeon worked on him, an ugly wound inside his armpit. The surgeon did not see who was watching; the wounded boy was looking up.

"Are you sorely hurt, lad?"

The boy was in obvious pain, surgeon leaning into him, the flash of a scalpel.

The boy tried to shake his head, face pale.

"Got it!" the surgeon exclaimed, sitting back on his heels, obviously intent on his work.

"Now don't move, son. I clamped the artery. Another five minutes and you'd have bled out and be as cold as this ice five minutes after that."

"Thank you," the young man said weakly.

"Don't move. I'll be back in a few minutes. Don't move a bloody inch. If that clamp let's go, your mother will never forgive you, or me. I got a few Hessian boys to look at. Then inside with you, and I'll stitch it shut proper like."

The surgeon stood up and for the first time realized that the General had been watching.

"Young Lieutenant James Monroe here, sir. I saw him lead the charge to take that gun back there. Artery cut, but he'll pull through if he doesn't move."

The surgeon wiped his bloody scalpel on his jacket sleeve as he went down the street where several Hessian wounded, one with an arm dangling loosely, blood pouring out, waited for help. Several American soldiers had gathered around trying to stanch the bleeding.

Monroe stirred as if somehow trying to stand and salute.

"You heard the surgeon, Lieutenant Monroe. Don't move."

"Yes, sir."

"I will look into this, lieutenant. So you led the charge?"

"Well, sir, a lot of the boys just surged forward and I went with them."

"Our country needs officers and leaders like you. Now wait for the surgeon to come back."

Monroe offered a weak smile.

Washington rode on, passing a house with the door smashed open. Hearing shouts from within, he slowed. A small knot of men were gathered outside, looking in.

"What is going on here?" Washington snapped.

One of the observers turned. It was Sergeant Howard from his headquarters company who, seeing his General, came to attention and saluted.

"Sir, the scout from Jersey that was with us. This is his home, sir."

"I want no looting, sergeant," Washington snapped.

"No, sir. Of course not, sir. Just it seems his family are Tories, sir. They're not too happy at the moment."

He could hear the shouting from within.

"Keep an eye on it, sergeant."

"I will, sir."

He rode the last few feet to where Knox had set up headquarters. A gunner standing guard in the doorway came to take the reins of his horse as he dismounted, still accompanied by Billy Lee and Wilkinson.

He nearly slipped on the ice as he climbed the stairs into the spacious three-story house.

He had been in the saddle since the crossing at Jacob's Creek. He was soaked clean through, as were all his men.

As he stepped into the house the sight of a glowing blaze in the fireplace beckoned from the parlor and he walked into the room. Several of Knox's young staff were already there, one of them with a half-devoured loaf of bread in his hand. They came to attention, and he motioned for them to stand at ease.

A chair of padded leather by the fireplace beckoned and he walked over to it woodenly and sat down.

Billy Lee was by his side, already kneeling down, as if to remove his boots.

"No, Billy. If I take them off I might not be able to get them back on."

"Sir, we don't dry your feet, you'll get the death of a cold."

He waved him off. "Find yourself something to eat, Billy. Just let me sit for a few minutes."

Billy did as ordered. In the kitchen in the back of the house, one of Knox's men announced that there was fresh pork roasting out there, the table still set for the breakfast of the Hessians.

Washington gazed at the fire. The room was hot, stifling hot after the long cold hours of what had seemed to be an endless night.

I must not sit here now, he thought. I've gone far longer than this without sleep.

He thought of his men, all that they had endured.

A feeble shaft of light crept into the room through the south-facing windows. A break in the clouds. Sunshine.

Paine. "Sunshine patriots . . ." How did

he do it? Did he really understand what it was he wrote? Such a profane, strange man, and yet so inspired.

Wearily, he leaned against the headrest.

There were no sunshine patriots here this morning. Oh, certainly they would come back in the months ahead and someday try to lay claim to this victory, to this moment.

The men here, though, these were the patriots of the cold and the night, the patriots without hope, and yet they had endured. God had most assuredly seen them even in the darkest of nights and heard their prayers. It had been the darkest of nights, followed by a storm-swept dawn, and a day filled with light and hope reborn.

When Billy Lee returned minutes later with a plate heaped with hot food, he found his General fast asleep, staff standing about him, watching over him in reverent silence.

"Say, Jersey, what is this place?"

It was several of the men from the headquarters company whom he had marched with through the night. He was not aware that, even as he argued with his brother, men were coming into the store and gazing about in wonder at the shelves heavy with goods.

"My family store," Jonathan announced.

There was no pride in his voice. He found he could barely speak, each breath a labored effort.

"Your store, you say?"

The three men looked hungrily at the shelves, all of them barefoot, ragged, shivering.

"Come on in." He looked over at his father, who was gazing at the three wide-eyed.

"Father, these are my friends. I don't know their names." As he spoke he labored for every word.

"They are, however" — he hesitated — "my brothers."

He looked at the three.

"Take what you want."

"You heard the orders about looting."

It was the sergeant, standing in the doorway, gazing in as well.

"Not looting, Sergeant Howard. A present from my family to our brave soldiers."

The three looked from Jonathan to their sergeant.

The sergeant winked. "Well, lads, be quick about it, and do as the boy says."

The three rushed toward the row of boots.

"Damn you, don't touch them!" Jonathan's father cried.

"Father!"

The old man turned, eyes blazing.

"Father, look at my feet," Jonathan whispered.

His father lowered his gaze, and he stood as if struck, than turned away.

"Take the boots. Take anything you want," Jonathan said again.

Several more came in, the sergeant joining them. In less than a minute a dozen or more were swarming through the small store, clearing the shelves.

"There's food in the kitchen," Jonathan announced.

The men needed no urging, flooding down the narrow corridor, loud shouts of delight echoing.

His mother stood pressed up against the side of the door, unable to speak, gazing in horror at the ragged, ill-smelling scarecrows pushing past her.

"Not as neat as your Hessian friends, are they?" Peter asked, addressing his words to Allen.

"I never said I liked their company."

"But you did keep company with them."

Allen nodded.

"We all took the king's offer of pardon. Reverend White suggested that those of us who joined the Loyalists would find far better treatment now that the war is all but over."

"The same reverend who urged us to fight six months ago, no less." Peter sighed, shaking his head.

Allen smiled sadly and nodded. "Then he was your preacher. Now he is their preacher.

"Since I know German, they made me an adjutant and liaison."

"Nice comfortable post, isn't it?" Peter snapped.

"I used to be able to cuff you down with one blow," Allen replied, features turning red.

"I wouldn't suggest it now," Peter retorted. Allen looked into his eyes and then seemed to sag.

"Remember, it was you who gave me that copy of Paine's first pamphlet," Jonathan added.

"Curse the day."

"I remember you saying he, in fact, did make some sense."

"Jonathan, that was nearly a year ago. Before the king sent his fleets, his armies, before thousands died. And you want it to continue?"

"I want it to end. But I doubt if we'll ever be brothers again," Jonathan whispered.

"I'll not hear any more of this," their

mother interjected. "Now, for heaven's sake, let's get some dry clothes on him, and then off to bed, my boy."

He looked at his mother and felt the weight of the months at war.

"I'm sorry, Mother. I am no longer your boy."

"Listen to her," Allen whispered. "At least rest for a while."

Jonathan looked into his brother's eyes, and at that moment the hatred he felt did start to melt away.

This war, this damned war did this to us. It divided us as so many wars have divided so many families across history. Though Allen was now the enemy, at least he had made a choice and stayed with it, doing so to try and protect his parents. He could forgive him for that, even as he knew he could never fully forgive James, who had turned his back on any belief other than his own needs.

He fought back the tears, and Allen, seeing the emotion, squeezed his shoulders.

From the kitchen came roaring laughter and cheers of greeting as Allen led his brother there and then to the fireplace, where he sat down on a small stool.

The men were at the table, gorging themselves; James standing sullen, leaning against the far wall, watching.

"This your family, son?" Sergeant Howard asked.

"It is," Jonathan replied weakly.

The sergeant stood and nodded politely to his mother. "Your boy is a brave lad, and we thank you for your hospitality, ma'am."

She glared at him, unable to reply.

"Did the Hessians here before us act so polite, ma'am?" one of the men cried.

"As a matter of fact they did. They're Christian men, they are, and eat with manners. Not like you heathens."

Her response was met with some laughter but no mocking retorts. The men were too busy cramming down what they could.

The sergeant stood up, came over to Jonathan's side, and knelt down.

"How you feeling, lad?"

"I'll be fine."

The sergeant looked to his mother. "Ma'am. He's had a bad night of it. May I suggest, ma'am, you get this lad stripped down and into a bed for a couple of hours before we move out."

"Exactly what I've been telling you, Jonathan," his mother exclaimed, actually smiling at the sergeant.

"Do that, and I won't move for days," Jonathan whispered. "No."

"Lad, come along now," the sergeant said in a fatherly way.

He shook his head. "Just let me warm up a bit by the fire. I'm so cold now."

"Your son's a brave one, he is," the sergeant said.

"Can't you order him?"

"Not under my command."

He looked past Jonathan to where Allen stood. The uniform coat was still on the floor, color revealed, and the sergeant's eyes narrowed.

"You a Hessian?"

"No, sergeant, his brother."

"A Tory then?"

"Yes. First New Jersey Loyalists. I'm posted with this garrison."

"A bad day for you then, boy."

Allen didn't speak.

The sergeant's gaze drifted to James.

"And your story?"

"He's nothing," Jonathan whispered. "Nothing at all."

As he spoke, Jonathan fixed James with a withering gaze, and James lowered his eyes, turned away, and stalked out of the room.

The sergeant seemed to sense something and turned back to Jonathan.

"Leave him be," Jonathan sighed.

"All right, lad. But you should get to bed.

We'll roust you out before the army moves."

"You'll have to move," Allen said. "You know what force is at Princeton, don't you?"

"Ready to turn traitor again and tell us?" the sergeant asked coldly.

"You don't need a traitor to tell you what you already know. Once they get word of this, they will be on you like an avalanche."

The sergeant forced a smile. "We'll see."

"You men!"

Jonathan looked up. It was an officer, hands on hips, standing in the kitchen doorway.

"What in hell is going on here?"

"Breakfast, sir," the, sergeant replied smoothly.

"Out! All of you, out! The General is getting set to move."

The officer turned to look at Jonathan's mother.

"Ma'am, have they been looting?"

She paused for a second and then shook her head.

"No. They're my guests."

He turned away. "Sergeant, get your men out. Now!"

"Sir."

The officer fixed Allen with his gaze. "Your story?"

"A Loyalist, sir."

The officer grinned slightly.

"Take him in tow then."

The officer stormed out of the building, shouting for the men to fall in and be ready to move.

"No rest for the wicked," the sergeant said. "Boys, take what you can."

He looked to Jonathan's mother. "How many did you have quartered here?"

"Twelve men."

"Their kits?"

"Upstairs."

"Josiah, Steven, Andrew, go upstairs. Take anything we can use."

The three ran up the stairs.

The men began to clear out.

Jonathan struggled to get to his feet.

"No, please, son." His mother, with hands on his shoulders, was trying to force him to sit back down.

"Can't he stay?" she pleaded, looking at the sergeant.

"Son, you're in no shape to march."

"Just find me some boots," Jonathan gasped.

"You can't make him go."

"Ma'am, your Tory son there is right. The lobsterbacks will be here before the day is out; most likely moving even now. He has to move. He stays here and they catch him,

Loyalist son in your house or not, it will be off to the prison hulks in New York with him. And in his shape he will die aboard those ships. I'm sorry, he has to go."

"You're killing him," she cried.

The sergeant looked down at Jonathan and then sadly at her.

"No, ma'am, I'm not killing him. It is this damn war that is killing him." Now his gaze lingered on Allen.

He sighed, patting Jonathan on the shoulder and then let fall the boots he had looted from the store.

"Put these on, boy," the sergeant said, shaking his head. "This war, this damn bloody war."

"Help me," Jonathan whispered.

Peter came to his side and was down on his knees, Allen joining him. The boots offered by the sergeant were a loose fit, but just drawing them on sent waves of agony through him so that he could not help but groan, his cries causing his mother to break down completely.

Peter helped him back to his feet.

The sergeant looked at him appraisingly.

"Son, we'll see if the ferry here can take you across. That or maybe ride one of the limbers for the guns."

"I can walk."

The sergeant clapped him again on the back. He spoke to Allen sharply. "You, too; come along with us."

"Sergeant?"

"What is it?"

"A request."

"What? Be quick about it."

"Will you take my parole?"

"Your what?"

"I offer my parole not to try and escape if you will let me help my brother here. Once across the river, you can send me with the others."

The sergeant looked at him appraisingly. "Fine, then." He pointed at the coat on the floor. "Turn that coat. Give him something warm to wear."

Allen picked up his uniform jacket, pulling the sleeves inside out, so that the blue with green facings was concealed. Stripping off Jonathan's tattered blanket he draped it over his brother's shoulders.

Jonathan slowly walked to the front of the house, trying to keep his balance with frozen feet stuffed into boots far too big. He could hear his mother crying.

"Maybe the war is over now," she said between sobs. "Maybe my boys can come home tonight or tomorrow?"

The sergeant looked at her, and wanted to

comfort her. "Maybe," he lied, and then was out the door.

Jonathan felt his mother's arms go around him, head buried against his back.

"You boys will take care of each other?" she begged.

"Yes, Mother," Allen whispered, his own voice breaking.

"Then take my blessing."

They turned to face her. Reaching up she kissed Allen's forehead, and then touched Jonathan's fevered brow with her lips.

"May our Lord watch over my boys and bring them safe back to me at day's end," she said slowly.

Jonathan fought to hold back his own tears. It was the same blessing she had given them every day across so many years as they had once rushed out together to go to school, to play, to explore the world beyond.

"And may the Lord watch over you, Mother, so that you may greet us at day's end," both replied softly, kissing her in return.

Jonathan glanced toward his other brother, James, silent, arms folded, with his father standing beside him, obviously in shock. Neither of them spoke, and he had nothing to say to them. Not now.

He stepped out onto the street. A column

was beginning to form up, orders being shouted for the men to make ready to move out.

A shaft of sunlight passed through roiling clouds, bathing him with its feeble warmth.

He fell in with his comrades, and did not look back.

CHAPTER FIFTEEN

The scent of lilacs drifted on the morning air.

Washington smiled. A dream? Strange that you can at times realize you are in a dream. But is it one?

Martha was standing in the open doorway at Mount Vernon, waving, calling his name, the way she had so often greeted him when he came home after a long trip, unable to contain her excitement, her delight showing when she first caught a glimpse of his horse trotting up the lane. Propriety forgotten in front of the house servants and field hands, she held up the hem of her dress as she sprinted, girl-like, down the steps and onto the graveled path.

It was a beautiful morning. To his left the broad sweep of the Potomac reflected the turquoise blue sky, whitecaps dancing across the river, a schooner, close-hauled, bow wake foaming, catching the sun, sparkling like diamonds.

It was an all so perfect morning. Warm, the kind of warmth that bespoke a hot day to come, but now, in the first hour after dawn, after a long night of travel, the warmth would soak into his bones and make him feel so alive. Looking forward to breakfast at home, catching up on the local news, sharing the day together.

She was coming closer. He could hear her laughing.

Mount Vernon. Strange, some of it was as he remembered it as a young man, still a bit of a rough-hewn look to the place, before her hand guided the creation of the finer touches, the change of paint, the new curtains from England, the expansion of the porch as a place for a score of friends to sit on a summer evening to watch the sky and river darken. And yet with another look it was indeed changed back again to his memories of an earlier youth.

It must be a dream, but he reveled in it as she drew closer.

"George!"

He slipped out of the saddle, the way he would sometimes do as a younger man, swinging right leg forward and over his horse's neck and then dropping to the ground, a bit of bravado, for, after all, was he not the finest horse man along fifty miles of the Potomac?

He alighted, grinned, and flung his arms wide.

She leapt into his embrace, still laughing, face radiant, eyes sparkling, brow and cheeks not yet lined with age. She kissed him excitedly.

"Oh, George, you should have been home ages ago," she exclaimed, kissing him again, and again as he held her high in the air. "What kept you?"

What kept me?

Had it been a hunt that went too far afield? He and the others deciding to just make it a night, building a fire and settling down, sleeping under the open canopy of the sky until first light of dawn, all of them then joking about how wives would be waiting, arms akimbo, ready to let fly with various accusations.

Or was he now just back from the Monongahela, bearing the first tidings of that terrible defeat . . . No, that was before Martha, long before her.

"You're cold, George," she exclaimed, cupping both hands to his cheeks. "Good heavens, you're chilled to the bone, and soaked clean through."

She pushed back slightly, and he let her

slip to her feet, stepping back slightly, her headed tilted in a manner that could always cut into his heart.

"George Washington, you'll catch your death of cold."

The front of her dress was stained, wet from his holding her, and he wondered if the fine blue silk would somehow be ruined. But she didn't seem to care. She reached out to take his hand, clasping it firmly with both of hers, chaffing it vigorously even as she turned to lead him back to the house.

"What have you been doing? We must get you inside at once! And get you out of those wet clothes this instant."

How he adored the way she could, at times, take command of him this way, her gentlest suggestion a wish for him to fulfill, her orders something he would accept with a knowing smile and follow if only to please her.

She began to chatter away, telling him all the news of what had happened since he left. How long ago was it? Yesterday afternoon? A month ago? Ten years? There was talk of the Richardsons and their newborn twins, of the storm that had blown down a favorite old chestnut tree where as a boy he had gathered nuts to roast. But when was that? Wasn't that eight years past, its wood now paneling a guest room?

Talk of a new colt from a favorite sire, the loss of a hunting dog — "poor thing, we buried him as you would have wished," she sighed — the arrival of new china settings for twelve and apologies that they had cost eight pounds more than expected and four of the cups arrived broken and how their agent in London would hear of it . . . Such a thing . . .

He laughed and shook his head. Four cups broken. Strange how important that now was, and he clucked, saying he would send a letter forthwith and insist upon proper replacement without charge for, after all, the entire set was useless until plates, cups, and saucers matched.

She squeezed his hand with delight and exclaimed again how cold he felt.

They were at the four steps that led up to the porch. One of his hounds, now aged, allowed to run free about the place, came out from under the porch, tail slowly wagging in greeting, head up, sniffing at him. Poor thing, nearly blind, but still he could recognize his scent and drew closer. He reached down with his free hand and scratched him behind the ears. Was it Scottie, Old George, or Max? But wasn't it Old George who had died long ago and was buried under the chestnut?

Accepting the greeting, the dog went back, and with a sigh settled into the soft warm earth under the porch.

She stopped on the third step, the place where when she turned she could meet him at exactly eye level.

"How I've missed you," she said, and leaning forward kissed him lightly on the lips.

He drew her closer and she laughed.

"You know everyone is watching us, George. What will they say?"

"They'll say that I'm home."

He kissed her and she sighed, leaning her head on his shoulder.

"When will you come home, George?"

He drew back slightly in surprise.

"But I am home."

He was on the porch of Mount Vernon, she was in his arms, the doorway was open, house servants coming out, smiling, ready to greet him. Neighbors were coming from across the fields beyond, waving, distant shouts.

"I am home."

"Sir . . ."

"Martha?"

"Sir!"

The voice was a whisper, masculine . . . It was Billy Lee.

"Sir."

A chill breeze swept in and around him as he opened his eyes. Billy Lee was leaning over him, hand resting gently on his shoulder, shaking him.

"Sir, you were dreaming, sir."

He started to say her name again and then stopped, embarrassed. The room was filled with a dozen or more men. They were standing politely, with backs turned, for no proper gentleman should hear the whispered dreams of another, but he could see a couple of them exchanging sidelong glances and grins.

"How long was I asleep?" he asked, an edge of embarrassment and then anger at himself in his voice for being caught up this way.

"Only a few minutes, sir. Just a few minutes."

He stood up, Billy Lee drawing back. Wordlessly he accepted the offer of a cup of coffee. He wanted to dress Billy down, to tell him never to allow that to happen again. It was undignified. How dare he allow me to fall asleep while my men still labored?

But he said nothing. Billy knew without

533

being told, and being Billy, he had allowed his General a brief nap, knowing that just twenty minutes or so would refresh him. Yet now he felt as if drugged. It was hard to shake off the sleep, and the softness of the memories.

He sipped the coffee Billy Lee offered, black and thick, not hot, but still warm enough, and drained the contents quickly, letting it go to work.

The room suddenly felt confining, hot. The doorway out onto the street was open. General Sullivan entered, mud spattered, wet breeches soaked, a broad grin lighting his face.

"They have over forty hogsheads of rum, by God," he exclaimed, and then, seeing the General, he fell silent, the others grinning again.

"Where?" Washington asked.

"Sir, in a store house behind the barracks."

"Order it destroyed. If our men get into that we won't have an army in another hour."

"Sir, I've already ordered that."

Washington said nothing more, but could clearly smell the rum on Sullivan.

Greene stood in one corner, Knox was over by the fireplace, extending his large beefy hands, rubbing them vigorously. Stirling and Mercer were leaning over a map spread on a table, the corners held down by pewter candlesticks, the map itself wet and stained.

He walked over to join them.

"Your reports?" he announced, signaling that a meeting had begun, and each, unable to contain his delight, told his story.

"Fifteen hundred or more prisoners . . . Three stands of colors . . . Six field pieces, four of them of bronze . . . The Hessian commander Rall is dying . . . Over a hundred enemy dead and wounded, with surgeons now attending to them . . ."

He nodded, taking the information in while continuing to gaze at the map, as if by looking at its lines he could somehow cross the spanning miles and divine all.

"First, gentlemen, any reports of British movement from Princeton?"

They looked one to the other and shook their heads.

"Do you know for sure? I want definite information, not assumptions."

"Sir, as ordered," Sullivan replied, "advance scouts were sent out along the Pennington Road, and from there on to the Princeton Road. None have reported in with any observations of movement. In fact,

535

the garrison at Princeton may not even be aware yet of our presence here."

"Do we know that for certain?" Washington replied again, and as he spoke he shot a glance to Billy Lee, who came, fetched his empty cup, and returned seconds later with a refill, this one scalding hot.

"No, sir, not for certain, but we do have agents afield who certainly would have reported in if they were moving."

He said nothing for a moment. None of them in this room, other than perhaps, interestingly enough, Billy Lee, fully knew just how many agents he did have in the field. Though he could never raise enough to pay the men of this valiant army, he had always placed the highest of priorities on the use of what little gold he had to purchase the right information from the right people, having cast his net wide even as the army withdrew across New Jersey. It was how he had known the disposition of the enemy here in Trenton, information that he was now finding was indeed accurate. It was how he knew the tenuous connection between the garrisons at Bordentown, Trenton, and Princeton and from there on to the main garrison at Perth Amboy which was two days' march away, perhaps three now, given this weather. Without such information from his secret network of agents and spies he never would have dared to begin this campaign. And he knew, as well, how to keep secret their existence.

And yet, news from them could only travel as fast as the swiftest horse.

Some of the Hessian dragoons based here in Trenton had, after all, escaped the net. He reached into his vest pocket and drew out his watch and opened it. Three hours had passed since the first shot was fired. Even in this blow a terrified rider could have driven his mount fifteen, perhaps even twenty miles, avoiding his patrols by using back lanes and cutting across fields.

"We must assume word has reached Princeton by now."

He looked carefully at those who had gathered by his side and around the table.

No one showed disagreement.

"Their garrison could even now be on the march, but if so, to where?"

There was no agreement, some pointing directly at Trenton, where the enemy could move to attack him directly. Greene, ever the strategist, pointed instead back to McConkey's Ferry.

"Cut us off first from our line of retreat," he announced. "That would be the move, then sweep down from the north and hold us in place while the garrison from Perth Amboy force marched."

"We attack in reply or simply fall back to the south," Sullivan replied, and the debate was on. Washington listened, saying nothing, as was his practice, letting their nimble minds fight out the varied arguments.

"Did anyone else cross? Was there no one else?" he finally interjected.

They looked one to another, and Greene shook his head.

"Sir. We got a message across the river from General Ewing. He begs to report, with regret, that ice prevented him from crossing as it also prevented General Cadwalader."

Washington took it in. "Why did it prevent them and not us?" he asked.

"Sir, I can see their side of it," Greene replied. "Just below the falls here at Trenton, the river is tidal. The ice is piled up three, four feet thick in places. Broken as well, so any man who tried to disembark while still in the river would have fallen through. It was impossible."

He finally nodded, accepting the answer.

"It was a miracle we even got across," Mercer interjected. "I know this river, sir. No blame to Ewing or Cadwalader should be placed. It's a wonder even we made it."

"Yes," Washington said softly.

He looked again at the map.

I am across on the enemy side of the river with fewer than two thousand five hundred men, he realized. He had counted on six thousand or more fording the river during the night.

We were alone, the enemy garrison should have been fully aroused and yet it was not. That foolish assault of the evening before, ordered by Stephens, who still would have to answer for doing so without informing him, had most likely aroused the garrison, had forced them stand to arms for several hours. Then the men, worn down by the weather, had simply retired, believing that surely, on such a night, there would be no additional peril.

Again a miracle.

Shall I push farther? he wondered.

The others were still arguing, Stirling exclaiming that, surely, with the advantage of surprise, the enemy would be on the run and if they marched now upon Princeton, before the day was done, the mere onset of their men, imbued now with the fire of victory, would create a rout.

Fired by enthusiasm he painted a picture in which, with luck, perhaps even Cornwallis might be present. What a prize that would be, to take the commander of the Jersey garrisons prisoner, a triumph that would trump even what they had accomplished this day. Perhaps even bring an end to the war.

Washington looked steadily at Knox, the ever steady Knox, who nodded his head, but without enthusiasm. His only comment was that his gunners were exhausted; it was a different story for artillerymen manhandling one-ton pieces along ice-slicked roads than for infantry who had only their muskets to bear.

Greene pointed out on the map that though the enemy garrison at Bordentown was small, still it was upon their flank and a threat. He pointed out that, beyond all else, they had to honorably deal with the prisoners taken here first.

There was no mutual agreement, the argument shifting back and forth.

If anything, at this moment Washington was aware of just how uncomfortable he felt. The room was warm, surely, but he was still soaked clean through, wool underclothing, shirt, vest, jacket, all heavy with the damp, his boots cold and clammy, feet so chilled he could barely feel his numbed toes.

If I feel this way in here, what of those out there?

He looked out the window where his men were milling about. They were in a jubilant mood, more than a few sporting captured Hessian headgear, strutting about like children at play. Others were trying on cast-off Hessian jackets, coats turned inside out so there would be no mistake as to which side they were on. And yes, more than a few were staggering, either from exhaustion or the fact that those hogsheads of rum had not all been smashed in immediately upon discovery.

Looking closer, he saw yet more of his men, curled up in doorways, or inside the yard beside the homes across the street, collapsed, sleeping, or just sitting.

There was a brief glimmer of sunshine, and yet, even as he watched, it darkened and a spattering of freezing rain began to come down.

"Gentlemen, we have been blessed." He spoke, and all around him fell silent.

They waited, expectantly, some eagerly, as if wanting to be unleashed; others silent, ready to follow orders no matter what they might be.

And under the weight of their attention, he felt a profound change within himself, his heart swelling.

Only yesterday when he had held his final

staff meeting, laying out the last details of the assault, he had seen that all were ready to follow him. They would follow him . . . but did they fully believe in him?

Now there was no longer any doubt. This day, this miracle at Trenton, had changed all. These men would follow him into hell if he asked it. They would follow him no matter how long it would take. No longer simply out of sense of duty and solemn oaths, but because they did indeed believe as he now most assuredly believed. Heaven would never have placed a cheap price upon such a celestial gift as freedom. We have realized it this day; we were willing to pay the price, even with our lives; and in return we have received our first glimmer of hope.

They were no longer a rabble, driven, humiliated, defeated, turning like an animal that, when cornered, would at least die game. They were an army. Regardless of all that had gone before, they could fight . . . and win.

"Gentlemen, we can be assured of but one thing this morning," he said. "We have won an astounding victory and I thank you for that. For without your inspired leadership, surely this venture would have floundered and gone down to ruin."

They looked one to another, coughed

politely, most now raising their voices, stating that the victory was his, and his alone.

He shook his head.

"Let us be in agreement then at least upon this. The victory belongs to our men out there." As he spoke he gestured toward the window, the men awaiting their orders, now turning their backs not in disrespect but because the wind was again kicking up, from the north, bringing with it a pelting rain.

"We must think of them first. They have done more than any soldiers should ever be asked to do. We must think of them now. That is our duty."

No one spoke.

"We have but two choices. We can attempt to advance, to exploit this gain, and as suggested, march upon Princeton."

Stirling looked up, eyes afire.

"What more can we ask of these men?" Washington said softly.

"They will fight for you, sir."

"I know they will. But to what end? God blessed our arms this morning with a victory unlike any seen upon this continent. I am not a profane man, General Stirling, so I will not speak of wagers with God, but indeed, sir, would we not be wagering all if we should hazard a second throw? Come now, think upon that."

He spoke solemnly but with a smile, and there were soft chuckles from a few.

"They have endured all because of their belief in our cause. But they are only men after all. We must remember that. Most of us rode this march; most of us have warm uniforms and capes and boots. We must think of their condition and always place that first."

"We march them to Princeton," Greene said softly, "and not one in ten will be fit for another fight, regardless of their belief in our cause. For them this battle was one of desperation, sir, knowing that either it would be victory or death. We can not ask that of them a second time on the same day."

Washington nodded in agreement.

"If I had Ewing and Cadwalader's men as reserves, or, better yet, rested and ready to lead the advance, I would reconsider holding this position on the enemy side of the river."

He forced a smile.

"Come now, General Stirling, your blood is still up, but this storm continues as well. I think we should place our hearts with our gallant men and see to their needs. Their need now is rest. A simple reward of rest, warm fires, fresh food, and then see what opportunities a few days hence will bring once their strength is renewed."

He looked around the room. Not one man showed disagreement. Even the firebrands deferred. Again a swelling of his heart. Not one challenged his decision as had so often been the case in the past.

This day had united them. No longer, at least for this moment, were they Virginians and Marylanders, men of Pennsylvania, Massachusetts, and New York. They were comrades, united by the shared bond of blood, suffering, and, at last, this victory. They were the army of these United States of America, and his duty now, if this Revolution was to survive, prosper, and eventually prevail, was to them above all else.

Strange, is it not? he thought. They believe in me. The doubts after Long Island, the tragedies of New York, Westchester, the Palisades, the bitter retreat — all washed away by this miraculous morning.

Merciful God, he whispered to himself. Please make me worthy of them.

"Our prisoners are to be treated with utmost respect and compassion."

No one spoke.

"Do I make myself clear? All transgressions of the past are to be forgotten. For when two armies contend for victory, often it is the gentler hand that in the end shall win. Let their brutalities and crimes be their shame, and our response a point of honor."

No one demurred.

"Let this be a mark, now and forever, of the ideal of what we Americans strive to be, even with a beaten foe."

He nodded at the looks of approval, even from such firebrands as Stirling.

"Ensure that Colonel Rall is well taken care of. The wounded are to be left behind under parole not to take up arms again. Their surgeons to be released free of parole. Their able men are not to be humiliated, and are to be treated with Christian compassion. That in itself will be a shock to many, a lesson to all, not just in their ranks but across this entire nation. I pray it will turn this conflict aside from the bitterness and brutality that has recently taken hold."

His orders, each like a commandment, he knew would be spread through the army.

"Prisoners are to be moved to the ferries above and below town and to the other side of the river. As for our army. Do you believe the road back to our ferry to still be secured?

Greene cleared his throat.

"So far, yes, sir. But why not recross the river here? There can be rest on the other side once across."

"Not enough boats," Knox interjected. "Moving the prisoners alone will take most of the day. Ewing's men on the far shore can take charge of them. But the road back to our encampments by the ferry we used is half as far as the roads on the Pennsylvania side. The direct route back is along the River Road. It will spare our men five miles or more of marching, and besides, most of the boats still await us there, not here."

Washington weighed the risks. If we linger here in this town it might not be until well past midnight before all have crossed. By that time the British garrison at Princeton might fall upon us with our backs to the river. Once across, the men would still have to march five or more miles to regain the primitive shelters of their camps.

He could not hesitate now before these senior officers.

"General Greene, my compliments to General Ewing. He is detailed to see to the embarking of the Hessians. I want our army formed immediately, ready to march as soon as possible. We make for our place of embarkation. Send word ahead along with any food we might garner here loaded on those wagons that can be found. Our gallant men are to be greeted on the far shore with hot coffee, tea even, and as much as they can eat. Have fires lit for them along the way."

Greene nodded, smiling with obvious agreement.

"Orders have already been given, sir. The men are forming ranks even now."

He nodded approval.

"Our forward pickets facing toward enemy positions are to be contacted as well and doubled. If there is even a remote sign of the Princeton garrison moving upon us, we will reconsider this plan. But, gentlemen" — he paused — "through Divine Providence we have won this day. Never forget that in the years to come. We shall regain our crossing and tonight rest victorious on the far shore. In the days ahead we will plan our next move. Can we not see that we have been blessed? Let us not flaunt it, or take it lightly. We who one day shall achieve old age when this struggle is finished. Let us remember this moment and tell our grandchildren of it and always thank our Creator for granting this blessing on us."

No one spoke.

Saying no more, he nodded, and headed to the door; Billy Lee falling in by his side.

He looked at the man and wondered. What in his heart did this man now think? Is this victory his as well? How do I someday make this victory his, if he does not believe it now?

Billy Lee held up his cape, offering it, still heavy and damp in spite of having been placed so near the kitchen fire in the back room that several holes had been burned through it. Washington accepted the offer, glad to feel its warmth.

Out in the street troops were ready to move.

He looked up the street. The column was ragged, few actually in marching order. Many were in white coats, Hessian uniforms turned inside out, and nearly all, at last, with boots on. More than a few were holding a piece of beef, roast pork, or a half-eaten loaf of bread already sodden from the pelting rain.

They gazed at him. Eyes afire.

Were these the same men who had fled in panic at Long Island? The same men who had fled in yet another panic from Fort Lee? The same men whom he had begged to serve for but thirty more days.

No. They were not the same men. Their physical forms might be the same, but they would never again be the same men. These were the men, who for the rest of their lives, whether that ended this day, or fifty years hence, would say they had fought and won at Trenton.

Some might go home when enlistments ran out, in five more days, but he could already sense that most would stay. They would stay and see it through. Whatever God's ultimate will might be on the fate of this cause, this nation, these men would stay and be part of that fate, for they had fought and seen victory at Trenton.

He drew his sword. A lone drummer gave the long roll as he pointed it forward.

More and more men were pouring out of houses. He caught a glimpse of several moving out of a house several buildings away, slowly coming out, two men with a third between them. He recognized the boy who was being half carried. It was the same one who had served as a guide, the one who had gone into the river. The lad was pale, gasping for air, one of his helpers wearing new breeches and vest coat, a captured Tory perhaps from the look of his clean uniform breeches. He could see a resemblance between the young boy and the Tory.

Dear God, another family sundered by this war. A sergeant was coming up to the three, calling for men to find a blanket to help carry their comrade.

His staff and officers issued from the house they had occupied. An orderly, after taking down Knox's flag, held it aloft and waved it high overhead. Several others holding up the captured Hessian flags and waving them, joined him.

He wanted to order no such display, but a cheer had erupted at the sight of the captured flags, and he let them have their moment. They were, after all, the first enemy colors taken since the start of the campaign nearly six months ago.

With lowered sword he pointed the way, and set off. A few blocks and then he turned north, onto the River Road. To his left the Hessian captives were being herded out of their temporary prisons in the barracks and churches, sullenly marching down to the Trenton ferries.

They looked humbled, forlorn, almost pathetic. Most were without uniform jackets or boots, shuffling along, dejected, looking back at the triumphal column turning on to the River Road, now wearing their boots, their inverted uniform jackets, filled with the breakfasts they themselves had been eating hours before.

Several of their officers, seeing Washington in the lead, broke away from their column shuffling toward the ferry, approached him, and with drawn swords saluted.

He slowed, motioning for the column to

press on, with General Greene moving to take the lead.

"General Washington," one of the Hessians cried, attempting to speak in English, and Washington looked down at the man, not sure of his insignia of rank, a major perhaps or a colonel.

"Yes?"

"Sir, on behalf of my men I wish to thank you for the mercy shown this day."

Again memories of Hessian brutalities at Long Island and Harlem. He did not speak.

"My men thank you, sir. You are an honorable foe. The glory of this day is yours."

"We do not fight for glory," Washington said coldly.

"Sir?"

"We fight for our liberty. Our freedom as free men."

The Hessian officer did not know how to reply.

"Your men shall be well treated. That is my pledge to you, sir."

"We already see that, sir."

He hesitated.

"It is the act of any Christian soldier, and I pray you learn from it."

The officer seemed struck but said nothing in reply. Washington could see the tears in the young man's eyes and relented, absolving him of the memory of the atrocities committed in the fighting around New York.

"Your commander. Rall, isn't it?"

"Yes, sir."

"Was he a good man?"

The officer could only nod in reply.

"Then he shall be in my prayers."

"Thank you, sir."

"Once back across the Delaware, I expect you to report to me as to how you are treated. Inform General Ewing you have my parole to do so."

"Thank you, sir."

Washington hesitated. "Sir, remember this day. Remember how we treated you. And when the day comes that this war is ended, tell the truth of what you saw here. This is what free men are like. In contrast to so many other fields of battle."

The Hessian lowered his head.

"I will not forget this, sir, nor shall my men."

Again Washington suppressed the desire to express his anger, his rage at so many reports of the massacres, the humiliation of his men taken by these mercenaries who fought not for a belief but simply because some petty prince paid them to do so.

But it was not their fault in any ultimate

sense. It was the way of their world, of an old world.

He and those with him this day were making a new world.

"See to your men, sir," Washington replied.

The officer hesitated.

"Sir, what is their fate to be?"

"If they pledge not to fight again in this war, they will be left in peace. Most likely they will be held for a time behind the lines, but if proper exchange is agreed upon, they will be allowed to go home."

The eyes of the officer brightened.

"I humbly thank you, sir."

He could not resist.

"Would your Colonel Rall have done the same?"

The Hessian lowered his gaze. "We will not forget this. I pray that in years to come, never will arms be raised between us again."

Washington sighed.

"I join you in that prayer, sir."

He rode on, the captives around their major looking at their former enemy with wonder.

McConkey's Ferry
4:10 P.M., December 26, 1776
"Hurry, men, hurry!"

The last of the column came slipping and sliding down the slope from Bear Tavern.

It had been a day that had shifted from radiant hope to increasing concern. A lone scout had come in claiming that the British garrison was indeed on the move and even now was approaching.

He trusted, as Greene had affirmed, that it was but a single report. Perhaps a probe sent forward, but the garrison in Princeton, even if caught so off guard, was indeed very slow to react.

Nonetheless, he would not rest until the last of his men were safely across the river.

Fires lined the banks of the river, men waiting to cross gathered around them.

His army was now collapsing from sheer, total exhaustion. They had marched twenty miles since this time a day earlier, marched through a storm which even now had not loosened its hold, shifting to a cold pelting rain.

The march back, in some ways, had been infinitely worse than the advance. At least during the night they had been driven by an inner fire, a belief that this was, in some way, a final march, to be crowned either with glorious victory or the oblivion of a death that would end their suffering.

Throughout the long day that energy had

been abating. The battle had been won. In its aftermath, the suffering was renewed, even made more painful as they trudged foot after painful foot toward the rude shelters and safety on the far shore.

Every dozen feet or so another man was down on his knees or just sprawled by the side of the road, passed out with exhaustion, comrades with some little strength left coaxing him to his feet for the final few hundred yards to the crossing.

Glover's men, who had marched with the column rather than stay behind with the boats, had pressed forward as they approached the river crossing, ready again to man the oars. Hardy New England fishermen. If ever again he heard a disparaging word from those of Virginia or Maryland who spoke with disdain about the men of the north, he would remind them of this final effort.

Manning the boats that waited for them, they were again at the oars, pushing against ice floes, helping to manhandle guns onto the Durham boats, helping unknown and unnamed comrades aboard, encouraging them that upon the far shore fires, food, shelter, and warmth awaited, even as they continued to cross the river again and again under the lash of the freezing rain.

Dusk was beginning to settle. He saw Knox in the shadows, hurrying along a team of men laboring to bring in a three-pounder, its axle tree bent, spliced with ropes and strips of lumber most likely torn from the side of a barn. There were no horses. At least twenty men were straining at the traces.

Knox, seeing Washington, rode to his side.

"My God, sir," Knox said, voice choked. "I told them to just abandon the gun. It took a direct hit, breaking the axle. Against my orders they refused, sir. Refused and said they would bring it out or die trying. They patched it up and have pulled it all this way."

He lowered his head.

"My God, sir," he whispered again.

The men slowly labored past, one exclaiming that the ferry was just ahead, none noticing the General watching by the side of the road.

"No sunshine patriots here this day, Knox," Washington commented firmly.

Knox could not reply. He fell in by their side, urging them forward, saying that a barrel of rum would be on him tomorrow. The men looked up, faces strained, and offered a feeble cheer for their gallant commander.

Wilkinson came riding up.

"Any behind you?" Washington asked.

"Just a few stragglers, sir. I fear we lost more than a few on the march here, though. Just played out."

"Heaven help them."

"Yes, sir. I doubt that the British, enraged after this, will offer them much mercy."

"Perhaps the locals will at least hide them now."

"Is that the last of them?" Washington asked, and he pointed toward a small group bearing a blanket litter.

"I think so, sir."

"Fine then, Major Wilkinson. I will never forget your service this day."

"Sir, the honor was mine, believe me."

In the gloom, the driving rain, he recognized the leader of the last stragglers. He gazed past them for an instant. There was no pursuit. His worst fear eased. They had pulled out and escaped.

The sergeant leading the group looked up and, recognizing his General, stepped to the side of the road, saluting.

"Report, sergeant."

"Sir, I think we're the last of them. At least the last who are still moving."

"Then down to the ferry with you, sergeant. Fires and good food await you."

"And you'll be with us, sir?"

"Of course, Sergeant Howard," he said

with a smile. "It would not be proper for me to be captured now."

"No, sir; I mean, yes, sir." The sergeant was, obviously so exhausted he was no longer sure of what he was saying.

"Who do you carry there?"

"The boy from Jersey, sir. The one who guided us. He just collapsed several miles back. Sir, we could not leave him."

"Which boy?"

"You might remember him, sir. The one who jumped into the river when we crossed and then spliced the tow lines."

Washington was himself so exhausted that for a moment he could not comprehend what Sergeant Howard was saying, and then memory returned.

He edged his mount forward a few feet down to the road, and gazed at the lad in the rough blanket litter.

Even in the settling darkness he could see that his features were gray, drawn, each rattling breath a labored gasp for life.

"Galloping consumption," the sergeant whispered.

Washington did not reply as he dismounted and drew closer, the men attempting to hold up the litter, slowing and then coming to a stop.

"How are you, son?"

The boy looked up at him, gasping for air, lungs rattling, unable to reply.

Washington looked over at the sergeant.

"Once across, take him directly to my surgeon. He should be set up in the ferry house!"

"Yes, sir."

General George Washington reached down, grasping the boy's hand. It was cold, icy cold.

"Son, my surgeon will see to you. You shall soon be well."

Jonathan gazed up at the General, unable to speak, no longer even sure that the man above him was even the General, General George Washington.

He could no longer speak or think clearly or even comprehend clearly. And yet one thought stood clear.

He fumbled with his wet, clammy jacket, trying to open it. Trying to draw something out.

He did recognize his brothers. His brothers Allen and Peter. Yes, Peter was now his brother as well. Allen hovered above him, tears streaking down his face. Even if he had chosen wrongly, and must now pay the price, Allen was still his brother.

He tried to open his jacket, to bring out the treasure within, the treasure that had sustained him, the treasure he wished to pass on to the General so that it might sustain him as well.

He tried but no longer had the strength.

The General looked down at him, hand touching his brow, and then pulling back.

"To my surgeon, now!" Washington cried.

The men holding the blanket labored on, the sergeant turning back to join them, holding his battered hat over the boy's face, in a feeble effort to ward off the stinging rain and sleet.

General George Washington looked back down the River Road.

No one was behind these last few men.

He fell in behind them and rode to the ferry. As was his custom and desire, he would always be the first to lead and the last to withdraw.

The miracle of this day was at an end. The day that had saved the Revolution to create America, December 26, 1776, was over.

EPILOGUE

McConkey's Ferry, Pennsylvania
6:00 P.M.
December 26, 1776

A gentle breeze out of the west drifted down off the high hills bordering the west bank of the Delaware River.

General George Washington stood on the shore of the river. The last of his men were safely across, the fires on the far shore extinguished.

The storm had at last abated. Nearly a full moon was showing through the high scudding clouds, the stars of winter revealing themselves overhead . . . Orion the Hunter, Gemini, Venus glowing bright on the low western horizon.

The wind had backed around, and the air was strangely warmer. The night of freezing rain, sleet, and snow, had changed back to rain and now this breath of relative warmth.

Heaven sent, he thought.

Generals Greene and Sullivan and even Billy Lee had long ago ceased urging him that a warm fire waited within the ferry house and that it was time for rest.

He could not rest.

He could not let go of this moment.

Has this been the moment my entire life aimed toward? he wondered.

Long ago, on the night after the disaster on the Monongahela, he had had the same thoughts. That fate had decreed him to be there upon that terrible day, to help lead the terrified survivors out of the trap into which Braddock had so blindly led an army.

But today? This day?

Was this indeed the day I was destined for?

Something told him it was not so, that more such days waited ahead.

Yes, a victory had been won. Won by the ragged men who had stayed with him when so many others had fled. Men who refused to give in, to surrender. Men who now, all strength drained, lay down upon frozen ground and drifted into exhausted sleep. It could rain again, freeze, bring down torrents of snow, but tonight they would sleep content. Their stomachs were filled, shoes on their feet, the turned coats of Hessians warming their backs. And their souls were filled with the warmth, the realization, that, after all, they could win, and if they endured, no force on the face of the earth could ever truly defeat them.

Today was only a single victory. But from it much would be shaped.

He might be tempted to dream that today, and today alone would bring an end to it all. That Cornwallis and Howe, dealt such a blow of defiance, would see the ultimate end and withdraw.

A fool's dream.

No. It would not be today. Perhaps, just perhaps, a year hence. But then again, five years might be more likely, perhaps a dozen years, a score of years.

As his men drew inspiration from him, so he drew inspiration from them.

If need be then . . . forever. Never will we surrender. On this day of days we proved something, and in that proving we will never go back.

We will never surrender . . . not now. Never.

He thought for a moment of his dream of the morning. Of going home one day to Mount Vernon. To lay down this burden.

No, even that, no matter how longed for, would have to wait. Mount Vernon — the peace of that place, the embrace of Martha

— he could not give in to that now. That must be his sacrifice, her sacrifice as well for a future yet undreamed. Maybe if it were to run several more years, she could come to him and bring some of the comforts of home. That would make it much easier to endure a long conflict.

"General Washington?"

He looked away from the ice-choked river.

It was his surgeon. Billy Lee, carrying a flickering torch led the way.

They saw him and hesitated to approach.

Again a difference, a deference not known before this day.

The surgeon drew closer.

"Sir, I felt I should report to you."

"Go on then."

"Sir, this army is worn to exhaustion and collapse. Not one man in ten will be fit to stand in the ranks come tomorrow."

He said nothing, the surgeon nervous, clearing his throat.

"I assumed that," General Washington finally replied. "Tomorrow is a day of rest unless some emergency requires otherwise. I want fresh beef brought up for the men. As much as they can eat. We captured some cattle in Trenton, and they should be driven in by afternoon tomorrow."

"My thoughts exactly, sir."

"What else?"

"Casualty list for today's action, sir," he paused. "Two confirmed dead from enemy action. Two wounded. One of them Lieutenant James Monroe, sir, who is expected to make a full recovery if his wound does not become moribund."

"Are you certain?" Washington asked intensely.

"That is it, sir," the surgeon announced gravely.

"This is indeed a wonder."

The surgeon said nothing, head lowered.

"Sir, I wish I could say the same for the days ahead. A hundred, perhaps two hundred or more are so gravely ill that today's exertions will surely lay them in their graves."

"What?"

"Sir, exhaustion, dysentery, consumption, exposure. A hundred, perhaps two hundred, will die within days as a result of what happened this day."

Washington did not reply. Could not reply.

"Are you certain of that?"

"I am sorry, sir. But this army is worn out. Disease, exposure. Even such a simple thing as want of shoes can be as deadly as any enemy bullet."

He nodded silently, his sense of elation

now damped.

"I felt you should know."

"It was your duty to report this," Washington replied sadly.

"Yes, sir."

The surgeon turned as if to leave, hesitated, then reached into his jacket and pulled out a crumpled piece of paper.

"Sir, I feel compelled to give this to you."

"What is it?"

"That boy, sir. The one you ordered to be brought directly to me."

"Yes?"

"Do you know his name?"

He stood there, unable to reply, and then wearily shook his head.

"I am sorry, I do not."

"Sir, he asked that I give this to you."

The surgeon held out the balled-up piece of paper.

Washington could not reply, taking it. It was sodden, wet.

"Go on with your report."

"Sir." The surgeon hesitated.

"Go on."

"He died an hour ago. Severe consumption and exposure, sir. I felt you should know."

"Did you get his name?" Washington asked woodenly.

"No, sir."

"I see."

"Before he died, the boy asked that I give this to you. 'General Washington, please ask him,' the boy said."

The surgeon hesitated, obviously filled with emotion.

"Sir. He pressed the paper into my hand and then just slipped away. Sorry, sir, but he was far beyond hope even when he was brought to me. He never should have joined the march last night."

Washington could not speak.

"I'm sorry, sir. Felt I should honor his wishes by giving you this."

"Of course," Washington whispered softly.

"Anything else, sir?"

General George Washington could not reply.

"I'll have a full written report by morning, sir," the surgeon said. "And pray there shall be no more fighting for a long time to come."

Washington looked over at him and sighed. "That, my good man, is a prayer I fear shall not be answered. The fighting has only just begun."

The surgeon, nodded his understanding and left, disappearing into the shadows.

Billy Lee stood silent beside him, torch in hand.

George Washington opened the paper given to him by the surgeon.

He held it up close. Of late his eyes were beginning to grow weak, a failing that only Billy Lee knew of, so far.

He held the paper close, Billy Lee by his side, gazing down as well.

"These are the times that try men's souls . . . ," he read aloud. Ever so gently General George Washington folded the paper up and slipped it into his pocket.

He looked to Billy Lee and nodded. The man who had been his companion for so many years understanding the gesture, lowered the torch and drew away, but not so far that he could not see.

Alone, in the dark . . . he knelt in the snow and ice. With head bowed General George Washington, commander of the armies of these United States of America, began to pray.

THE AMERICAN CRISIS
NUMBER I*

DECEMBER 19, 1776

These are the times that try men's souls:
The summer soldier and the sunshine
patriot will, in this crisis, shrink from the
service of his country; but he that stands it
now, deserves the love and thanks of man
and woman. Tyranny, like hell, is not easily
conquered; yet we have this consolation
with us, that the harder the conflict, the
more glorious the triumph. What we obtain
too cheap, we esteem too lightly: — 'Tis
dearness only that gives every thing its
value. Heaven knows how to set a proper
price upon its goods; and it would be
strange indeed, if so celestial an article as
FREEDOM should not be highly rated.
Britain, with an army to enforce her tyranny,
has declared, that she has a right (*not only*

* Text from *Common Sense and Other Writings,*
edited by Gordon S. Wood [The Modern Library.
New York: Random House, 2003].

to TAX) but "*to* BIND *us in* ALL CASES WHATSOEVER," and if being *bound in that manner* is not slavery, then is there not such a thing as slavery upon earth. Even the expression is impious, for so unlimited a power can belong only to GOD.

Whether the Independence of the Continent was declared too soon, or delayed too long, I will not now enter into as an argument; my own simple opinion is, that had it been eight months earlier, it would have been much better. We did not make a proper use of last winter, neither could we, while we were in a dependent state. However, the fault, if it were one, was all our own; we have none to blame but ourselves. But no great deal is lost yet; all that Howe has been doing for this month past is rather a ravage than a conquest, which the spirit of the Jersies, a year ago would have quickly repulsed, and which time and a little resolution will soon recover.

I have as little superstition in me as any man living, but my secret opinion has ever been, and still is, that GOD almighty will not give up a people to military destruction, or leave them unsupportedly to perish, who have so earnestly and so repeatedly sought to avoid the calamities of war, by every decent method which wisdom could invent.

Neither have I so much of the infidel in me, as to suppose, that HE has relinquished the government of the world, and given us up to the care of devils; and as I do not, I cannot see on what grounds the king of Britain can look up to heaven for help against us. A common murderer, a highwayman, or a housebreaker, has as good a pretence as he.

'Tis surprising to see how rapidly a panic will sometimes run through a country. All nations and ages have been subject to them: Britain has trembled like an ague at the report of a French fleet of flat bottomed boats; and in the fourteenth century the whole English army, after ravaging the kingdom of France, was driven back like men petrified with fear; and this brave exploit was performed by a few broken forces collected and headed by a woman, Joan of Arc. Would, that Heaven might inspire some Jersey maid to spirit up her countrymen, and save her fair fellow-sufferers from ravage and ravishment! Yet panics, in some cases, have their uses; they produce as much good as hurt. Their duration is always short; the mind soon grows thro' them, and acquires a firmer habit than before. But their peculiar advantage is, that they are the touchstones of sincerity and hypocrisy, and bring things and men to light, which might otherwise have lain for ever undiscovered. In fact, they have the same effect on secret traitors, which an imaginary apparition would have upon a private murderer. They sift out the hidden thoughts of man, and hold them up in public to the world. Many a disguised Tory has lately shown his head, that shall penitentially solemnize with curses the day on which Howe arrived upon the Delaware.

As I was with the troops at Fort Lee, and marched with them to the edge of Pennsylvania, I am well acquainted with many circumstances, which those, who live at a distance, know but little or nothing of. Our situation there was exceedingly cramped, the place being on a narrow neck of land between the North river and the Hackensack. Our force was inconsiderable, being not one fourth so great as Howe could bring against us. We had no army at hand to have relieved the garrison, had we shut ourselves up and stood on the defence. Our ammunition, light artillery, and the best part of our stores, had been removed upon the apprehension that Howe would endeavor to penetrate the Jersies, in which case Fort Lee could be of no use to us; for it must occur to every thinking man, whether in the army or not, that these kind of field forts are only for temporary purposes, and last in use no longer than the enemy directs his force against the particular object, which such forts are raised to defend. Such was our situation and condition at Fort Lee on the morning of the 20th of November, when an officer arrived with information, that the enemy with 200 boats had landed about seven or eight miles above: Major General Green, who commanded the garrison, immediately ordered them under arms, and sent express to his Excellency General Washington at the town of Hackensack, distant by the way of the ferry six miles. Our first object was to secure the bridge over the Hackensack, which laid up the river between the enemy and us, about six miles from us and three from them. General Washington arrived in about three quarters of an hour, and marched at the head of the troops towards the bridge, which place I expected we should have a brush for; however, they did not chuse to dispute it with us, and the greatest part of our troops went over the bridge, the rest over the ferry, except some which passed at a mill on a small creek, between the bridge and the ferry, and made their way through some marshy grounds up to the town of Hackensack, and there passed the river. We brought off as much baggage as the wagons could contain, the rest was lost. The simple object was to bring off the garrison, and march them on till they could be strengthened by the Jersey or Pennsylvania militia, so as to be enabled to make a stand. We staid four days at Newark, collected in our out-posts with some of the Jersey militia, and marched out twice to meet the enemy on information of their being advancing, though our numbers were greatly inferiour to theirs. Howe, in my little opinion, committed a great error in generalship, in not throwing a body of forces off from Staaten Island through Amboy, by which means he might have seized all our stores at Brunswick, and intercepted our march into Pennsylvania. But, if we believe the power of hell to be limited, we must likewise believe that their agents are under some providential control.

I shall not now attempt to give all the particulars of our retreat to the Delaware; suffice it for the present to say, that both officers and men, though greatly harassed and fatigued, frequently without rest, covering, or provision, the inevitable consequences of a long retreat, bore it with a manly and martial spirit. All their wishes were one, which was, that the country would turn out and help them to drive the enemy back. Voltaire has remarked, that king William never appeared to full advantage but in difficulties and in action; the same remark may be made on General Washington, for the character fits him. There is a natural firmness in some minds which cannot be unlocked by triffles, but which, when unlocked, discovers a cabinet of fortitude; and I reckon it among those kind of public blessings, which we do not immediately see, that GOD hath blest him with uninterrupted health, and given him a mind that can even flourish upon care.

I shall conclude this paper with some miscellaneous remarks on the state of our affairs; and shall begin with asking the following question, Why is it that the enemy have left the New-England provinces, and made these middle ones the seat of war? The answer is easy: New England is not infested with Tories, and we are. I have been tender in raising the cry against these men, and used numberless arguments to shew them their danger, but it will not do to sacrifice a world to either their folly or their baseness. The period is now arrived, in which either they or we must change our sentiments, or one or both must fall. And what is a Tory? Good GOD! what is he? I should not be afraid to go with an hundred

Whigs against a thousand Tories, were they to attempt to get into arms. Every Tory is a coward, for servile, slavish, self-interested fear is the foundation of Toryism; and a man under such influence, though he may be cruel, never can be brave.

But, before the line of irrecoverable seperation be drawn between us, let us reason the matter together: Your conduct is an invitation to the enemy, yet not one in a thousand of you has heart enough to join him. Howe is as much deceived by you as the American cause is injured by you. He expects you will all take up arms, and flock to his standard with muskets on your shoulders. Your opinions are of no use to him, unless you support him personally, for 'tis soldiers, and not Tories, that he wants.

I once felt all that kind of anger, which a man ought to feel, against the mean principles that are held by the Tories: A noted one, who kept a tavern at Amboy, was standing at his door, with as pretty a child in his hand, about eight or nine years old, as most I ever saw, and after speaking his mind as freely as he thought was prudent, finished with this unfatherly expression, *"Well! Give me peace in my day."* Not a man lives on the Continent but fully believes that a seperation must some time or other finally take place, and a generous parent would have said, *"If there must be trouble, let it be in my day, that my child may have peace;"* and this single reflection, well applied, is sufficient to awaken every man to duty. Not a place upon earth might be so happy as America. Her situation is remote from all the wrangling world, and she has nothing to do but to trade with them. A man can easily distinguish in himself between temper and principle, and I am as confident, as I am that GOD governs the world, that America will never be happy till she gets clear of foreign dominion. Wars, without ceasing, will break out till that period arrives, and the Continent must in the end be conqueror; for though the flame of liberty may sometimes cease to shine, the coal can never expire.

America did not, nor does not want force; but she wanted a proper application of that force. Wisdom is not the purchase of a day, and it is no wonder that we should err at first sitting off. From an excess of tenderness, we were unwilling to raise an army, and trusted our cause to the temporary defence of a well meaning militia. A summer's experience has now taught us better; yet with those troops, while they were collected, we were able to set bounds to the progress of the enemy, and, thank GOD! they are again assembling. I always considered a militia as the best troops in the world for a sudden exertion, but they will not do for a long campaign. Howe, it is probable, will make an attempt on this city; should he fail on this side the Delaware, he is ruined; if he succeeds, our cause is not ruined. He stakes all on his side against a part of ours; admitting he succeeds, the consequence will be, that armies from both ends of the Continent will march to assist their suffering friends in the middle States; for he cannot go every where, it is impossible. I consider Howe as the greatest enemy the Tories have; he is bringing a war into their country, which, had it not been for him and partly for themselves, they had been clear of. Should he now be expelled, I wish with all the devotion of a Christian, that the names of Whig and Tory may never more be mentioned; but should the Tories give him encouragement to come, or assistance if he come, I as sincerely wish that our next year's arms may expell them from the Continent, and the Congress appropriate their possessions to the relief of those who have suffered in well doing. A single successful battle next year will settle the whole. America could carry on a two years war by the confiscation of the property of disaffected persons, and be made happy by their expulsion. Say not that this is revenge, call it rather the soft resentment of a suffering people, who, having no object in view but the GOOD of ALL, have staked their OWN ALL upon a seemingly doubtful event. Yet it is folly to argue against determined hardness; eloquence may strike the ear, and the language of sorrow draw forth the tear of compassion, but nothing can reach the heart that is steeled with prejudice.

Quitting this class of men, I turn with the warm ardour of a friend to those who have nobly stood, and are yet determined to stand the matter out; I call not upon a few, but upon all; not on THIS State or THAT State, but on EVERY State: up and help us; lay your shoulders to the wheel; better have too much force than too little, when so great an object is at stake. Let it be told to the future world, that in the depth of winter, when nothing but hope and virtue could survive, that the city and the country, alarmed at one common danger, came forth to meet and to repulse it. Say not, that thousands are gone, turn out your tens of thousands; throw not the burden of the day upon Providence, but *"show your faith by your works,"* that GOD may bless you. It matters not where you live, or what rank of life you hold, the evil or the blessing will reach you all. The far and the near, the home counties and the back, the rich and the poor, shall suffer or rejoice alike. The heart that feels not now, is dead: The blood of his children shall curse his cowardice, who shrinks back at a time when a little might have saved the whole, and made *them* happy. I love the man that can smile in trouble, that can gather strength from distress, and grow brave by reflection. 'Tis the business of little minds to shrink, but he whose heart is firm, and whose conscience approves his conduct, will pursue his principles unto death. My own line of reasoning is to myself as strait and clear as a ray of light. Not all the treasures of the world, so far as I believe, could have induced me to support an offensive war, for I think it murder; but if a thief break into my house, burn and destroy my property, and kill or threaten to kill me, or those that are in it, and to *"bind me in all cases whatsoever,"* to his absolute will, am I to suffer it? What signifies it to me, whether he who does it, is a king or a common man; my countryman or not my countryman? whether it is done by an individual villain, or an army of them? If we reason to the root of things we shall find no difference; neither can any just cause be assigned why we should punish in the one case, and pardon in the other. Let them call me rebel and welcome, I feel no concern from it; but I should suffer the misery of devils, were I to make a whore of my soul by swearing allegiance to one, whose character is that of a sottish, stupid, stubborn, worthless, brutish man. I conceive likewise a horrid idea in receiving mercy from a being, who at the last day shall be shrieking to the rocks and mountains to cover him, and fleeing with terror from the orphan, the widow and the slain of America.

There are cases which cannot be overdone by language, and this is one. There are persons too who see not the full extent of the evil that threatens them; they solace themselves with hopes that the enemy, if they succeed, will be merciful. It is the madness of folly to expect mercy from those who have refused to do justice; and even mercy, where conquest is the object, is only a trick of war. The cunning of the fox is as murderous as the violence of the wolfe; and we ought to guard equally against both. Howe's first object is partly by threats and partly by promises, to terrify or seduce the people to deliver up their arms, and receive mercy. The ministry recommended the same plan to Gage, and this is what the Tories call making their peace, *"a peace which passeth all understanding"* indeed! A peace which would be the immediate fore-runner of a worse ruin than any we have yet thought of. Ye men of Pennsylvania, do reason upon these things! Were the back counties to give up their arms, they would fall an easy prey to the Indians, who are all armed. This perhaps is what some Tories would not be sorry for. Were the home counties to deliver up their arms, they would be exposed to the resentment of the back counties, who would then have it in their power to chastise their defection at pleasure. And were any one State to give up its arms, THAT State must be garrisoned by all Howe's army of Britons and Hessians to preserve it from the anger of the rest. Mutual fear is the principal link in the chain of mutual love, and woe be to that State that breaks the compact. Howe is mercifully inviting you to barbarous destruction, and men must be either rogues or fools that will not see it. I dwell not upon the vapours of imagination; I bring reason to your ears; and in language as plain as A, B, C, hold up truth to your eyes.

I thank GOD that I fear not. I see no real cause for fear. I know our situation well, and can see the way out of it. While our army was collected, Howe dared not risk a battle, and it is no credit to him that he decamped from the White Plains, and waited a mean opportunity to ravage the defenceless Jersies; but it is great credit to us, that, with an handful of men, we sustained an orderly retreat for near an hundred miles, brought off our ammunition, all our field-pieces, the greatest part of our stores, and had four rivers to pass. None can say that our retreat was precipitate, for we were near three weeks in performing it, that the country might have time to come in. Twice we marched back to meet the enemy and remained out till dark. The sign of fear was not seen in our camp, and had not some of the cowardly and disaffected inhabitants spread false alarms thro' the country, the Jersies had never been ravaged. Once more we are again collected and collecting; our new army at both ends of the Continent is recruiting fast, and we shall be able to open the next campaign with sixty thousand men, well armed and clothed. This is our situation, and who will may know it. By perseverance and fortitude we have the prospect of a glorious issue; by cowardice and submission, the sad choice of a variety of evils — a ravaged country —

a depopulated city — habitations without safety, and slavery without hope — our homes turned into barracks and bawdyhouses for Hessians, and a future race to provide for whose fathers we shall doubt of. Look on this picture, and weep over it! — and if there yet remains one thoughtless wretch who believes it not, let him suffer it unlamented.

ABOUT THE AUTHORS

Newt Gingrich, former Speaker of the House, is the author of several bestselling books, including *Gettysburg* and *Pearl Harbor.* He is a member of the Defense Policy Board, cochair of the UN Task Force, and is the longest-serving teacher of the Joint War Fighting course for Major Generals. Gingrich served in Congress for twenty years and was *Time* magazine's 1995 "Man of the Year." He is the founder of the Center for Health Transformation, the chairman of American Solutions, and a commentator for Fox News Channel. He resides in Virginia with his wife, Callista, with whom he hosts documentaries, including their latest, *Ronald Reagan: Rendezvous with Destiny.*

William R. Forstchen, Ph.D., is a Faculty Fellow at Montreat College in Montreat, North Carolina. He received his doctorate from Purdue University and is the author of more than forty books. He is the *New York Times* bestselling author of *One Second After,* published by Tor/Forge of St. Martin's Press. He resides near Asheville, North Carolina, with his daughter, Meghan.

The employees of Thorndike Press hope you have enjoyed this Large Print book. All our Thorndike, Wheeler, and Kennebec Large Print titles are designed for easy reading, and all our books are made to last. Other Thorndike Press Large Print books are available at your library, through selected bookstores, or directly from us.

For information about titles, please call:
(800) 223-1244

or visit our Web site at:
http://gale.cengage.com/thorndike

To share your comments, please write:
Publisher
Thorndike Press
295 Kennedy Memorial Drive
Waterville, ME 04901